I0819179

STRANGE FAMILIARS

STRANGE FAMILIARS

BOOK ONE OF
THE SEAMERE COLLEGE DUOLOGY

KESHE CHOW

ACE
New York

ACE
Published by Berkley
An imprint of Penguin Random House LLC
1745 Broadway, New York, NY 10019
penguinrandomhouse.com

Book design by Nancy Resnick
Illustrations: cat by Shakil_Mahmud/Shutterstock; bearded dragon by Emre/Adobe Stock

Library of Congress Cataloging-in-Publication Data

Names: Chow, Keshe author
Title: Strange familiars / Keshe Chow.
Description: New York : Ace, 2026.
Identifiers: LCCN 2025024228 (print) | LCCN 2025024229 (ebook) |
ISBN 9780593956489 hardcover | ISBN 9780593956496 ebook
Subjects: LCGFT: Fantasy fiction | Romance fiction | Novels | Fiction
Classification: LCC PR9619.4.C48 S77 2026 (print) | LCC PR9619.4.C48 (ebook)
LC record available at https://lccn.loc.gov/2025024228
LC ebook record available at https://lccn.loc.gov/2025024229

Printed in the United States of America
1st Printing

For my husband,
the best thing to come out of five years at vet school

CONTENT WARNING

Light gore, mentions of murder, depictions of animal birth, depictions of self-harm, depictions of surgical procedures, on-page sexual activity, discussions of racism, discussions of class, discussions of privilege, nonlegal prescription sedative use, and alcohol consumption.

STRANGE FAMILIARS

1

Gwendolynne

The cat reclines on the cold steel table, his skin fizzing slightly, sparks flying off him like a shower of falling stars.

"Exactly how long has he been like this, Mrs. . . . er . . ." I glance down at my chart, my cheeks heating. "Mason?"

Damn it! I should've checked her name before entering the room. Now that we're almost fully qualified, we're not just assessed academically. We're evaluated on our client communication skills, too. Tonight, when Mrs. Mason leaves, she'll be asked to give her feedback.

Will I be marked down for forgetting something so, well . . . basic?

The urge to check the strap on my wrist rises, and I fight it down with difficulty. It's an action that's become so reflexive I often do it without thinking. But I shouldn't. Not in front of a client. If I annoy her, it'll make it even more likely she'll give me a poor review.

Later. I'll check my marks later. Right now, I need to focus on the current problem: the once-fluffy black cat who, quite obviously, is brimming with *too much magic*.

The client, Mrs. Mason, shifts in her hard plastic chair and waves a hand sporting five manicured fingernails. "Oh, maybe one or two days." As she speaks, she flips open the top of her burgundy leather handbag and digs through it, producing a small silver compact mirror, which she uses to check her perfectly coiffed blond hairdo.

I'm suddenly self-conscious about my own appearance. My hair, which is black and frizzy, is scraped into a messy bun, tendrils of it stuck to my sweaty forehead. My nails are chewed. My robes are rumpled. Mrs. Mason, on the other hand, is the epitome of understated luxury: from the soft cream jumper casually knotted around her shoulders, to the pink-tipped toes peeking from her sandals, to the expensive designer handbag she has perched upon her lap. The bag's flap is still open, and I squint at the small logo printed on the inside. *De*—something? *DeCar*—something? I can't read it; it's upside down.

With some effort, I tear my gaze from Mrs. Mason's handbag and eye the cat dubiously. Percy, the name on the chart says. That detail I *did* check. I never forget to check the animals' names. Memorize their signalments. My attention always zeroes in on what I'm most interested in . . . the patient.

It's only ever the humans whose names I forget; who I tend to see as an unfortunate, unavoidable side effect of a career working with animals.

He's fourteen years old, according to the notes, but to be honest he looks much older. His hair has fallen out in patchy clumps. His tail has a kink in it from a poorly healed break. And he's missing one eye, the sunken divot in his skull covered with fuzzy black fur. I know from reading his history that he hasn't visited a hospital since he was a kitten—when all witches' familiars receive their inoculations against magical diseases—but even without reading his chart I can trace the resonant echoes of previous injuries. The lingering aura of magic, so dulled with age it tells me he was forced to heal over a very long period of time.

What happened to him? Had he been kicked by a horse? Hit by a car? Stomped by a dragon as it landed from flight? With my magical senses, I can see the ghostly outline of an eyeball popped out of its socket, the optic nerve stretched, frayed, blood collecting in the anterior chamber and obscuring the yellow iris. The eye itself would've been unsalvageable. It probably died, withered, and dropped off instead of being properly enucleated in hospital, under anesthesia . . .

Bile churns in my belly. This poor cat suffered injuries that would've caused him unimaginable pain and yet . . . his family just *left* him?

Swallowing down my revulsion, I raise an eyebrow. "One or two days, you say?"

She narrows her heavily mascaraed eyes at me. "That's right," she confirms, though we both know she's lying. Even without the extensive hair loss, the sheer amount of excess magic coming from this cat indicates that he's been sick for weeks, at least. This level of magic would need to gradually accrue, the animal's body acclimatizing to it in slowly increasing increments. If he'd had a sudden spike over just a few days, it would be incompatible with life. If that had happened, he'd have come into the hospital dead, and I wouldn't be locked in this room trying to decipher the upside-down brand name on Mrs. Mason's bag.

I lean over the cat, but he swipes at me with one bedraggled paw, then jumps off the table. He approaches his owner, who by now is absorbed reading something on her strap, but she just frowns and pushes him away with her foot. Instead, he leaps onto one of the other chairs and turns to stare at me, his back arched, his ears flattened, the hairs on his tail puffed up.

"It's okay, Percy," I murmur, drawing closer and slowing my movements until they're barely detectable. "I'm Gwen. Your doctor. I'm here to help." People sometimes look at me strangely for talking to my patients like they're human. But whatever. They're magical. They're familiars. Clearly, they understand more than they let on.

He gives a soft hiss but allows me to put my hands on him—gently, so gently—as I begin to catalog his vital signs and carefully palpate his abdomen.

The excess magic feels like tiny electric shocks every time I touch him, but I grit my teeth and continue. I don't just *want* to do a good job. I *have* to do a good job. We're nearing graduation, which is when we receive our final marks, and I really need to beat Harrisford-fucking-Briggs.

My mind whirs as I poke and prod, tracing the source of Percy's magic. The low pulse of it thrums through my body. *Vital signs normal,* I think. *Evidence of old healed injuries. Patchy alopecia, but no skin excoriations or obvious inflammation.*

While I'm examining, I try to remember if I've read anything relevant in one of the textbooks I pore over on a nightly—and daily—basis. For some students, magical medicine is an art form, like listening to a piece of music and then knowing instantly how to play it. But for me? For me, it involves grueling study. Hours spent shackled to my desk, memorizing complex passages of text and drinking obscene amounts of tea. For me, medicine is like building the entire orchestra, one painstaking instrument at a time, only able to construct music from it once I've figured out all the parts.

I've read through hundreds, possibly thousands of textbooks by now. Was there ever anything about magiphilia, the term for when one is suffering from elevated levels of magic? This, here, is like nothing I've ever seen before. And granted, I'm just a student in her final year of training . . . But after seven years at vet school, four of them spent in and out of Saint Gertrude's Hospital for Magical Familiars, I've seen enough to know that magiphilia is extremely rare. And magiphilia to this degree? Even rarer.

"Can you hurry up?" Mrs. Mason's voice cuts through my thoughts. "I have a dinner reservation in fifteen minutes."

Pressing my lips together, I do my best to speed up. I really don't like to be rushed during consultations, especially ones this complex, but I'm well aware that the hospital has already closed for the night.

The cat gives me a halfhearted swipe when I'm finished, the movement so apathetic it could almost be a friendly gesture. Still, I straighten and step away, since the tiny burns from embers of his wayward magic are starting to sting a little.

"Mrs. Mason—" I start.

"Mrs. Mason-*Price*," she says, smug, and it hits me: I've seen this woman before. She's the wife of Nathaniel Price, head honcho at Magecorp, and a committed socialite. I've seen her on my tiny strap screen—that's how I watch all my news, since I can't afford my own television—standing next to her CEO husband as he delivers speeches, flashing her dazzlingly white teeth at the many cameras pointed in her direction.

I don't really have time to process this information, since I still have to outline my findings, explain my recommendations, perform diagnostic tests, send them to the laboratory, record everything in the magical database, and then type up a report. But it's a relief to know that she's well-heeled enough to be able to afford this. If there's one part of magical vetting that I absolutely *loathe* (apart from my nemesis, Harrisford Briggs), it's this: talking about money. It always feels vaguely distasteful, like biting into a peanut cluster but finding it full of cockroach bits. I have to tell myself I'm not *selling* things, I'm *recommending* things, and always in the animal's best interest, and always, *always* because I care. I hate the moment the owner's face falls, when they've heard how many magecredits the treatments will cost and they realize they can't afford it; they can't afford the best option for their beloved familiar, their closest friend.

But the Prices have *money*, so at least this time that won't happen.

"Mrs. Mason-Price," I say, correcting my error. "Percy here seems to be suffering from magiphilia—that's too much magic. It's quite an unusual presentation, and I'm going to have to run some tests—"

"No."

I pull up short and gape at her for a moment. "N . . . No?" I hadn't expected her to be so abrupt.

She stares at me, her eyes hard. "Just, no. No tests."

Flustered, I shuffle through some scrolls that contain price lists, trying to find one that itemizes the tests I want to perform. "If it's about the money, I can try to modify the diagnostic plan to find the least expensive way of—"

"It's not the *money*," Mrs. Mason-Price snaps, obviously affronted. "It's the hassle of it. I don't want this cat continuing to soil my furniture. Ruining my best clothes with magic. Setting fire to my antique rugs."

My mouth is open; I shut it. "He—he can't help it . . ."

"I don't care. I want him gone."

"But he's your familiar!" I can't help the note of outrage that creeps into my tone. Witches' familiars—which help magical folk tap into magic from the atmosphere—are usually closely connected with their owners. The human-familiar relationship is supposed to be one of the strongest bonds there is.

"He's not mine," she says icily. "He's my husband's. And Nathaniel can afford to buy another."

Percy, the cat in question, glares at the woman, his one yellow eye slitted. He's now settled himself into the curved seat of the chair, his crooked tail thumping against the plastic.

I'm lost for words. This has never happened before. Sure, people decline treatments all the time, because they can't afford them. But here is an owner who *can* afford it, and she's declining because of what? Convenience?

Slowly I restack the scrolls and glance at Percy. He's lolling again, leisurely licking one paw. But his feigned indifference doesn't fool me—his tail is still twitching. He's heard, and understood, what his owner has said.

"Well," I venture, trying to think through my options. "We have a no-adoption policy here. You'll need to take him to the shelter—"

She scoffs. "*I* need to take him? I don't have time for that!"

My irritation is rising; I try to tamp it down. Instead, I smile, my teeth together, my words edging out through the cracks. "Like I said, Saint Gertrude's has a no-adoption policy."

She gives a hard, bitter laugh. "Then put him down."

There's a long pause. The only sound is of Percy's spiny tongue dragging through his shabby coat. He's enthusiastically licking at his belly now, which is almost entirely hairless—soft, pink, and wrinkled.

"Put. Him. Down?" I repeat, not sure I heard correctly.

"Yes, you heard me. Put him down."

"Like, to sleep? Put him to sleep? Not . . . down on the floor?"

"Do you not understand English?" she says, enunciating each word, as though my East Asian appearance suggests I'm fresh off the boat and not a BBC—British-born Chinese—who was literally born and raised in England. "Put him down. To death. With your toxic potions, or whatever it is you magical quacks do."

My throat tightens; my mouth runs dry. I drop my gaze to Percy, watching as he begins to lick his crotch. Even by usual cat standards he'd only be middle-aged: far too young to contemplate putting him to sleep for a potentially treatable condition. And since he's a witch's familiar, it's even worse. Some familiars can live for centuries. By magical standards, he's practically a baby.

"Please," I say, my voice coming out small. "Won't you reconsider? I know I don't have the answers yet, but if you'll just let me run some tests I'm sure we can get to the bottom of it . . ."

Mrs. Mason-Price leans forward, gripping her designer handbag. Her voice has turned acerbic, her pink-painted lips twisted in a sneer. "I'd advise you to do as I say, little quack, or it may be that my husband has a little . . . word . . . with the hospital board. And *you* might find yourself unexpectedly expelled." She sits back, satisfied.

My swallow is painful, my throat thick. "Yes, of course."

Just minutes later, I watch through the window as Percy's owner speeds off in her red sports car. She skids around the corner, tires squealing, spraying mud all over my rattly old bike in the process.

As soon as she's out of sight, I turn to face Percy again. He stops grooming and regards me with one bright yellow eye.

My heart pounds. I don't want to do it. I can't do it. The glow of his life force, his qì, envelops him, bright as a polished penny, and I know that apart from the magiphilia problem he's in fine, robust health. But it's the rules, and the piece of parchment Mrs. Mason-Price signed to consent to his euthanasia lies on the table behind me. Effectively, it's Percy's death warrant. So noxious it could well be burning a hole right through the steel-topped surface.

He looks at me. I look at him. I clench my fists, my palms sweaty, a pulse hammering in my inner wrists. The euthanasia potion bubbles, bright green, in the stoppered flask that I've already taken out of the usually locked safe.

I push up the sleeves of my robe, grab a needle and syringe, attach the two components, and uncap it. Slowly, and with shaking hands, I unstopper the flask of venenmort and draw up a measure of the poisonous fluorescence.

Percy seems to know that something important is happening. He sits up straight, on his haunches—an unusual position for a cat—and watches me.

I draw closer to him, biting back a sob. I'm expecting him to hiss, or swipe, or at least flatten his ears. He and I haven't got off to the best start, and now, after only ten minutes of acquaintance, I'm expected to effectively dispatch him into his next life.

But he doesn't hiss. He doesn't swipe. He doesn't even flatten his ears. All he does is half close his eyes and start purring . . . then he bumps his head against my hand.

My heart stutters and I reel, staggering backward, the green-glowing syringe clattering to the ground. "No," I say to myself, beneath my breath. "*No.*" Rule or no rule, this is wrong. Killing an otherwise healthy animal for the sake of convenience is *wrong*.

Mrs. Mason-Price and her smarmy husband can threaten to get me kicked out of Seamere College of Magical Veterinary Sciences all they want. I'll just have to outsmart them. I'm a resourceful person; I mean, I've survived this long on not much more than my wits and intellect, haven't I? I'll just have to do everything within my power to not get found out.

Scooping the still-full syringe off the floor, I toss it into the sharps bin. With a flick of my wrist, I harness the last of my day's ration of magic and set the parchment on fire. It curls in on itself, like a spider dying, until it's nothing more than a pile of ash.

Then I shrug out of my white robes, shove an outraged Percy beneath my shirt, and hurry out of the room.

2

Gwendolynne

It's after closing time, which is lucky, because everyone's already gone home. Technically, Jenna Rutherford should have hung around until I left, since she's my supervisor and all. But only a few weeks into term, she had me pegged. She saw how responsible I was. And since we final-year students are considered close enough to being qualified to work with minimal supervision, soon after that she just . . . took it to the next level. She started leaving bang on closing time, waving to me cheerily as she got on her motorbike, her tattooed arms wrapped around her girlfriend's waist.

"I trust you," she'd say with a wink. And "What they don't know won't hurt them."

I admire Jenna, I really do. The way she's effortlessly cool, blasé without being reckless, enthusiastically willing to break rules. I admire all of it, especially the rule-breaking bit—something that doesn't come naturally to me at all.

Not that anyone would know it right now. Percy's a wriggling lump beneath my clothing, and by the time I reach my bike I swear he's already gouged me with his claws upward of a dozen times. I'm sure he doesn't much like being swaddled in my scratchy brown cardigan, a vintage charity shop find that looks more expensive than it actually was. Neither do I, for that matter, but needs must.

My bike isn't locked up; I don't really need to secure it since it's too shabby to steal. And now, after being subjected to Mrs. Mason-Price's dramatic car park exit, it's even muddier than before. Percy continues squirming, but I somehow manage to keep him contained with one hand while awkwardly steering my bike with the other.

I check my strap and sigh. It's already after seven p.m. I still need to read up about magiphilia *and* replenish my magic stores. Without more magic, I can't do my job, which is not only bad for the animals but also bad for me. I can't risk losing more marks, especially since my instincts were right: I *was* docked a mark for forgetting Mrs. Mason-Price's name. I sigh again; after processing the payment, she must have picked the frowning face on her post-consultation survey.

Luckily I'm still top of the class, though only just. Harrisford Briggs trails me by only two points.

Twilight is falling as we walk along, the rhythmic clicking of my bike wheels chittering into the night. There's sweetness in the air, which is suffused with mellow pink light, and the distant laughs of students playing Flaugball float by on the breeze. Eventually, Percy stops struggling and goes still, as though calmed by the soothing hum of magic and the soft sounds of dusk.

It should be calming me, too. Usually dusk is my favorite time of day. It's when I can finally leave behind the stresses of Saint Gertrude's, Seamere's magical familiars hospital. When I can drag my weary feet toward my dorm room, eat a bowl of cereal for dinner, and scroll mindlessly on my strap for an hour before settling in for my nightly study.

But tonight I'm feeling jittery. I've flagrantly broken the rules—it's possibly the first time in my twenty-four years of life that I've done so. And while I'm content in the knowledge that I did what I felt was right, I still have to deal with the ten pounds of scruffy fluff concealed beneath my clothes.

At least Percy's fluctuating magiphilia seems to have eased a little. By the time we reach one of the campus vending machines, his magic is an almost-pleasant tingle against my skin, rather than outright incineration.

The machine is a shiny black monstrosity, emblazoned with the Magecorp logo. My lips flatten. Of course it had to be *this* machine, didn't it?

Magecorp, Mrs. Mason-Price's husband's company, is one of the two major suppliers of magic. The other supplier is Linksphere, but their vending machine is located across the paddocks at the opposite end of campus, and I really don't have time for a detour.

Gripping Percy, I take a few deep breaths, trying to steady myself. My gut feels hollow, and not just because I missed out on eating lunch. Seeing the Magecorp logo is dredging up all of tonight's memories. Everything that has happened is playing on a loop inside my mind.

Suddenly, I have the urge to call my parents and confess everything. About the cat I've rescued. About my run-in with his owner. I need to tell *someone*, or it feels like I might explode. And since my mum and dad live in Manchester, with zero connections to the vet world—apart from me—it should be safe to tell them my secret. Right?

Fishing around in my jeans pocket, I locate my magecredit card. At the same time, in an effort to multitask, I switch my strap to speaker mode and dial my parents' number.

My mother answers after two rings. "Guiying?" she says, using my Chinese name. "Is everything all right?"

She's clearly worried, since normally I video call my parents on Mondays, when they're off work. And today is, in fact, a Wednesday.

"Yes, Mā. I . . ." I pause. My confession teeters right at the tip of my tongue.

At the last minute, though, I balk, and stop myself.

It would only worry her. This close to exams she'd think of a new pet as a distraction. So instead I say, "Everything's fine. I . . . just miss you is all." Absently, I swipe my magecredit card through the slot in the machine.

My mother's voice softens. "It only a few weeks now, and then you be home with us."

My heart aches with such longing that my next words come out thick. "Yeah. I know."

The vending machine beeps, a red error message flashing on-screen. I glance at it, barely registering what it says, since my attention is being commandeered by my phone conversation. Perhaps I swiped too quickly.

So much for multitasking.

"And when you home, we make you your favorite, yes?" my mother is saying. "Stir-fry bean curd in black bean sauce—"

"How *is* the restaurant?" I cut in, just to change the topic. My parents' bean curd has been my favorite thing on their menu since I was a child. The thought of eating it again sends bittersweet nostalgia spiking through my chest. I swear, if she goes much longer like this then I'm going to end up blubbering right in the middle of Seamere's courtyard.

I swipe my card again. Again, the vending machine beeps red. Percy gives a wriggle against my chest, and I tense, holding him steady, shifting our positions so he's more secure.

"It all fine," my mother says immediately. "No need for you to worry."

I frown at her response. Sometimes I wish she'd be more open about what's happening. But it's not surprising, really. My parents never discuss their financial woes with me. They've always insisted that it's not my problem, believing that it's their job to take complete care of me—at least until I complete my studies. Then, when they are old, it'll be my job to take care of them.

I guess they're hoping they can hold out until then.

The trouble is, I'm not so sure.

There's a long, uncomfortable pause before my mum's sharp voice cuts through the silence. "Have you eaten?" To anyone else the tone change might be startling—but not to me. After all, my mother is Asian. Scolding is her love language.

"Not yet," I say. "I was just about to." At this, my mother makes a sound of disapproval before launching into a tirade of advice, interspersed with reprimands. The only words I can get in edgewise are the occasional "Yes, Mā" or "No, Mā."

Finally, I manage to say my goodbye and click off the call. I exhale. Now, at least, I can focus.

For a third time, I swipe my card. Again, the error message flashes up, and this time I can finally concentrate. *Invalid credits*, it says on the screen.

Shit.

I shove my card into my pocket and press another button to check the cost of today's magic, which fluctuates from day to day, much like regular car fuel. Apparently it's due to market forces, though everyone knows there's a lot of politicking involved. Whatever the reason, *today's* magic prices are nearly double what they were last night.

Shit. Shit shit shit. My head starts to pound and I suck in a breath, trying to ease the tightness in my chest.

It's okay. It's okay. I'll just need to restock my magic another way. A shiver ripples down my spine at the thought. With my free, non-

Percy-restraining hand, I massage my right temple, digging the pads of my fingers into the hollow.

I've just closed my eyes when someone speaks from behind me. "Trouble with the machine, Chan?" they say. Their voice holds an obvious sneer, their clipped accent the result of privilege, international tutors, and basically being an insufferable twat.

My eyelids spring open. It's Harrisford, because of course it is. Harrisford Briggs: straight-A student and grade-A git. It's just like him to want to rub it in.

After letting my breath out slowly, so that it's more like a pained sigh, I grudgingly turn around. "None of your business, Briggs."

I edge in front of the machine, obscuring the error message. It's still flashing, like an extremely irritating alarm clock that's been set for a six-minute snooze. A prickling heat has started to creep up my neck, but I ignore it, raising my chin to glare at him.

Harrisford makes no effort to hide the fact that he's trying to see the screen. "Do you need me to lend you the money?" He pulls his own magecredit card from his pocket and waves it in my direction. "I could get you a discount, even. You know, mate's rates and all." With a condescending lift of his eyebrow, he smirks.

"No, thank you," I say abruptly. I'm positive he's just using this as an excuse to flaunt his wealth. Harrisford's father—Darghan Briggs—is one of the top executives at Magecorp. Mr. Briggs works closely with Nathaniel Price, the ex-owner of the *Felis catus* currently stashed under my shirt.

They're like one big, happy, nepotistic family.

Harrisford himself is the top student in the Mythological Creatures stream, the rival academic stream at Seamere. While the students in my cohort, the Magical Familiars stream, are considered the refined intellectuals of veterinary medicine, those in the

Mythological Creatures stream are like the renegades, the cowboys, the ones who get a rush from lassoing a dragon, pinning it to the ground, and performing some hacksaw surgery with nothing but local anesthesia. They do most of their work in the field—in paddocks and stables and crushes—unlike us magical familiars folk who work inside the hospital, like *civilized* people.

It's a bona fide boys' club, with Harrisford at the helm. Sure, there are women, genderfluid folk, and enbys who pursue that stream too, but they're considered the exceptions. And all the myth.creat students sneer at those of us who pursue magical familiars training, calling us "city folk" and teasing us for being "soft."

Harrisford has been my number one rival since the first day of vet school, when he found out I was a scholarship student and singled me out as one of the "smart ones"—and therefore a threat to his supremacy. Back then, we hadn't yet split into streams, and our entire year took combined classes together: Anatomy of Magical Beings, Paranormal Parasitology, Pharmacology of Potions, and the like. It was during Pharmacology that he stole one of the ingredients that I needed to make an elixir, forcing me to use an inferior substitute, which led to me exploding every single one of my beakers over an entire class of unsuspecting first years. Harrisford himself, of course, had managed to excuse himself to go to the bathroom, and swaggered in just as the rest of us were picking bits of toad guts from our robes. With the teacher occupied, he'd flaunted the shriveled bit of rat cecum he'd pilfered from my stash of rations, tossing it into the air and catching it again, all the while sporting the most rage-inducing, shit-eating grin.

Ever since then we'd been enemies. Competitors. Rivals. Nemeses. He at the top of the myth.creat cohort, and me at the top of the mag.fam cohort. Some years, one of us would come out on top, but more often than not we'd tie for a draw.

I grit my teeth. This year will be different. It has to be. I'll beat him, once and for all, and knock that smarmy smile right off his face. If I want to save my family from financial ruin, there is, quite literally, no other choice.

Harrisford shrugs. "Suit yourself." He returns his card to his pocket. His eyes—one icy blue, one brown—drop to the bulge beneath my shirt. "Are you off somewhere?"

I swallow, ripping my gaze away from him. It's infuriating how well Harrisford's heterochromia suits him; on anyone else I might find the difference in eye color jarring, but on him . . .

My cheeks heat and my heart begins thrashing in my chest. I pray that Percy won't hear it and start struggling again. I'd been so distracted by my hatred for Harrisford—and my stress over the price of magic—that I'd briefly forgotten I was sneaking illegal contraband through the school in full view of everyone.

Not only had I flouted Saint Gertrude's no-adoption policy and directly disregarded a client's wishes, I'd also broken one of the most fundamental Seamere rules. It's categorically prohibited for students to acquire familiars, except for those that were brought from home. A rule that was introduced almost fifty years ago, as a way to stop bleeding-heart vet students from acquiring dozens and dozens of strays.

I know it, and Harrisford knows it. And he also knows my family can't afford to buy a familiar, even if we obtained an official license. In fact, the first time I ever encountered real-life familiars was once I'd already entered vet school.

Which means if he spots Percy, he'll realize I've stolen a hospital patient. And if he discovers that secret, it'll all be over. My education. My future career. There is nothing, and I mean *nothing*, Harrisford would delight in more than witnessing my illustrious downfall. I've been his number one nemesis, the stick in his side, for coming on seven years now. And we're so close to the end, so close to exams and to receiving final grades, that if there was ever a moment to take me out . . . it'd be now.

My gut is churning and my skin is sweaty—not helped by the fact that Percy has just let off a zapping spark beneath my clothes. *I need this more than you do, Briggs*, I think. Harrisford is rich. He'll graduate easily and land a good job whatever grade he gets. He only wants to beat me for the glory of it. Whereas me? I *need* to come top of the class. I need that position. I need all the benefits—the prize money, the well-paying Ministry job—attached to it.

"I'm just going to my dorm," I say through gritted teeth, tightening my hold on Percy.

"Right." Harrisford's eyebrows knit, just a little, and he stares harder at my stomach. I desperately hope he didn't notice Percy shift slightly. Perhaps he'll think I've accidentally infected myself with some sort of rapidly growing magical parasite, and not that I'm smuggling an illegitimate feline into the residential halls.

I swallow, grasping for conversation, anything to stop Harrisford from staring at me *down there*. "Where are *you* going?" My question comes out more belligerent than I intended, but whatever—it's Harrisford, after all—so I decide to run with it. Jutting up my chin, I blurt out, "You look like you're going to a jiāngshī's funeral." He's all dressed up tonight, his usual myth.creat coveralls swapped for an expensive-looking black cloak, his golden blond hair combed back from his face, his cowlick causing a single curl to fall down over his one brown eye. On his feet are shiny patent leather dress shoes with absurdly pointed toes. His bearded dragon familiar is perched atop one of his broad shoulders.

I honestly don't know how Harrisford manages to look so put together all the time, given he spends his days crawling through paddocks covered in mud and filth and unicorn shit. I suppose he must be so rich he can afford to change his clothes every hour. He probably owns hundreds of slouchy linen shirts and unnecessarily tight designer slacks.

His head whips up, his eyes narrowing to slits. "A *what?*"

I forgot he wouldn't know what a jiāngshī is, since they're native to China and rarely seen here in England. My parents talk about them all the time, but here they're barely recognized. "Vampire . . . zombie-type thing," I mutter. My face heats; he wouldn't have understood the reference. "They don't . . . well, die."

Harrisford is silent for a moment, regarding me. Then he says, "You know, it's a little sad when you have to explain the punch line of a joke, Chan."

"I only explain my jokes," I retort, in the haughtiest tone I can muster, "to those too stupid to get them."

His eyes narrow further. "Touché." Is it just me, or is there a hint of a smile hovering about his lips?

Thankfully, Harrisford has stopped looking at my chest-lump-that-is-Percy. Instead, his attention has slid up to my face, which I'm pretty sure is sheened with sweat. I mean, it's a warm night, plus I'm being intermittently electrocuted by a magiphilic cat.

Besides, being near Harrisford always invokes an incendiary sort of fury. And when I get angry I get all hot and irritated, like a phoenix about to combust. The knowledge of how horrid I must look compared to him really does pain me.

"As a matter of fact," Harrisford says, tilting his head to one side. "I *am* going to a funeral. Someone very close to me, in fact."

My stomach lurches. I didn't know. "I—I'm sorry," I stammer. As much as I hate Harrisford Briggs, I never mean to intentionally hurt anyone, even if I often inadvertently do. I have two default emotional states: extreme awkwardness and wretched guilt. Unfortunately, one often leads to the other, and it's a ghoul's guess which one I am at any given time.

Harrisford stares at me for a long while before throwing his head back and letting out a huge guffaw. My mortification hardens inside me, petrifying like an ossified cancer, and my hand twitches, wishing it could slap him.

It takes several long moments before Harrisford's laughter dies out, until he's still hiccuping and wiping his eyes with the back of one long-fingered hand. "Good lord, you're gullible, Chan," he says, still chuckling. "So worth it, though, to see your face."

I draw myself up to my full height. "You're disgusting," I snap. "Funerals are nothing to joke about—"

His laughter stops abruptly, his voice turning to ice. "So it's all right when you do it, is it?"

I glare at him and clamp my mouth shut—because he's right, of course, and I have no comeback.

That's it. I'm done here. Trying to tamp down my fury, I turn and stride off, the wheels of my bike squeaking. Percy, warm and furry, snuggles against my chest.

There's no point trying to act civil to Harrisford Briggs.

No point at all.

3

Harrisford

She's hiding something. I have no idea what. All I know is that Gwendolynne Chan is most definitely hiding something.

I watch as she stalks off in the direction of the Heywood Residential Halls. She has something stashed beneath her cardigan—an abomination of knitted acrylic if I ever saw one—and, perhaps I'm imagining it . . . Perhaps the thought of tonight's impending tedium is going to my head, but I could have sworn that it actually *moved*.

I am immediately suspicious. Is it something she's using in an attempt to best me at our final exams, which are in only a few weeks' time? Maybe she's gathering ingredients to make a potion that will somehow incapacitate me. I wouldn't put it past her. For almost seven years, she's been my most bothersome rival, the one student at Seamere who I find impossible to beat.

Everyone else is easy, with rather obvious human weaknesses. All it takes is for me to root these out so I can determine how to exploit them. To tell the truth, when it comes down to it, I probably shouldn't be one of the top students at Seamere. Yes, I'm clever, but not necessarily the cleverest. It's just that I have two things that give me an edge above all the others: one, the motivation—my father would absolutely slaughter me if my grades ever slipped. And two, I *know* people. I'm good at figuring them out, at finding out what provokes them, what distracts them, even what gives them joy.

Not with her, though. Gwendolynne Chan is infuriatingly private, cagey, and closed off, keeping everyone at a distance and barely ever socializing. It's as though no one can get close enough to her to even find out her weaknesses.

Irritation flares, hot and pestiferous, in my chest. Good god, she is exasperating. *What the hell was that bulge beneath her clothes?*

The strap on my wrist buzzes, jolting me from my speculation. I check the wide-angle screen. It's Father. Two words: You're late.

No "How are you, son?" or even a "Hello." It's been a week since we last spoke and as usual, all he can do is point out my failures.

Scowling, I recommence walking to the front gates, where my father's vehicle is waiting. It's a monstrosity, sleek and black and far too large to be suited to city streets. There is a chauffeur leaning against the passenger door, even though he's somewhat superfluous, considering the car is powered by magic. Like everything my father does, it's all for show.

I hitch up my cloak and climb into the cool, leather-lined interior. Mozart is playing softly from the speakers and there are bottles of sparkling water nestled in the ice bucket.

The car starts, its magic-powered engine making no noise whatsoever. As we glide through the streets, we somehow dodge pedestrians who don't even seem to see us. We narrowly avoid oncoming vehicles, slipping past bright red double-decker buses on narrow, one-way roads. We squeeze through alleyways and gaps in traffic that a car this size has no business fitting through.

It takes mere minutes to reach the Natural History Museum, right in the midst of London, even though Seamere is well outside the city. So many magecredits go into powering this car: into making it faster, more malleable, more invisible. Too many credits, really. Honestly, I could have just left earlier this evening, and we could have driven at a normal speed without spending the extra money. But I know Father considers the car a tax write-off. As chief financial officer of Magecorp, he'll just put it all on the company expenses.

It's lucky I left later, anyway, since otherwise I would not have run into Gwendolynne, and I wouldn't have seen that she was up to something. My jaw clenches, the muscles tight and painful. What the hell is she playing at? I'll have to figure it out before our first exam.

Get a grip, Briggs, I chide myself. I'm not scared of that mediocre witch, and whatever nefarious plans she has to thwart me being rightfully awarded the top spot.

Except she's not mediocre, is she? a spiteful voice within my mind whispers.

Immediately, I shut that thought down. I should not be thinking of her, or her pathetic plans. Not tonight. Tonight I need to focus on what truly matters: my future.

As soon as we pull curbside, the chauffeur promptly jumps out, earning at least part of his wage by opening the car door for me. I quickly sequester my bearded dragon into an inner pocket of my tuxedo robes before climbing out. "Thanks," I mumble, and he nods, the movement stiff because of his high-necked uniform.

The museum's ornate, gothic towers jut up into the amethyst sky, the two arched entrances glowing like twin mouths of hell. As expected, Father is waiting for me at the top of the stone steps.

He looks positively unimpressed. Exhaustion clings to him like a mantle—the grim lines that bracket his downturned mouth are even more pronounced than usual, and there are dark smudges beneath each eye.

"Decided to finally grace us with your presence, have we?" he sneers as I trudge up the stairs.

I sigh, my shoulders involuntarily slouching. "Hello, Father."

"I hope you'll leave that attitude outside, Harrisford." His frown deepens. "Do not forget that tonight I am—"

"Doing me a favor." I finish his sentence for him, since I have it memorized. There's no way I could have forgotten since he has reminded me around ten thousand times. "I haven't forgotten."

Tonight is ostensibly a charity gala, but Father says he's only throwing it for my benefit. Since I'm nearing graduation, he wants me to rub shoulders with the best and brightest of the magical community: ministers and MPs, CEOs and celebrities. "It will be an opportunity to network," he's told me, over and over again. "In case you don't get that job at the Ministry."

I will, though. I *will* get the job. I'll ace my examinations and come first, and no gutter-born witch from Manchester is going to stop me.

We join a line of magical folk, and I can't help but notice that Father is acting twitchy. He crosses his arms and drums his fingers on his biceps as we're waiting to clear security. He jumps when a man in minister's robes taps on his shoulder to greet him. His eyes dart around as though scanning for something, and small pinpricks of sweat are dotted along his receding hairline. Now that I think about it, he's been acting strange for a while now. Months, in fact.

It takes me a while to place his emotional state: He's nervous. Which is strange. My father is never nervous. Angry, spiteful, sardonic, disapproving, yes—but I have never seen him nervous, not like this.

"Is everything all right?" I venture, when we're finally checking our cloaks.

"Everything's fine," he says, curtly, as he shrugs out of his outerwear and tosses it at the clerk.

A pause. "It's just . . . you seem tense."

He stares at me for several long, uncomfortable moments, before he finally speaks. "You have one job tonight, Harrisford," he says. His voice has taken on a didactic tone, as though he's delivering a lecture. "To meet important people. To ingratiate yourself with them and make a good impression. You do *not* need to be concerning yourself with anything else—and certainly not sticking your nose where you're not wanted."

A flash of anger, white and sharp, knifes through me, and my heartbeat kicks up in my chest. I open my mouth to respond, but my father is already striding off—uninterested, as always, in what I have to say.

I tear off my own cloak and shove it at the clerk. I don't know why I continue to try, why I continue to attempt reaching across the chasmlike space that divides us.

When I was younger, he was always too busy. Too busy to go anywhere, to play, or to spend any time with me at all. I had half fancied that when I grew older and mature enough to follow his interests, perhaps things would change. But no matter how much I tried—modeling my hobbies after his, reading about current events he seemed invested in, even dressing like him—he never bothered to treat me as anything but an inconvenient waste of space.

Ignore him, Harrisford. The voice in my head interrupts my dour thoughts. *This is your night; don't let him ruin it.* Since we're not technically supposed to bring familiars, I'm hoping no one will notice the reptile-shaped lump talking to me from my chest pocket. It's lucky that human-familiar communication is conducted mind-to-mind.

I sigh, shove my hands inside my trouser pockets, and stomp in after my father.

As much as I don't want to be here, I have to admit that tonight, Hintze Hall does look magnificent. The vaulted roof, the ornate archways, and the illustrated panels on the ceiling are fancy enough at the best of times, but tonight the event planners have gone all out. Thousands of floating magelights hover in midair, like tiny suspended fireflies, and live pine trees sprout right through the tessellated tile floors, festooned with more lights on strings.

Tonight, it's a Winter Wonderland theme. Stalactites are suspended from the high, domed roof, and waitstaff glide around on ice skates that float a foot above the floor. Snow—presumably enchanted to never melt, considering how warm the room is—lines the balcony railings.

The ceiling too has been enchanted to produce flurries of actual snowflakes. They spin in the air currents, floating gently to the floor before disappearing altogether. The magelights illuminate their icy fronds as they flutter down, light beams scattering into iridescent rainbows that wink and spark through the air. And finally, above us, the hanging blue whale skeleton has been enchanted to move, undulating as though it is actually swimming.

I'm impressed, in spite of myself. To charm something that heavy to move for an extended period would take some considerably advanced magic. I squint up at it, trying to figure out the mechanics. Truly, it's an extraordinary feat of engineering.

The whole place is glittery, and magical, and utterly pretentious, especially since we're currently well into summer. That's Magecorp's modus operandi, really: doing the most ostentatious thing ever—such as holding a winter-themed ball during one of the hottest months of the year—just to prove that they can. The overpowering smell of too much magic permeates the room.

Father's nowhere to be seen, which is absolutely fine by me. I grab a drink from a passing tray. The champagne explodes, fizzy on my tongue, tasting like the promise of memory loss and oblivion and an actually enjoyable night.

"Is that alcohol, Harrisford?" someone says from behind me, and I turn to see Samuel Sloane, talk show host and B-list celebrity, gesturing at my drink. His usually tanned skin is matte with white powder, which has collected in the creases, and he's wearing the corpse of a polar bear as his costume, his face peering out of its wide-open mouth. As he draws closer, the polar bear's eyes blink at me and it roars. I fight the urge to roll my eyes. Magic tricks, of course.

"On a school night, too." Samuel sticks out his lower lip in an exaggerated frown and shakes his head. "Tsk, tsk."

"I'm twenty-five," I snap. "And I'm only having one." Samuel is one of Father's friends. I've been to countless parties with him, and he's always trying to befriend me.

"Pity." He winks. "That's even more disappointing."

Ugh. He's looking to get me drunk. Again. I start to nudge my way past him, but he stops me with a hand on my shoulder.

"Let me go, Samuel." I try to shrug his hand off me. He doesn't move, just leans closer and closer until I can smell the alcohol on his breath.

"Why?" He's already slurring. "You afraid of getting drunk around me?" His fingers dig harder into my shoulder.

"No, I—" Then I stop, for I've noticed something about Samuel's polar bear hat.

It's sparking. Not just sparking, but thin plumes of smoke are spiraling up from both its eyes. And the boozy smell of Samuel's breath is being replaced by something far more sinister . . . The acrid tang of singed fur.

"Get off me," I bellow, shoving Samuel away from me. "You—you're on fire. Take that thing off!"

"On fire?" His unfocused eyes fix on me, his forehead creasing. "Whatever do you mean, Harrisford—"

I point. "Your hat. Take it off. Unless you want—"

I never get the chance to finish my sentence, because the next moment Samuel's entire polar bear hat has gone up in flames. Spontaneously combusted. Conflagrated. He screams, trying to bat at his head, then screams again when he burns his hands in the process.

Without thinking I toss my drink over his head before diving for a pitcher of water on one of the nearby tables. And it's immediately after I've dumped its entire contents over Samuel's head that I notice: The entire room is starting to shake. The magelights are quivering. The branches of the pine trees rustle, even though there is no wind. And the blue whale skeleton hanging suspended from the ceiling trembles, the bones clacking together.

"GET DOWN!" I shout as I dive to the floor and cover my head with my hands . . .

Just as the explosion hits.

4

Gwendolynne

Fortunately, since no one else at Seamere is as nosy as Harrisford-fucking-Briggs, I manage to get Percy safely inside my dorm room before encountering anyone else. He tumbles out from his knitted prison, clawing my stomach with his hind limbs as he does so.

"Ouch!" I cry, but Percy doesn't seem to notice, or he doesn't care. He just darts under the bed, navigating stacks of paper and odd socks and embarrassing amounts of dust. I drop to the floor and flatten myself, peering into the darkness—he's crouching in the corner, blanketed by shadows, every now and then emitting a shower of sparks.

Figuring he might be hungry, I rustle through my bar fridge for something potentially suitable. It's too late to get any actual cat food tonight, but I'll go first thing tomorrow. In the meantime we'll just have to make do.

The inside of the fridge is dark; the magelight has long since blown and I haven't bothered to replace it. All I find is some wrapped cheese, hardening at the edges, and a half-empty carton of soy milk. My snacks drawer isn't much better—it's mostly cereal, and things that are easy to stuff into my mouth when studying, like nuts and pretzels and an old pack of leathery beef jerky my mother once bought me "for the iron." Finally, I scrounge up an old tin of tuna-for-one and empty it into a bowl.

I set it down on the floor beside the bed. Percy vehemently ignores me. He also ignores the beef jerky I toss at him, and the piece of cheese that I'd pulled out in desperation.

"Seriously?" I ask him, incredulous. "You don't like *any* of this?" But of course there's no answer. The Office of Magical Animals at the Ministry is the only entity that issues permits allowing a person to keep a familiar. And it's only once they've granted one that they'll perform the bonding ritual enabling direct communication between a permit holder and their pet.

I already know I'll never be able to get a permit. Seamere rules forbid it, first of all. And besides, there's no way I could afford one.

Plus, I don't even know if the Mason-Prices will bother to cancel Percy's current permit. Probably not, since they're so loaded with money, they wouldn't care about getting the partial refund, especially now they think he's dead. To me, without a permit, Percy will always be nothing more than a regular old cat. And he'll stay bonded to the horrible Magecorp CEO, Mr. Nathaniel Price.

Suddenly, something occurs to me, and my blood runs cold. All my extremities feel numb. I clutch at my face, barely feeling it.

The Prices think Percy is dead. But Percy is not dead. He's very much alive. And humans can communicate telepathically with their animal familiars. Which means . . .

"Percy," I say, dropping back down to the floor. "Whatever you do . . . Don't speak to your master, yeah? Nathaniel thinks you're dead. In fact, he *wants* you to be dead. If you say anything, they'll figure it out and send someone after you. But if you stay quiet . . ."

Percy continues to stare out of the darkness at me, his one eye glowing a reflective green. After several drawn-out seconds, the eye disappears briefly as he gives me a slow blink, and I know he's understood.

Letting loose a relieved sigh, I push myself off the floor and then flop into the worn seat of my desk chair. I lean my elbows on my desk for a second, massaging my forehead, dreading what's coming next.

Most of the other students, the ones whose families can afford to send them to Seamere without needing scholarships, can buy unlimited stores of magic. To them, buying magic is no more onerous than stocking up on pens, or parchment, or textbooks, or spare robes.

Me? I have to purchase the bare minimum whenever it's affordable and then diligently ration it out. I need magic for everything I do: studying, sitting exams, working shifts at Saint Gertrude's . . . even charging the battery of my strap.

While there are some smaller companies that sell magic, Magecorp and Linksphere are the two main distributors, and they have a complete choke hold on the market. They harvest it. They control the supply chains that circulate it around the globe. And they trade the familiars that allow humans to more efficiently channel and store atmospheric magic. They haven't started breeding them yet—but everyone says it's just a matter of time.

It's a massive, massive industry, which we learned in Economics of Magic 101 is actually a *good* thing. Magecorp—headed by Nathaniel Price and Harrisford's father—and Linksphere are two of the biggest employers of magical humans worldwide. And while stores of magic *are* pricey, the economies of scale mean that without these two corporations regulating the market, magic would be even more prohibitively expensive.

I don't understand it fully, but it makes sense. The quaint little corner stores that sell magic do so at a far higher cost. And as much as I wish I could support them, I simply can't, not when they sell at such inflated prices. Here on campus, I'm forced to buy it online, or from the Magecorp and Linksphere vending machines in a pinch. So I can't really complain about the market when I, like so many in the magical community, am one of the cogs that keep it turning—even if Magecorp does result in unfortunate side effects like the existence of Harrisford Briggs.

Sighing, I push my sleeves up to get to work, ignoring my clammy palms. Whenever I can't afford to buy magic, I have to replenish my supplies by using an extremely obscure rationing spell, which makes what I have stretch further. Back in first year, I had to trawl through some pretty complex magical textbooks to figure out how to do it.

Since it's so horrible, most people don't bother—they'd rather just buy more. That's not a luxury I have, however.

Sometimes I wonder if I should've studied medicine. The truth is, magical doctors need less magic to do their jobs than we vets do. Something about the way we treat so many species drains our magic more quickly, more thoroughly. But those thoughts are fleeting, and honestly far between. Even on the hardest days, I wouldn't change it. I chose to go into vet school—even though both my pay and my status in magical society will be lower than other careers—because I love animals. Because I want to help.

Also, honestly . . . humans are *disgusting*.

I unwrap a scalpel and close my eyes, beginning to mutter the incantation, one that I know so well I could probably recite it in my sleep. But I'm interrupted by a loud moan and then the unmistakable whack of a headboard banging against the wall. The walls here are paper-thin, a fact that I've become uncomfortably aware of since Bridie Masters, my neighbor, started hooking up with her new boyfriend, Danny Wong.

Damn it! They've broken my concentration, and after everything that's happened today . . . I'm exhausted.

"Masters! Wong!" I thump the wall between our rooms. "Keep it down!"

There's a pause, and a giggle. "You could always join us, Gwen!" Bridie's singsong voice floats across the plaster.

I wrinkle my nose. "Just quieten down, will you?"

In fine Bridie form, she responds by moaning even louder. I glower at the wall before powering up my strap, then turning the volume up high. Maybe it'll drown out the noise, at least partially.

The familiar buzz of the nightly news spills into the dank air of my dorm, and I push up my sleeves again, which have annoyingly fallen down.

"—tonight's charity gala, which was being held by Magecorp CFO Darghan Briggs to raise funds for the Society of Magical Veterans—"

My ears prick up at the mention of Harrisford's dad, and I stare down at the screen. A charity gala? Was that where Harrisford was headed tonight?

The news anchor is wearing a salmon pink jacket and a tiny downturned frown. "The entire museum has been cordoned off in an attempt to identify the source of the explosion, though eyewitnesses say it seemed to originate from multiple locations at once."

A face I recognize, TV presenter Samuel Sloane, flashes onto the screen. He's wearing a large furry sort of hat that has been scorched beyond recognition. "It was my hat at first," he rants, pointing at the blackened lump atop his head. "It seemed to start here, and then, just . . . boom!"

The camera cuts to a scene outside the Natural History Museum, which has been barricaded behind yellow tape and is crawling with journalists and police. I sit forward in my chair, my heart thumping. A field reporter stands before the camera, holding a large gray magephone emblazoned with the news station's logo. "While a number of suspects, including several high-level members of the Magical Liberation

Organization, have been brought in for questioning," the reporter says, "no group has yet come forward to claim responsibility for this act of terror, which so far has resulted in zero casualties."

I blow out a breath. Zero casualties. That's good. Just some random explosion that affected a bunch of rich people who don't concern me in the slightest.

Not that I care what happens to Harrisford.

Chewing my lip, I frown at my strap screen. The fact the authorities are questioning the Magical Liberation Organization is interesting. The MLO, an extremist group that actively works against the Ministry, are activists who want to dismantle the tight regulations on magic; their mission statement is that everyone should have equal access to it.

While they haven't been too active in recent years, in the past they've been known for agitating, for disrupting, sometimes even for violence. Years ago, the Ministry officially labeled them a terrorist organization.

I shake my head. I have no idea why the MLO would try to blow up a charity gala, but right now I need to focus on my own problems. Turning my attention back to my rationing spell, I prepare to make the first cut with the scalpel. Slowly, I unwrap the blade, then shimmy my jeans down past my thighs.

Sometimes I do my forearms, but my legs are easier to hide—so most of the cuts I make are there, on top of the already present, unsightly mess of scars.

I'd started doing this for practical reasons, but after a while it became routine. A sort of anchor to my anxiety. Often, the pain helps me to stop thinking—even if only for a few moments—about the stress of vet school. About my family and how much I miss them. About how they're on the brink of losing the restaurant they've owned for as long as I can remember.

Or about how, since they've sunk all their money into the business and put none toward a pension, they'll end up destitute . . . unless I can win.

Each year, whoever comes first at Seamere is automatically offered a lucrative graduate role at the Ministry's Office of Magical Animals. To be honest, if I could choose anything, I'd probably prefer an internal medicine internship, but the low pay wouldn't be enough. Whereas with the Ministry job, I'd be able to help haul my parents back from impending bankruptcy.

It's why I want to beat Harrisford. Scratch that, it's why I *need* to beat Harrisford. The thought steels my resolve. We're weeks away from exams; if I want to win, there are no two ways about it: I *need* more magic. I inhale. Exhale. Then continue.

The news I leave running in the background. I'm only half listening, and there isn't much more information—just some interviews of patrons who'd been at the gala. But neither Harrisford's father nor Harrisford himself shows up on-screen.

Again, I'm interrupted, because there are the sounds of footsteps running down the hall outside. A scream. Then—a bang. Another bang. And a shout. Percy streaks out from under the bed and leaps into my lap, trembling.

What the hell is going on? I need to complete this ritual without being continuously interrupted. Clenching my teeth so hard my masseter muscles ache, I try to ignore the noises. But when the footsteps and shouts and bangs and screams don't stop, I fling the scalpel down, tug up my jeans, scoop Percy up with one arm, and cautiously crack open the door.

The corridor is dark. The fluorescent magelights have gone out. There are more distant shouts and thumps and something that sounds like . . . an explosion?

"Gwen! Gwen!" Pen Ferguson rushes up, their generous curves

swathed in a purple dressing gown, their hair in rollers, their feet shod in fuzzy slippers. "You'd better come—"

I'm about to ask why when Pen cuts me off. "The animals are going wild," they say, panting. "There's been an explosion."

I tear after Pen, following them to Heywood Hall's enormous common room. We arrive to find a scene of total pandemonium. Students are crammed in there, many of them already in nightwear. It's where most of them hang out before bed, chatting and socializing and playing games over their straps. Not me, though. I'm normally shut up in my room, studying.

Those who had brought their familiars into the common room are struggling to keep ahold of their pets. There's Danny Wong, already out of Bridie's room, wrestling with his carpet python, Artemis. Isla Ennis is grappling with her flapping, squawking eclectus parrot, and Conall Peters is there too, pleading with his guinea pig, Gary, who is glowing like a firework and throwing off sparks. Outside, Heloise Chapman is being dragged along by her unicorn, Lightning. Lightning is usually stabled overnight, but somehow he's managed to burst out of his pen and is bolting across a paddock. Even though it's nighttime I can see that Heloise's skin is flushed, her braids flying, her eyes wide with panic.

What is going on? I take in the scene, my mouth falling open. First the museum explosion, and now this? What on earth is actually happening?

I startle when I hear the voice echoing through my head.

This is what happens, the voice says, sounding weary and jaded and thoroughly bored, *when there is simply too much magic.*

5

Gwendolynne

My head jerks down to eye Percy, who is still tucked beneath one arm. I'd been so shocked by the news of the explosion that I'd forgotten to keep him hidden. Luckily, everyone else is too caught up trying to pacify their own pets, and no one seems to have noticed.

"Did you . . . speak?" I ask, staring at his one unblinking eye.

He narrows said eye and turns his head away.

Of course I did. His voice is still inside my head. *What do you think I am doing? Does it appear as if I am performing a jaunty song and dance?*

My pulse is drumming in my ears, and I squeeze my eyes shut, shaking my head. "But you can't . . . I can't . . . I don't have a permit." I open my eyes again, my brows knitted. "You can't be my familiar."

It appears that I am, Hairless One. Believe me, I'm not happy about it either. First, you stuff me beneath that awful cardigan. And then you attempt to feed me fish from a tin. *A travesty!* He huffs out a breath. *This is not how I envisioned my life going, either.*

My mouth is still open, and I shut it again. To be honest, I've never thought about how familiars don't get a say in the decision to bond with a human. It's the human who purchases the permit, and the Office of Magical Animals that opens the connection post-approval. This revelation brings up all sorts of uncomfortable thoughts about the bodily autonomy of sentient creatures.

And, aside from that, this whole situation is just so very *wrong*. Percy might not be aware of the Ministry's rules and regulations, and how serious a transgression it is to have an unregistered familiar, but I am. For Percy to have connected with me without the official bonding ritual . . . Something has gone seriously awry. The normal procedure has been circumvented, as though the magical world has tilted on its axis, and the usual controls have just slipped away.

Was it some sort of power surge? Has an unprecedented swell of magic somehow short-circuited everything?

I don't have time to find out. Already the animals, who are all going feral, have started to cause injuries to their human hosts. Conall's arms are covered in burn marks from where his guinea pig has scorched him, and Isla's blond hair is a snarled mat from her parrot's grasping claws. Danny is nursing a bite wound inflicted by Artemis's fangs, and Heloise . . . I don't even want to know what injuries Heloise is sustaining, being dragged along by a unicorn that can gallop at up to sixty miles per hour.

"Can you help?" I ask Percy. "Can you channel the excess magic?"

He raises his nose, sniffing the air, then wrinkles his lips back in a Flehmen response to taste it. Then, finally, he says, *I certainly can. Unlike these amateurs,* I *have been adapting to excess magic for months.*

My voice is breathless. "Then do it. Please."

What will you give me?

My heart lurches in my chest. I don't have time to negotiate, but the cat isn't giving me much choice.

"I've already offered you everything I have," I say, flustered.

"Fish . . . cheese . . . beef jerky." My voice is rising with my stress levels. "The only other thing I have is a tin of baked beans—"

Sold, Percy says, and I only have half a second to shoot him an incredulous look before he shifts his weight beneath my arm and lets his eye fall shut.

For several seconds, nothing happens. "What are you doing?" I ask.

He doesn't bother to open his eye. *I am asking the other familiars for their consent*, he says, as though it is the most obvious thing ever. *Before I drain their magic.*

"Oh." Of course he is, and rightly so. I fall silent, chagrined, thinking about the myriad of ways animals are better than humans.

Eventually, his small body starts vibrating, his black hair standing on end . . .

And then slowly, slowly, the magic starts to stream into him. The other animals begin relaxing. They stop thrashing and writhing and biting and scratching, and their owners slump their shoulders, letting out sighs of relief.

Percy, meanwhile, is getting hotter and hotter. Sparks begin to fly off his fur, and although at first I can ignore it, it starts becoming more frequent, more relentless, the amplitude of the electricity higher. And my arm starts to burn where he touches my bare skin, smoke billowing from his black patchy coat.

"You're getting *hot*," I whisper-hiss, and Percy just opens his eye. I could swear he raises one eyebrow at me, even though logically I know cats lack pronounced facial expressions.

Of course I am. If you thought that I could channel this amount of magic and remain at 38.6 degrees Celsius, then your common sense is sorely lacking.

I clench my teeth. Just my luck; I finally get a familiar and it turns out he's a colossal jerk. Girding myself against the pain, I try to stay quiet. But just as the other animals all calm down, Percy has a surge of extreme heat that sears into my arm like a brand.

"Dragon's balls!" I yelp, dropping him, and the other students all look up. Percy—the little shit—sprints off like a black blur, slipping into the forest of legs.

I bolt after him. I can't risk him being caught, and me being found out. It was foolish for me to even pick him up—I only did because I had thought that he was *scared*.

So foolish.

He sprints down one corridor, and the next, and I follow, cursing him the whole while. "Come back, you little turd!" I shriek, the words choked off by my shortness of breath. "As soon as I catch you I'm sending you right back to Gertrude's!" It's an outrageous lie, and I'm sure he knows it as well as I do.

As we run, I notice that many of the doors have been flung open by the magic surge. Some of them are hanging on their hinges, some of them are burned, some of them have had holes blown through. It's a fucking mess. Magical Maintenance are going to have their work cut out for them tomorrow.

Finally, he slips into a room at the end of one corridor, through a jagged hole in the door. I don't recognize this place—it's a wing I haven't been to before. It looks . . . nice. The doors here, though ruined, are all paneled mahogany, unlike the cheap MDF doors in the dorm rooms of my wing. There's plush carpet on the hall floor—a far cry from our scuffed laminate—and actual magetorches in sconces line the walls instead of fluorescent lighting.

This must be the south wing, where the rooms cost a bomb in boarding fees. *No matter*, I think. Likely all the rich folk would have been at the charity gala, or else drinking in the bar downstairs where cocktails are like, thirty magecredits apiece. They often do that of an evening rather than hanging out with us plebs in the common room (not that I hang out there, anyway).

I creep along the shadowed corridor, careful to keep quiet so that Percy doesn't hear me and get spooked. I'm practiced at approaching skittish cats, and the plush carpet swallows the sound of my footfalls, so I'm practically silent as I enter the darkened room.

It takes a moment for my eyes to adjust, and when they do, I have to stifle a gasp. This room is so far beyond anything I'd imagined. Our dorm rooms, the ones that the likes of me and Bridie Masters and Pen Ferguson occupy, are utilitarian, consisting of nothing but worn carpet, a single bed, a desk, and a wardrobe made of pine. We try to make them look as nice as we can, we really do. Some of us stick posters up, or perform decorating charms. And I have the bar fridge stashed beneath my desk—a lucky find I picked up off the pavement because a neighbor no longer needed it.

But this room? *This* room! It's absolutely stunning. The walls are a dark sort of paneled wood, and there's an actual fireplace set into the far wall, though it's not lit. The bed is big, a four-poster, and lined with silky white curtains. The bedclothes are rumpled, but in that styled-for-a-magazine-shoot kind of way: a navy duvet spread over crisp white sheets; pillows and cushions piled high at one end, leaning against a carved wood headboard. I nearly salivate at the walls of bookshelves, all stuffed with leather-bound books. And the antique desk is enormous, also mahogany, an elegant magelamp with an actual lampshade perched atop it.

I edge closer, unable to stop myself from running my fingers along the desk's varnished surface. There are pieces of parchment scattered about, a fountain pen in a stand, and a high-backed leather chair. It's all very elegant, and refined, and . . .

Where is Percy?

I drop to my hands and knees and begin to crawl around. I'm trespassing in some rich person's room, someone who has way more money to pay lawyers than I do. I need to get in and out, fast.

Percy isn't under the desk, and he's not beneath the bed. I search behind a cushy, wingback armchair that sits in what I presume is the "library." I even paw through the unnecessarily extravagant number of pillows. Who needs this many pillows, anyway? Fucking royalty? I roll my eyes. Perhaps someone has stashed a pea under the mattress.

There's only one more place to look. A door, fitted into the wooden wall, is standing ajar. I tiptoe over and push it slightly. It opens silently, without resistance.

The scent of men's cologne hits me immediately, something that smells vaguely familiar. Ignoring this fact, I whisper softly into the darkness.

"Percy? Are you in here?"

There's no answer. And it's dark. So I flip on the magelights, which flicker into brightness.

Oh hell no. This wardrobe is *enormous*. It's almost as big as my entire dorm. And no—oh no. Oh no no no no no.

I recognize the clothes here.

Lining each rack are rows and rows of linen shirts and equally many neatly hung trousers. Hanging in the far corner are several clean, pressed coveralls, and on the opposite wall are scores of fancy robes; I spot dress robes and tuxedo robes and travel cloaks and numerous long, soft, woolen scarves. A neat row of ties have their very own rack, and displayed on a shelf beneath the window there are cuff links, a spare strap, and a shiny silver fob watch, imprinted with the initials *HFB*.

Oh, lords save me. *HFB*.

I'm in the bedroom of my worst fucking enemy.

I need to get out. And quickly. Dropping back to the floor, I begin searching through the many shoe racks, all lined with shiny, expensive-looking shoes. There are studded boots and loafers and dress shoes and—thank the gods—Percy himself. He's wedged himself unceremoniously behind a pair of brogues. Or at least I think they're brogues. From the looks of it, Percy's let off a mini explosion, and the leather is kind of charred.

Good, I think vindictively.

"Percy," I whisper, keeping my voice low and urgent. "Come on. Quickly! We need to get out of here."

He's silent for a moment, before his voice rings, loud and clear, inside my head. *I don't think I shall*, he says. *I am comfortable here, and besides, perhaps it would do you good to be exposed to someone with better fashion sense.*

I scowl at him. "My fashion sense is just fine, thank you very much."

He gives me an appraising look with his slitted yellow eye. *The cardigan you are wearing says otherwise.*

I give a groan of exasperation. It really isn't my fault that I'm forced to buy clothes at charity shops. "This isn't *funny*, Percy. Do you know whose room we're in? If we're caught, we're going to be in so much fucking trouble. Harrisford Briggs is a selfish, pompous, arrogant prick and—"

And it's like this—on the floor, insulting Harrisford, with my bum high in the air—that I hear the drawling voice behind me. The voice that never ceases to fill me with incandescent rage.

"Chan? Is that you?" Harrisford says. Then, he adds, as my heart pools in my stomach, "What the *fuck* are you doing in my room?"

6

Harrisford

Gwendolynne crawls out backward from beneath a row of my best Italian wool trousers. Wisps of her hair—normally silky and black—have escaped from her messy bun and are hanging in frizzy waves around her flushed face. She's still wearing that horrible baggy cardigan, and beneath its loose neckline her normally pale chest is reddened too, all the way down to her—

I snap my gaze back up to her face and scowl. "I asked you a question, Chan. *What are you doing in my room?*"

She must have snuck in, not expecting I would be back so early.

After the explosion at the gala, I'd fought through the crowds to locate my father, only to find him already giving an interview to some reporters. *Fine*, I'd thought, bunching my fists in my pockets. It wasn't unexpected, really: that he'd be more interested in doing damage control than finding out whether his only son was safe.

So, not bothering to say goodbye, I had walked out the door, hailed the valet, and promptly left.

And now my evening has only got worse. What are the chances I'd return to my room to find Gwendolynne Chan rummaging through my wardrobe?

After how shifty she'd looked earlier, and how obvious it was that she was hiding something beneath her clothes, I am immediately suspicious of nefarious intent. I'm so certain of it that I'm willing to stake my considerable inheritance on the fact that she is trying to sabotage me. By what? Blowing my door apart and breaking into my room? Creeping into my wardrobe and planting something to get me in trouble?

As if *I* would truly get in trouble. Frankly, the idea is laughable. Just like every other time, Father would make a phone call, gift a hefty donation to Seamere, and everything would be smoothed over by supper.

Not that he cares about me, of course. He just wouldn't like the optics of his son causing controversy at one of England's most prestigious colleges.

Gwendolynne straightens her shoulders and blows a strand of hair from her eyes. "I . . ." she starts, then swallows, the smooth column of her throat rippling. "I was looking for my cat."

I stare at her. "You don't own a cat."

She raises her chin. "I do."

My eyes narrow; so do hers. "No you don't."

"Listen, Briggs—" Her voice has taken on a slightly hysterical edge. "Just because you're too *priggish* and self-centered to notice anyone else around you and whether or not they actually have a cat doesn't mean that I do not have a cat! And I do have a cat!" She takes a step toward me, fists clenched. "So there!"

I step forward too, until we're chest-to-chest. She's bluffing. I know she is. I've watched her for the past seven years and never once have I ever seen her with a blasted cat.

"Oh, it's like that, is it? Very well, then. Why don't you show me the reason you're trespassing in my room? Why you've blown a hole through my fucking door?" I allow the corners of my lips to curl up into a sneer. "Go on, Chan—show me this alleged 'cat.'"

She shoots me a look of unfettered loathing before dropping back onto her hands and knees and crawling back under my clothes racks. I watch her narrowly, trying not to make eye contact with her backside, though it's difficult considering it's stuck high up in the air and her jeans are hugging her curves in all the right places—

Fucking stop it, Briggs. I swallow, tearing my gaze away from her wiggling arse. Gwendolynne is the *enemy.* She's snuck into my room, she's trying to frame me for something, she's trying to steal the top spot from me, and she's . . .

She's holding a cat. Bloody banshee's balls. She actually *does* have a cat.

I glare at her as she climbs to her feet, hugging a black ball of fluff to her chest.

"See?" she says, victorious. "I got him." Her eyes meet mine and she blushes again. "Thanks for, er—letting me look for him. I'll just be off now, yeah?" She's looking nervous. She shuffles closer, trying to push past me, heading for the wardrobe door.

Realization clicks into place. Was this what she was concealing under her clothing earlier? When she was on the way home from Saint Gertrude's? Nothing but a goddamned *cat*?

"Wait." I put a hand on her shoulder to stop her, and she sucks in a breath. I freeze, my muscles rigid, then snatch my hand away. She was warm, so warm, beneath my palm.

I realize it's the first time I've ever touched her.

In all of seven years.

"Why?" she snaps. She's annoyed now.

Flustered, I rake my hand through my gelled hair. I am well aware I'm not looking my best. My robes are scorched and I'm pretty sure I have a smudge of charcoal somewhere on my forehead. "Is this cat one of your patients, Chan?"

She begins to tremble, just slightly. We're standing entirely too close in this confined space. I can feel the heat radiating off her and smell the scent of her chain store perfume.

"No," she says.

She's a fucking terrible liar.

"You're lying," I say accusingly.

She begins to shake even harder. "I . . ." She's stammering. Shaking her head like a kid caught with a hand in the biscuit jar. "I'm not."

"Give it to me." Even I'm surprised by the firm tone my voice has taken on.

Her trembling stops, and she scowls at me. "*Him*, not *it*," she says, and it's as though defending the furball has given her courage. "And I'm not giving him to you!"

"Come on, just let me look at him—"

She clutches him to her chest tighter. "No!"

As she squeezes, though, the cat gives an incensed yowl. His head pops up. He thrashes—Gwendolynne manages to keep ahold of him, just—before he swivels to look at me, fixing me with one devilish eye.

I stare, disbelief tearing through my bones. I know this cat. With his flea-bitten ears, his single eye, his crooked tail . . .

"Percy," I spit out, and the cat pulls back his whiskers and hisses. A little torrent of sparks flies from his open mouth.

Gwendolynne's eyes widen, and she glances from me to the cat, then back again. "Wait—you *know* him?"

"Of course I know him, Chan," I snap. "He's my father's boss's familiar—"

"*Was* your father's boss's familiar," she says, resigned, and it's obvious she knows that it's all over. She's been caught. There's nothing she can do or say now to feign her innocence. "Mrs. Mason-Price was going to euthanize him, and I—"

"You took him." I'm horrified, of course, but not surprised, that

Mrs. Mason-Price would do such a thing. I mean, I used to *play* with this cat when I was a kid, and he a kitten.

Still, I can't show Gwendolynne any sign of weakness. This is the first time ever I've had an ounce of leverage over her, and if I want to exploit her fear I need her to believe—without question—that I do not care one iota about this cat.

It takes tremendous willpower to hold in my maniacal laugh. Finally, after so many years, I've figured out what the indomitable Gwendolynne Chan actually, truly cares about.

I tilt my head, regarding her for several long moments, watching as she withers beneath my stare. "Look at you, being all rebellious. I wonder what the dean would think if she found out you broke a Seamere rule?" Professor Anika Kaur, the dean of Magical Veterinary Sciences, is a no-nonsense woman who has a zero-tolerance policy for rule breaking. I know this because my father has had to go above her before to settle issues with *my* rule breaking.

And there's something else I know: Gwendolynne absolutely idolizes her.

All of the color drains from her face. "I haven't." Her voice cracks and I almost—*almost*—feel sorry for her.

Or at least I would, if she hadn't been caught breaking and entering my room. "Oh, but you *have*, Chan. Imagine that! The mag.fam princess, top of every class, never-broke-a-rule-in-her-life Gwendolynne Chan, stealing patients from Saint Gertrude's." It's difficult in this cramped space, but I manage to lean even closer, so that our breaths mingle in the heavy air. "I can see the headlines now, Chan, and let me tell you . . . They're glorious."

She visibly gulps, her face pale, her fingers twisting into the cat's fur. Then she seems to gather herself, and her chin tilts up. The movement brings her lips close to mine, and my heart begins to pound. Involuntarily, my breath catches in my throat; I hold my ground, just managing to stop myself from stepping back.

“What do you want, Briggs?” she says, her eyes suddenly hard. “I’ll do anything you want as long as . . . As long as you don’t tell.”

Anything I want? She doesn’t know what a dangerous proposition that is for a man like me. Again, I conceal my derision. She is so tragically naïve.

Good god, I hate her. I’ve always hated her beating me in class and being so difficult to read and acting so uppity even though she’s laughably poor and her family comes from *nothing*.

And I really fucking hate her now.

I hate the way she’s affecting me. How rattled I feel that I found her here, on hands and knees, in my walk-in wardrobe. The way I seem unable to stop noticing how her face flushes when she’s angry, or how full her lips look at close proximity.

Her heat. Her smell. The way her shoulder felt beneath my touch.

And I suddenly feel the insatiable need to make her suffer, as I’ve suffered.

So I turn on the full force of my charm. Reaching out, I finger a loose strand of her hair, listening to how her breath hitches. Then, so slowly, so deliberately, I tuck it behind her ear.

“All right, Chan.” I smirk, allowing my fingers to linger at the soft skin of her neck. Her breaths are coming ragged, uneven. “As a matter of fact, there *is* something that I need from you.”

7

Gwendolynne

"You want me to treat your lizard," I repeat, my voice flat. The familiar in question rests on Harrisford's forearm, perfectly still and unblinking.

"My *dragon*," Harrisford says, scoffing. "Good lord, Chan, you could at least *try* to be more specific. Exactly what sort of vet student are you?"

My face heats again, and irritation expands in my chest like a bubble. "The type that says *lizard* to differentiate it from the actual *dragons* that are stabled outside. You know, the enormous, classic, fire-breathing ones?" When a dragon is brought in ill or injured, they keep them confined in a series of fireproof concrete pens, tethered to prevent them from flying away. Occasionally the Mythological Creatures Hospital has to treat a wingless Chinese dragon too—those ones don't breathe fire—but since they're non-native we only ever get captive ones from the zoo.

As usual, Harrisford is acting like a typical myth.creat student: completely lacking nuance.

"I should think you'd be able to differentiate them given the considerable size difference," he drawls.

I roll my eyes and then turn my attention to the lizard. "Well, what's wrong with it, then?"

"*She*, not *it*," Harrisford shoots back, echoing my words from before. "And she—I'm worried she got injured—"

"In the explosion?" It all suddenly makes sense. Harrisford's familiar had been sat on his shoulder before the gala. She would have been there when the explosions hit.

I knit my brows, confused. "Can't *you* do it?"

"No, Chan." His lips twitch with something like amusement. "I'm not accustomed to handling things so . . . small."

I narrow my eyes at him suspiciously. "Why don't you take her to the emergency hospital?" Being open 24/7, it costs a lot more than the regular hospital, even with our student discount—but that wouldn't really deter Harrisford, would it?

His gaze slides away from mine and he shifts the lizard up to his shoulder. "Well, I . . ." Seemingly automatically, he begins to stroke his familiar's chin. She raises it slightly, arching into his touch. "If you must know, I wasn't supposed to bring her. Familiars are banned from events such as these. You know, for security reasons."

Inside my head, Percy utters, *Bah!*

"Oh," I say, ignoring my cat. "I didn't realize. I've not been to one before." I guess it makes sense. Familiars allow their bonded humans to drain magic from the atmosphere, and in a crowded event like a gala, it could quickly deplete levels to zero.

His eyes lock on mine, cold and calculating. "Of course you haven't."

Chewing on my lip, I cast a glance at the lizard, who by now has turned her head and is regarding me with one black beady eye. "So you want me to check her over and patch her up without telling anyone why she was hurt? And in exchange you'll, what? Keep quiet about my cat?" I let out a short, sharp laugh. "Harrisford Briggs, are you *blackmailing* me?"

He cocks his head. "What's a little blackmail between friends, eh?"

Friends? Is that what we are? I weigh the word in my mind, frowning, finding it woefully inaccurate. We're more like enemies. Rivals. Competitors. Nemeses.

Still, this is my one chance of escaping the wrath of Professor Kaur. My one chance to get away with all the rules that I've broken within the last six hours. So I square my shoulders, heft Percy's weight into my other arm, and nod.

"Okay, then," I say. "I'll do it."

Harrisford follows me to Saint Gertrude's, which takes a while since we're both on foot. We march along, carrying our familiars, neither of us saying a word. I'm still stewing over the look Harrisford gave me when I asked if he owned a campus bicycle.

Night has fully fallen, and the sound of chirruping crickets laces the balmy air. We're walking through one of Seamere's ancient, ornate outdoor corridors, and residual heat from the day is radiating from the stone. It's abnormally hot for nighttime, even for a London summer, and I wonder whether this funny weather we've been having is somehow connected to the magic surge. I drag a hand across my sticky forehead, sweeping hair out of my eyes.

Is it much farther? Percy's voice whines in my head. His tail jerks back and forth like a metronome that can't keep time.

Unbelievable, I think. *You're not even walking!* But he just lets out an impatient sigh.

Thankfully, the elaborate turrets of the hospital building eventually come into view, the stone grotesques leering at us from high up on their perches. Saint Gertrude's isn't a regular, modern vet hospital. It's an imposing, ivy-clad gothic structure, cracked and crumbling and held together by magic—much like the rest of Seamere.

When we reach the staff entrance, I set Percy down and pull out the big brass key that Jenna had once slipped into my pocket. She'd patted it, given me a knowing look, then sauntered off. The key slides into the lock without making any noise.

"You have a key to the hospital?" Harrisford's tone is incredulous. It sparks with wicked amusement. "Two rules in one night, Chan. It must be your personal record."

I turn to face him. Moonlight spills across the pavement, but his face is shadowed by the eaves. There's really nothing I can do to explain this, to hide Jenna Rutherford's crime. I only hope I don't get her in trouble, too.

"Yes, I have a key. But"—I swallow, the movement painful—"you can't tell anyone, all right? My supervisor gave it to me so I could lock up of an evening. And if you tell, it won't just be me who gets in trouble . . . She will, too. It doesn't seem fair, that." I stare up at him, into his darkened eyes, challenging him.

"It's perfectly fair," he retorts, his whisper getting louder. "Since she has, in fact, broken the rules." I bristle, but he quickly adds, "Don't worry, though. I won't tell. I'm quite certain that Jenna Rutherford scares me more than she does you."

I almost laugh, but manage to stop myself just in time. Instead, I narrow my eyes, scrutinizing, trying to determine if he's being genuine. In the end, I decide that he is. I mean, he's right, really; Jenna *is* a little scary.

"Thank you," I say, my shoulders relaxing. "I appreciate it."

"You're welcome. Though I must point out, Chan, the list of *your* demands seems to be getting inequitably longer."

"What's a little blackmail between friends?" I flash him a small, sarcastic smile and turn to push open the door.

The interior of the building is dark and cool, the mage-powered air-conditioning running on high to keep patients comfortable. Machines and monitors beep and blip, and one of the canine patients huffs out a soft bark.

We slip inside; I stealthily deactivate the alarms just like Jenna showed me.

Percy strolls in as though he owns the place, his crooked tail up and curled around like a question mark. He sniffs at the leg of a table and hisses, puffing up all over like a bottle brush.

Someone's been here, he spits out. *A* cat.

I manage—just—to suppress my eye roll. "Percy, we're in a veterinary hospital. Of course you can smell other cats." I pause, then add, "Are you sure it's not *your* smell, from a few hours ago?"

If you could smell this too, Hairless One, he says, clearly offended, *then you would understand how insulting that is*.

I shake my head and power on the fluorescent magelights. The hospital flickers into visibility, the patients blinking in the sudden brightness.

"Put her on the treatment table," I instruct Harrisford, grabbing my white robe from its hook and throwing it on over my street clothes.

Carefully, Harrisford places his familiar on the stainless steel surface, then backs away a few steps.

I approach cautiously. Although we treat all types of companion animals at Saint Gertrude's, reptiles are a less common type of familiar. Therefore I'm not quite as used to handling them. And I don't want Harrisford to think that I'm, well . . . incompetent. He'd never let me hear the end of it.

Pushing up the sleeves of my robes, I hover my hands mere millimeters away from the bearded dragon's skin. She stays stock-still, her black eyes fixed on me, as I lean into my magical senses and start palpating the lizard's qì.

Like all the other familiars that went a bit feral tonight, I'm immediately hit with the sensation of way too much magic. The magiphilia pulses through the familiar's life force like an oncoming tide; her skin is scorching, when she should be relatively cool since it's nighttime and she's ectothermic. I run my hands along the palpable aura, muttering when my hand catches on something—an injury.

It's on her underside. There's a burn there, deep enough to warrant dressing.

"She has a burn," I say softly, checking the rest of her over. "I can easily heal it. It'll be a bit uncomfortable, though. I'll need to lightly anesthetize her. Are you okay with that?"

When I look up, Harrisford's face is pale, his jaw clenched. "Go ahead. Please."

Automatically, I reach for the drug safe key, but then hesitate.

"What's wrong?" It seems impossible, but Harrisford's grown even paler.

"We might have an issue," I say. "Someone's going to realize if there are drugs missing. I could use gas, but—"

"But what?" Harrisford's shoulders are tensed, his fists clenched.

I grimace. "It won't work if she holds her breath."

He looks squarely at his familiar, a stern slant to his eyebrows. "Don't hold your breath, Pudding."

A laugh escapes my lips, involuntarily, and Harrisford scowls at me, his expression dark. "What's so funny?"

I'm still trying to stifle my giggles, but I manage to choke a response out. "Your familiar's name is *Pudding*? You—Harrisford Briggs, the most intimidating final-year at Seamere—named your lizard *Pudding*?"

"My dragon, Chan," he snaps, his cheeks going pink. "And I was just a kid when I got her. I was four years old, and friendless, and I really liked pudding, okay? So I named her after what I liked best."

Immediately, I stop snickering, pondering Harrisford's words. Imagining him as a small, lonesome child is oddly unsettling. Like peeking behind the curtain of a fancy house and finding that it's dilapidated, dirty, and deserted. Our gazes meet—his steely, mine flustered—and I quickly look away.

"I get it," I mumble awkwardly. "I mean, I like pudding too."

To break the tension, I fetch the plexiglass induction chamber and hook it up to the anesthesia machine.

The machines require magic to function, which under normal circumstances would be a problem since I've pretty much depleted my magic stores for today. And this evening, having been interrupted by the scene in the common room, I never got the chance to complete the rationing spell to replenish it.

But luckily, as a result of recent events, I've unexpectedly acquired a familiar, meaning I can now channel magic directly from the air.

Some people believe that all magic comes from an alternate universe called the Void, which Magecorp and Linksphere tap into, somehow. In reality, though, it's probably just atmospheric magic that the corporations siphon—or else a reservoir of magic harvested from mines—not that mystical, pseudoscience Void shit. It doesn't help that both Magecorp and Linksphere are so secretive about their harvesting methods, calling it proprietary knowledge.

Gently, I place the dragon into the box before I reach for the anesthesia machine and press the refill button. Since Percy absorbed all the excess magic in the common room, the magic flows easily: power flowing from the atmosphere, through him, and then into me, coalescing in my hands.

I let it run into the machine, filling its reservoir, before turning the dial on the vaporizer and letting the magic flow into the chamber.

There's an uncomfortable hush during which Harrisford and I both stare at Pudding, who is crouching completely motionless in the clear plastic box. I begin preparing the heat mat and the equipment I need for intubation. But I quickly run out of things to busy myself with, and we lapse back into an awkward silence. Finally, Harrisford breaks it.

"So you find me intimidating, huh?" The vulnerability is gone from his voice; instead, there's a smirk hidden within his words.

Now it's my turn to blush. "About as intimidating as a baby rabbit." It's supposed to be an insult, but its impact is lessened by the way my voice happens to crack midsentence.

Luckily Harrisford doesn't seem to notice. "I was bitten by a rabbit once," he says thoughtfully. "At a birthday party. I thought the magician was using real magic. Didn't expect the blasted creature to still be in the hat." He frowns and shakes his head. "Horrid things."

"There you are, then," I say. "They're exactly like you."

He raises one elegant eyebrow but doesn't respond. Then he gestures to Pudding, who by now has lain down and is breathing slow and deep. "Is she ready yet?"

"I think so." My voice has inadvertently dropped to a whisper. "Do you know how to hold her to intubate her?"

"You want me to *nurse* for you, Chan?" His eyes widen in mock horror.

"Just shut up and do it." I'm losing patience. "That way we can get this over and done with faster."

Of course, as usual, Harrisford performs his role impeccably, and I manage to get the endotracheal tube in with no drama. Together, we roll her belly-up onto the heat mat, hook her up to the anesthesia machine, and connect all the monitors, which begin to beep reassuringly. At my instruction, Harrisford takes the rebreathing bag and manually ventilates her, his eyes glued to the monitoring screen the whole time.

I work quickly, bathing the wound to ensure it's clean and performing a healing spell. Since the skin will likely be more delicate for a few days, I wrap a little bandage around the bearded dragon's middle. Lastly, I inject her with pain relief and a small amount of antibiotics so that the wound won't fester, and switch the anesthesia machine off.

Recovery is always the most dangerous part of anesthetizing animals, so I leave the breathing tube in and the monitoring equipment on and continue to give Pudding small puffs of air as slowly she comes back to consciousness.

"So why did you take her, anyway?" I ask Harrisford as I check her vitals. Her carbon dioxide levels have crept up, so I give her another breath. "To the gala. Since you weren't supposed to."

Harrisford won't meet my gaze. "That's none of your business." His tone is short.

"You've kind of made it my business," I say. "When you coerced me into sneaking into the hospital at nighttime and secretly fixing your pet."

"Coerced you?" he says, outraged, the muscle in his jaw jumping. "May I remind you that the *only* reason you agreed is so I'll keep quiet about *your* rule breaking—"

My anger flares. "They were going to *euthanize* him, Briggs!"

Harrisford narrows his eyes at me, his voice stony and deceptively soft. "They probably had their reasons."

My fury explodes, running over like an overfilled cup. "They *didn't*," I hiss. "He was only house-soiling because he has too much magic."

Percy's voice cuts into my thoughts. *Actually, I did rather relish targeting that horrid woman's shoes—*

Not. Helpful. Percy! I silently grit out.

Harrisford's eyes have snapped to mine, and he looks stunned, like I've slapped him. "What did you say?"

Ignoring Percy, I attempt to explain. "Percy—he has too much magic. Like the rest of the familiars. Except his magiphilia has been going on for months." I pause, suddenly aware that Harrisford hadn't seen what had happened in the common room. "The animals were all going feral tonight, in the residential halls and the stables. Bolting and kicking and biting and escaping. You didn't see it because you were at the gala." I cast a look around the hospital room and at the patients resting quietly in their cages. "I think these guys only escaped it because the hospital must be protected against magical surges." There are all sorts of protective wards and charms built into the walls of Saint Gertrude's. I'm not sure how old the hospital is, but the building itself has been here for a very long time.

Harrisford paces away from the treatment table, raking both hands through his hair. Then he strides back to me, his eyes wild. He leans over the table, his fingers gripping the edges, his knuckles white. "That's what happened at the gala, too."

I'm speechless for a moment. "The explosions were because of a magical surge?" I say finally.

He stares, hard, down at the stainless steel surface. In it, his face is reflected, his mirrored features all dull and blurry. "I think so," he says, enunciating the words carefully, as though he's thinking things through. "I'd put Pudding in my pocket to conceal her. Normally, she's pretty good there. She knows the drill and she'll stay quiet. But she suddenly started thrashing about, and got really hot. That's . . . That's probably when she got burned. And then Samuel Sloane's hat exploded." He pushes off the table and swipes his hair off his forehead, clasping his hand against his head.

I stare at him, my heart drumming double time in my chest. "Do you think it's connected?" I whisper. "I heard on the news they're questioning MLO members . . ."

Harrisford doesn't answer immediately. He watches his familiar as she begins to twitch and recover. I glance at Percy. He's now lying in the corner, flopped onto his side, staring at us, unblinking.

Finally, Harrisford's icy gaze slides back to me, and he stares at me with cold determination. "You know what, Chan," he says, slowly. "I think it is."

8

Gwendolynne

Harrisford insists on walking me back to my dorm room, though I know it's only because he's worried I'll run off and snitch about the lizard he snuck into the gala.

As we walk, he tells me about how his father has been acting weird for the past few months. Which is, coincidentally, precisely when Harrisford noticed the first magical power surge—at home.

"It was just a small one," he explains, cradling Pudding with both arms. "We were having breakfast when all the lights went out, even the chandelier."

I squint sideways at him. "You eat breakfast beneath a chandelier?" He just shrugs, and doesn't respond.

My magic levels started rising a few months ago too, Percy says, sounding thoroughly unimpressed.

Hugging the cat tightly, I consider this new information. "Percy was the first, I think. His magiphilia started at around that time, too. And at some point since then, it started in the other familiars." I purse my lips, thinking hard. "I suspect they've all been channeling slightly higher levels of magic for a while now, else the surge tonight would've killed them."

Harrisford nods. "That's probably why Samuel's polar bear blew up. I'm sure he bought it new and only enchanted it for the night. It hadn't had a chance to acclimatize."

My mouth pulls down in a frown. "But what does it all mean?"

Harrisford's expression mirrors mine. "I don't know," he says. "But given my father has been acting so peculiar, I wonder if he—or Magecorp—is involved?"

I throw him a look. "You think it's Magecorp, and not the MLO?" Glancing at the scorch marks that flare up the corridor walls, I involuntarily give a shudder. If it *was* the MLO, then it means that somehow they've infiltrated us here, at Seamere.

Harrisford pauses for a moment. "I rather think it could be either, at this stage."

We've arrived in front of my room. I'm suddenly hyperaware of how shabby our surroundings are. How messy things are inside. I mean, if we were to open the door we'd see a rank, open tin of tuna, torn-up bits of beef jerky, and pieces of dried-out cheese strewn across the worn, stained carpet.

"Well," I say, falsely jovial. "This is me." When Harrisford doesn't move but just continues staring at me, I add, "Good night, then."

Adjusting my grip on Percy, I reach my free hand out and turn the doorknob. But Harrisford's own hand whips out and clamps around my wrist. His touch is hot, almost burning. We both jerk our heads down to look at where he's grabbed me, and for a moment I sense we're both holding our breaths. But by the time that detail registers, he's already let me go.

It might just be the light, but his pupils are blown so wide his eyes—even the blue one—look almost black. "Wait," he says, his voice low and slightly hoarse.

I start to panic, my heart pounding. What does he want? Not to come in, hopefully? I *really* don't want him to see the inside of my room. "Why?"

The faintest line has appeared between the graceful curves of his eyebrows, and he runs a hand across his chin. "Don't you think we ought to . . . you know . . . *investigate* things?"

I let out a most undignified, and skeptical, snort. "You don't mean together, Briggs? Surely!" I'd already been pondering the magical surges, of course, but Harrisford is the last person I want to ponder them with.

Somehow, the expression in his eyes morphs from liquid to steel in less than a single heartbeat. "I don't fancy the idea much either. But don't forget: We both have a stake in this."

"No, we don't," I clap back. "It's *your* father involved. Your father, your father's company, possibly the MLO. It's got nothing to do with me." Huffing, I push open the door, which is slightly ajar, trying to slip inside.

Harrisford, displaying impressive reflexes, catches the door handle so that it stops swinging. I smack face-first into the cheap painted wood. My nose throbs and I cry out, more from shock than pain.

"Let go!" I shriek, not caring whether anyone—like Bridie or Pen—might hear me. But Harrisford gives me a look of grim determination and continues holding the door.

"Listen, *Chan*," he says, through clenched teeth. "It has *everything* to do with you. If there's some sort of cover-up happening, over whatever is causing these magic surges, then it has the potential to affect everyone. And not only that"—his lips pull up into a sinister smile, though his eyes stay remote, detached—"but if our familiars are affected, or the flow of magic is disrupted, do you really think we have any hope of passing exams?" His smile curves even more when he sees my sharp intake of breath. "You hadn't thought of that, had you?"

My heart lurches. Harrisford has pulled out the big gun, the golden ticket, the one thing he knows will stop me in my tracks. And annoyingly, he's right. The final exams aren't run by Seamere, but by the Magical Education Regulatory Authority. And based on past years, MERA doesn't give concessions for extenuating circumstances. The idea is that we graduating students are supposed to be resilient and adaptable and capable of doing our job under actual, real-life conditions.

With a third of our final assessments being practical exams, we really need a stable, reliable flow of magic in order to demonstrate our skills. And with these surges randomly occurring at unpredictable times, they definitely have the potential to put our academic performances at risk.

I hadn't thought about how the surges might affect me, personally or academically. But if I can't perform at my exams, and I can't come first, then it's not just me who will suffer. It's my family too. It's my parents' livelihoods. And we definitely need the money more than Harrisford Briggs.

A faint, pounding pain is building behind my eyeballs. If there's one thing I can't bear, it's the thought of Harrisford-fucking-Briggs working this out on his own. I bet if he did, he'd keep the knowledge to himself, fixing his own flow of magic so that only *his* spells worked. He'd get top marks, and I—

The Ministry position hangs between us, unspoken for, like an existential carrot dangling between our noses.

I need to come first, I tell myself. Drawing a deep breath, I correct myself. *I* will *come first.*

So, despite the fact that my pulse is hammering like a warning drum in my ears, I raise my face to Harrisford's, speaking through gritted teeth. "Fine. I'll help you investigate the surges, Briggs."

In my head, I add, *And then I'll fucking win.*

Harrisford and I had grudgingly agreed to meet in the library after class the following day. The aim? To track down any historical precedent for magical surges and research how often—and where—they've been occurring recently. Before we parted, we'd both conducted a cursory search on our straps. Except for what had happened at the gala, which was too big an event to cover up, we'd found that none of the surges had been reported by mainstream media.

"It's very odd," Harrisford had murmured, scrolling with a frown.

I don't much want to meet with my nemesis tomorrow, but right now I have to put it completely out of my mind. Tonight my priority is to stash Percy safely in my room, so he's hidden, and then go to see Heloise. After the incident earlier where she'd been dragged by her unicorn familiar, I really need to check to make sure she's okay.

Heloise Chapman is who I consider my closest friend at Seamere—though in truth, she kind of intimidates me. I've always been a little confused as to why she bothered befriending me at all, considering the Chapmans are, like, the richest Black family in London. Her parents are both doctors: her mum holds a prominent position as president of the British Magical Medical Association, and her dad teaches magical biomedical sciences at a prestigious university. He's famous for having invented a spell that gives gym-goers the effects of hours of cardio from just minutes of moderate exercise. Apparently it's the magic solution to our modern, sedentary society. Years ago, he and his research group sold the patent to Big Pharma and basically set themselves up for life.

Heloise's older brother and sister are both doctors too, and Heloise often jokes that she tried to rebel against following in her family's footsteps. Instead, she became an animal doctor—about as rebellious as she'd dared.

When I find Heloise in the infirmary, she's reclining in a hospital bed, against a heap of puffy white pillows. Several floral arrangements are clustered around her, and Dr. Dennis, the school healer, is busy dabbing at a cut on her cheek. The wound needs to be cleaned before it's magically healed so it doesn't become infected.

She's wincing at the sting, but when she spots me her face brightens immediately. "Gwen," she calls out. "Hey!"

I hurry over, eyeing all the gifts on her table, wishing I'd thought to bring something too. Not that I can afford to buy flowers, especially after hours. And it's not like I have anything suitable in my room—I highly doubt she'll want a pack of Knobbly's Premium Unsalted Nuts.

"Hiya, Heli," I say, pulling up a chair beside her bed. "How are you feeling?"

She flashes me a wide smile, her perfect rows of white teeth a striking contrast against her dark skin. "Oh, you know. I'm much better now. Dennis has healed most of my major injuries." She leans forward, her eyes widening. "I had three cracked ribs, a compound fracture of my left tibia, and bilateral shoulder luxations!"

I wince. "Ouch," I say. "Sounds nasty."

"It was." Heloise frowns slightly, her brow furrowing. "I don't know what got into Lightning. He's normally so placid, and tonight he just . . . wasn't."

I glance around the room to make sure we're alone. Dr. Dennis, having finished healing Heli, has put away her medical supplies and disappeared into her office at the far end of the ward. And there's only one other patient here, who I think might be a fourth-year, sound asleep in the far corner.

Still, I lower my voice. "Heli, I don't know if you realize, but . . . Lots of familiars went kind of wild tonight. There was a surge of magiphilia. It was really weird."

She lets out a little gasp. "Really?"

I nod. "Really. I'm actually surprised there aren't more injured folk here. Some of the familiars were like, biting their own humans and stuff."

Heloise scrunches up her face. "It did get kind of busy earlier. I didn't take much notice 'cause I was really zoned out on pain meds. But there was a flurry of activity and then everyone left, except us." She gestures at the sleeping student, then raises her eyebrows at me. "What gives, Gwen?"

"I don't know," I say slowly. "Did you hear there was an explosion at the Natural History Museum earlier? At some sort of charity gala."

"Yeah. My mum and dad were supposed to go, but they got hit with gastro, so they stayed home." Heloise wrinkles her nose. "Lucky, huh?"

"I think it might be related." I bite my cheek, wondering if I should tell her about Percy, and the fact he's had slowly elevating magiphilia for the past few months. *And* that somehow the magical surge bonded him to me, so now I happen to have a familiar.

But I decide against it, because the fewer people who know about him, the safer. I'm already deeply uncomfortable with the fact that the only person who knows my secret is my enemy, Harrisford Briggs. It's already a precarious enough situation, considering I'm relying on Percy, a rather capricious cat, to keep quiet enough so Nathaniel Price doesn't notice his missing pet is still alive.

So I veer away from talking about familiars. "Do your parents know if anything like this is happening in humans?"

"Magiphilia?" Heloise reaches beneath one of her pillows and whips out a brand-new-looking laptop. “Hang on,” she says. “I’ll ask.” She takes a Magecorp-branded powerbank and plugs it in, booting the computer up.

I lean back in my chair as Heloise taps out a message to her mother, her long fingers flying across the laptop’s pristine keyboard. It’s not long before we hear the *ding* that tells us Dr. Chapman has replied.

Heloise’s eyes scan the screen, and she reads out her mother’s message, paraphrasing it slightly. “She says that there are sporadic reports of magical surges affecting humans too.” I grip the armrests of my chair as my friend continues reading aloud. “People have been randomly disappearing. Apparently there have even been deaths, though they can’t identify a pattern. There’s been an increased incidence of bites and scratches from magical familiars. And some hospitals across the country have been experiencing random magic outages.” Heloise raises her big brown eyes to meet mine. “It’s chaos.”

“Deaths.” My mind has snagged on that word, which tumbles from my mouth like a stone. I do a quick search on my strap, tapping the cracked screen. My heart starts pounding until all I can hear is roaring. “People have *died*, Heli . . .” I shake my head in disbelief. “But it hasn’t made the news.”

Heloise frowns and returns her attention to her computer screen. “Listen to this: Mum also says she’s been trying to secure some grant funding to study this phenomenon, since nothing like this has ever been reported in any of the medical literature. She says there’s a group in Bristol who are keen to spearhead the research, but the Ministry keeps on declining their application . . .” Heloise trails off, two fingers pressed against her lips. “That almost never happens, Gwen. Everyone knows that with my mum’s connections, if she backs a grant application, it almost *always* gets approved.”

My stomach churns, and all of a sudden I feel sick. Deaths in the magical community. Explosions at a charity gala. Familiars going feral. Hospitals randomly losing magical power.

And behind it all, Darghan Briggs acting strange, and the Ministry declining grant applications that should technically be a shoo-in.

I force myself to dig my fingers into the cracked vinyl of the hospital chair to keep from clawing at my face.

As much as I'm loath to admit it, Harrisford Briggs is right. This problem is big. Bigger than I'd initially thought. "All the way up to the Ministry" big.

And if we don't figure out what's behind it, it could destroy us all.

9

Harrisford

Gwendolynne appears rather frazzled when she arrives at the library, a full twenty minutes late. Today, she's ditched the horrid brown cardigan and is wearing a scrub top over a long-sleeve blue-and-white striped top. Her long black hair is pulled back into a braid.

Pudding, who's perched on the desk beside me, turns her head—very slightly. Her melodious voice echoes through my mind. *For someone who claims to hate this woman, you seem to be noticing a lot about her appearance—*

Oh, shut it, I think back. Pudding just chuckles and goes back to being a statue.

"Sorry," Gwendolynne says, dropping her bag onto the table. "I got held up at the hospital, and then I couldn't find you." She glances at my familiar, who is still wearing her bandage. "Oh, hiya, Pudding. Glad to see you're looking better."

Pudding raises her chin, preening. I roll my eyes, but my lips twitch with a smile.

It's not surprising that Gwendolynne couldn't find me. I suppose I should have been more specific with the location. The library is five levels of stone archways, sweeping staircases, and scores of crumbling books. It's a veritable rabbit's warren of shadows and hidden nooks and crannies, the dimness not helped by the stained glass windows. I had to choose our location strategically, so that the books wouldn't listen in on our conversation.

Being from a magical legacy family, I haven't had much occasion to visit regular human facilities. But according to what I've read, regular libraries are *nothing* like ours. In regular libraries, the books are there only to impart information. And while in the Seamere College library, there are plenty of books and scrolls that do that, there are also whole sections devoted to *listening* books: books that are designed to absorb information.

The idea being that you can take a book to a lecture at a magical sciences symposium, for example, and it will absorb all the most up-to-date information. Within hours, you'll find it all logically arranged into volumes and chapters, printed like a regular textbook. You can even take an existing listening book along and it'll update the information already there. They're rare, expensive, and tremendously important: They're one of the ways that magical knowledge has been kept, recorded, and passed down through the generations. And it's one of the reasons the librarians are so hell-bent on keeping visiting students quiet.

The issue is that the books even listen when they're shelved, dormant, in the library. On more than one occasion, I've pulled out a volume about some dry topic, such as the history of magical revolutions, and been reading a passage about the 1642 civil war, when all of a sudden the text will segue into something like *oh yes, oh god, just like that, that's it* and it's obvious that at some point a couple of irresponsible students got overly frisky between the stacks.

Which makes for interesting, but irrelevant, reading.

So for tonight I'd had to find a desk that was expressly out of range of any listening books. *Not* because I'm planning on getting frisky with Gwendolynne Chan, of course, but because I don't want us to get caught discussing a potential UK-wide magical conspiracy.

Gwendolynne slides into her chair and pulls out a bunch of scrolls. I arch an eyebrow at her. "What are those, Chan?"

She glares at me, as though I said something rude instead of asking her a simple question. "They're dates," she says. "Dates of when human deaths have occurred due to magiphilia. Periods of time when human hospitals have experienced surges and magical outages, and records of all the injuries sustained from magical familiars treated at public hospitals over the past year." She taps one of the scrolls, her lips pursing. "Even Heli is listed here."

I don't really know who Heli is, and I don't much care. I just lean back in my chair and level a look at her. "I must say, I'm impressed."

She seems to swell with pride before realizing who she's talking to. The joy drains from her face and is replaced by her usual scowl. "Yeah, well, it wasn't me, really. It was Heloise who got it all from her mother."

I say nothing, and Gwendolynne raises her eyebrows in disbelief. "Nora Chapman? You know, the president of the British Magical Medical Association?"

"Riiiiight," I say. "I believe I've met her before, at a function."

"Figures," Gwendolynne mutters beneath her breath. "Anyway, Dr. Chapman was so happy her daughter was showing an interest in human medicine that she was happy to give Heli all this information. I think she's hoping that Heloise might transfer to medicine—"

"Why?" I cut her off, genuinely shocked. "Why would one transfer when humans are—"

"—disgusting." Gwendolynne gives a delicate wrinkle of her nose. "I know, right?"

She lapses into silence, and I take her cue, lowering my reading glasses from where they're perched on my head and turning my attention back to my book. It's maddening. I've trawled through dozens of history books already, and have found nothing about magical surges in any of them.

Is it because it's never happened before? Or because . . . the records have been wiped?

We continue researching for ages, only exchanging a couple of words here and there. About an hour into our session, she slips her feet out of her shoes. Ten minutes after that, she draws her feet beneath her, tucking them under her backside.

I catch myself watching her more often than is strictly necessary: at the way she chews her lower lip absent-mindedly when she's concentrating. At the way she periodically rolls her head and rubs at the back of her neck. At the way she tugs at her braid as she reads, until strands of smooth straight hair come loose and fall haphazardly around her shoulders.

I force myself to look away. I'm stiff, sore, and agitated; something is uncomfortably hard and it's not just my chair.

Abruptly, I stand, my chair scraping against the floor. Gwendolynne glances up, a distracted expression on her face. She seems utterly unaffected by the fact that she's been sitting for hours, doing nothing but perusing scrolls.

I flatten my lips in disapproval. She really is an incurable swot.

"Where are you going?" Since she's barely spoken a word since her arrival, her voice is a little husky, and it's doing something to my nether regions that I'd rather not analyze too closely.

"To get a drink," I say, jamming my glasses into the chest pocket of my shirt.

I wait at the library café on the ground floor, wondering how much longer I can do this. Sit in close proximity to Gwendolynne while she reads scrolls and bites her lower lip. I wonder what's going on in her head, what she's thinking, whether she's been studying so much that she'll actually beat me and win that coveted top spot.

You seem troubled, Harrisford. Pudding's tone is full of worry.

I sigh. "It's nothing to concern yourself with. I'm just tired. Hopefully coffee will help."

By the time I return with both of our drinks, Gwendolynne is gripping a scroll so hard it's almost shaking, and simultaneously staring at her strap screen.

"Briggs," she breathes. She looks up at me, brown eyes wide, excitement wrought plain on her face. Something twists inside me to see her looking so goddamned . . . happy. I don't think I've ever seen that look on her face before. "I think I've found something!"

I set her drink in front of her. It's still steaming since I have, very considerately, put a keep-warm spell on it. Then I flop down into my own chair and take a swig of my coffee, hoping the caffeine buzz will hit soon. "What is it, then?"

She pushes the scroll she's holding toward me. It's covered in pencil marks from where she's crossed off each date. I frown at it. "And what am I looking at, exactly?"

Drawing the scroll back to her, she shows me her strap screen. It's so small that I have to squint to see anything, even with my glasses on.

"It's the Witches Truths Society web page," she jabbers, excited. "All the big news sites have been completely silent on the magical surges, but WTS have reported on every single one."

"WTS?" I scoff. "Come, now, Chan. Be serious. Everyone knows that they're deranged conspiracy theorists. Everything they print is rubbish."

Her face flushes red and she glares at me. "No it's not, you twat!

Look"—she jabs a finger at the marked-up scroll—"every single date Nora Chapman gave us matches up."

I snatch the page off her and stare at it, double-checking Gwendolynne's assertion against the WTS's list. Fucking hell, she's actually right. Even the mini power surge we'd had at the Briggs family breakfast table is listed on the WTS website.

As I read, Gwendolynne picks up her drink and takes a sip. "Oh!" she gasps. "It's tea."

I'm so absorbed in cross-checking the lists that I don't look up at her. I just mumble, preoccupied, "Yes. Earl Grey with one sugar and soy milk, right?"

She doesn't respond, but I feel her eyes on me, so eventually I raise my head and frown at her. "That's your usual, is it not? Or did I get it wrong?"

She has a curious sort of look in her eyes. She keeps staring at me for several seconds, then blinks and looks away. "Uh, no, you didn't get it wrong. I . . . um . . . thanks."

The back of my neck burns, and I duck my head again, pretending I'm perusing the scroll. I suddenly understand why she's acting so flabbergasted. I'd gone and ordered her favorite drink without even fucking realizing it. And it occurs to me that, embarrassingly, the reason—the *only* reason—I know it by heart is because I'm more aware of her than I'd care to admit.

It's just because you need to beat her, my mind insists obstinately. And it's true—I've been watching her for years, attempting to sniff out her weaknesses, trying to figure out her methods and why she's so smart and how I can one-up her in each exam. She's my ultimate rival, the only witch who has ever unseated me from top place.

Though it still doesn't really explain why I've noticed her in the lunchroom. Or why I've memorized the way she makes her tea when she thinks no one else is looking.

And perhaps it doesn't explain why I insisted that *she* dress Pudding's wounds, when I probably could have taken my myth.creat knowledge, applied it to a smaller reptile, and managed it myself.

No. I was just worried about my familiar last night, that's all. I wasn't thinking straight. After all, Pudding came into my life at a particularly vulnerable time, and since then I've been very protective of her . . . Some might say overprotective. I most definitely was *not* trying to spend more time with Gwendolynne Guiying Chan.

I swallow, suddenly extremely conscious of the movement my throat makes as I do so. Gwendolynne is no longer looking at me, but instead is staring very hard at her scroll, a faint tinge of pink dusting the tops of both cheekbones.

"Chan?" I say eventually.

"Yes, Briggs?" she responds, still determined to not look at me.

"Do you have plans for tomorrow night?"

She gives a nervous laugh, a flush creeping across her décolletage. "Oh, you know me," she says, rubbing at her neck. "I'll just be chained to my desk, studying."

I almost spit out my coffee but manage to swallow it down. "Can you take a night off?" My hands are clammy; I tighten my fingers around my cup. Something about the dates on Nora Chapman's lists has given me an idea . . . and unfortunately, it involves my father.

Finally, she looks up, giving me a wary look. "Why?"

"Because," I say, my mood darkening, "we need to break into my father's study."

10

Gwendolynne

The next day at our weekly dean's lecture, the dean, Professor Kaur, is away. Apparently she's unwell, so Seamere's vice dean, Professor Thomas Pickering, is standing in.

The vice dean's speech is all about the magical power surge that happened in the common room two nights ago; Professor Pickering assures us all that it's a "one-off event" and that "no students were harmed" and that we should all focus on our studies and exams in a few weeks' time.

The professor's speech baffles me because for one, there's no mention of the other power surges that have been occurring across London—including the one at the charity gala. And two, students *were* harmed. Several students, in fact. Heloise is still in the infirmary, and her empty chair is like a burning hole beside me.

At the conclusion of his lecture, Professor Pickering invites questions from the audience.

A fifth-year student at the back of the hall raises her hand. "What about the rumors about MLO involvement, Professor? Some people have been saying that it might be connected—"

Professor Pickering harrumphs and cuts her off. "I would encourage you not to listen to unfounded gossip, Miss Larsson." With one finger, he pushes up his wire-rimmed glasses. The overhead lights catch the beads of sweat that have sprung out on his forehead. "There is absolutely no evidence that a terrorist organization like the MLO could breach Seamere security. However, if anyone has any concerns about the matter, or wishes to discuss these . . . *rumors* . . . in more confidence, see me in my office."

I mull over this as the vice dean continues to answer questions, fielding several related to how much time students can legitimately take out of classes in order to tend their injured familiars.

While it's true that the MLO sneaking into Seamere is unlikely, that doesn't necessarily make it better. Even if it isn't them that caused the explosion, shouldn't that still be a cause for concern?

I cast a surreptitious look around the room. What if it's one of *us*?

Professor Pickering doesn't seem worried, however. Any further questions about magical surges or explosions are quickly and expertly shut down. I begin to suspect that the professor has been given some sort of media training.

It's only when we're finally dismissed that I realize I'd been clenching my fists the whole session. My palms are covered with little red crescents from where they've been indented by my nails.

I'm supposed to meet Harrisford by the large paddock tonight, fifteen minutes after the end of class. I'd suggested we meet somewhere outside since I didn't want to risk him coming by my dorm again. When the time comes, I rush to my room: Fifteen minutes is just enough time to throw on some clean clothes and smear on some lip gloss. It's silly, but I'm actually nervous, my pulse erratic.

My thoughts keep sliding back to what had happened in the library yesterday. How—and why—had Harrisford known the way I take my tea? As far as I can remember, I've never told him. He can't have been watching me that closely, can he?

Unless . . . I pick up my brush and drag it through my hair, barely noticing it snagging in my knots. *No.* It's probably just because Harrisford is highly observational and likes to figure people out. I suspect he wants to know everything he can about his rivals—including me—so he can properly destroy them.

Percy watches as I try to scrape my hair back into something resembling a hairstyle. He's lying on my brown cardigan and has burned a hole right through it. It could well have been intentional, but I'm not brave enough to ask.

I still don't understand why you humans insist on grooming yourselves with those dreadful plastic things, he observes dryly, as my flat hair fights a losing battle against Earth's unconquerable gravity, *when a tongue is clearly so much better.*

"I don't have spines on my tongue, Percy. It's less functional than yours." I let out a sigh, then give up on my hair, letting it tumble loose around my shoulders. Momentarily, I consider trying a hair-volumizing spell. But I'm not well practiced at doing them, so I decide it's not worth the bother.

This is true, Percy replies. *I suppose you do have less hair overall anyway. You're all . . . ugly, and hairless, and beige-colored.* He yawns and shifts position, tucking his paws tighter beneath him. Then he squeezes his eye shut, as though he cannot stand to look at me for even one second longer.

I battle the urge to point out the state of his own coat and decide, on balance, it's not worth it. So, ignoring his musings, I scoop a cup of cat food into his puzzle feeder and grab my bag before dashing out the door. I'll be just in time.

But as I'm passing Conall Peters's room, I hear a great, heaving sob from within.

I pause, chewing my lip, staring at the cracked-open door.

"Conall?" I say, peering into the darkness within. "Are you all right?"

There's no answer; just the sound of more weeping.

I try again, this time gently knocking. "Conall?"

Finally, footsteps approach, and Conall's tear-streaked face appears in the crack. His light brown hair is all mussed up and he has burn marks along both arms, and I realize in retrospect that he hadn't shown up to Saint Gertrude's *or* to today's lecture.

I stare at him in alarm. "What's wrong?"

He lets out a snivel, then chokes some words out. "It's—it's Gary."

My heart sinks. "What happened?"

Conall doesn't respond, just swings the door wide and goes inside. I follow, not quite sure if I'm doing the right thing. I don't know Conall well; he's only been at Seamere since fourth year, when he transferred from another degree.

This is the first time I've been inside Conall's room, and the first thing I notice is that the walls are plastered with geometric ink drawings. Although I'm no artist, I recognize that they're really good—the line work is intricate and precise. I'm guessing they were made by Conall.

By now, Conall himself is kneeling in the center of his room, cradling the tiny brown-and-white body of his familiar, Gary. And considering the guinea pig's matte, glassy eyes and straight, stiff little legs, it's quite clear that Gary is stone-cold dead.

"Oh no, Conall," I say, sinking to my knees beside him. "I'm so sorry."

Conall blinks, and several tears slide out from beneath his eyelids, dripping down his long pointy nose before pattering onto the floor. "It was"—he sniffs, then swipes at his eyes with his forearm—"the magic surge. The other night. I tried to save him, Gwen, I really did, but he never quite came good . . ."

Pity twists itself into my chest and I reach out, awkwardly placing an arm around Conall's shoulders. I give him a squeeze as he dissolves into a cacophony of wails.

"He was such a help, you know?" Conall continues, his voice catching between sobs. "Before, I felt so alone, so dysphoric . . . but Gary always knew who I was. He always saw me as a boy." Conall raises his red-rimmed, watery eyes to mine. "He *understood*, you know? Like only a familiar can."

I think about my own newly acquired familiar, who doesn't seem in the least bit understanding. If I'm being honest, Percy's actually a massive jerk. But from what I'd seen of Conall's familiar, Gary the guinea pig had been a gentle, empathic soul—much like Conall himself.

Multiple emotions are warring inside me: grief and pity, because of what Conall's lost. But also . . . rage. Rage because of what is happening, and how little the higher-ups are taking it seriously. My chest tightens at the memory of Professor Pickering so casually dismissing students' questions.

It was bad enough when Heloise told me that people had actually died from the magical surges. But they were nothing but names written on a screen. Now it's Conall—who, if not necessarily someone I'd consider a *friend*, has always been unflappably kind—and his poor guinea pig that have suffered. And it's brought it that much closer to home.

Putting my arms around Conall, I let him cry and cry, his tears dampening my shoulder, until he is all cried out. Then I hand him some tissues and say, my voice gentle, "Come, Conall. I'll help you fill out the paperwork for cremation."

It's six forty-five p.m. before I manage to make it down to the paddocks, a good half hour after I was supposed to meet Harrisford.

As I hurry toward our meeting point, I let out a relieved sigh. Harrisford hasn't finished up yet. He's still in the paddock, holding a dragon by a tether.

I edge closer, not without some trepidation. I haven't been this close to a dragon since third year, before our year level split into our respective streams. Prior to this, we'd all had to take Dragon Studies, learning not only their lore and history and the extent of their magical abilities but also the particulars of their anatomy, physiology, and nutrition. At the end of third year we'd been assessed on our knowledge; I'd fumbled at the point where we were supposed to label the dragons' markings and colorings. But the examiner, knowing that I was dead-set destined for the Magical Familiars stream, had taken pity on me and given me a passing grade. I think it had come with the unspoken caveat that I never touch a dragon in a veterinary capacity again.

The truth is, I'd found that exam kind of difficult because dragon colorings make no fucking sense. It's like horses, where a white horse is gray and a brown horse is bay and still other brown horses are called chestnut. To a non-horsey person like me it seems completely illogical. For dragons, orange dragons are labeled red, black dragons are called sable, and—because they're the most common—green dragons aren't given a color at all. They're just called dragons.

This one is a red, its burnished scales glowing in the mellow light of the early-evening sun. The flap of its gargantuan wings creates a gale that blows my hair back, and the ropes attached to its tethers snap and strain. The air becomes noticeably hotter the closer to the paddock I draw; the dragon stamps its foot and snorts, emitting small licks of flame from each nostril.

I have to admit—it's actually kind of . . . majestic?

Harrisford hasn't noticed me yet. He's with Danny Wong and three others—one of the myth.creat vets, and two other strangers who I presume are vet nurses. All of them are wearing enormously thick leather gloves and steel-capped work boots.

The supervising vet watches from the sidelines, arms folded. Meanwhile, the others are stationed in the four corners of the paddock, each holding the end of one rope. The dragon continues to flap its wings, rising and sinking with the movement, but its restraints stop it from flying off. I lean my elbows on the fence, one foot propped on the stile, and take a moment to observe, with both personal and academic interest, the intricate knots the veterinary students have tied. There is no way that dragon is escaping tonight, and for that I am very thankful.

Eventually, Harrisford gives a shout, and all four ropes slacken. He's obviously been assigned as the lead student for this particular case.

The humans slowly let the dragon down, allowing it to descend, until finally it hits the ground with a judder. Carefully, Harrisford approaches the beast, inspecting a neat line of sutures beneath its wing.

Even though we have spells for healing, we still need to use sutures for severe lacerations. Just-healed skin remains fragile for days—stitching a wound closed allows it to heal without re-tearing. Plus, in a mobile place like beneath a wing, the tension on the skin is even greater, the risk of wound breakdown too high to leave the healing solely to magic.

Harrisford spends a long time poking and prodding at the wound and muttering to himself. Once he's satisfied, he nods and signals to the others.

"She's healing well," he says to his assistants, then taps the dragon on the rump. "Take her back to the stables; then you're free to go." The nurses slip all but one of the ropes off the dragon, then begin leading her away.

Harrisford confers with his supervisor briefly. I can't hear what they're saying, but based on Harrisford's expression I can guess the subtext. When they break apart, the supervisor claps him on the back before walking away.

I check my strap and grimace. It was as I guessed: Harrisford got full marks for this case, which means he's drawn even with me.

"Nice job, mate," Danny says. "Keep doing what you're doing, and that Ministry job is yours." He slings an arm around Harrisford's shoulders before ruffling up his hair. Harrisford bats him away, grinning. I exhale forcefully through my nose, my jaw clenching.

Harrisford isn't getting that job. I am.

I haven't quite hidden my irritation when Danny finally spots me. "All right, Gwendolynne?" he booms, flashing me a smile, dimples blooming in his round face.

"Hiya, Danny," I say, trying to smooth away my scowl. Danny is a right idiot, but at least he's always been kind. Not like Harrisford-fucking-Briggs.

As though he'd just noticed me, Harrisford finally looks up. Pointedly, he turns to face me and tugs off his gloves—first one, then the other. He doesn't say anything, just stares at me, and I glare right back. All of the warm feelings I'd gleaned from watching the dragon have fully dissipated, and now I'm just annoyed.

Danny looks between me and Harrisford, the smile dying on his lips, before saying, "Well, see ya, then," and speeding off.

"Late again, Chan?" Harrisford calls, tucking his gloves into a pocket of his coveralls. With the dexterity of someone who has done this many times before, he swipes a rope off the ground and begins to rapidly wind it.

My scowl deepens. I have a good excuse, but it's not my place to tell Harrisford about Conall Peters's grief. "You weren't even done here, anyway."

He looks up and cocks one eyebrow, still working on coiling the rope. "What if I was hoping to show off to you a little?"

I press my lips together and look away. I'm trying not to notice how the navy coveralls strain against his broad shoulders or how his hair is all sweaty and damp and plastered to his head. "I think I saw enough," I mutter. *Cocky bastard.*

He doesn't respond, just returns his attention to the rope. When I look at him again, he's grinning.

"How are we getting to your place, anyway?" A breeze dances across my skin, ruffling my hair.

He tosses the coiled ropes into a large crate on my side of the fence and then climbs over right where I'm standing, forcing me to shuffle sideways. I sigh. Why do men like Harrisford always have to take up so much space?

Hefting the crate into his arms, Harrisford starts toward the building, which houses upward of a dozen of the world's most dangerous monsters. From within its concrete confines, chains jangle, wings rustle, and there's the occasional whooshing sound of fire.

"We're going to fly," he says, not looking at me.

Reflexively, I reach out and grab him by the arm, my fingers digging into hard muscle. "*Fly?*"

He stops, then jerks his chin at the building full of dragons, which is apparently our destination. "Yes, Chan. Fly."

"Oh no," I say, backing up and crossing my arms tight across my chest. There's absolutely no way I'll be entering that stable. Sure, dragon-riding is a common enough transport method—but not for me. I'm not even comfortable going too *near* a dragon, let alone riding one. Watching from a distance, with a fence between us, is close enough, thank you. "No, no, no. Not that. Anything but—"

"We don't have a choice." Harrisford's growing frustration is evident. "I don't own a car, and since we're planning to sneak into my father's study, I can't exactly borrow his."

"Then we'll catch the train!"

"The train!" He has the audacity to look horrified. "Listen, Chan." He sets the crate down, rubs his face with both hands, then spreads them wide. "We can't take a car. Trains are filthy and take too long. It's either a dragon or my bike."

I've seen Harrisford speeding out the gates on his motorbike before, trails of dust suspended in his wake. I try to picture myself perched behind him, my arms wrapped around his middle. My hands gripping his firm abs and my face pressed against his back.

A shudder rolls right through me.

Then again, even on a dragon we'd have to be wedged up close. At least, though, the trip would be over quicker. Chewing my lip furiously, I finally concede defeat.

"Fine, I'll ride the bloody dragon," I mutter, stalking toward the stables, not bothering to check if he is following.

Harrisford dumps the crate full of ropes inside the stable office, pulls off his boots, then proceeds to peel off his coveralls. Beneath them he's wearing one of his signature white linen shirts, sleeves rolled up to the elbow, leather braces, and a pair of beige riding jodhpurs that hug his muscular backside distressingly well. Thankfully, I only catch a glimpse of these clothes for a second before he throws his travel cloak on over the top.

He frowns at my skirt as he does up the clasp at the neck. "I thought I told you to dress warm," he says, his tone disapproving.

Irritation rakes its way through me. "I brought a coat."

"Yes, but . . ." With one hand, he gestures vaguely in the direction of my bare legs.

My gut clenches, and I tug my skirt down. "Well, I wasn't exactly aware we'd be riding a fucking dragon, was I?" Now that I'm here, I regret not wearing trousers. What if my skirt rides up? What if he sees the scars on my legs?

Harrisford yanks his boots back on more forcefully than is necessary—his right first, then his left. "Believe me," he mutters, lacing them. "I am *acutely* aware of that."

When he's dressed, he opens the gate to a pen with a creak. I peer into the darkness. A standard green dragon—I mean, a standard *dragon*—crouches in the corner, its fire-filled eyes glinting.

"This is Arkany," Harrisford says, as though introducing his skittish nemesis to one of the college dragons is a normal, everyday occurrence. "Arki for short. She's one of the most placid dragons at Seamere." He's already altogether much too close to the beast, stroking the leathery scales of her neck.

Placid? My heart is bashing itself against my ribs so hard that I'm quite sure she can hear it. "Hello, Arkany," I recite obediently.

There's a long pause before Harrisford hisses out the side of his mouth. "*Chan!* Where are your manners? Introduce yourself back!"

"Oh," I stammer, my face flushing. "I—I'm Gwendolynne Chan."

Using the supernumerary claws on her wings, Arkany toes her way forward, her snout raised high in the air. She turns her head sideways, appraising me with one of her reptilian eyes, then lets out a little puff of smoke.

Harrisford beckons me over. I creep forward so slowly I may as well be staying still. When I'm finally close enough to feel the heat radiating from Arkany's skin, I hesitate, hovering about a meter away, clutching my coat to my chest. My legs are trembling so hard they feel like they're about to collapse, and patches of sweat are gathering at my armpits.

Reaching out, Harrisford places a hand on the small of my

back—surprisingly gently—and draws me even closer. I stumble a little, resisting weakly, until we're both standing right by the dragon, our bodies flush. Harrisford is much taller than me, so my eyeline is somewhere at his upper chest. And it makes absolutely no fucking sense, but Harrisford's heat through his clothes feels even warmer than the actual dragon.

"It's the same principle as approaching a unicorn," he says, his voice low, and he's close enough that his breath stirs the fine, loose wisps of my hair. "If you stand closer to them, it's actually safer." He pats one of the dragon's powerful hind legs, which is unnervingly close to my face. "See? If she kicks you, it will have less power behind it. It'll do significantly less damage."

Briefly, I consider asking him to define *significantly* and *less damage,* but then think better of it. Honestly, it's probably best that I don't know.

Instead, I raise one skeptical eyebrow at him. "You say that as though I regularly associate with unicorns."

Harrisford chuckles, turning to me. "Come. We've no time to waste. I'll give you a hand up."

Awkwardly, I clamber onto the dragon's back. Even with Harrisford pushing me from behind, it takes me three tries to swing my leg over; I'm pretty sure he cops an A-reserve, front-row view of my bum in the process. Eventually, though, I'm stable enough to scramble forward and wedge myself in the furrow in front of Arkany's wings.

Harrisford springs up infuriatingly easily and settles himself behind me. I can smell his cologne and a faint trace of sweat. I can feel the hard lines of his chest snug against my back and his hands palming my hips. Immediately, my pulse begins racing. My palms grow hot and horribly clammy.

How the hell am I going to hold on?

I don't need to wonder for long, because the next moment Harrisford is winding his strong arms around my waist. *Oh*, I think, and my mind briefly goes blank.

Then, too soon, Arkany is lumbering forward, out of the open gate and into the warm summer eve. I suck in a sharp breath as the dragon crouches low, ready to take off, and Harrisford tightens his hold.

"Ready?" he says, the rumble of his voice tickling the back of my ear.

"No—" I start to say, but the dragon shoots into the sky, and my words are lost to the wind.

11

Harrisford

I really, really wish she'd listened to me and put on something warmer.

We're soaring over Surrey when she starts shivering, the movement so violent her teeth clack together. Even though it's summer, at the altitude we're cruising the air is bitterly cold.

Adjusting myself in my seat, I throw my cloak around the both of us, but she continues to tremble, her backside bumping against my crotch.

"Christ, Chan," I snap, trying not to think about the heat of her body against mine, or her scent wafting off the skin of her neck, or the movement that's happening down below. There's a very embarrassing reflex happening that I've no control over, and the shivering is *not* helping. "Will you stay still already?"

"Cant . . . help . . . it . . ." she says, perfectly oblivious to my torment. "It's . . . so . . . cold . . ."

"Well, I told you to wear—"

"Shut it, Briggs." She's still chattering. "Or I won't . . . hesitate . . . to push you off."

I narrow my eyes at the back of her head. "And lose the extra warmth from my cloak? You wouldn't dare."

She snorts, but doesn't respond. All she does is wriggle back against me more firmly.

Goddammit.

It's not long before we're descending, our hair streaming in the wind, and we land in a remote corner of the Briggs estate. Fortunately, Father and me traveling by dragon is a common enough occurrence that we have special stables set up for such trips.

Gwendolynne immediately slides off, putting a few meters of distance between us. As I drop to the ground, her gaze flicks down to my trousers, then away. She flushes. *Fuck.* She wasn't so oblivious after all.

The house is still and quiet, which is not surprising since Father's recently taken to doing overtime at the Magecorp offices. His study is at the end of a long corridor, a good distance from the bedrooms, and as usual it is locked.

Gwendolynne hovers in the shadows behind me as I try my master key—but frustratingly, it doesn't work, even though it used to.

"It's locked." I give an exasperated sigh and lean my shoulder against the wall.

Yesterday in the library, when I'd been perusing the WTS website, a striking detail had suddenly become clear. The dates and locations of the power surges correlated almost exactly with places my father frequented. Not precisely, of course, but pretty closely. And it seems so obvious in retrospect, but he's been acting strangely—so strangely—for months now. Staying late at work; trying to mask his signs of obvious stress.

And now? Now he's gone and changed the bloody locks.

My suspicions, which were once as hazy as shifting smoke, are solidifying within my mind. I'm certain Magecorp, and my father, are connected with the magical surges somehow. It would make sense, since Magecorp is the biggest worldwide manufacturer and distributor of magic. It would also explain why Percy, who until recently was the CEO's familiar, was one of the first animals to suffer from magiphilia.

Perhaps they've lost control over the magical harvesting system and are trying to cover it up by leveling accusations at the MLO.

Whatever the reason, if Father truly is hiding something in this study that could affect me, affect Gwendolynne, even affect the entire world, then I have to stop at nothing to find it.

Thinking hard, I unlock my strap screen, tapping out a quick message to one of my less . . . savory . . . contacts.

"What are you doing?" Gwendolynne asks, her eyes narrowed.

"Definitely nothing illegal. Now hush."

She watches me suspiciously as I continue texting back and forth. Finally, after what feels like a million years, there's the *ping* that tells me the spell has arrived in the inbox of my burner account.

I hurriedly download it. The magic unfurls in my fingertips, feeling warm—a tingling caress. They glow as I reach forward, my hand hovering midair. Then, squinting at the doorknob and summoning all my concentration, I deliberately rotate my hand.

The lock clicks and the door unlatches, settling slightly ajar.

Gwendolynne makes a surprised noise from somewhere deep in her throat. "What? How?" she stammers. "That was—"

"A *resignio* spell," I murmur, pushing open the door. It swings wide, completely silent on its hinges.

"But that's . . . It's impossible, it's—"

I arch an eyebrow at her. "Illegal?"

She crosses her arms and raises her chin. "Well . . . yes."

Gwendolynne is right, of course. There are a handful of spells on the Ministry's Dangerous and Restricted list, and *resignio* is one of them. Mostly they're spells that could be used for crime, torture, or homicide. They're highly regulated, accessible only to specific groups of people—such as the magical police or certain first responders. To the rest of us, they're banned, and there are hefty penalties for their use.

Which is why I had to venture into the dark side of the web to get it.

"For the right price," I say, smirking, "*nothing* is impossible."

She considers that for a second, then lets out a breath. "I don't know whether to be impressed or horrified at how easily you throw around money."

I stride through the door, not looking at her. "How about both?" I say. But what I don't tell her is that I've just drained a third of my trust fund to do it. Restricted spells cost a lot. The thought makes me feel faintly ill.

When we're finally both in the study, the reek hits me. A singed smell, like something's burning, alongside the distinctive scent of too much magic. Gwendolynne and I glance at each other. Her eyes betray her concern—wide, the whites showing, her brown irises like deep pools of liquid in the darkness.

I reach out with my magical senses, ascertaining that the energy is just residual; there are no active wards or security protections to bind the room. I curb my grin—it's lucky that my father did not think to protect his private sanctum with anything but a simple lock.

"You check the desk," I whisper. "I'll take the shelves and the filing cabinets."

We set to work, methodically searching through Father's personal belongings. We're looking for anything that might incriminate him, suggest he's privy to the cause of the surges. The desk drawers scrape as Gwendolynne opens and shuts each one.

The bookshelves are neat and orderly, but the sheer amount of magic shows me where my father has been. Like a footprint left on wet sand at low tide, his magical presence is absolutely smeared across his stuff. I just have to follow the spark of his life essence until it leads me to a small stack of books stashed in a corner behind a truly horrible pink floral vase. Groping at my chest pocket, I fish out my glasses and jam them on top of my nose.

"Son of a witch," I mutter as I pick each book up and flick through the pages. All of them are historical volumes, and a quick scan shows that each of them delves into incidences of magical surges that occurred over the millennia.

I'd wondered yesterday why I couldn't find anything at the library. Now I actually know.

I'm still perusing the books when Gwendolynne lets out an audible gasp. Immediately, she clamps her hand over her mouth in horror. Luckily there's no one around but me to hear.

"What is it?" I say, shutting the book and sidling up to her. She's bent over the third drawer, fingers still pressed to her lips.

She doesn't respond, just points at what she's been looking at. A scattered mess of ID cards on lanyards. The type of ID card I've seen hundreds of times before.

"Yes, and?" I say, confused. "Those are just Magecorp staff passes. My father works there. It's not so strange."

Gwendolynne finally finds her voice, though it wavers more than usual. "But it's not just any old Magecorp staff. Look." She rummages through the bag she has slung over one shoulder, pulls out Nora Chapman's creased, marked-up scroll, and flings it at my chest.

I catch it and unroll it, but not before shooting her a disapproving look for being so needlessly loud. Then I start to read what's written on it.

It's a list of names. They seem familiar. I grimace.

"What am I looking at, Chan?"

Gwendolynne rolls her eyes, then taps the parchment with her finger. "Look at the names. Compare them with what's on the cards. These are all the people who've gone missing. They match. Every single one."

Gorge rises in my throat as I stare at the list. Elouise Forrester. Hani Nguyen. Benjamin Purcell. Dr. Demi Wallan. Even a pimply-faced teenage intern called Li-wen Tan. All names confirming that my father does, in fact, have a drawer full of missing—presumed dead—people's IDs locked inside his study.

My organs feel frosted with ice, while outside my skin is scorching. A bead of sweat detaches itself from my hairline and runs down the back of my neck, catching on my collar.

Gwendolynne plucks the parchment from my limp fingers and rolls it up. "Maybe there's an explanation." Carefully, she tucks the scroll back in her bag. "Maybe they're just . . . in hospital, being treated for magiphilia, or something."

I frown, thinking.

"If that were the case, surely Nora Chapman would have a record of their treatment," I say eventually. "Besides, why cover it up? Why weren't these disappearances all over the news? And why keep their photos locked inside a drawer?" I've watched enough true crime documentaries to know that this isn't normal behavior. In fact, this feels more like trophy-collecting, serial-killer-type behavior.

In truth, my father hasn't been acting normally for *months*. Maybe even longer. Perhaps I'd just been too caught up in my own life to notice.

What the hell are you up to, Father? I'd always known he was an arsehole. But tonight is the first time that I'm beginning to suspect, a tiny bit, that he might also be a homicidal maniac.

"What do you think happened to them?" Gwendolynne's voice is just a whisper. "Do you think Magecorp could have . . . could've *killed* them?"

"I'm not sure," I say, my voice cracking. "But we certainly can't rule it out."

After searching the rest of the study and finding nothing else of interest, Gwendolynne and I leave my father's study, the door clicking shut behind us. She's clutching one of the staff IDs she found—Hani Nguyen's—and I'm holding one of the history books, the one that seemed to contain the most detail. We'd thought it safer to only filch the bare minimum; if we take too much my father will notice.

We're almost around the corner when I hear footsteps approaching.

"Shit," I hiss, then yank Gwendolynne back into the shadows. I recognize the heavy tread—the cadence of it—and fear twists itself into my gut like a knife. "My father is coming."

Even in the darkened corridor I see her face blanch until it's as pale and white as the risen moon. And of course she's scared. She's right to be scared. Hell, even *I* am scared. After all, my father is approaching, and we've just discovered a bunch of possible dead-people trophies hidden in his third desk drawer.

It's too late to escape; we can't slip past him without him noticing, and we can't retreat into the study since that's where he's probably headed. And if he catches us here . . .

Before I can overthink it, I do the only thing that might work. I lean into Gwendolynne, pressing her body against the wall with my own.

"What the hell are you doing?" she hisses. Her hands are at my chest, trying to shove me off.

"Shhh," I urge, my voice low at her ear. "Just go with it." My blood is pulsing through my head and I want to plead, want to beg, want to make sure she does not give us away. But there's no time. All I can hope for is that she'll somehow catch on to my plan.

I press against her harder and, as she lets out a little gasp, I slide the book I'm holding beneath the hem of her shirt. She's trembling against me, I can feel it, and I am pretty sure she's holding her breath.

Shifting slightly, I keep my hand beneath her shirt, securing the book in place, then push my free hand up into the hair at the nape of her neck. Twining my fingers in her hair, I tilt her head, then move my lips down to the little hollow beneath her ear. My nose skims her hairline; her scent fills my nostrils.

She lets out a ragged breath, which hitches as my lips just brush the soft skin of her neck. "Briggs." Her voice is shaky. "Don't."

"Don't worry, Chan," I murmur, my words vibrating against her skin. "I'm not going to kiss you. Now slip the ID into my pocket."

Her lips part in surprise. "What?"

My voice drops to a whisper. "Slip. The ID. Into my pocket." I can't risk my father finding us with the evidence.

Locked in the same position, her hands fumble a bit, her fingers tracing along my belt before sliding the card into my front pocket. Her touch is hot, searing, leaving a trail of electricity prickling across my skin. The sensation makes me flex my hips unconsciously, and I draw in a sharp breath, grasping her hair tighter.

If anyone were to stumble across us, they'd see an amorous couple: the woman pushed up against the wall, the man kissing her neck, one hand shoved up her top.

The footsteps approach. Slow. Stop. "Harrisford." My father's deep voice is stern, his intonation disapproving.

I raise my head and blink at him slowly, letting my lips curl up into my cockiest grin. "Why, hello, Father."

He doesn't move for several moments, just stands there peering owlishly at me through his glasses. Then he shakes his head and sweeps past us. "Take it to your room, Harrisford. I shouldn't need to tell you again."

I do not move. Do not blink. Instead, I stay pressed up against Gwendolynne, a smirk plastered across my face. It's only when he's slammed the door behind him that I allow my expression to morph to a scowl.

I'm still staring at my father's closed door when Gwendolynne's voice sounds in my ear.

"*Briggs*," she hisses. "You can move now."

My gaze swivels to her face, to the flushed sheen lining her cheeks; her slightly parted lips; the languid, liquid brown of her large, long-lashed eyes.

I don't know what I'm thinking, but I seem incapable of stopping myself. Perhaps I'm not even thinking—not with my head, anyway. Leaning down, I press a gentle kiss against her neck, right where my lips had hovered mere moments ago.

Then I push away from her and stride off, leaving her panting against the wall.

12

Gwendolynne

We'd come so close to getting caught.

It takes me several rapid heartbeats to regain my breath, and even longer to gather my wits. And then I'm hurrying after Harrisford as he strides through the corridors of his mansion.

What did he mean by kissing me on the neck? Mr. Briggs's words are seared in my brain: *I shouldn't have to tell you again*. Which means that Harrisford has done this before, in this house. It doesn't surprise me, really, given his reputation.

Still, I can't help wondering . . . exactly how many women has he pushed up against one of the Briggs mansion's many walls?

My mouth twists in disgust. He's a right royal shit and I feel quite sure he only did it to toy with me. To throw me off my game. He didn't actually *want* it. He didn't actually want me. He probably wasn't enjoying himself at all.

But then . . . My mind strays to the way he'd physically reacted to me on the dragon. And again, when I slipped the card into his pocket. That second time, my fingers had inadvertently bumped the evidence in his trousers that he was, in fact, enjoying himself. Very, *very* much.

It's nothing, Gwendolynne, I scold myself. *Just a physical reaction. Nothing more, nothing less.* We were only in that compromising position so we wouldn't get caught raiding Darghan Briggs's study.

Harrisford moves faster than me, so I'm breathless by the time we stop in front of an opulent set of double doors. "My room," he says curtly.

My stomach gives a sickened lurch. His father had told us to go to his room, so he took us to his room.

Inside, it's much like his dorm room at Heywood Hall—except even more extravagant. The comforter on the bed looks like gold-shot silk, the marble mantelpiece is stupidly large, the ceiling is vaulted with a painted mural. A fucking *mural*, for Chrissakes! It's ludicrously, preposterously, and nonsensically lavish. It makes me even more determined to stop him from *ever* entering my room.

I slip the book out from under my shirt, unthinkingly dumping it on a nearby table. My attention is elsewhere—my head swiveling, taking in my surroundings—unaware until too late that my mouth is hanging open.

When I catch sight of Harrisford's smirk, I shut it, my teeth clicking together, and give him a tight-lipped smile. "I suppose we should make a plan." I lean against his desk, grasping the edge with both hands.

Harrisford disappears into his walk-in wardrobe for a few seconds and reemerges holding a fresh shirt, which he drapes across a chair. "We should," he says, shrugging out of his braces so that they're hanging below his waist. Then, facing away from me, he tugs his shirt over his head.

It's the first time I've ever seen him shirtless and . . . he is more muscular than I'd ever envisioned. Not that I make a habit of envisioning Harrisford Briggs without clothes, of course, but I'm amazed at what he's managed to hide beneath his scores of shapeless coveralls and loose linen shirts. He's all carved muscle, thick biceps, and broad shoulders tapering to a narrow waist, and his unnecessarily tight trousers display the thickness of his legs. There are old, healed scars—probably from his time working with mythical beasts—covering his back and neck.

I swallow, my mouth dry.

Harrisford looks up suddenly, over his shoulder, and grins. "Like what you see, Chan?"

Heat floods my face and neck, and I grab a book off his desk, flipping it open and burying my nose in it to hide the redness of my face. "No." I stare hard at the words on the pages, but they don't seem to make any sense. They're bleeding and blurring together, and my ears are roaring, and it kind of feels like I'm drowning, being pulled underneath the water.

In my peripheral vision, I see Harrisford putting the new shirt on. He buttons it, leaving the top three open as usual, and saunters over. I stare even harder at my book.

Harrisford tips the book toward me so that he can read the cover. His smile widens, becoming almost exultant. His murmur is sultry and velvet soft. "*Reproductive Biology of Monstrous Creatures*," he reads out. "Really, Chan?"

Ugh. Of all the books I could have grabbed off his desk, I had to grab *this*?

My cheeks are burning, but I refuse to be cowed by him. "Yes. It's a bit of an interest of mine."

His eyebrows raise in mock surprise. "What a coincidence. It's one of mine, too." He grins. "Perhaps we should study . . . together." He's entirely too close. Uncomfortably close.

"Sure," I say, and shut the book with a snap. "How about we start with all the different methods of castrating a male?"

He chuckles, and I throw the book at his head, unfortunately missing it when he manages to duck out of the way. The book tumbles to the ground. We both leave it.

"So?" I say, putting my hands on my hips. "What now?"

Harrisford runs a hand through his hair, leaving the back sticking up. "I suppose . . . I suppose we should try to figure out the source of the actual surges. It definitely seems as though Magecorp are doing something shady, but to find out what, we need to know how—and where—they mine the magic."

I frown at him. "You don't know?"

"No. That information is restricted to a select few, and kept hidden in the vault at Magecorp HQ. They say it's for security reasons, and because it's their intellectual property, but I suspect it's actually so they can control the market."

I pause for a moment, thinking. "We'll need to sneak into their offices, then," I say finally.

Harrisford paces to his desk chair, bracing his hands on its back. He stares at the ground for a long while, then shakes his head, defeated. "I don't know if it's even possible. My father's study is one thing. But Magecorp HQ? That's a whole other layer of difficulty. The levels of security they have there are tremendous."

He straightens as I approach him, watching me with wary eyes, until I'm close—near enough to feel the heat emanating from his body. I reach out, slipping my hand into his pocket. He goes rigid beneath my touch.

"Luckily, then," I say, pulling out the card, "I have a staff ID."

The next morning, Harrisford's gaze slides to my face, then back to the card he's holding, then back to my face.

"You look nothing like her," he says, his voice flat.

I shrug. "She's Asian, I'm Asian . . ."

He squints at the small photo on the staff ID. "You still look nothing alike."

It's Saturday, and I'm standing in the place where I'd least like to be on a Saturday: Harrisford's dorm room. Well, it's where I'd least like to be any day of the week, really.

I've spent a good half hour trying to do my hair like Hani Nguyen, the Magecorp employee who's pictured on the card. And I'm wearing the business attire that Harrisford pilfered from his mother's closet.

I had always known that Mrs. Theodora Briggs had died, but I'd never considered how or when. Now, I'm still too hesitant to ask about it—and Harrisford doesn't seem keen to elaborate. But I hadn't missed the lifeless expression that had settled across his features when I walked in wearing his dead mum's clothes.

Moving closer, I snatch Hani Nguyen's ID from him and shove it into my pocket. "Trust me, Briggs," I say. "I've been mistaken for other Asian women often enough. Literally no one is going to notice."

He frowns, still skeptical. "Surely not."

I let out a heavy, long-suffering sigh. Why won't he just believe me? "I promise you, it happens. I had one client recently that *swore* I'd treated her Dogue de Bordeaux with an entire six-month course of chemotherapy."

"And let me guess—it wasn't you?"

Shaking my head, I sigh again. "No. It was Marika Yamata, who graduated last year."

The vein on Harrisford's temple dilates, and he splutters, "But that—it's ridiculous—she's not even Chinese!"

I raise an eyebrow at him. "Do you really think that matters?" I rub at my face and blow out a breath. "It's not just clients, either. Professor Bartell still gets mixed up between me and Alice Chu . . ."

"Then he's a fool," Harrisford mutters, crossing his big arms. "An ignorant fool."

"Yes," I say. "So many people are. I guess you're just lucky you don't have to notice it."

He tugs at his lower lip, his blue and brown eyes boring into mine. Then, after a long silence, he says, "Regardless. I think we should think of another way. It's too dangerous."

I resist the urge to roll my eyes. "There is no other way, Briggs. You know that as well as I do."

We've been over it a hundred times. Maybe more. We'd even discussed using a glamour, but I had to admit that I've never cast one and don't actually know how. Harrisford does, but he refuses to use them for reasons he can't—or won't—explain.

So here we are. I'm banking on the fact that Hani Nguyen's staff ID will still be functional. Since Darghan Briggs is seemingly trying to obfuscate what's happened—as evidenced by the IDs he's keeping locked inside his study and the fact that it's somehow been kept out of the mainstream news—there's a chance he hasn't yet deactivated Hani from the system.

Still, this is risky. Very risky. We're entering the workplace of someone who may or may not be a murderer, to steal some top-secret information that is kept I-don't-know-where. Added to that, I have no idea how close Hani was to her colleagues—all it would take is for one to not recognize me, and the entire farce would all be over.

But I know I at least have to try.

Harrisford swallows, his Adam's apple rippling beneath the skin of his throat. I guess he's so nervous because he's about to defy his diabolical father. "Just—be careful, all right?" he says quietly. "And stick to the plan."

I nod, straightening the hem of the late Mrs. Briggs's pencil skirt.

It's a tweed skirt suit with shoulder pads and an alarmingly nipped-in waist.

Before we leave, I decide to head back to my dorm and stock Percy up with food. I'm hoping we'll be in and out in the span of an afternoon, but if something goes awry . . .

I push open the door to my room. Percy's curled up in a tight ball on my bed. The entire room is spattered in scorch marks, including my shabby old quilt. I sigh. Another victim of Percy's magiphilia. At some point I'll need to rustle up some extra magic, and the spare time, to repair it.

For a minuscule moment, I can *almost* empathize with Mrs. Mason-Price's frustration . . . but then I look at Percy's adorable little sleeping face and I'm rapidly past that feeling.

I don't want to interrupt the twenty-three hours of sleep he seems to need each day, so I tiptoe over to his puzzle feeder and start doling out scoops of food.

There's a little squeaking noise as Percy wakes, yawns, and rolls onto his back, both of his back legs stretched out. Then he curls his upper body toward me and looks at me upside down. *You look . . . nice.*

"These clothes aren't mine," I say, distracted. I've lost count of how many cups of kibble I've scooped.

Ah, Percy says, righting himself. His voice sounds bored inside my head. *That makes sense, then.*

My head jerks up and I throw him an arch look. "I'm going out, Percy. I might be back soon, but in case I'm not, I've left you some spare food." Casting a final, appraising look at the mountain of dry food I've heaped into his feeder, I straighten, brushing off my skirt.

Where are you going? Percy asks, though his tone suggests he has absolutely no interest in my response. If he had opposable thumbs, I swear he'd be filing his nails.

Still, he's my familiar, and we are supposed to be closely bonded.

So I decide to tell him at least part of the truth. "I'm trying to break into Magecorp."

Magecorp? His ears swivel to face me, as though his interest has been piqued—slightly. *The conglomerate that packages and supplies magic?*

"The very same." I grimace. What Harrisford and I are about to attempt seems . . . insurmountable.

Are you stealing some? Percy pauses. *I suppose that makes sense, given you seem to be able to afford very little.*

My head grows hot with frustration, and I snap, "Well, aren't you my familiar now? Aren't you supposed to help me channel more magic, or something?"

I'm a cat, he retorts, and sniffs. *Not a rechargeable battery.*

I stare at him, open-mouthed. Before, I'd always thought getting a familiar would signal the end of all my problems. Now I'm realizing that maybe, just maybe, it might end up causing more.

Percy just closes his eye and turns his head away, ignoring me. Tamping down my irritation at my arrogant jerk of a cat, I start heading back out. It's time to go—with or without Percy's help.

As I'm slamming the door behind me, his voice sounds in my head again.

Best of luck, Hairless One, he says.

Magecorp HQ is open seven days a week (the demand for magic is, after all, 24/7), but as it's a Saturday the office is a bit less crowded than usual. Since Harrisford is instantly recognizable and therefore can't go in, he and I part ways at the entrance; he lopes into a side street to park his motorbike while I totter through the enormous glass doors, slightly unsteady on my borrowed heels. They're a size too big and I've packed the toes with tissues, but my feet still slide around inside.

Inside, the lobby is enormous, with marble floors and steel sculptures and a massive concrete reception desk. Harrisford told me reception would be unoccupied on a weekend, and he was right.

I take a deep breath, my fingers curling into fists by my sides. I can do this. I can be brave. Over the past few days, I've stolen a cat, I've ridden a dragon, and—perhaps the most reckless thing of all—I've spent time, alone, with Harrisford Briggs. Compared with those things, breaking into Magecorp HQ is nothing . . . or so I tell myself.

Trying to look like I belong, I march up to the row of turnstiles, my high heels clicking on the floor. I hold up Hani's ID, which is now looped around my neck, my pulse going haywire as I wait for the magical scanner to complete its identification.

It takes an excruciatingly long time, and by the time the turnstile clicks open I'm practically hyperventilating. I pass by a cleaner mopping the shiny, pristine floor and slip into the lift. Harrisford has told me that the high-security section, where all the most confidential information is kept, is on the top level.

It feels like a long ride up to the fifty-second floor, and by the time the lift doors ping open, my clothes are clinging to my sweaty back. I edge out, checking the corridor for any people, before heading toward the stainless steel vault at the end of the hall.

There's a magical scanner just outside. Is it too much to hope that Hani Nguyen's card will work? I swipe it, but the door just gives a plaintive beep and doesn't open. *Damn it.*

Leaning my back against the wall, I think. This is the room that Harrisford said would contain the information that we need, and somehow I have to get inside. An idea is forming; it's not something I relish doing, since I don't want to break more rules, but I simply can't think of another way. Besides, it's not like Harrisford Briggs will miss the money.

I open the Messages app on my strap. Briggs, I type out quickly. I need the resignio spell to get in.

There's a brief pause during which he doesn't reply. Is he . . . still there? Has that bastard abandoned me to do this myself? Or even worse—has he *betrayed* me? Is this all a ruse to frame me, to get me caught breaking the law?

Perhaps he's down there laughing his arse off, expecting the burglar alarms to go off any second.

I swallow down the thick lump in my throat.

But then my strap vibrates, and there's a message from Harrisford. No words, just a single, no-effort, apathetic thumbs-up. That twat. He makes me so fucking furious.

I wait for several minutes until the magic infiltrates my fingers, then hold my hand above the steel door handle. Mimicking what I'd seen Harrisford do at his mansion, I mime opening up the door.

Nothing happens.

It didn't work.

Fucking fuckity fuck. Did I do it wrong? I'm the first to admit that while I'm exceptional at performing veterinary work, I'm not that great at non-vet spells—mainly because growing up I never had enough spare magic to play around with simple charms.

My breath is starting to feel tight in my chest. The clamminess has crept up my back and now laces my neck and my forehead; my sweaty feet slip around in my shoes. What am I going to do? How am I going to get inside?

Then—the worst thing possible happens. The lift doors *ding* as they slide open.

Fuck. Fuck fuck fuck fuck fuck fuck fuck. Someone is coming.

And here I am, stuck on this side of a security door.

13

Gwendolynne

The footsteps are approaching. I claw at the door, jiggle the door handle, try the *resignio* spell again and again. But nothing works.

My heart beats, thunderous, deafening in my ears. *Please, God*, I think. *Help me.* Fear is making me desperate—I haven't prayed since I was six years old.

Then, a voice, my salvation, flickers into in my head. Just in time, I stop myself from crying out. I'm not alone.

You do realize that you cannot open a reinforced door with the resignio *spell, don't you?* It's Percy's voice.

"I—you . . . I can *hear* you?" I had no idea we could communicate over such a distance.

I can almost picture the irritated thump of his tail. *Of course you can.*

"But why haven't we . . ." I splutter. "Why did you not say . . ."

There was never a need before, Hairless One. But you called for me, did you not?

I shake my head, my eyes scrunched shut. "No, I'm pretty sure I called for—oh fuck it. Never mind." I don't have time to contemplate Percy's inflated sense of ego. "I really need your help. I'm in danger. I need to open this door."

You'll need an explosion, Percy says. *Or a massive power surge that will short-circuit the door's integrated magic system. Not normal levels of magic, mind you. More like the ones that have been occurring recently.*

My thoughts have become ragged, hysterical. Luckily, then, there's so much excess magic swirling around in the world. "Can you do it from where you are? Tap into the surging magic and channel it into me?"

A pause. *I can channel the magic through you, yes, even at a distance. But the sheer amount will be painful. And I must warn you, Hairless One: After that, you will be on your own. Once you are inside that room, the security door will break any connection we have.*

I'm kind of shocked he's agreeing to this. Regardless, I straighten my shoulders and draw myself to my full height, trying not to notice the slow shuffling of footsteps approaching ever closer. I don't much like pain, but I really have no choice. Harrisford and I need to figure out what's causing these surges—not just so I can pass exams, come first, and save my family's restaurant, but *also* so we can stop people, and animals, from getting hurt.

"Do it," I say, steeling my resolve. "Push the magic through to me."

Percy falls quiet, but I sense the strain of his concentration over our telepathic bond. It quivers, trembling with the influx of energy, straining beneath the surging current he's sending through the ether.

At first it's warm, pleasantly so, but pretty soon it becomes uncomfortably hot. Needles of pain stab through my body, my staticky hair stands on end, and I shake with the effort of containing the sudden burst of magic.

"Are you. Almost. There?" I grit out, clenching my teeth against the pain. Is this going to kill me? I haven't acclimatized like Percy has. I'm not used to magiphilia. I mean, most of the time I'm struggling to make use of too *little* magic, not too much.

But at this stage, there's little else I can do. I'm here, I'm stuck, and I have to see it to the end. The fate of the magical world rests upon my shoulders, and if I fail . . .

I shove my fist into my mouth to curb my scream.

Finally, Percy speaks again in my mind. *You're ready*, he shouts, inasmuch as a cat can shout, and I hold up my palms to the security door.

The magic explodes from me, blanching my entire vision in stark white light, and I place my hand on the door. The shock is like a stampede; it's like being struck by lightning. My entire body goes rigid and my back is thrown into an excruciating arch as the current tears its way through me. Magic runs from my hands into the metal door. I'm fused to the steel, in agony and searingly hot. With a grunt, I manage to tear myself from the contact, and I'm thrown onto the floor. The door makes some sounds—several clicks, followed by a deep, metallic scraping—then swings wide open on its hinges.

I slump there, almost weeping, almost unable to move. Percy . . . He came through. I wasn't sure that he would help me, but when it came down to the literal wire . . . he did.

The footsteps are growing closer and I don't want to get caught. I don't want to be imprisoned; I don't want to be killed. So, ignoring the pain that knifes its way through my body with every movement I make, I commando-crawl, inch by excruciating inch, until I'm finally through the door.

The cleaner's mop comes into focus, and I know now who followed me up here. It's the woman I saw downstairs, now washing the top-story floors.

With the toe of my high-heeled shoe, I manage to wedge the door shut behind me . . . just as she rounds the corner.

Flashing forks of magical power streak like lightning across the door. It's still live-wired, crackling with surplus energy.

I sag, panting, against the wall for a moment, trying to catch my breath. It takes a while for the room to stop spinning.

When I can finally gather myself, I raise my head and look round. The vault is . . . surprising. I'd been expecting something high-tech, like everything else at Magecorp, but this room looks like a gothic, arcane library.

The walls are brick, laced with lichen and artfully distressed with age. An illusion, perhaps? The floor is polished hardwood, with magelights embedded into it at regular intervals. Like reverse spotlights, they shine upward, illuminating the still air with a muted golden glow.

There are small wooden pigeonholes lining one wall, each containing a single scroll. A low-pitched hum slithers below my skin and up my spine, and as I move into the room the air thickens, heavy with potent magic. So overpowering that it becomes more and more difficult to breathe.

Everything here is antiquated, as though I've stepped right back through time, except for some electrical cords and plugs hanging from the ceiling and one that circles the perimeter of the room. I remember from studying magical history that Magecorp has been in existence, in some shape or form, since as early as the Middle Ages. It wasn't called Magecorp then, of course, and ownership has changed hands several times because of corporate buyouts and business mergers—but the company secrets have been passed down through many iterations.

I approach cautiously. My feet disturb the silence, sending dust motes spinning into the filtered light. There is so much information here, sequestered into the Magecorp vault. Where the hell do I even start?

Quickly, I tap a message out to Harrisford on my strap. What should I be looking for?

The message swooshes off, but less than a second later a big red dot appears on my screen. **Message failed to send.**

Of course. Percy had warned me that the room's security would cut off human-familiar communication. I can only imagine that it interferes with telecommunications, too. Sighing, I reach out to finger one of the scrolls. All I can do is start.

Quickly, and silently, I pull out one scroll after another, unrolling them, flattening them, and snapping pictures on my strap. They're mostly plans, maps, and blueprints of what I presume are magical machines, and even if I understood it all I wouldn't have time to properly decipher them. My bag slips off my shoulder; annoyed, I hoist it back up.

At least if I have some photographic evidence, then I'll be able to scrutinize them properly, maybe with Harrisford's help. How much has he picked up subconsciously, just from being the Magecorp CFO's son? It's possible that he's heard snippets over dinner tables; absorbed information without even knowing it.

I take pictures of as much as I possibly can before moving farther into the room. There's a central, circular structure—a room within the room—made of what appears to be reinforced concrete. Another steel door is fitted into it, this one curved and flush with the wall. There's a sort of subliminal pulsing emanating from inside, as though there's something contained within that's not meant to be seen by outside eyes.

With a shaking hand, I reach out and try the door handle. Miraculously, it turns, and the door swings open with no noise or resistance at all.

Immediately, I squint, for inside the room is a painful, blazing glow. The glare is coming from something in the center of the circle; I shield my eyes, the webbing of my fingers glowing red as I move closer.

It's some sort of rock, radiant with a pulsating light. The exterior of it is all pockmarked, but not irregularly like the moon. It's more like a uniform honeycomb pattern imprinted on its surface. It's not just the rock's appearance, though, that has me all flustered. It's also . . . a feeling. It's like . . . it's calling to me. As though it's putting out feelers, trying to burrow beneath my skin, trying to get inside my mind and learn everything about me.

It's exquisite and horrible all at once, and I feel as though I'm frozen, rooted to the spot. It's almost as if I can't look away.

But then I notice the shadow of something: a man with almost-white hair, steel-framed glasses, and a receding hairline. The man is standing near the glowing rock. And even though the details of his face are hazy, silhouetted against the glare, I recognize his profile instantly.

Darghan Briggs.

Harrisford's father is here. With me. In this room.

My scalp tightens. Cold dread drenches my body. My heart begins to pound, flooding my entire vision red. It can't be true, because Harrisford told me he'd be out of town, and—

Fury snaps into place. Harrisford must have lied. This is a trap. The arsehole must have lied to me to trap me up here with his killer dad. But for what? Is it to sacrifice me to the cause—use me to figure out what's behind the surges while saving his own slimy skin? Or was the investigation just a ruse, something he used to gain my trust, and he's actually been working with Magecorp—and his father—all along?

I don't have time to ponder it; all I know is this is bad. Very bad. And if I ever get out of here, then I'm going to fucking kill him.

Trying to not make any noise, I immediately start backing away. When I reach the curved steel door, I turn to flee.

I don't make it far, though. I skid to a stop in front of the outer door—the one that I'd failed to open with Harrisford's gifted *resignio* spell. It's still sparking, brimming with unspent power.

Desperately, I try to contact Percy, but there's no response. I tap out a message to Heloise too—just one word: HELP—on the off chance that being near to the door might allow a single message to slip through. But straightaway the red dot appears again and I grind my teeth, panicking.

There's only one thing I can do, and that is brave the electric hum of magical charge still flashing across the door. *You've done it once*, I tell myself, taking a steadying breath. *You can do it again.* But would I survive a second shock?

Either way, I don't really have a choice.

Raising my palm, I go to push on the door, intending to make my escape through it.

I haven't quite touched the sparking metallic surface when I feel a hand twist in my hair. My entire body jerks back. I thrash and struggle, kicking out, trying to claw back to the door, but Darghan Briggs's hold on me is relentless, and he continues dragging me back into the room.

"What are you doing, witch?" he hisses in my ear. His hot breath washes over my neck. I scream into the dead air, but his forearm clamps across my throat, choking my scream to silence.

"Nothing," I whimper, struggling to voice the words. "Nothing."

His voice drops low and deceptively soft. "Then why are you snooping around in the vault? Do you work here?"

I don't have any way to escape this, so I try to bluff my way through. "Y-yes," I say shakily. "I've been allocated to a new department and I . . . I just lost my way."

I can tell he's not buying it by the way he tightens his hold in my hair and gives me a little shake. "Your name and department, girl?" When I don't answer immediately, he shakes me again. "Name and department! Quickly! Or mark my words: You'll be disciplined *severely* for your disobedience!"

I blink, and tears run down my face, soaking into his hairy arm. "H-Hani Nguyen," I stutter, unable to think of any other excuse. "You can ch-check my ID."

Darghan Briggs lets me go, and I fall forward onto my hands and knees. Then he's already in front of me, hauling me forward by the ID hanging around my neck.

He says nothing for several moments. Just stares at the small rectangular card. Then, eventually, he relents, drops it, and squints right at my face. I scuttle backward, pressing myself against the wall, trying to put as much distance as possible between Harrisford's father and me. Will he realize I'm not Hani Nguyen? Will he recognize the suit I'm wearing, which once belonged to his now-dead wife?

Hopefully not. I'm desperately hoping he's the kind of man who lacks basic observational skills. The type who thinks all Asians look identical, and who'd pay no attention to the clothes his spouse once wore.

The silence stretches on for so long I almost think that maybe, *maybe*, I've got away with it. But then his wrinkled eyes narrow, and his lips curl into a sneer.

My heart thrashes even more wildly. It's disturbing how similar Harrisford's smile is to his.

"Hani Nguyen is no longer here," Mr. Briggs spits, his voice full of venom.

Then he raises his palm and shoots a spell at me, hitting me right in the middle of my chest. I'm thrown back against the brick wall. Pain shoots through my body. Black spots explode in my vision. And as I slide down the wall into a crumpled heap, the world wobbles, goes foggy, and completely fades to black.

14

Gwendolynne

When I come around, I'm slumped against the wall, my body still throbbing with pain. I'm cognizant of that fact that Darghan Briggs must've hit me with some sort of stunning spell. It had knocked me out for long enough for him to restrain me, because I'm now tied up, my wrists bound together with one of the electrical extension cords.

I struggle against my restraints, to no avail. Raising my hands before my face, I squint at the bindings, my vision hazy.

"Who are you?" Darghan Briggs is oddly calm. He's pulled a chair up in front of me and is leaning back in it, his legs crossed at the ankles. A gun lies across his lap. "Where are you from?" If he genuinely doesn't know, maybe Harrisford *isn't* working with him?

"No one." My voice is raw and scratchy, my words sounding choked. "I'm no one."

"Are you from the Magical Liberation Organization?" He shifts in his chair, one hand palming the handle of his gun. His eyes—so pale blue, like two chips of ice—are fixed on me.

"What? No!" He's jumped to that assumption so quickly; maybe, despite what Harrisford thinks, there's some merit to the idea that the MLO was behind the gala explosion.

His eyes burn. "Then which organization are you from?"

I chafe at my bindings, the cords pinching my skin. "I'm not from any *organization*," I grit out, wincing at the pain. "I'm just—" I pause, trying desperately to figure out the best angle; how I might get him to talk. "Hani . . . was my mother. And when she disappeared I—" I take in a big, exaggerated sniffle. "I just wanted to know what she was working on."

Mr. Briggs's expression softens, just slightly. "Well, I can assure you that you won't find anything here."

"I was just curious, you know, to see if there was a reason for her disappearance."

He's silent for a moment. "People run away all the time. Does there have to be a reason?"

I swipe at my eyes, wiping away nonexistent tears. "She would never, though . . . She'd *never* leave. My high school graduation is coming up soon and I . . ." I cover my face with my bound hands and heave a great, shaking sob.

My captor lets out a sigh. "Listen, Miss Nguyen. I imagine that it's difficult to accept your mother leaving. But you never know what someone is going through internally. She might have been deeply unhappy. She might have had a breakdown. She might have needed to escape." He adds, his voice gentling, "Wouldn't you want your mother to be happy?"

A trickle of cold floods my insides and I shake my head, letting out a shivery breath. Darghan Briggs acting all sympathetic *now*, after everything else he's done, is confusing me. "It's not that. It's just—I don't buy her missing it on purpose. She was *so* excited to see me graduate! I was wondering whether it, you know, had anything to do with the surges."

Harrisford's father's eyes immediately harden to flint. "The surges? Whatever do you mean?"

I raise my face. It's already tearstained from before, so it's not too hard to look miserable. "The surges that are happening around London. I was wondering if . . ." I trail off, because Mr. Briggs has risen to his feet and is now pointing the gun at me. Dread slithers up my spine, and my pulse begins to hammer. Harrisford's mother's suit is swelteringly hot, the collar of my buttoned shirt too tight.

"You can stop now," he says. His voice has turned acidic, a sinister whisper that slides effortlessly beneath my sticky, sweat-laced skin. "You can stop lying, girl. Did you really think I would believe that *ridiculous* sob story?"

And then I realize: He'd been humoring me, all that time. I start shaking. All I can see is the barrel of the gun. Deep inside it, there's a tiny glow—the kernel of magic that will explode if he pulls the trigger. Magical guns are much like normal guns, bullets and all, except they're triggered by magic instead of gunpowder.

"I'm not lying," I say, but the words are weak and lack conviction.

Mr. Briggs adjusts his grip on the gun. "Oh, drop the charade. You really think I don't conduct background checks on all my employees?" He tilts his head to one side and regards me through narrowed eyes. "I know that Hani Nguyen didn't have a daughter. And I know her ID was locked in my study. I don't know how the fuck you got it, but you can stop lying and tell me where you're from."

That's it. My cover is blown. My pulse is racing, and my mouth has run dry. But a reckless sort of abandon is tearing through my body. The adrenaline, probably—my sympathetic nervous system has kicked into overdrive.

I know the signs: the effects of adrenergic receptor activation. My pupils are dilating, my heart rate is increasing, my lungs are expanding to full capacity. Blood is being diverted from my extremities and pooling at my core.

I know the adrenaline is clouding my mind and my judgment

and giving me courage I don't possess. Logically, my brain understands this—that my bravery is artificial . . . But honestly, in this moment, I don't even care.

Physiology fucking *rules*.

I raise my chin, glaring at him. "Where is Hani Nguyen, Mr. Briggs? You say she's no longer here. What does that mean? Is she dead?"

"You're riding a dangerous wave, little witch," he spits out. "You don't know what you're getting yourself into."

I struggle against my bindings again. "I know that you're responsible for the power surges, Mr. Briggs. I know that you're involved in a cover-up. I know that Magecorp is *killing* people—"

"No." He takes a step closer, still holding the gun with both hands. A shadow slides across his face, his pale eyes gleaming in the dim light, but I don't fail to notice that his hands are shaking. "You know *nothing*."

I swallow. My heart thumps louder. My eyes lock on the gun.

It's probably just the adrenaline talking, but if I might die here, murdered by Darghan Briggs in the Magecorp HQ vault, I may as well make sure he knows his actions aren't going unnoticed. "Are you going to kill me like you killed Hani, Mr. Briggs? Elouise Forrester? Benjamin Purcell?"

Mr. Briggs's face pales, his forehead a slick sheen of sweat. It gives me a heedless sort of courage, and I continue to push. "What about Dr. Wallan, Mr. Briggs? Or Li-wen Tan? Do all their families know they're dead?"

When Harrisford's father speaks again, it comes out as a whisper. "Who are you?" His fingers clasp the gun so tightly that his knuckles have gone all white. "How do you know those names? Are you a reporter? Are you from the WTS?"

I ignore his questions. "Was it the surges that killed them? Why are they happening? Does it have to do with the mines? Is there trouble with the workers there?" I am relentless, stubborn, flinging questions at Darghan Briggs as though I am not the one tied up and he's not the one with the gun. "Have you lost control of your magical mines, Mr. Briggs? Does Magecorp have issues the public doesn't know about?" I shake my head, my eyes wide. "What will your shareholders think, Mr. Briggs?"

"Mines?" he scoffs. "There are no *mines*."

My heart falters for a moment, then resumes at a rapid pace. My jaw is clenched so hard it's like I'm pulverizing my teeth to dust. "Then how do you harvest magic?" My bound hands shake, my fingers curling into fists.

Mr. Briggs huffs out a laugh, his eyes still hard and cold. "Good grief. Mines! If only it were that easy!" He moves even closer, the gun inching incrementally closer to my face. "There aren't any mines. There isn't even a reliable source of magic. There's only our world—the real world—and the other world . . . the Void. And it's Magecorp's job to tear holes in the universe so that the magic flows to us."

I freeze, shocked into silence by this revelation. The Void? The Void is *real*?

All this time I'd assumed that Magecorp had some secret supply that they mined and harvested for magic. When it actually sounds like Magecorp destabilizes the very fabric of the world in order to steal power from the Void.

Since my family are not really religious, I'm not well versed in the theories surrounding the Void. I know there are certain religious denominations that worship it, but neither I nor my family ever believed it to be real. How strange that now, just as I'm about to die, I find out that it is.

"So, what?" I ask. "The magic is flowing from the Void too quickly? Is that what's happening?"

"No, girl," Mr. Briggs says, and frowns. "It's that too many holes are being ripped in the world at once."

"And Magecorp is doing that? Why? Greed?"

"God, no! You've got it all wrong. We don't know why the extra holes are forming—"

"But you were willing to let your employees die to find out," I snarl. "*And* cover it up."

He lets out a disdainful laugh. "They sacrificed themselves in the name of research. It's for the greater good."

Right, I think. *Like Percy.* Revulsion rises in my throat; the Magecorp CEO and his wife considered their cat expendable, and now Darghan Briggs is talking as though his employees are, too. "And I bet you convinced them they were safe, didn't you? That launching an investigation into the surges wouldn't put them at risk. Maybe you even promised them promotions—"

"If the surges go on unchecked," Mr. Briggs says icily, "then many more lives will be lost. More than a few Magecorp employees." He says it almost as though he . . . cares . . . about the threat to the greater population.

The room lapses into silence. It suddenly strikes me as ominous that Mr. Briggs is so willing to share information. "Why are you telling me this?" I ask, challenging him. Trying to sound courageous.

Mr. Briggs doesn't hesitate. Swiftly and surely, he raises the gun and presses the barrel of it against my forehead. "Because it doesn't matter what you know," he says, his face a blank, emotionless mask, "when I'm going to kill you anyway."

I freeze. My throat has seized up, every muscle tense and rigid. *He's going to murder me*, I think, *and bury the evidence.* Just like the dead Magecorp staff. And it may be completely illogical, but my first and only thought is that I don't want to end up as just another photo in his drawer.

You won't, my brain tells me, stubborn and insistent. *You won't end up like them.* And my brain is right, because Mr. Darghan Briggs has got one thing very wrong.

Like most arrogant men, he has underestimated me. He thinks I'm weak; that I won't fight back.

But I'm not just some silly girl trying to play with the grown-ups.

I am Gwendolynne Chan, the smartest witch at Seamere, and what Mr. Briggs doesn't know is that in third year I'd blitzed the Restraint of Mythical Beasts exam. And one of the sections that I'd scored perfect marks in?

The module on knot-tying.

At the time, I'd thought it was fucking useless, considering I never planned to work with livestock—but now I'm glad I put the effort into passing.

I'd recognized the knot Darghan Briggs had used on me immediately. And while I'd kept him talking and spilling all his incriminating secrets, I had been quietly working on undoing it. I'd drawn my knees up to my chest, as though I was simply frightened and trying to shield myself. I'd shoved my hands between my legs to hide my efforts.

If he'd had half the knowledge we vet students have, he would've realized . . .

That he had used the wrong fucking knot.

And just as Mr. Briggs clicks off the safety, I burst out of my electrical cord restraints.

If you've ever worked with large animals, you'd know that controlling them is not about physical size or force. It's about intelligence. Work smarter, not harder, as the lecturers say. Even the smallest veterinarian can tip a sheep, compel a unicorn to move, or restrain a dragon inside a crush.

So, calling on the last vestiges of my myth.creat knowledge, I use momentum to sweep Mr. Briggs's legs from under him and then kick the gun from his grasp.

He flips over onto his stomach, scrabbling for it unsuccessfully as it skitters across the floor. And as he reaches out, clamoring for his weapon, I slam my foot between his shoulder blades, pinning him to the ground. My brain is nothing but static. There's only buzzing in my ears. And in this fractional moment I'm back in the livestock yards, about to hog-tie a beast.

I'm still holding the cord Mr. Briggs had used to tie me up. And in less than a second, I take the end of the wire and hurl it against the electric door.

15

Harrisford

It's only minutes after Gwendolynne disappeared through Magecorp's automatic doors, and I am already pacing.

It's not time to panic just yet. Pudding's voice, reassuring, echoes in my mind.

"I'm not panicking," I say too quickly.

She tilts her head, just slightly. *Of course you're not.*

I reach the end of the alley and peek into the road. Everything is quiet. We're in the business district of the city; during the week, it would be bustling, but it's quiet on weekends. A listless breeze gusts down the street. Empty food wrappers spin along the ground, scraping the concrete pavement.

Reaching into my open satchel, I draw Pudding out and nudge her onto my shoulder. Her claws dig into the thick leather of my jacket. It's chilly, so I turn my collar up in an attempt to shield her from the wind.

Normally, Pudding is the only individual I worry about. The fact I'm worrying about someone else is . . . different.

Gwendolynne looked good in that outfit, Pudding says after a beat. *It suits her.*

I'm chewing the corner of my thumbnail. "It does." I don't say what I'm thinking out loud: that I'm quite partial to how she looks in jeans, too. I'm not quite quick enough to shield my thoughts, but Pudding is gracious enough to pretend not to notice.

"Do you think she'll be out soon?" I pace to the end of the alleyway again.

Relax, Harrisford. She's probably still going up in the lift.

My strap pings, and I immediately check it. It's Gwendolynne. I let out a breath and tap open the message.

Briggs. I need the resignio spell to get in.

"She's there," I say to Pudding. "In front of the door."

I know speed is of the essence so I send her a simple thumbs-up, then text my contact. I need another resignio, I type. My fingers feel stiff and my stomach is churning.

The message comes back almost instantaneously. Two in two days? Whatcha up to, man?

My chest twists in irritation, and I tap out a grumpy reply. Cut the questions. It's my job to pay. Your job to provide.

All right, all right, settle down. Wire me the money and I'll get it right to you.

It takes several minutes for the money to transfer—another third of my trust fund, gone—and for the spell to land in my account. I forward it to Gwendolynne, hoping desperately that it works.

There's radio silence from her, but I try not to message again. I know she is in a precarious position and I don't want to risk distracting her. But before long, I can't stand it anymore, so I send her a message. Did it work?

A red dot pings back. **Message failed to send.** That's good, I tell myself. She must have made it into the vault.

Now all I can do is wait.

The seconds crawl by, agonizingly slow. My chest hurts and I feel like I'm going to vomit. This was a bad plan. A very bad plan. If

Gwendolynne gets caught and my father figures out she's working with me, then . . .

A shiver rolls through me, and I brace myself with one elbow against the graffiti-covered wall. *Breathe, Harrisford*, I think, but my chest is tight and everything around me is spinning. *She won't get caught.*

I've witnessed the wrath of my father before. Too many times. And I definitely don't want Gwendolynne subjected to it.

And then I see it. Out of the corner of my eye. A sleek black car, a chauffeur in the front seat, the vague outline of a man in the back seat blurred by the tinted windows.

It's exactly the kind of car that Magecorp executives use.

What the fuck? I'd checked our family calendar, and Father should be out of town. Was he lying? I pluck Pudding off my shoulder and plonk her down on the seat of my bike. Bile rises; I taste it in the back of my throat. "Wait here," I say, breathless, and start running.

The car pulls up to the curb, stopping in a No Parking zone, and the suited man inside steps out. I skid to a stop—it's Nathaniel, the CEO, not my father, who is striding through the Magecorp entrance.

"Shit!" The word bursts from my lips. This isn't much better—my father is Nathaniel's lackey. And whatever shady thing my father is up to, Nathaniel is up to too.

My insides are a mess, my organs writhing.

Harrisford, Pudding says, her voice a warning. *Don't. You'll only make things worse.*

I bury both hands in my hair. "But Nathaniel's just gone in, Puds, and Gwendolynne—"

My instincts are going off, my panic is rising, and some indistinct intuition is telling me that something has gone wrong.

And then, it happens . . . My worst fear, confirmed. The roof of Magecorp HQ explodes.

The entire top floor shatters, flames flaring, black smoke billowing up into the blue arch of the sky. Debris rains down, and I don't hesitate before I bolt full speed toward the building.

The alarms are sounding as I dash through the door, my heart pounding like a drum in my throat. My strap pings, a delayed message coming through from Gwendolynne. What should I be looking for? My chest constricts. When the hell had she sent it?

Fortunately, the lift is still functional. I fling myself in, jabbing repeatedly at the top floor button as the doors close—too slowly.

But something is wrong with it. The lift grinds to a halt, its gears creaking, just when I reach floor 40. The doors struggle to open, but I manage to wrench them apart just enough to get through and burst out into the hall.

I'm immediately choked; the building is filling with rolling waves of thick, pervasive smoke. I pull my shirt over my mouth, trying not to breathe the noxious air. After locating the fire escape, I bash open the door and sprint up the remaining twelve floors. My heart is about to give out and my breath is coming in harsh pants as I reach the top of the stairwell on the fifty-second floor.

It's a fucking mess. The roof has blown off, and smog clogs the air, and everything, *everything* smells like burning.

"Gwendolynne!" I bellow, my voice sounding not at all like my own. "Gwen!"

Everything is ash, and soot, and twisted bits of metal. Some of the walls are still standing, electrical cords trailing. Sweeping them aside, I struggle through the wreckage, scanning the rubble for any sign of her.

Finally I spot her; she's lying beneath a pile of bricks. My mother's suit is scorched, and her hair is all frizzy. I shove the rubble off her, pricks of panic crowding the edge of my vision, and fall to my knees amid the layer of ash.

"Gwendolynne," I say, and her name comes out choked. "You're okay. Tell me you're okay."

She doesn't answer. I can't quite catch my breath. When my fingers find her neck, I feel her fluttering pulse, and thank the lords, she's breathing.

What the hell happened here? She's alive, but . . . not moving. My heart is thumping so hard that it's threatening to burst from my chest. "Gwendolynne." I sweep some hair away from her face, and her eyelids flutter open.

"Briggs?" Her voice is weak as she squints up at me. She tries to sit up, but then groans and falls back down. I manage to catch her just in time, cradling her body to mine.

Her lips are moving, but I can't quite hear. So I bend my ear to her mouth. "Your father," she whispers, almost inaudible.

"My father?" I blink, confused, casting a look around. My gaze catches on something: a flash of singed white fabric.

Confusion clouds my mind. Even though he's lying face down, I recognize the back of his head.

None of this makes sense. He was supposed to be in Wales; he wasn't supposed to be in London, or at Magecorp HQ. I don't know where Nathaniel is, and I don't know why the roof exploded; all I know is that I need to get Gwendolynne to safety. I need to do it straightaway.

My hands are shaking, and I keep making errors, but I manage to tap out a message on my strap. It's the only person I know who can help me: the same person who sent me the *resignio* spell.

Get me a dragon, I write. Now. Rooftop of Magecorp HQ.

16

Gwendolynne

Everything is hazy when my eyes first blink open, and I'm staring at a row of fluorescent magelights. There are dozens of tiny insect corpses shadowed against the brightness—their pattern looking oddly familiar. And as my vision comes slowly back into focus, I figure out where I am: my dorm.

And even worse, sitting among the drab mass-produced furniture, leaning back in my tattered desk chair, is the last person I would want in my room . . . ever.

Yep. Harrisford-fucking-Briggs.

I struggle up to my elbows, disrupting Percy, who's sitting on my chest. He gives an outraged howl and holds tight, digging his claws into my skin.

"*Briggs*," I say, bordering on a shriek. "What are *you* doing here?"

He swivels the chair around to face me, an infuriating smirk on his face. "Why, hello, Chan." There's a sarcastic slant to his greeting. "It's *so* lovely to see you, too." Behind him, Pudding is sitting on my desk, basking in the light from my desk lamp.

My entire body hurts like I've been dragged through a meat grinder, but seeing his smarmy face makes me remember. Brings back all the fury I have over how he'd tricked me, how he'd trapped me in the Magecorp vault with his father, how I'd almost died because of him and his fucking lies.

I try to sit up, but my head spins and I fall back against my pillows. Percy lets out an indignant growl before settling himself back on my chest. Clutching my forehead, I let out a groan. "I'm going to fucking kill you."

Harrisford shifts to sit forward in my chair, elbows on his knees. "Bloody hell, Chan." He shoots me a scandalized look. "That's no way to speak to someone who just saved your life."

I drop my hand and glare at him. "What do you mean, saved my life?"

"You don't remember?" He passes a hand over his chin and frowns at me.

"The last thing I remember was the explosion."

"But you were talking to me . . . On the way here. You *fought* me. I had to sedate you to get you on the dragon—"

"The dragon!" It occurs to me that I'm more pissed off about the dragon than about the fact Harrisford forcibly sedated me.

"It was the only way to get you here quickly enough to save you!" he thunders.

I cross my arms, my eyes narrowing to slits. "It's big of you to talk about saving me, Briggs . . . when you're the one that almost got me murdered."

And for the first time since I woke up, Harrisford's self-satisfied mask slips. "Murdered? Did my father . . . Did he try to *kill* you?"

I shudder, suddenly cold. Placing a hand on Percy, I elaborate. "He had a gun. He threatened me. He"—I touch my forehead, where I can almost still feel the cold kiss of steel—"held a gun to my head."

Harrisford is suddenly on his feet. He strides to the bedside, eyes wild, both hands buried in his hair. "Oh god. Oh god, Chan. I'm so sorry, I—"

"Lied to me?" I finish his sentence off for him, my voice acidic. "Told me he was out of town? Got me trapped in a locked room with your violent, gun-toting father?"

He stops and stares at me, his mouth open. "I swear," he says, and his tone is almost pleading. "I swear I didn't know he was in London. He told me he'd be in Wales, for fuck's sake, and I believed him." Harrisford shakes his head and curls his hands into fists. "If I'd known he might be there, I would *never* have taken the risk . . ." He turns away, bracing both hands on the desk.

I stare at his back, at his bowed head, trying to work out if I believe him. I can't believe him, I shouldn't—I ought to not trust this man who has been my rival for so many years . . . And yet. He brought me here, didn't he? After the explosion, he somehow managed to get me back to Seamere, back to my bed . . . And not only that, he's still here.

And anyway, wasn't it my idea to break into Magecorp? It was me who insisted on it, who assured him it would be safe for me to impersonate Hani Nguyen.

It was my fault things went so badly.

I don't want to ask, but I have to. "Your dad . . . Is he dead?" My voice is small; it catches in my throat. The stark reality is starting to hit: *I blew up the top floor of Magecorp.*

A pause. Harrisford won't look at me. "He's alive."

I blow out a relieved breath. Yes, Darghan Briggs is a scumbag, and he threatened me with a gun . . . But the idea of actually killing someone—even if it was accidental—sickens me.

Harrisford drops back into the seat of my chair and scrubs at his face with both hands. Neither of us speaks for several moments. Percy starts purring, the vibrations reverberating through my body. "Thanks, Percy," I whisper, and scratch him under the chin. There's an unsubstantiated theory that cats purr to heal their bodies from within, and I wonder if by sitting on my chest he's trying to help me heal, too. Either way, having his warm fluffiness on top of me *is* making me feel better—even if it's purely psychosomatic.

Eventually, Harrisford breaks the silence. "What happened in there, anyway?"

I quickly recount everything that happened up to and including the explosion. As I talk, Harrisford's hands grip the armrests of my desk chair, holding on so tight I fear the brittle old plastic might crack.

"How did you know the door would cause an explosion," he asks, "when you flung the wire at it?"

I draw the bedsheets around Percy and me both, enveloping us in the draping warmth. This is the first time Percy's sat on me—ever—and I really don't want him to leave.

"Well," I say slowly, trying to order my thoughts. "I knew the air would be ionized, because of the huge reservoir of magic they keep in the circular room. And I knew that the door was still live-wired from the initial shock. So I figured that if I managed to ground the current from the door to the floor, it'd create a magical explosion."

"Fucking brilliant," Harrisford says, more to himself than anything. Then he glances at me sidelong. "I have to say, Chan, you secretly being an evil mastermind is . . . frankly rather frightening."

I stare at him. "You say that like it's a good thing."

"Well," he says, one corner of his mouth lifting. "Maybe it is."

I rip my gaze away, my cheeks heating, and pick at a stray piece of lint on the sheets. "Yeah, well, that's the last thing I remember. The explosion." My brow creases as I try to untangle the sequence of events further. "If you brought me here on a dragon, how did your dad get out?"

Harrisford's gaze drifts away from me and fixes on the opposite wall. "The ambulance helicopters were just arriving as we were flying off. They took him to the London General Magical Hospital. But . . . he's apparently in a coma."

My eyes linger on Harrisford's profile, silhouetted against the light from my lamp. I'm trying to work out why he's frowning. Is it because he loves Mr. Briggs and is mad at me for endangering his dad's life? Or is it because he actually hates his father and wishes that the blast had killed him proper?

"I—I'm sorry, Briggs."

He waves a dismissive hand at me. "Don't be. We both know that he would've killed you."

A shudder tears through me, and I clutch at the sheets. Percy's claws dig in again. The memory of Darghan Briggs's attack is still all too fresh in my mind—and my body. It's like any mention of it triggers a visceral reaction deep in my organs and flesh.

Which is why, when Harrisford tentatively broaches the subject, I don't feel up to elaborating. "Exactly what did he say to you?" Harrisford says. He seems to be holding his breath.

I swallow, my tongue scraping the dry roof of my mouth. "It's—it's all in the listening book."

Until now, he'd been slouching, tipping my desk chair back. But now he sits up straight, giving me a sharp look. "You had a listening book?"

I nod and point. "In my bag. I nicked it from the library."

He stares at me for a second, as though trying to work out who I am and why I'm suddenly flouting school rules with impunity. But soon enough he breaks eye contact and rummages through my bag.

"There are a lot of packs of Knobbly's nuts in here." He raises an eyebrow and I scowl at him.

"Keep looking."

After a while, he locates the book and pulls it out triumphantly.

Flipping it open, he jams his glasses on and starts reading, his blue and brown eyes scanning back and forth.

I watch him as he reads. It's always incredible—and disconcerting—how different Harrisford looks when wearing his spectacles. They're slightly rounded, with thick tortoiseshell rims, the kind you'd expect an Oxford graduate to wear. Or those male models on posters in opticians' shops, who you know never actually wear glasses but are used in advertisements anyway just because they're pretty.

And as much as I hate to admit it, Harrisford *is* pretty, in that haughty, rich-boy way. The way his golden hair sweeps back in gentle waves from his face. The oceanic blue of his left eye and the deep mahogany of his right, framed by lashes so dark they really don't belong on a blond. The way his high cheekbones and straight nose and sharp jaw frame his perfect, pouty lips . . .

I sigh. Not only did Harrisford win the wealth and privilege lottery, it seems he won the genetic lottery, too.

On me, glasses would just look nerdy. On him? It's patently unfair, but on him they lend him a certain aristocratic air. As an average person—a mere mortal in the looks department—it would be horrible dating someone like him. You'd always pale in comparison.

Not that I'm planning to date him, of course. The prick.

Something in the listening book has caught Harrisford's attention, and his usual pale complexion is deepening to puce.

"What's wrong?" I venture, but he snaps the book shut.

"It's nothing," he says curtly, tossing the book on my desk. Then he levels a look at me. "It sounds like Father was saying Magecorp isn't behind the surges."

I can tell from the escalating pitch of his purring that Percy's had enough of chin scratches, so I move on to his ears. "Right." The memory of Mr. Briggs's words ricochets around my head. *You've got it all wrong. We don't know why the extra holes are forming.* And his chuckle—the chuckle I can still hear in my marrow every time I close my eyes—is a sound that still reverberates painfully around the caverns of my mind.

I wipe my clammy palms on the bedsheets. "Can we really trust anything your dad says, though? I mean, he lied to us about being in Wales. He . . . *attacked* me."

"But wait." Harrisford spins in my chair to grab a book from the desk. I recognize it as the one we'd stolen from his father's study. He starts riffling through the pages until he reaches a section of interest, then peers at it. "I think that in this case, my father might be telling the truth. Because, listen—

"*Although the Great Fire of London in 1666 is commonly attributed to a blaze that started in a bakery,*" Harrisford reads aloud, "*magical experts now believe that the conflagration was triggered by rogue magic. Records of the time indicate that there had been at least a year of magical destabilization, as well as several incidences of surges recorded throughout the city. Many of the earlier deaths were erroneously declared as being due to bubonic plague. However, reports of fatalities due to injuries inflicted by familiars, as well as recorded fluctuations in the levels of atmospheric magic, have led many historians to believe that the fire was a result of a massive power surge.*"

"Okay," I say. "Assuming the London fire *was* due to a magical surge. What does that have to do with us, now?"

"Hold your unicorns, woman," Harrisford chides, though his tone is not harsh. "I'm just getting to that."

He continues reading. "*Indeed, analysis of the records from King's Court Prison documents the incarceration of one Reginald Pius Navum, a well-known heretic of the time. Navum was imprisoned for opening illegal portals to the Void in an effort to create discord—an act of sabo-*

tage that amplified the flow of magic and now is thought to be the cause of the surge."

"So are we thinking that maybe someone is . . . sabotaging Magecorp?" I rub my forehead. "But who?"

Harrisford gazes at me, his expression thoughtful. "I don't know. But I do think that my father could be right. It could be someone on the outside, trying to interfere with Magecorp. I've been reading up on all the previous surges listed in this book"—he holds up the tattered tome—"and virtually all of them have been due to sabotage. The Great Library of Alexandria fire. The fire in Rome back in 64 AD. Even the Black Friday bushfires in Australia last century . . . They all have evidence that points to magical surges, even though the governments at the time worked hard to cover it up. The authorities have kept a tight control on magic ever since the Dark Ages, Chan, but *every* time they've lost control, it's because someone has managed to breach their defenses."

"So it's likely someone who wants to bring down Magecorp." But that doesn't really narrow it down. There are so many people, and groups, who have reason to hate them. Linksphere, for one, being their single major competitor. The Magical Liberation Organization too who are anti-capitalist at the best of times. Or even just disgruntled ex-employees of the corporation. Any one of them could be the culprit, and we're no closer to figuring it out.

Lifting Percy off my chest, I swing my legs out of bed. He gives a plaintive yowl, shoots me a loathsome look, and leaps right into Harrisford's lap. *Traitor.*

"Chan," Harrisford says. "What are you doing?" In the ultimate act of betrayal, Harrisford is scratching the spot above Percy's tail, and he has his bum stuck in the air, his crooked tail vibrating with pleasure.

I reach for my wardrobe and yank the doors open, intending to pull out some jeans. "I'm getting up. We need to report this, Briggs." But just as I close my fingers around a hanger, a bout of dizziness grips me and I sway, clinging on to the wardrobe for support.

"You're too unwell," Harrisford says disapprovingly. After tucking Percy beneath one arm, he stands and guides me back to the bed. "You almost died, remember? You really need to rest."

I don't want to rest, but I can't deny that my body is staging a protest at being upright. So I sink onto the bed with a sigh. It's then that I notice: I'm no longer wearing the tweed suit.

I stare at my body in dismay. I'm wearing a ratty, oversized old T-shirt that I use for going to sleep. It has a picture on it: the entire cast of the *Twilight* saga, terrible wigs and all. I'd bought it back in my Twihard days and got the last XL because it had sold in all the other sizes. I hope Harrisford hasn't seen the state of my arms, or . . . even worse, my legs.

"Briggs," I say, my voice shaking with suppressed horror. "Did you . . . Did you *undress me*?"

Harrisford's back to petting Percy. "You were injured." He gives a maddeningly nonchalant shrug. "Anyway, you have nothing to worry about. It's nothing I haven't seen before." But I don't fail to notice the pink tinge in his cheeks, or the fact that he seems to be refusing eye contact.

"And who"—I swallow, gathering my courage—"who healed me?"

This time, he does look up, his blue and brown eyes meeting mine. "Why, I did. Of course."

A bubble of madness is expanding in my brain, threatening to explode. I fancy that given long enough, cerebrospinal fluid is going to start leaking right out of my nostrils.

"*You* healed me?" I hiss. "You can't do that! What about taking me to the bloody hospital—"

"And risking them finding out we broke into Magecorp?" he

sneers, as though it's the most ludicrous thing anyone has ever suggested. "No, thank you."

I cross my arms tightly across my middle. Vets have a saying: Real doctors treat more than one species. But that isn't supposed to include *humans*. "It's wrong," I say, and I'm aware of how holier-than-thou I sound. But I don't care. "You've probably broken dozens of laws—"

"And you've probably broken hundreds!" His voice is rising too, and the pink in his face is turning into a deep, angry shade of red. "So where does that leave us, Chan? Are you going to dob me in? Report me? What happened to a simple 'thanks'?"

"Thanks for what? For drawing me into this stupid circus?"

He lets out a frustrated roar. "For saving your bloody life!"

We stare at each other, chests heaving, neither of us willing to back down. For god's sake—the moment Harrisford starts to finally seem human, and then he comes out with this? What a fucking bastard.

He did save you, you know. Percy's imperious voice rings loud and clear down our bond. *He rescued you from that ruined rooftop, brought you here, and used his own magic to heal you . . .*

Oh, shut it, Percy. Even in my mind, my voice sounds choked with tears. *You're just on his side because he's currently scratching your bum.*

Percy half closes his eyes. *He's a very good bum scratcher, to be fair. Perhaps you ought to try it.*

I grimace. *I am* not *letting him scratch my bum!*

But aloud, I finally concede. "Thank you," I mutter, crossing my arms even tighter.

"You're welcome," Harrisford says, his tone equally acerbic.

By the time Harrisford convinces me to lie down again, I'm feeling weak and shivery. Our quarrel has depleted the last of my energy, and I roll onto my side, my head pillowed against my hands.

"You should go to sleep now," Harrisford says. He's still annoyed with me; he doesn't look at me, instead just stares at his book.

"I'm not tired." I try, unsuccessfully, to stifle my yawn. "Keep reading. I want to know if there's anything else that'll help us."

Harrisford raises an eyebrow at me. "Are you sure? It's pretty dry."

I don't want to tell him that I need this—that after two days away from study, my brain is craving stimulation. Instead, I just say, "Perhaps your boring voice will send me off to sleep."

He shakes his head. "Christ, Chan, you really are a callous witch." But there's a faint smile playing about his lips. He draws my desk chair closer, its rolling wheels squeaking, then leans back, propping his sock-clad feet on my bed.

I close my eyes as he starts reading, the deep timbre of his words lulling me into calm. And soon enough, I fall asleep . . . to the sound of my enemy's voice.

17

Harrisford

I continue reading until long after Gwendolynne has drifted off, and by the time I finish my throat is raspy, my body is stiff, and my bladder is full to bursting. Percy gives a small whine of protest as I scoop him up off my lap and plop him by Gwendolynne's side. Gently, I draw the covers over the two of them, stopping just short of stroking her hair. She looks so peaceful when she's not wearing her customary scowl.

It's Sunday, and I have a whole day off from classes. According to my research, visiting hours at the London General Magical Hospital start in exactly twenty-five minutes. That's enough time to get there on my motorbike if I turn on the magical boost.

Still, I dawdle, deliberating over whether I should go. On the one hand, it *is* my father—the closest person who shares my DNA. And from what he said to Gwendolynne, neither he nor Magecorp are responsible for the surges.

On the other hand, he held Gwendolynne at gunpoint. He threatened her life. He lied to me, not just about being in Wales but about so many other things.

I'm floundering, trapped in a spiraling vortex of indecision. In the end, it's Pudding who convinces me. *Go*, she says. *At the very least it'll give you a chance to speak your mind, for once.*

Thirty-six minutes later, I'm pulling into the basement car park at the hospital. I'm pretty sure my father donated a wing here once; in any case, I'm greeted like an old friend as I stride past the main reception, Pudding perched high on my shoulder.

Father is in the intensive care unit, up on the fifteenth floor. He has a private room all to himself, and out his window is the most phenomenal view of the River Thames. It's almost a pity he can't appreciate it, because my tyrant of a father is still completely unconscious.

He's on an intravenous drip that feeds fluid into his body. A second line feeds him the magical anesthesia. His gown is splayed open, his chest dotted with round circles, cords trailing to the ECG. I squint at the small writing printed on each machine: *Powered by Magecorp*, it reads.

I snort. Figures.

Beside him, a ventilator creaks, performing the task that his lungs won't, because of too much swelling.

Noncardiogenic pulmonary edema, the consultant had said, back when they phoned me yesterday. *Compartment syndrome. Persistent cardiac arrhythmia. Marked swelling of the brain.* The doctors have healed his burns and broken bones with magic, but internal organ damage—especially all the excess fluid—is much harder to treat. And the list of things wrong with my father's body is *long*. I understand the terminology on a theoretical level, but hearing it out loud still makes my mind reel.

As I stare down at him, an odd, hollow feeling creeps outward, into my extremities. He looks so small in the big white bed. Usually, even though I've outgrown him—I'm taller by several inches—he always manages to make me feel small. But now he's the one looking thin, ill, and, dare I say it, fragile.

I pull up a chair, which scrapes across the linoleum, and collapse into it. It feels strange to have gone from one sickbed and come straight to another. I'd spent so long waiting for Gwendolynne, hoping that she would wake up. Now I am waiting beside my father, half hoping that he won't.

"Father," I say, and for a moment I wonder if he can somehow hear me. Whether I'll see a spike in his heart rate or a flicker of his eyelids—anything to tell me he's still there, locked inside. But there's nothing, of course. Just the wheeze of the ventilator and the beeps of the machines, dividing his life force into neat little packets of time.

I'm sure he can sense you're here, Pudding says kindly. She's still sitting on my shoulder.

Carefully, I shift her to my lap. I don't even know if I want him to sense my presence. My voice drops to a whisper. "When you wake, Father, I need you to tell me . . . what on earth have you been hiding?"

There's no answer, of course. Pudding was wrong; I won't get to speak my mind, since I'm quite certain that he cannot hear me.

This all seems so utterly pointless. When he wakes—*if* he wakes—he probably won't remember anything. Gwendolynne didn't; a small blessing, since it would pain me if she'd noticed how distraught I was for her safety. How my knees almost gave way as I ran to her. How, when I called out to her, my mouth could barely form her name because my throat was closing over.

How, even though my own father was buried beneath the rubble, all I could think about was Gwendolynne. Gwendolynne being in danger. Gwendolynne getting hurt. Getting *Gwendolynne* to safety.

Gwendolynne, Gwendolynne, Gwendolynne.

I'd cared more about her than I had about my own blood relation.

Is that how desperate Father felt, when my mother disappeared? Perhaps I'm following in his footsteps—maybe I am my father's son. If that is true . . . then I really am royally fucked.

Pulling out the stolen listening book, I flip it open, trying to see if there's anything more I can glean, anything that I'd missed. I'd started reading it in Gwendolynne's bedroom, but then I had to stop. For when I reached the part where my father had tried to explain Hani Nguyen's disappearance, the grief and fury that had risen inside me had threatened to rupture me open.

People run away all the time. Does there have to be a reason? my father had said to Gwendolynne while they were both locked inside the vault.

Already, I'm feeling that tide rise again, prickling at the backs of my eyes. *But you never know what someone is going through internally*, he'd gone on to say later. *She might have been deeply unhappy. She might have had a breakdown. She might have needed to escape.*

I pinch the bridge of my nose, squeezing my eyes shut. When he'd said that, it didn't sound entirely like he was talking about Hani Nguyen.

Pudding makes a sympathetic noise that burrows inside my brain. *I know it hurts*, she says from my lap. *But you have me. I'm here for you. I'm here.*

I grind the heels of my hands against my closed eyelids and force myself to take several deep, drawn-out breaths. Despite my best efforts, though, the memories still flood back, threatening to pull me under.

I was only four years old when it happened. Too young to really understand it, or to comprehend why one day my mother was there—hugging me with her warm body, comforting me when I got hurt, playing with me on the floor—and the next day she simply wasn't. My memories of those times are indistinct, as though I'm deep underwater, looking up, watching the wavy shapes of things shifting and moving somewhere above the surface.

But what happened afterward is sharp and clear: how not even a day after she had disappeared, my father had hired a dumpster and started systematically discarding all of my mother's things.

It was only because I managed to break open a box and pull out a pile of her clothes that I was able to salvage anything at all. My father threw out every photograph, every keepsake, every piece of jewelry . . . But I distinctly remember dragging a small cache of my mother's garments—blouses, T-shirts, a pair of shorts—into my bedroom and stashing it in my own wardrobe. Oh, and the tweed suit that Gwendolynne wore: That too was one of the pieces that I somehow managed to save. Seeing her in it was confusing, distressingly so. She looked beautiful, yes, but also it was awful—a knotted web of emotions all snared together. Grief. Wonder. Attraction. Shame.

I remember that every night, in the darkness, four-year-old me would pull out a piece of my mother's clothing. And I'd hug it, smelling the faint trace of perfume that reminded me of my mum, as I drifted off to sleep.

I suppose I can't really judge my father. Who knows what he'd gone through in those early days, when the pain was still fresh and raw? I suspect he'd acted out of grief, or rage—or maybe both. I don't know. We've never talked of it since. But no one visiting the Briggs mansion would know that anyone named Theodora Finlay-Briggs had ever lived there.

There's so much knowledge buried deep in the dungeons of Father's mind. His memories of my mother. What he remembers of our time together. What, if anything, he knows about the surges.

And if he dies . . . then I'll never know any of it.

I sit there, beside my father's bed, for a long time. Too long. Way past the end of visiting hours. And no one bothers to tell me to leave. Even the nurses who shuffle in and out at regular intervals barely cast me a second glance.

When you're the son of a man who's donated a whole wing, you get afforded certain privileges.

It's just a shame that being loved by your father isn't necessarily one of them.

18

Gwendolynne

By Tuesday morning, I'm nearly climbing out of my skin, so I go to class despite being not quite one hundred percent.

Today, I've been rostered onto hospital duty, along with Pen Ferguson, Conall Peters, and Isla Ennis. Heloise is doing consultations, and Tuesdays are open clinics, which means no scheduled appointments—clients can walk in at any time.

There aren't too many patients in hospital today. Which is lucky, because Professor Kaur's recovered from her mystery illness and has stopped by to deliver our fortnightly tutorial. Even though she's the dean, she still finds time to be in the clinics at least once every two weeks—"Just to keep an eye on things," as she likes to joke. It's worlds apart from the vice dean, Professor Pickering, who almost never descends from his temperature-controlled second-floor office.

Lenny, the dean's German shepherd, who is both a familiar and a guide dog, stays close by Professor Kaur's side. The only other dog in hospital is a Labrador who ate an entire pan of brownies laced with an invisibility tincture. We'd made him vomit, of course, and he was fortunately unaffected by the chocolate. But the magic absorbed too quickly into his bloodstream for us to save him from the effects of the spell. He's spent the morning periodically popping in and out of visibility, which has made for some instances of high-key panic from the staff.

It's lucky Professor Kaur is so perennially unflappable. Even when the invisible dog slips past us and escapes, she somehow manages to catch him and usher him back into his cage. I guess she doesn't need to "see" him, relying instead on other senses to know where, exactly, he is.

She really is so incredibly competent.

In the cat ward, there's just one patient, a Ragdoll who has been vomiting up tiny, real-life frogs for the past few days. The dean takes the opportunity to refresh us on how paradoxical aciduria develops in patients with gastric vomiting—a phenomenon that always makes perfect sense when she explains it, but precisely zero fucking sense later.

The cat is booked in for an abdominal ultrasound; until then, every now and then, we have to run around the ward with nets, catching dozens of hopping amphibians.

"Well, this is tiresome," Isla whines the third time we have to catch the frogs. "Why can't the cleaners do it? This really is *not* contributing to our education."

Tell her I'm happy to eat some, Percy says, speaking through our bond. I'd left him back in my room, curled up inside the filthy cardboard box that the hideously expensive leopard-print cat bed I'd purchased came in. *I mean, look at me: I am starving. I am the most starvingest cat of all the world's starving cats—*

You have an entire bowl of kibble, I point out, while Percy's words taper off into a grumble. *Plus, I fed you* two *breakfasts this morning.*

"The cleaners are a little busy." Conall deftly catches three frogs at once and tips them into a lidded bucket. "The invisible dog keeps escaping and pooping all over the wards. Anyway, isn't it good we're getting practice with our frog-handling skills?" Frogs are common both as familiars and for use in spells, so what Conall says is true. He's always trying to see the bright side of things. Even though I can tell that he is still mourning Gary, he's putting on a brave face.

"Mr. Peters is right." Professor Kaur scoops up another of the frogs with her net. "Miss Ennis, do try to see this as a learning opportunity."

Isla rolls her eyes, retreats into the corner, and starts scrolling on her strap. Conall and I raise our eyebrows at each other. There's no way either of us would ever *dream* of disrespecting the dean in such a way.

But Isla doesn't really have to worry, does she? Just like Harrisford, she grew up disgustingly wealthy—which explains why now, as an adult, she's such an entitled little witch.

When we've finally finished catching the frogs, I start taping down the lid of Conall's bucket. It's as I'm poking more holes in the lid for ventilation that Pen opens their mouth, daring to utter the sacrilegious word that no veterinary student should ever say.

"How weird is this?" they muse, staring at the rows of empty cages. "The fact that it's so qu—"

Conall and I both leap at them, exactly at the same time. Conall even scrambles over a table in an effort to stop Pen from saying the Q word:

Quiet. One should never, ever say that it's quiet.

It's just inviting trouble.

Conall, having better reflexes and just generally being more physically competent, reaches Pen first, clamping his hand over Pen's still-half-open mouth and smearing their fuchsia lipstick.

But it's too late. The rest of the word has already slipped out, and the three of us stare at each other in abject horror. This is it; we've done it. We've invoked the wrath of the gods.

And right on cue, Heloise bursts through the door.

"I'm admitting a cat," she says, panting slightly, as though she's actually run from the consult rooms. This hospital is so old, the hallways so convoluted, that it's honestly extremely impractical. "Matilda. Sixteen years old, female, neutered, Norwegian Forest Cat. Has been flat for three days and started vomiting around twenty-four hours ago. Owner presented her moribund. There's been two, maybe three months of increased drinking."

I peek into the carrier at the fluffy cat lying, completely immobile, on one side. Straightaway, we all jump into action.

Pen starts setting up a fluid bag and Conall cuts several small lengths of tape. Meanwhile, I gently lift the cat out, settle her on top of a clean blanket on the treatment room table, and quickly check her over.

"Hey, are you okay?" Heloise moves closer and touches me on the arm.

"Yeah," I whisper back. Pen and Conall have finished setting up the fluids, so I grab clippers to shave a patch of fur from the cat's foreleg. "Are *you* okay?"

"You wouldn't even know I got hurt," she says, grinning. "Except that my left tibia tingles when it's humid."

I give her a quick smile back, and Heloise mouths *Good luck* before heading back out the door.

Like a well-oiled machine, Conall, Pen, and I place a fluid line with no issues and start rehydrating the cat. After the flurry of activity, we still for a moment, catching our breaths and thinking about what to do next.

I glance at Isla. She's still absorbed with something on her strap, and I scowl. Since we're all working on the hospital wards together, she'll get at least baseline credit for whatever we do.

It can't be helped, though. We need to figure out what's wrong with the poor cat so that we can save her life. At least Professor Kaur will know, since she's still here typing something on the hospital computer.

"What do we do, Gwen?" Pen nervously smooths an escaped curl of red hair back into their ponytail. "She's really, really sick."

"Yeah, she is," I say, and frown. Old cats that come in like this can have any number of issues—kidney problems, diabetes, liver issues, cancer. I recommence my examination, carefully checking Matilda's mouth for any ulcers, her abdomen for any masses, her gums for any signs of paleness.

Despite his earlier gripes about not letting him eat the frogs, Percy helps me to channel magic via our connection, allowing me to also assess Matilda's qì. There's nothing obvious except that her life force is waning. Something on the inside, then.

"We need to do some bloods," I say. "As well as measure her magic levels." I pause for a moment to check her bladder, then add, "I'm pretty sure there's enough urine to collect a sample." I glance at Professor Kaur, who's listening avidly to our discussion.

Pen clutches the blood tubes that they've gathered tighter. "You do it, Gwen. You're best at blood draws."

Pen gets really anxious, something that Conall, Heloise, and I are trying to help them get past. I hand the syringe over to them, instead. "It's your turn," I say. I want the dean to see Pen do it. Conall nods his agreement with fervent enthusiasm.

"Are you sure?" Pen chews their lip, uncertain.

"They didn't hit the vein last time," Isla says from her corner, finally noticing what's going on at exactly the worst possible moment. She still hasn't looked up from her screen.

"Oh, shut up, Isla," Conall snaps, and Isla flips her blond hair over one shoulder and smirks at him. She must have really riled him up, since he never gets cross at anyone.

Pen takes their position, with me restraining the cat and Conall hovering, ready to hand Pen the tubes. As Pen uncaps the syringe, someone else walks through the door.

I immediately sense his arrival, not only because I can smell his cologne, but also because I've become weirdly, annoyingly attuned to the presence of Harrisford Briggs.

He strides into the cat ward like he owns the place, even though he's a myth.creat student and shouldn't even be in the mag.fam wards. I straighten, my head whipping around, about to tell him to shove off, when he takes a deep sniff and then exhales.

"Who has ketoacidosis?" he says.

"I . . . what?" I snap, scrunching up my nose. "What the hell are you doing here, Briggs—"

He takes a step closer, his eyes glittering under the magelights. "Diagnosing your patient, Chan." He gestures toward the cat. "It's DKA. Can't you smell it?"

I curl my hands into fists. Isla's finally raised her head, a wry smile on her lips, and Conall and Pen are watching us with a mixture of dismay and curiosity. And Harrisford? Harrisford is staring at nothing but me, looking mighty fucking pleased with himself.

"I can't," I say, my nostrils flaring. I force myself to take a deep breath. In, then out.

Some people are gifted with the genetic ability to smell ketones on an animal's breath. In this way, they can diagnose diabetic ketoacidosis, or DKA, with just a single inhale. Not me, though. I cannot smell a single thing right now, except Harrisford's fucking cologne.

From the corner, Professor Kaur pipes up. "Good pick, Mr. Briggs. You've saved us a hell of a lot of time."

Our straps ping, and all five of us check our wrists simultaneously. And as the class rankings notification flashes onto the screen, all I can do is clench my teeth to stop myself from screaming.

The dean has allocated *my* marks to Harrisford. Which means his diagnosis has helped him to slip ahead of me . . .

By one measly bloody point.

It's not even enough that Harrisford won the wealth, privilege, *and* genetic lotteries. He also won the "can diagnose complex diseases with nothing but his nose" lottery.

What a joke. Anger rips its way through me, beating at my chest, and everything in my vision goes fuzzy. I'm barely thinking as I reach out, grab Harrisford's arm, and haul him out the door.

The drug cupboard is annoyingly cramped, and it occurs to me that this is the second time in just a few days that I've been shut in a cupboard with Harrisford—though whether one can call his palatial wardrobe a cupboard is still up for debate.

It's dark, so Harrisford flicks on the magelights, throwing his features into sharp relief.

"Chan," he says, his forehead creasing. "Are you *mad* at me?"

"Did you have to interrupt like that?" I hiss, ignoring the way our proximity is forcing his muscular, coverall-clad body against mine. "Pen was *just* about to do a blood draw and you had to come and interfere!"

He rakes a hand through his hair, though it just flops right back down onto his forehead. "Oh. I had no idea. I was just trying to help—"

"Well, you didn't help." I go to cross my arms but only succeed in bumping our bodies together even closer. It's upsetting—and mortifying—how quickly my heart rate speeds up in response.

Harrisford frowns at me. "I actually just came by to see how you were doing, after, you know . . ."

"Your father nearly murdered me and I exploded the roof of his workplace? Yeah, I'm just jolly, obviously." I still have some cuts and bruises, but who's really keeping count?

Despite our crowded surroundings, Harrisford reaches up, touching a small wound that's still on my chin. "I missed one," he says, running the pad of his thumb across it. "Do you want me to heal—"

"I'm good, thanks." My face heats, and I bat his hand away.

We lapse into an uncomfortable silence, during which Harrisford won't stop looking at me, and . . . why won't he stop looking at me?

"I brought back your book," he says finally, producing it from some inner pocket of his coveralls.

The listening book. I hadn't even noticed he had taken it, so focused was I on catching up on my studies. With some maneuvering, I manage to take ahold of it and clasp it against my chest as though it is a shield. And it occurs to me that in a way, it is. Since it contains Darghan Briggs's full confession, it's my insurance against being charged for endangering life and property, should Harrisford's dad ever wake up and think to accuse me.

In fact, perhaps I should pre-empt that possibility, even before Mr. Briggs wakes up. "I think we should take this to the police," I say to Harrisford, who's still staring down at me.

His expression hardens, his brows drawing way down. "Why?"

"Because I think this is getting beyond what we can feasibly handle ourselves. We think it's sabotage, but we have no idea who it could be, or even where to bloody look." And also I don't want to get in trouble for what I did at the Magecorp vault.

Harrisford's gaze slides away, his jaw working, before returning to me. "No," he says, his eyes becoming cold, like ice. Once again, even though they look nothing alike, I'm painfully reminded of his father. It's the little details that are similar—like father, like son.

"What do you mean, no?" I try to keep my voice steady, try to stop it from rising in pitch. We're in a drug cupboard just off the main corridor, and I don't want to be overheard. "We have a written record of your father's confession—we should be reporting him to the authorities."

"Chan," Harrisford says, and sighs. "I see what you're saying, but I can assure you, we really can't trust the authorities."

I tilt my head, regarding him through narrowed eyes. "Is this about protecting your father?" I ask. "Because don't you forget that he held a *gun* to my head—"

"It's not about protecting him!" Now Harrisford is sounding frustrated. I can see the pulse in his neck distending.

"That's dragonshit and you know it, Briggs! You're refusing to hand in his confession, right? And from where I'm standing, that looks a lot like you're trying to protect him." White-hot rage is tearing through my body, collecting in my extremities, making my heart pound and my head heat up and my skin feel barely held together. After everything we went through . . . After everything *I* went through to procure that goddamned book, it'll all amount to nothing because of Harrisford's misplaced loyalty?

He shuts his eyes and massages his temples. "You know, for a smart woman, you really can be incredibly obtuse."

"Obtuse? Going to the police is not *obtuse*!"

Harrisford lowers his hand to glower at me, and when he moves even closer his eyes become shadowed. Then he leans in and says, right in my face, "It's instinctive for you, isn't it, Chan? To be a goody two-shoes and run off to whoever's in charge as soon as something happens." His lips spread into a grin, and he shakes his head. "You just cannot help yourself, can you?"

I bristle, fighting the urge to slap his face. When I speak, my words are a snarl. "This isn't about being a *goody two-shoes*, Briggs.

These surges have the potential to destroy all of us, and you just want to sit back and let that happen?"

He raises his hands and actually clutches at his face. "I don't mean to sit back, for fuck's sake, we can figure it out together—"

My anger brims over. Reaching up, I put my hands on his chest and shove him away from me. He crashes into a shelf full of drugs, rattling all the bottles. "I'm done, Briggs," I say, trying to fight my tears. "I'm *done* doing anything together." And with that, I turn and smack open the door, ready to stalk out.

Harrisford's hand on my shoulder stays me for a second, and I go to shrug him off. But he's leaning over me, his chin at my shoulder and his lips right by my ear. "Fine," he says, his breath caressing the back of my neck. "You do things your way, and I'll do things mine. But Chan?"

And despite being so angry, I don't move. Like the world's biggest idiot, I stay to hear what he has to say.

"If you go to the police," he says, his voice low and deadly, "then I *will* tell Professor Kaur about your stolen cat."

19

Gwendolynne

I hate him, I hate him, I really fucking hate him.

It's been a few foolish days of a strange and tentative truce—but clearly Harrisford and I are back to blackmail. I'm almost tempted by Percy's offer to pee on Harrisford's pillow, but it's too much of a risk. With Harrisford's threat hanging over our heads, I simply cannot risk Percy getting caught.

Still, I appreciate the solidarity.

I barely notice anything as I storm back to the hospital ward. When I burst in, a trail of rage like a cloud behind me, Conall and Pen glance at each other, concern etched on both their faces.

Isla finally lowers her strap. "Snogging Briggs in the drug cupboard now, are we, Chan?" Her upper lip curls.

"I wasn't snogging anyone," I snap, reaching into a cupboard and yanking out a syringe pump. While magic can heal traumatic injuries like cuts and bruises and even broken bones, internal diseases are a different story. Magic is powerful, obviously, but this cat is diabetic and in desperate need of insulin. And even the most skilled magical veterinarians cannot conjure hormones from thin air.

First, though, I have to rehydrate her and balance her electrolytes. As I unwind the cord wrapped around the pump machine, I spy the small lettering on its underside: *Powered by Magecorp.* I sigh. Of course it is.

Isla moves closer, the overhead magelights casting a halo on her head. "Just be careful he doesn't break your heart right before exams." She gives a contemptuous toss of her blond hair and flashes me a simpering smile. "I'm sure you're well aware of his reputation. I'd *hate* to see your grades slip because you're fawning over some man."

She's mocking me, but I know what she's really doing. Isla and Harrisford were a thing back in fifth year. They'd dated for ten months before Harrisford had illustriously broken things off with her. Rumor has it that she never quite got over him, and she likes to stake her territory whenever she sees him getting close to, well, literally anyone else.

What she doesn't realize, though, is that zero territory staking is necessary. Harrisford's and my circles had briefly overlapped, like a particularly distasteful Venn diagram. But now our circles have separated and are so far apart from one another they're not even touching. They're not overlapping . . . they're underlapping.

I don't look at her as I begin setting up the pump, plugging in the magical charging cord and powering it up. "I'm not foolish enough to make the same mistakes you did, Isla."

She scoffs and moves away again, talking to her parrot familiar through their bond. Her comments sound rather snippy, and I'm pretty sure I hear the words "snot-nosed swot" and "ugly cow" muttered beneath her breath.

Conall moves closer to help me calculate the electrolyte concentrations and infusion rates. "Are you all right, Gwen?" he whispers. "You seem kind of . . . off."

I stab at the buttons with my finger, taking my ire out on the machine. "I'm fine, Conall," I say. "But meet me after class, yeah? I think I need your help."

It's the second time I've been inside Conall's room, and this time I have more opportunity to examine the displayed drawings. They're beautiful—all intricate lines and tightly drawn circles and scribbles that should look messy, but in this context, they are not.

"Are all of these yours?" I touch one of them with the tip of my finger.

"Yeah," he says, shrugging. "It's what I do to decompress."

He comes to stand behind me, silent for a moment. I'm not exactly sure, but I feel like there's a new drawing, one that wasn't there the night Gary died. It's the most beautiful and ambitious one yet, and I can almost feel the grief and rage and agony pouring out from the page.

"So what do you need help with?" Conall says, fixing his big brown eyes on me.

"I wanted to know if you can help interpret some blueprints." Conall started out doing an engineering degree. But from the little he's said, I gather he found the toxic masculinity too triggering to his dysphoria, so he transferred to veterinary science after completing third year. He got some credits for the pure sciences and then worked hard to catch up to the rest, joining us in fourth year, a few weeks into term one. If anyone here can figure these blueprints out, it'd be him.

Unlocking my strap, I show him some of the photos I snapped of the scrolls stored at Magecorp HQ. The lines are faint and scratchy on the parchment, and I'm reminded of how old they were. Guilt swoops through my belly. They would have all been blown to bits.

Conall squints at my small, cracked screen, then extends his fingers toward me. "May I?" he says, and I nod, slipping the strap off my wrist.

He swirls his fingers through the air in a complicated figure-eight pattern, and all of a sudden the screen is projected into midair, suspended like a slightly translucent billboard. The projection shows the plans and blueprints, magnified, and he spends some time swiping through them.

I watch him, fascinated. It's incredible, really, how everyone here seems to so casually wield their magic. Conall's family isn't super wealthy—he *does* room in my dorm wing, after all—but from what I can gather, they're comfortably middle-class. Well-off enough, at least, to use magic on a whim. For someone like me, who's always had to carefully control my magic quotas, it's such an unfamiliar concept.

His eyes are two bright sparks as he finally turns to me. "What *are* these? Where did you get them?" There's barely leashed excitement quivering in his voice. "And more to the point . . . how?"

"I . . . well . . . I can't say how I got them, sorry. But they're from Magecorp HQ. Can you read them?"

Conall's gaze swivels back to the magnified blueprints. This time, when he speaks, he allows the excitement to fully fizz over. "Gwen, these are amazing! I've no idea what dark magic you did to get your hands on them, but everything is here: how to open portals, how to keep them open, how to harvest the magic that comes through . . . This is bloody *brilliant*."

The blueprints are tapping into Conall's innate love for the hard sciences, and my heart twists, wondering whether he might've stuck with engineering if circumstances had been different.

"I didn't even realize magic came from multiple portals," he murmurs. "I thought it came from mines." With one finger, he reverently traces the lines in midair. "Do you think this is related to the surge?"

Surge. Singular. Conall's only experienced one, and doesn't know about the others—the media has been busy telling everyone what happened at the charity gala was the result of a terrorist attack, and someone powerful has managed to quash all mentions of the rest. But even this one surge has impacted Conall in a big way. He lost his familiar, Gary; he lost his best friend.

"I think so," I say, and even though my voice is quiet, it lands heavily in the hush of the room. "I'm trying to . . . work out why it happened and whether there's a way to prevent one from ever happening again."

Conall's eyes are distant—he's clearly working things out in his head. When he speaks again, he speaks slowly, rubbing at one of his elbows. "According to these plans, once a portal is torn open, the tear is held in place by using some sort of . . . tether. An object, I think. It probably needs to be quite magically powerful to tether open a hole in reality."

My stomach flips. A tether. If someone is tearing open too many holes, is it because they've got hold of a tether? And if so, if there is indeed a rogue tether being used to sabotage Magecorp, could someone like me steal it back? Without knowing what the tether is, I can't be sure.

A twinge of guilt twists itself into my gut. Perhaps Harrisford's dad was telling the truth all along: that Magecorp aren't at fault but are, in fact, the ones being sabotaged.

Now, at least, we have something else to investigate—and I don't even need the assistance of a certain pompous, annoying blond.

After supper, Conall and I head to the common room, earning ourselves a slew of strange looks. I understand why: While Conall is sociable in his own quiet way, I almost never frequent any of Heywood Hall's communal areas. In fact, the closest I usually get to mixing with other people is when I pull long study sessions at the library.

Even then, I try to secrete myself in a hidden corner and talk to other people as little as reasonably feasible.

I mean, humans are disgusting, right?

But tonight I have a singular aim: Search the common room with Conall to see if there's anything vaguely resembling a tether, the theory being that it might still be in the vicinity after causing such a huge explosion. The thing is, it's difficult when we have no idea what to look for. The one saving grace is that Harrisford is happily absent, and nowhere to be seen.

To avoid suspicion, we wait until the room is mostly empty—the majority of the students having gone to bed—before we perform a thorough search. Pen joins us, after their rostered evening check of the hospital patients. They tell us Matilda the Norwegian Forest Cat is doing well, which is a huge relief.

We search beneath couch cushions, flip back all the rugs, run our hands along the filigree-patterned wallpaper. I rummage through the games cupboard, and Conall searches all the bookshelves, but none of us finds anything remotely useful. While all the objects are completely coated with magical traces—residual life force from the other students' use of them, none of them have any echoes of being magical itself. The only actual sources of magic here are two Magecorp-branded MagePoints—which, unlike typical electrical power points, you need to pay to plug into—that are set into the far back wall.

At one o'clock in the morning, after hours of searching, we're finally forced to acknowledge defeat and retire to our rooms. I'm exhausted; I've worked a full day and conducted an investigation at night, and I'm not even yet fully healed. As I struggle into my *Twilight* T-shirt, I wince a little—some of the bruises are a little tender—and briefly regret not letting Harrisford treat the rest of my injuries.

No, I scold myself. *Don't even* think *that.* I don't want Harrisford-fucking-Briggs to touch me ever again. He might be attractive—as much as I hate to admit it—but he's a slimy, conniving git with all the personality of a broken pencil.

Why are you so late? Percy asks me from where he's sleeping on my bed. His ears twitch as I pull out my toothbrush and begin to brush my teeth.

"I was searching for a source of the magic surges in the common room," I say, scrubbing at my teeth unnecessarily hard. I pause—suddenly picturing my dentist's spiel about enamel wear—then start brushing again, softer this time. "We think that maybe someone is trying to sabotage Magecorp."

Someone's sabotaging Magecorp? There's undisguised glee in Percy's mind-voice. *My megalomaniac ex-owner's company?*

I rinse and spit. "That's the one." Leaning over the sink, I splash water onto my face, then towel-dry it off.

Percy sits up and fixes his bright yellow eye on me. *Wasn't it you? Weren't you there over the weekend, breaking in?*

I sigh. "No, it wasn't me. I have no idea who it could be."

Percy gives a disappointed sigh, then lies back down, his head positioned very precisely at the center of my pillow.

I frown. Was that the only reason Percy helped me? So he could get back at Nathaniel Price?

Waving away that unpleasant thought, I slide my feet out of my slippers. I stand there, my feet sinking into the wiry carpet, twisting the towel with both hands.

It has suddenly occurred to me that, once upon a time, Percy had a front-row seat to all of Nathaniel's thoughts and actions.

"Actually . . ." I stuff the towel back on its railing and pad over to the bed. When I perch on the edge, dipping it, Percy grudgingly raises his head. "Did you notice anything unusual? Back when you lived with Nathaniel Price? Thoughts he had, or things he did, or . . . well, anything, really."

Rolling to an upright position and folding both of his front feet beneath him, Percy is silent for a long moment. Finally, he swivels his head to look at me. *As a matter of fact, something did happen.*

I sit forward, my heart pounding. "What?"

It was a few months ago. Someone broke into the Price family mansion.

My breath tears, harsh, through my throat as I gawp at him. Someone broke into Nathaniel Price's house? Is that when they stole the tether?

"A few months ago?" I say. "Can you . . . be a bit more specific?"

He narrows his eye at me. *Does it look like I carry a pocket watch around, Hairless One?*

I press my lips into a line; there's only one person I know who owns a pocket watch, and I absolutely do *not* want his help. "What did they steal?"

I cannot be certain, Percy says, his tail flicking. *All I know is that Nathaniel was tremendously angry. He spent copious amounts of time imagining the perpetrator being subjected to an array of increasingly creative torture methods.*

Shuddering, I turn out the light and climb beneath the bedcovers. Percy growls as though it's actually his bed and not mine. "There's room enough for us both," I gripe at him, but he pointedly leaps off the bed.

Perhaps there is, he says, stretching his back legs behind him, one at a time. *But you thrash around in your sleep too much. Also, you snore.*

"I do not snore!" But already he's coiled up tight on my desk chair. Seeing him there brings back memories of Harrisford: Harrisford reclining in it, Percy on his lap, his feet propped up on my bed, reading.

He'd at least had the decency to take his shoes off at the door, a detail that only occurred to me later. It's taboo in Asian culture to wear shoes inside, so I always slip mine off before I enter my room.

Harrisford had done so too—his stupidly expensive loafers had been placed neatly next to my scuffed-up trainers on the doormat.

I scowl at my ceiling. Expensive shoes, expensive shirts, expensive trousers that are tight enough to hug his perfect . . .

Stop it, Gwen. My face is burning. *Stop thinking about his fucking trousers.*

I sigh. It's sickening and irrational, but it would be a lie to deny that I find Harrisford Briggs good-looking—even if he is a total wanker. But that's the thing, isn't it? He already won the looks, wealth, and ketones-smelling lotteries; it would be too much for him to also have a half-decent personality.

Oh well. It doesn't matter. I am a full-grown, mature adult, and I can definitely appreciate a man's beauty while staunchly hating everything else about him.

I lie awake for almost an hour, stewing over my memories of Harrisford. Eventually, the last of my resolve crumbles, and I allow my fingers to sneak beneath my waistband. And soon enough I fall asleep, the liquid warmth of pleasure settled deep within my belly, the echo of Harrisford's name still lingering on my lips.

20

Gwendolynne

When I jerk awake, it's still dark, and the sheets are tangled around my waist. There's also drool pooling on my pillow. I swipe it away and squint at my buzzing strap. 2:37 a.m.

What the hell? The vibration on my bedside table woke me up at what should not be considered an actual time.

I scrub at my bleary eyes before focusing on the screen. It's a call-out, which is weird, because I'm not meant to be on duty. We final-year students are allocated eleven at a time, every eight weeks, to be on call. Each time, it's seven draining days and nights of managing the entire Seamere caseload, whether myth.creat or mag.fam. I dread my on-call weeks, because it means I might have to actually work with large animals (shudder) . . . but thankfully there are usually enough Mythological Creatures students rostered on that I can manage to avoid it.

Tonight, though, there's no such luck. Someone is calling me to the unicorn yards, and from the sounds of it, it's urgent.

I roll out of bed, finger-combing my hair, then pull on my neglected coveralls. Since I'm not officially rostered on, I could just refuse and go back to bed. But the memory of our class rankings after hospital wards yesterday is branded painfully on my brain: Harrisford, a mere one point ahead of me because he fucking stole my diagnosis.

So I do up all the studs on my coveralls, slide my feet into my waterproof boots, and—leaving Percy snoozing deeply on the cushioned seat of my chair—head out into the muggy night.

The unicorn yards are a maze of reinforced fences, designed so that male unicorns can't spear each other through the bars. Moonlight spills across the concrete, the trees casting skeletal shadows that stretch across the ground.

It's in the foaling stable that I find the myth.creat tutor who'd paged me on my strap. He's a newly graduated vet with dark curly hair and pale skin, and I can never remember his name.

"Ah, good, you're here," he says. "Follow me."

He wanders into one of the stalls, and I pull up short at the door.

The animal inside isn't a unicorn . . . instead, it's a qílín.

Qílíns are considered the Chinese equivalent of unicorns, though they don't look like unicorns at all, not really. For one, they usually have two antlers instead of one horn, and their heads are dragon-esque with long thick beards and manes. In fact, the only thing that qílíns and unicorns have in common is that they are both four-legged and have hooves.

I don't know why a qílín has been brought to Seamere. As far as I can recall, the zoo's qílín is rainbow-colored, so this one must be from a private trader. There are collectors that import mythical beasts from all over the globe, bartering and negotiating and spending way too much on those that are strange and rare.

This qílín is luminescent, her coat gold-and-red ombré, the golden scales darkening to a deep red at each of her four hooved feet.

And she's clearly in labor. Her golden tail is flicking, and every few minutes her entire abdomen contracts, her jewel-like eyes rolling.

Dystocia. She's having difficulty giving birth.

But the qílín isn't the only reason I stay frozen at the door. The other reason is a very familiar bearded dragon that is perched upon the railings. And if *she* is here, then so is . . .

Ugh. Harrisford.

Just my luck. I guess that's why he wasn't at supper, or in the Heywood Hall common room. It's because this must be his week on call. Did he ask them to call *me*, the prat? And if so, why? To make me suffer?

As soon as he catches sight of me, though, I immediately know it wasn't him. His eyes splay open wide, and his mouth opens and shuts a few times. A violent flush steals across his face, and he flings a hand in my direction.

"Marcus!" He's practically spitting. "What is *she* doing here?"

I narrow my eyes at him, wishing that I could vaporize him with the force of my targeted wrath. After our fight in the drug cupboard, he clearly wants nothing to do with me. Well, good, in that case—because I want nothing to do with him, either. There's no way Marcus (we'll see how long I remember his name) really needs the both of us. This must have just been a huge bloody mistake.

Marcus dunks his hands into a bucket of water. "I called her."

Oh. So it wasn't a mistake.

A muscle jumps in Harrisford's jaw. "Why? We don't need her here. She's not even myth.creat—"

The supervisor grabs a towel hanging over the railing and begins to dry his hands. "Isn't it obvious, Briggs? She's Chinese. This creature is Chinese. I think having her here will help." He's talking about me as though I'm not even present.

Having toweled off his hands, Marcus tosses the towel back over the railing and clasps Harrisford's shoulder. "Anyway, mate. It's late, I'm tired, and I'm going to bed. I've already cast the sedation spell. Good luck, kids."

And then Marcus is gone.

We both watch him leave. Me, livid; Harrisford wearing a scowl. Honestly, the supervisor's reasoning is ridiculous. First of all, I'm not the only vet student of Chinese descent currently studying at Seamere—there's also Alice Chu. Why he called me instead of Alice I have no idea. Either he, like Professor Bartell, thinks the two of us are actually the same person, or maybe he just called me first because Chan comes before Chu in class listings.

And second of all, I hardly know anything about qílíns. My parents may have come from China, but I was born here, and the fact that Marcus assumed I'd be an expert is actually quite offensive.

Still, there's not much I can do about it now. Clearly, Marcus has already put us both down as the allocated students for the case. So either I stay and help, or I leave Harrisford to tackle it on his own—*and* write the report. He'd probably find some way to make me look bad—say I skived off the call, or something.

Fuming, I roll up the sleeves of my coveralls, right up to the shoulder, and begin pulling on a full-length plastic glove.

Harrisford's already wearing a glove, but he uses his opposite arm to swipe some strands of hair away from his forehead. Then he fixes his gaze on me. "You should go."

From a large pump container on the ground, I squirt out a generous measure of lube, smearing it all over my glove. "What, and let you take all the glory? Not going to happen, Briggs."

I stalk past him, approaching the qílín. Remembering what Harrisford had said just before we rode the dragon—how standing close to large creatures is actually safer—I sidle in so near to the qílín's hindquarters I'm practically inside her.

Harrisford gives me a funny look. "She's not going to kick you, if you're worried about that. Qílíns are placid. They won't even walk on grass for fear of crushing the blades." He lets out a long, protracted sigh. "Listen, Chan, I don't expect you to know about qílíns, considering that you're mag.fam . . ."

But he trails off, because I've already positioned myself behind the creature and swept aside her tail. And, holding my breath, my heart hammering with the fear that I might do something wrong, I start pushing in my arm.

I feel the foal immediately, passing my hand around its gangling form. It's all lanky folded legs and a slimy-slick maned skull, and I carefully palpate, trying to determine which end is its front half and which end is its back.

"I think its head is bent backward," I say, my face scrunched up in concentration. I can do this. I can do this. It hasn't been *that* long since I did my myth.creat modules . . .

I feel around again, and confirm, with more conviction this time, "The head's definitely backward."

Planting my feet against the straw-covered ground, I try to grab hold of the foal's muzzle. But it's too slippery, and I can't get enough purchase. The qílín lets out a low bellow, eliciting a shower of sparks.

Wait—sparks? I force myself to notice what is happening rather than hyperfocusing on the foal. The qílín's skin is heating up, becoming searingly hot, and no, oh no . . .

I think we're on the cusp of another surge.

"Briggs," I hiss, my arm still buried inside the mare. "She's getting really hot. I think that maybe . . . there's another surge coming."

Harrisford utters an expletive beneath his breath. "We'll need to hurry, in that case. If the surge happens with the foal inside, it'll kill it—"

"I know that!" I'm panicking now. Even without a surge, we'd only have maybe thirty minutes, tops. But *with* a surge? Maybe this was a bad idea. Maybe I've . . . overcommitted. "You do it! You'll be quicker—"

Harrisford moves beside me, resting a hand on the qílín's rump. "No. You're already in there. You can do it, trust me. Just take a deep breath and do as I say."

I blink, and tears blur my vision. "Please take over—"

"Chan!" Harrisford's composure is fraying. With his ungloved hand, he grabs my chin and turns my face to look at him. "Just listen to me, all right? You will be fine. Just do. As. I. Say."

I nod, my forehead clammy with sweat, and blink my tears away. "Okay." I take a deep, steadying breath, and steel myself. "Tell me what to do." Under normal circumstances, I'd never let Harrisford Briggs boss me around. But this isn't a normal circumstance.

"You need to push the foal back toward the uterus to begin with, to give yourself more room to work. But be careful. You don't want to do any damage."

I heave, trying to shift the foal, and eventually I feel it move. "It's there, it's there." The birth canal is getting worryingly hot. "Now what?"

"Can you reach its head? If you can hook your fingers around its jaw, or even a nostril, you'll be able to ease the head forward."

I grope around, rising onto tiptoes, pushing my arm in as far as it can possibly go. Finally, I feel the foal's head. It takes some maneuvering, but eventually I'm able to grab hold of its lower jaw and gently ease it around.

It's difficult at first, but once it reaches a critical point, the head swings around quickly. "It's forward!" I'm almost crying again, though this time it's with relief.

I feel Harrisford's hand touch my lower back, just fleetingly, before it's gone. "Good job," he says. "Now you just need to pull its front legs—"

And then I'm pulling, and I'm pulling, and the qílín is becoming scaldingly hot, and then two little feet are poking out of her back end, and Harrisford and I both take a leg each and we're pulling and pulling and then finally—

The foal slides out, Harrisford supporting it, and lands in a crumpled little heap upon the straw.

I stagger backward, panting, then brace my hands on both knees. The qílín is starting to let off more sparks, and in a moment she'll go up in flames.

It's fortunate that qílíns are fire-resistant, I think, but then I realize—

"The foal!" I scream. But Harrisford came to the conclusion even more quickly than I did.

"Get down!" he bellows, barreling into me and knocking me to the ground. The next moment he's already thrown himself over me and the newborn, shielding us both with his body.

I shiver beneath him, covering my head with both hands, while the qílín's flames flare before slowly flickering out.

And then we're both climbing to our feet, Harrisford backing away, the qílín taking a few shaky steps closer to her newborn foal.

She nudges it with her nose. It doesn't move. My pulse stutters and my stomach begins tying itself in knots. Were we too late? Perhaps the foal died, suffocated during birth. Or maybe we didn't pull it in time and it *did* get hit with the surge.

Both Harrisford and I hold our breaths. The seconds tick by so slowly, and everything is oddly silent, like the few moments before a thunderstorm when all the sound is sucked away. Each thump of my heart is almost painful in my chest.

But suddenly, the foal puts its little head up, and its mother starts licking it clean, and I let out a huge, grateful sigh. Tonight, we've managed to mitigate disaster—for this mother and foal, at least.

For the first time in forever, our marks don't matter. Who's coming first in class rankings doesn't matter.

And, so—for the first time in forever—neither Harrisford nor I even bother to check our straps.

21

Harrisford

I lean back against the stable wall, the foal's head resting on my lap, feeding him via syringe.

The qílín, exhausted from both the surge and her difficult, extended labor, had sunk onto the floor, all four legs folded beneath her. Knowing that the foal needed colostrum, I'd gently milked some from the qílín's teat and was now busy administering it to the baby.

"Can I have a go at that?" Gwendolynne is sitting against the opposite wall, cross-legged, staring wistfully at the foal. Her coveralls are splashed with muck, her hair is all messy and sticking out in odd directions, and she . . .

She looks more beautiful than ever.

I never thought I'd live to see Gwendolynne Chan with her arm up a mythical beast's back end. Or witness her pulling a qílín foal with nothing but her hands. And perhaps I'm odd, perhaps it's a strange sort of thing to find attractive . . . but honestly, she was incredible.

The truth is, in that moment, I'd *wanted* her to succeed. I wanted to share in *her* victory. For the first time in seven years, I hadn't cared about my marks, or her marks, or which of us was besting the other.

I'd thought of nothing else in that moment except the foal's welfare, Gwendolynne's safety, and my urge to give her the win.

Perhaps I just have a competency kink.

Regardless, I feel like something has shifted between the two of us. So I immediately hand her the syringe and relinquish my hold on the foal. "Sure. Go ahead. You delivered him."

She crawls closer, sliding in beside me, until I can feel the fierce heat of her body. Something twists deep inside me at the memory of it pinned beneath mine. She takes the foal's little head, beaming as she squeezes drops of colostrum onto its tongue. My eyes trace her features, lingering on the curve of her lips.

She did so well, Pudding says from her perch on the fence. *So did you.*

I allow myself a smile. *We did, didn't we?*

A peaceful sort of quiet blankets the four of us: Gwendolynne, me, the qílín, and the foal. For a few minutes, the only sounds are the lapping of the foal's quick little pink tongue, the occasional gust of wind that creaks through cracks in the walls, and the soft snorts and pawing hooves of unicorns in adjacent stalls. The foal, a little boy qílín, is entirely red, and I wonder if qílíns fade as they age and he will end up colored like his mother.

I'm mighty glad that Marcus didn't listen to me when I told him to send Gwendolynne home. I'd seen her face when I'd said it; she looked like she wanted to sodding kill me. And I don't blame her, really. She probably thought I was trying to get rid of her because of the rivalry we have—she as much as said so—as well as the animosity that had arisen after our fight earlier in the drug cupboard. But in truth, I was just livid that Marcus fucking *thought it was a good idea* to drag Gwendolynne out of bed just because her parents come from China. She was born in Manchester, for god's sake! And there was no reason she—a proper mag.fam student—should have been able to pull a malpresented foal under pressure just because of some new grad's fucked-up ideas about race.

Though I'm not about to explain all this to her, of course. I was incensed at the time, but now that things have calmed down and I'm thinking logically again, I understand it isn't my place to comment. It's bleeding obvious to me now that a man like me, who has privileges I've never even had to consider, has no business making decisions for a woman like Gwendolynne Chan.

I drag my thoughts back from the darkness and turn my attention back to the foal. Watching Gwendolynne handling him so gently makes my breath catch in my throat. After everything that happened with my mother, every maternal sight I see makes me tear up like a baby. It's honestly kind of pathetic.

Though, to be fair, most humans are . . . so at least I'm not alone.

You're being too hard on yourself, Harrisford, Pudding says.

Internally, I sigh. Maybe I am.

Still, I don't need Gwendolynne knowing the full extent of my wretchedness. I don't want her to be a witness to my weakness. So I try to distract myself. Try to steer my thoughts away from the nausea-inducing sight.

"I take it you haven't gone to the police?" I hope not—because if whoever is behind the surges finds out, it would definitely put Gwendolynne at risk. The image of her lying motionless under the rubble on the roof of Magecorp HQ flashes through my mind; it feels like my legs are giving out all over again.

Her smile immediately dissipates, melting into an irritated scowl. "I haven't," she says, her voice curt. "Your precious dad is safe for now."

"But you will, won't you?" I can't help but dig my claws in further. "Now that there's been another surge, I'm assuming you'll run straight to them and tattle?"

She actually flings the syringe down until it lands nestled in the straw. "No! As a matter of fact I've figured out that—" She stops abruptly, her lips pressing thin, and I know she's shared too much. More than she wanted to share with me. And for some reason, that realization weighs heavily in my gut.

"Figured out what, Chan?" I press her. Then, when she doesn't answer, I repeat, louder this time. "Figured out *what*?"

Picking up the syringe, she begins carefully feeding the foal again. I can tell she's trying to decide how much to actually tell me.

I swallow, my nausea intensifying. Somehow, between breaking into Magecorp and now, I've lost her trust and I . . . don't actually know how to get it back.

It's because I never really needed to try before. Gaining people's trust was never an issue for me. I was born a cherubic, blond-haired baby, who grew into an angelic-looking child. Coupled with the fact that I'm rich and clever, and I never had to work hard to make friends. I guess that's why Gwendolynne frustrated me so. No matter what I did, whether it was playing nice or teasing her or even being downright mean, she would keep me at a distance. Treat me with disdain. Push me away.

It was as though she always knew my true nature: that I'm extremely, irredeemably fucked up. That the smooth confidence I project is just a front to hide the absolute mess, the turmoil, below.

Finally, she speaks, without looking at me. "I showed Conall Peters the photos of the blueprints. They explain how Magecorp opens the portals."

I draw in a sharp breath. "To the Void?"

Gwendolynne nods, swiping up a small drop of leaked colostrum with the tip of her index finger. "Yep. Apparently it requires a tether—some sort of magical object—which anchors the tear to our world and keeps it open."

Rubbing my forehead, I consider this information. "So you think that Magecorp has some sort of magical object?"

She frowns. "I don't know. I mean, logically the tethers would have to be positioned close to the tears, right? But we searched the common room pretty thoroughly tonight and found nothing."

"Maybe it's something that they keep at Magecorp?" I wonder aloud. "What if it works remotely, at a distance?" I remember her describing the circular room in the vault, where my father was secreted the day he was supposed to be in Wales.

Gwendolynne sticks out her lower lip. "It's possible. But if there was something as important as a tether, they'd probably have locked it in the vault. There was a glowing rock there, but unless that rock is made of something that can withstand severe damage, then it should have been destroyed in the explosion—and it wouldn't have caused tonight's surge."

Tipping my head back against the rough wood wall, I let out a long, slow exhale. "That's true. Then I guess we need to keep looking at the sites where surges happened. Where have you checked so far?"

Finally, she raises her head, her brown eyes meeting mine. In the moonlight, they look almost black. But not the black of shadows, or funerals, or even the absence of light.

They're dark like the star-spangled arch of a cloudless sky, or the soft space beneath your bedsheets when you burrow beneath them at night. They're a *warm* sort of dark, a color that evokes pleasure, not something that causes pain.

"Just the common room." Her teeth dig into her lower lip. "We haven't had a chance to look anywhere else."

"We could look here." I cast a look at our surroundings. "That's a start."

We need to do *something*. The fact that the surges appear to be occurring with increasing frequency is worrisome.

Beside me, the qílín raises her head, nuzzling against my hand. And I scratch her in her mane until she whickers and lets out a little puff of air.

When I look up, Gwendolynne is watching me, a curious look upon her face. "What?" I say, suddenly self-conscious.

"It's just interesting, that's all. That the qílín likes you." Her gaze drifts across to my newfound golden friend. "Apparently, according to the ancient myths, they're only drawn to good people. To those who are pure of heart."

It's as though everything around me darkens, and I grimace, quickly withdrawing my hand.

"Well, Chan," I say. "I suppose we must assume that the ancient myths are false."

22

Gwendolynne

We spend the remainder of the predawn hours searching around the stables, while also keeping an eye on the qílín and her foal. At some point, Percy wakes from his slumber, and, from where he's lounging in my room, asks me what happened. I assume he senses the stress-related cortisol spike still percolating in my bloodstream.

I manage, just, to stop myself from rolling my eyes; somehow my familiar managed to sleep through one of the most singularly traumatic events of my life.

It's only when the morning students come in to relieve us that Harrisford and I trudge back to Heywood Hall. I'm so tired that fog has settled into every sulcus of my brain. My movements feel two steps behind, delayed somehow, as though I'm trying to run a marathon underwater. I'm thinking of nothing but my bed and the quilt my grandma made—it's still comfortable, even with all the scorch marks burned into it thanks to Percy.

But even with the fatigue, my mind still tries to cram in as much study as possible. *It's my amygdala. My amygdala's having trouble talking to my forebrain.* Then I shake my head. "Quit it, Gwen," I mutter to myself beneath my breath. I steal a look at Harrisford, to check that he hasn't heard.

He hasn't. Thankfully, he's so exhausted himself that he's merely walking along, both hands shoved in his pockets, his eyes trained on the ground. I study his profile, then duck my head, flushing with embarrassment at what I'd done last night to get to sleep.

When we reach the entrance of Heywood Hall, he turns his red-rimmed gaze on me. "Well, good night, then. Or good morning. Or . . ." He waves a long-fingered hand, somehow managing to make the movement look regal. "Never mind." For a moment, he pauses, as if on the cusp of saying something . . . But he says nothing, and instead starts walking off in the direction of the south wing.

For some reason, this irks me. He's really going to just . . . leave . . . after we'd done something as magical as delivering a qílín? Though I suppose, for him, it isn't that extraordinary. I'm sure Harrisford-fucking-Briggs has pulled many a calf out of dragon mothers, and other equally heroic shit. Still . . .

"Hey," I blurt out, before I can stop myself.

He pivots slowly, blinking at me in the watery light of dawn. "Yes, Chan?"

"You didn't think I could do it, did you?" *Fuck.* Not only is my amygdala not talking to my cerebral cortex, the latter has clearly removed all its inhibitions on my speech center, too.

His eyebrows knit. "Do what?"

"Pull the foal."

Understanding dawns in his eyes, and he stares at me for some moments, still slouching, still with his hands stuck in his pockets. Then he straightens and says to me, "No."

There's buzzing in my ears, and I don't think it's my good friend tinnitus. I clench my fists. "Is that why you told . . ." My brain scrabbles, trying to remember the new grad's name. "*That guy* to send me home?" *Shit.* I didn't even last one night.

There's a long, weighty pause, his gaze now searching my face. "Yes."

I knew it! The arsehole. It's lucky I stayed, and didn't quail, and—with his guidance, to be fair—managed to do it. Otherwise he'd still be thinking of me as a weak little mag.fam girl.

This time, it's my turn to roll my eyes and turn away.

"Chan." Harrisford's hand encircles my wrist, spinning me back around. "I was thinking . . ."

"That's a first," I mutter, jerking my hand away. He shoots me a filthy look, so I give him my falsest, most saccharine smile. "*Do* go on."

"Since there are no signs of the tethers in the common room or the stables, perhaps we're not thinking big enough." He drags his fingers through his hair, making it stick up all over, though annoyingly even messy hair suits him. "What if the tethers are only needed to keep open the biggest holes? And cause the biggest explosions? What if all the other surges are like aftershocks—"

"Like an earthquake?" The idea is starting to invigorate me, in spite of my tiredness. "Briggs, you could be right! Maybe we should search the Natural History Museum."

At this, he grins, in a weary sort of way. "How serendipitous," he says. "Since I've just been told that they're planning another gala."

Being a veterinary student basically means being the bottom of the hierarchy—way below the nurses and interns. *Shit flows downhill*, our supervisors like to say as they leave us with full hospital loads and head out for beers, or have us clean up a temporally triggered invisible dog's feces, or make us telephone the most vexatious clients, like Mr. Featherstone from Chelsea, who goes on long tirades about how unethical we were to implant a microchip into his beagle. He's adamant that they have GPS capabilities and cannot be convinced otherwise.

So it's for this reason that, despite being up half the night on call, neither Harrisford nor I get to rest before we're expected to show up to class.

"You're going to the gala?" Heloise says as we're walking some dogs in the yards. "With *Harrisford*?"

"Do I have to go, Heli?" I say, my voice pleading. "I don't want to go."

"Oh, come on." Heloise stops to untangle the dogs' leashes. "It'll be fun. I'll be there with Mum and Dad. We'll get tipsy on wine and judge everybody."

I chew my lip, thinking, as we resume walking. If Heloise is there, then perhaps it won't be so bad. She'd be a bit of a buffer, at least, between Harrisford and me. And maybe if I can monopolize Nora Chapman's attention for a bit, then I'll be able to quiz her about the surges and how they're impacting the medical community.

"Yeah." I smile. "Sounds good, that."

At precisely 7:00 p.m. that night, Harrisford raps on my door. It's as though he wants to rub in the fact that he, unlike me, is a punctual sort of person.

I glance in the mirror, smoothing down my skirt. After I'd told him I literally had nothing in my wardrobe but jeans and charity shop cardigans (and a T-shirt from one fandom that shall remain nameless), Harrisford had arranged the delivery of a ball gown. An actual ball gown. I assume, like the tweed suit, it had been one of his mother's, though this one seems much more modern.

The dress is one-shouldered and made of deep plum silk. It's modest enough so that I don't feel self-conscious, but it clings to my curves in every spot that matters. The skirt hugs my hips until it reaches my knees, where it flares out into what I'm pretty certain is called a fishtail hem.

And . . . it is absolutely stunning. In fact, I actually feel ridiculous wearing it. Despite trying all evening, I haven't been able to do anything half decent with my hair, and my makeup skills are less than rudimentary. And now I've run out of time. The dress is so commanding that it seems to be wearing me, not the other way round.

With jangling nerves, I try to fix my atrocious updo, attempting to twist some loose bits of hair into my bun.

In my head, Percy gives me a disdainful sniff, from where he's crouching atop the bar fridge that's wedged beneath my desk. *You look as though you are fighting a losing battle, Hairless One.*

"Ugh!" I let out a sharp, frustrated sigh and let the bun go. It flops down, as flaccid and deflated as a neutered minotaur's scrotum. Standing with my hands on my hips, I grimace at my reflection. Then, because I'm irritated, I unleash my ire onto Percy.

"Why do you call me Hairless One, anyway?" I snap, giving my hair one last tug. "Clearly I have hair, even if it does look like shit. And besides, that's not my name. My name is Gwen. G-wen."

Percy swooshes his tail back and forth, his ears flattening slightly. He narrows his eye at me. *Yes, well, my name isn't really Percy, you know. It's* actually *Lord Percival the Second, Purveyor of the Flesh of Small Defenseless Creatures, Destroyer of Carpet, Scratcher of Doors, and Usurper of Recently Vacated Chairs . . . but I don't insist that you call me by* my *proper name now, do I?*

"Fine," I grumble, my annoyance giving way to a sort of pained defeat. I guess he means the hair on my body, of which I have comparatively little. The rapping at the door resumes, louder and more insistent. "All right! I'm coming!" And, as though my heart rate is correlated with the speed of the knocking, my pulse begins to race.

Resisting the urge to rub my sweaty palms on my dress—my clothes are the only thing going right tonight, and I really don't want to stain the silk—I finally cross to the door and yank it open.

I've no idea what to expect. When Harrisford had first seen me in his mother's suit, his face had immediately turned cold: a lake freezing over in winter. I guess it had triggered some grief-stricken memories. As pretty as they are, I almost wish he'd stop putting me in Theodora Briggs's clothes.

So, as soon as I fling open the door, I scrunch my eyes shut, waiting for him to make some haughty remark about my paltry lipstick, or perhaps the messiness of my hair. But there's no sound so, apprehensive, I crack open one eye.

Harrisford is staring. Brazenly, openly staring; he's leaning slightly forward, one hand gripping the doorframe. The tendons are standing out on his hand, and his knuckles are the palest white.

"You look . . ." He trails off, reddens, then clears his throat.

Oh god. He can't even say it. He can't even articulate how ridiculous I look in such a fancy dress. My stomach clenches, feeling hollow. "It's too much, isn't it?" I clasp both cheeks with my hands. "Yes, you're right, it's too much—I'll take it off."

Harrisford moves into the room like a predator, forcing me to take two steps back. In the dim light of my desk lamp, his pupils are dilated—scorching his irises black. "No." A command, not a request. "Leave it."

I swallow, frozen under the force of his stare. He is . . . intimidating. And sexy. Intimidatingly sexy. He's wearing a similar tuxedo robe to what he'd worn to the first gala, except this time his bow tie is plum, the exact color of my dress. Tonight, his blond hair is slicked back from his face; on anyone else it might look severe, but on him it just accentuates his model-sharp cheekbones, the intensity of his eyes, the perfect curve of his shell-pink lips . . .

It is so completely unfair. That he seems to have been dealt all the good cards right from the moment of birth. That such a beautiful exterior can mask such a shitty person beneath. That said beautiful exterior is having an effect on me that I *really* don't want it to have.

Realizing I'm gawking, I shut my mouth and tear my gaze away. Regardless of how striking he looks, I cannot forget that this man is actually *blackmailing* me, and threatening to get rid of my cat.

"I . . . uh . . . haven't been able to do anything with my hair." With a resigned sigh, I pull the hair tie out of my pitiful bun, and my hair falls loose around my shoulders. While I haven't been to an event like this before, I've watched Heloise prepare for several. Her routine involves long sessions at the hairdresser's, bespoke tailored formalwear, and professional makeup artists. I can't believe I'm about to attend my very first gala with a crappy updo and a dress borrowed from a dead woman.

Harrisford's eyes sweep up to my head. "Your hair is fine."

My palms are sweating again, and now so are my armpits. "No, it's a mess, and—" I pause, feeling slightly sick. Then, to myself, "I wish I knew how to cast a glamour."

Reaching out, Harrisford takes a loose lock of my hair between his thumb and forefinger. For a long time, he doesn't say anything, just stares at it, frowning. Then he drops it. "I can assure you, it really is unnecessary."

Right. Harrisford doesn't care what I look like tonight, even with my scruffy hair. I'm just a convenient way to help him investigate the surges so he can happily sit his exams.

The thing is, though, this isn't Harrisford's first gala. But it *is* mine. And while he might not care, I do.

"I'll just be a minute. I'm sure it's dead easy." Surely there'll be a simple tutorial on the internet? I'll just look up the method and then ask Percy if I can siphon some of his magic to do it.

I faff around, unlocking my strap. After finding what looks to be a promising website, I click into it, only to be hit with a paywall.

Goddammit. I used up most of my weekly magecredits buying Percy's stupidly expensive (and as yet unused) bed. It was the dearest cardboard box I've ever purchased.

The next website too charges for its tutorials. The next is the same. And the next. And the next.

My hope deflates like a burst balloon. How ironic. Finally, I have enough magic to cast the glamour, but I can't even afford to learn how to bloody do it.

Frazzled, I start mentally calculating whether I can budget enough magecredits for the download, when suddenly I become aware that Harrisford too is watching my strap.

My cheeks flush hot. I shut down my screen. "You know what? Never mind."

"Chan." Harrisford sighs, resigned, and I look up from my wrist. "You're being absurd, obviously. But if you truly wish it, then I can cast the spell."

My eyebrows knit. I'm suddenly curious. "Didn't you say you don't do them?"

For a long moment he doesn't respond, he just stares at my face, scrutinizing me. Eventually he says, "I'm willing to make an exception."

My mouth is dry; I swallow. I must look fucking terrible for him to willingly break his own rule. Oh well. It doesn't matter, I guess, if it means he will actually do it.

Lifting his hands, he raises his eyebrows at me: an invitation. And although my stomach is threatening to crawl right up my throat, I nod my consent.

I study his features as he works, his eyes narrowed in concentration. "Do *you* wear a glamour, Briggs?" It would make sense if he did—explain why he always looks so frustratingly perfect.

He snorts out a laugh, then shakes his head. "No. I don't."

Damn. There goes that theory.

I fall quiet. I've never worn a glamour before; mainly because I've never really had an occasion to wear one, but also because it uses magic that I've never had to spare. And as Harrisford casts his spell, I'm simultaneously nervous and excited. What am I going to look like, once the spell is done? Will I even recognize myself? Will I be disappointed with my features when, at the end of the evening, the magic finally wears off?

My face heats as the glamour penetrates, and I let my eyelids fall shut. When I feel that the spell has settled, I reopen my eyes and spin to face the mirror. And I look . . .

The same.

Exactly the same. "Oh."

Percy pipes up from where he's sat. *Is that the best that man can do?* he scoffs. *Because if so, it's not very good.*

"Hang on." Harrisford is looking flustered, his cheeks a little pink. "I didn't do it right. Let me try again."

This time, the glamour takes, and when I look into the mirror it's almost as though a different Gwendolynne is peering back. My skin is glowing; my eyebrows are sculpted, my lips a deep plum color that perfectly matches my dress. The glamour has smoothed my hair into glossy Hollywood waves that hang over my smooth, bare shoulder.

"Better?" Harrisford says.

"Yes," I say, pulling on my coat, my gaze still lingering on my reflection.

He goes to the door and opens it with a jerk. Is it just me, or are his shoulders looking a wee bit stiff?

"After you," he says, gesturing out the door with one hand. And as I sweep past him with a rustle of shiny plum silk, he does not look at me again.

23

Harrisford

I can't even look at Gwendolynne as we ride to the gala in the back of my father's car. And it's not just because my body instantly reacts each time I so much as glance her way . . . it's also because I'm absolutely mortified for fucking up the glamour. If only she knew *why*, she'd probably think me a total loser. Though, to be fair, she already does.

It's not that I don't know how to cast glamours. I do. In fact, I'm rather good at them. Danny Wong and I used to mess around with them all the time when we were teens. On certain occasions, when we were bored, we'd enchant each other's faces for a laugh. It was a waste of magic, sure, but we'd always had enough surplus for that not to be an issue.

What I'd forgotten about glamour charms is that the final effect lies with the person casting it—*not* the person receiving the spell. If it were listed in a textbook, the section under glamours would read: *This spell alters the recipient's appearance, allowing their features to change in such a way that is most desirable to the caster.* That is, it can be someone else you find attractive, or the most pleasing version of oneself. This is why most of the time people cast glamours on themselves.

Danny and I, on the other hand, used to turn each other into girls and guys we fancied, and then give each other total shit for it. Until the last time I'd cast a glamour back in fifth year . . . It had gone badly, and I'd sworn off them for good.

But tonight, so desperate to put Gwendolynne out of her apparent misery, I'd put a glamour on her, not stopping to think about what the end result would be. And when she opened her eyes and saw her unaltered reflection . . .

Well.

Sure, I'd tried to cover up my mistake by immediately pivoting to a hair and makeup spell, and even though it had been clumsy spellwork she'd seemed happy enough with the result.

But I was shaken. I'm still shaken. It was the sudden, horrible realization that what I desire most is Gwendolynne—exactly as she is. Loose hair, ugly cardigans, beat-up trainers, jeans. And that if she knew anything at all about glamours, then she would know exactly what I had done.

It was even a revelation for me, though it shouldn't have been, considering the elaborate fantasies I've been having about her of late. In fact, when she'd mentioned taking off the dress, it took all of my willpower not to grab her and growl, *There's only one person that's allowed to take that thing off, Chan . . . and that's me.*

Somehow, I'd managed to restrain myself. To stop myself from blurting out those foolish, foolish words. I know she doesn't think about me that way—she's both told me and shown me on a number of occasions how hateful she thinks I am. And to be honest, she's right. I'm not a good person. I'm cocky, I'm short-tempered, I'm extremely judgmental. I'm the son of a harsh, murderous tyrant, and I'm quite sure my genes are just as rotten as his. I'm so fucked up that I can't even bring myself to feel bad about the fact that my father is in a coma.

I'm so fucked up that not even my own mother considered me worthy enough to stay.

And even if Gwendolynne didn't detest me—even if by some miracle she got past her deep-seated hatred—then I *still* wouldn't want her falling for me. After what happened with Isla, I can't guarantee that I wouldn't break Gwendolynne's heart. I had lost interest in Isla after less than a year, until even looking at her sickened me. What if that happened again? I simply cannot risk it.

No. I'm just going to have to appreciate that Gwendolynne is an extremely attractive woman without ever letting her know how I feel.

"Can you pass some water?" Gwendolynne says, jolting me out of my thoughts. I push one of the chilled bottles into her waiting hand, and for the briefest of moments our fingers brush. Hers are so warm, her skin so smooth. Uncomfortable, I shift in my seat, then go back to staring out the window and jiggling my leg.

I'm nervous. It feels as though a lot is riding on tonight. Plus, after what happened at the museum last time I'd begrudgingly left Pudding back at Heywood Hall.

"Hey." Gwendolynne leans over and puts a hand on my knee, stilling it. "Don't stress. It's just one night—Pudding will be fine." It's as if she can read my fucking mind.

It's lucky she can't, though, because if she could, she'd know that there appears to be a direct connection from my left knee to my groin. She'd see that my brain is thoroughly preoccupied with images of me grabbing her face and kissing her. Pushing her back against the leather seats, her legs wrapped around my waist. Sinking to my knees, lifting her dress, worshipping her with nothing but my lips and hands and tongue . . .

I blink, forcing myself to look away. I'm both glad and not glad that I ordered that dress; she looks fucking good in it, but it is really not helping my composure.

"I'm not stressed," I say curtly, tugging on my collar and studying the scenery outside.

It's started to rain, that heavy, muggy rain that wets the windscreen in big, round, splashy drops. It streaks across the car windows as we zip along the motorway far faster than a normal car. There's an awkward tension in the air; Gwendolynne keeps fiddling with her hair, twisting the elaborate curls, and several times she opens her mouth and then closes it, as though unsure of what to say.

Finally, she spits it out. "I think we should make a plan for tonight."

"Very well," I say, throwing a glance at her. "We go in, look for a powerful magical object, and then get out again."

She scowls at me. "That's not very comprehensive. How about we split up and try to interrogate people? I'll start with Nora Chapman, I can probably get Heli to—"

"Chan, this is a gala, not a fucking police procedural. We can't just round up the guests and start firing questions at them."

The words explode out of her. "I wasn't going to—" She stops short, pauses, then continues. "I didn't *actually* mean interrogating them. I just meant trying to eke out some information by asking a few questions, that's all."

I raise one eyebrow. "That sounds an awful lot like interrogating."

She folds her arms across her chest and glowers. "What's your plan, then? If we don't find any tethers, how do *you* propose we best make use of our time?"

I can think of many activities I'd rather do with her, but I don't say it. I just narrow my eyes, staring back, silent for a few stretched-out moments. Then I say, finally, "We drink. We eat. We socialize." I pull an open wine bottle out of the ice bucket and start to pour myself a glass. "We *charm* people. Get them all buttered up, loosen their tongues with champagne, and wait until they spill their secrets." With the bottle still poised, I tilt it at her, offering her a drink.

She ignores my offer, her irritation tangible. "It doesn't actually work like that—"

Very deliberately, I replace the wine bottle in its bucket, then lean back and take a sip. "Of course it does."

I can almost see her inflating with rapidly expanding anger; can almost see actual sparks flying from her eyes.

She uncrosses her arms and flings them out until both hands are braced on the car seat. "It doesn't for *me*!" she hisses. "Just because *you* can get away with your charm and good looks doesn't mean the rest of us can!"

My stomach dips at her words; my fingers tighten around my glass. Uncrossing my legs, I lean forward until I'm entirely too much in her space. Our breaths mingle, my lips parted, a gasp hitching in her throat.

I grin, cocking my head to one side. "You think I'm good-looking?"

She stares at me for a moment, then looks away, out the window. "Some people might think so," she mutters. "Not me, though. *I* happen to think you're dead disgusting."

My heart is thumping so hard I can almost taste it, and I can't stop my smile from spreading. Reaching up, I cup her cheek with my hand, turning her face to mine. "Yes," I say. "I *am* disgusting. But then again, Chan . . . all humans are."

Our eyes lock. My gaze drops to her darkened lips. My breath feels trapped in the labored rise and fall of my chest.

Good god. This woman . . . *This woman.* She is utterly impossible.

She infuriates me constantly, more than anyone else has, ever. If something were to happen—if I were to kiss her, right here, right now, right in the back of this limo—then I'm quite sure yet another hole would tear right through the universe.

But then what? If we were together, we'd bicker all the time, much like we're doing now. We'd be frustrated, and miserable, and probably wind up loathing one another. And hating Gwendolynne, after all these years, is not a valid option.

So I force out a breath, let her face go, and lean back—just as the car pulls up to the curb.

24

Gwendolynne

Harrisford had explained earlier that tonight's gala would have extra security, given what happened last time. Tonight is supposed to be a demonstration, "a shining example," proof that Magecorp are not afraid.

Considering the hundreds of police stationed around the cordoned entrance, though, I can confidently say that the CEO of Magecorp must be very, very afraid. It takes us a ridiculous amount of time before we're even let through the front doors. As we wait among the crowd of shuffling rich folk, I keep stealing glances at Harrisford's face.

The way he'd looked at me in the car, right after I'd admitted that I find him attractive . . . I cringe, remembering my unplanned confession. *What the hell were you thinking, Gwen?*

But then he'd leaned forward. He'd cradled my face. His gaze had dropped, hungrily, right down to my lips. And all of a sudden we'd arrived. The spell was broken; we'd sprung apart.

What was he playing at? Was he trying to rattle me? Lull me into a false sense of security?

What might have happened if the car ride had been a mere five minutes longer?

I can't allow myself to dwell on these thoughts, or get suckered in by his games—already Harrisford is murmuring his thanks to a guard, who is languidly waving us through. Tonight, I must only concentrate on trying to find the tether. And if I'm unsuccessful at that, I'll corner Heloise and her mother, since it seems like Harrisford is planning to be absolutely zero fucking help.

According to the heavily embossed and gold-foiled invite, tonight's theme is Magical Masquerade, so Harrisford reaches into his pocket and pulls out a gleaming mask. It's silver, embroidered with a complicated brocade pattern, and is flanked by two feathered wings. When I pluck it out of his hand, the wings actually flap, showing off the tiny diamonds woven through them. I feel Percy's interest prick up through our bond. I suppose he *is* a cat, and any feathery flapping thing is bound to catch his attention.

Harrisford helps me tie my mask on, then dons his—also silver, but wrought from metal, the body and head of a roaring dragon wrapping around the periphery.

As we enter Hintze Hall, where the function is being held, I have to stifle a gasp. The space is vast, the roof an enormous paneled arch above our heads. There's a skeleton of some sort—a dinosaur, perhaps?—hanging from the ceiling, and stone arches line both sides of the room. At the opposite end there's a sweeping staircase, cathedral-like windows set into the far wall. Instead of magelights, real-life faeries flutter about, each one holding a tiny lantern. And dozens of roving magicians perform magic tricks. Every now and then a huge flame goes up, followed by whoops and cheers.

"It's . . . beautiful," I manage to choke out. Glancing up at Harrisford, I add, "I've never been here before."

Immediately, his entire demeanor changes. Up until now, he's been tense, brooding—but now he seems to brighten, as though my innocuous words have instantly lifted his mood.

"Well, then," he says. He flashes me a quick smile. "Allow me to give you a tour, Miss Chan."

After grabbing two champagne flutes from a passing waiter and handing me one, Harrisford proffers his elbow. I take it, my fingers curling around the well-defined muscles of his forearm. Something jolts inside me at the contact, but I ignore it. "Why, thank you, Mr. Briggs," I say, in my fakest, poshest accent, as he steers us past several small clusters of people.

I'm buzzing at the atmosphere as Harrisford leads me to the first display, an enormous fossil skeleton. My scientific curiosity is instantly triggered—I let Harrisford's arm go and press up against the glass. I study the large, curved tusks; the thick skull; the unusual, cone-shaped molars, which are like nothing I've seen before. It's a little bit like an elephant, but also . . . not.

I squint at it through the glass. "Is this . . . a mammoth?" I could read the card, of course, but I'm loath to tear my eyes away.

Harrisford comes up beside me. "No. It's a mastodon. *Mammut americanum.* It's sort of like . . . a distant relation."

I turn to look at him. "Do you have to study these? In myth.creat? Even though they're all extinct?"

"No." He stares at the skeleton, thoughtful for a moment, then takes a swig of his drink. "I just spent a lot of time here as a kid."

We move on to the next exhibit, which Harrisford tells me is a *Mantellisaurus atherfieldensis* skeleton, and once again my love for anatomy kicks in. I analyze the way its digits articulate; the disparity between its front and hind limbs; the sharp thumb claws located where dog and cat dewclaws should be. I'm so busy looking at the dinosaur that I don't notice Harrisford watching me. When I glance up, I go red because his gaze is so intense.

He swallows, then says, "Come, Chan, we need to hurry. The official program will be starting soon."

I nod, chagrined. We're still in the pre-drinks reception, and most of the guests have crowded into one of the two adjacent galleries, leaving Harrisford and me among the few couples wandering around the main hall. And I want to soak up as much of this glorious science as possible before more people start streaming in.

We continue down one side, seeing fossilized tree trunks; an ancient, colorful rock; even a sparkling meteorite. At some point, Harrisford's hand strays to my lower back—so hot, it's like his fingers are searing right through the thin silk. The offhand way he's touching me makes my breath catch; has he even noticed he's doing it, or is it just reflex for him, since he dates so many women? Perhaps he's just playing the part since we're pretending to be a couple.

Yes, that's it, I'm sure of it. It's all just part of tonight's elaborate act.

But as I bend to read the meteorite's plaque, his hand drifts up, his thumb stroking—just once—across the bare skin of my shoulder. It feels like . . . *more*. And it makes me shiver.

His touch feels electric, sparks tingling across my skin. I straighten, and we're close—so close—standing chest-to-chest. He looks down at me, his lips slightly parted, the faerie lights glinting off the burnished gold of his hair.

"Did you feel anything?" I ask finally, slightly breathless.

His breath quickens, his pupils dilate, and he somehow manages to move even closer. "Feel what?"

And I'm looking at him . . . *everywhere*, at the broadness of his shoulders, at how his hair curls around his ears, at the way his eyes look so dark in here—a deep and fathomless sea. He's traded his normal loosely buttoned linen for a dress shirt and bow tie, and my mouth goes dry as I trace the way it hugs his neck. This close, I can smell his cologne: something crisp and woodsy, like cold winter air before it snows.

Oh god, I am in trouble. The gala hasn't even properly started, and I'm already fantasizing about ripping off Harrisford's fancy shirt and bow tie. *No*, I tell myself. *Remember, he's nothing more than an arsehole. A stupid, sexy arsehole.*

I inhale slowly and force myself to focus. "Did you feel any magic from those objects that would suggest they may be tethers?"

He's still staring at me. Studying me. Finally, he tilts his head slightly, his eyes glittering behind his mask. "No. I didn't. Did you?"

I shake my head, then bite my lip. "We've only looked at half the hall, though. We should take a look at the other side."

"We should." He rips his gaze away, and this time, he doesn't do the gentlemanly thing of offering me his arm. Instead, he rests his hand on the small of my back.

We drift back out to the main hall, aiming for the opposite side. But the hall has got far more crowded in just the past few minutes. Harrisford shakes his sleeve back and checks his strap. It's eight p.m., and the gala is about to start.

Right on cue, a chamber orchestra in the corner begins to play. The strains of elegant classical music echo around Hintze Hall, amplified by magical speakers placed strategically around the room. Half of the crowd cram into the center dance floor, in the middle of the linen-lined tables, and start to partner up.

"The opening dance," Harrisford murmurs, taking our drinks and depositing them on a table. He slants a look at me. "Shall we?"

"Oh hell no." I start to pull away, self-conscious, but Harrisford pulls me back. I stumble forward into his arms, less stable than usual on account of my high heels—silver-colored stiletto-type things that Harrisford also sent. I'd been a bit confused when I'd opened them and found them to be exactly my size, since his mother's work shoes had been slightly too big.

I'm collapsed against the hard planes of his chest, feeling the lines of muscle beneath the soft fabric of his shirt. I blush, remembering how I'd ogled those muscles in his actual bedroom . . . And before I notice anything further he has me fully clasped against his body, his hand splayed against my back.

"Just dance, Chan." His voice is commanding, even though he's leaning down and whispering the words against my ear. "It'll look suspicious if we don't. And we don't want people to start asking questions . . ."

"But, Briggs," I hiss back. "I don't know how to—"

And then we're doing it. It's unbelievable, but I'm dancing. Spinning around the floor with the melody swelling all around us and colorful couples, all wearing masks, sashaying around the room. There are two old white-haired men together, every now and then giving each other an affectionate peck on the lips. There's a father dancing with his daughter, a little wisp of a thing in a floaty lilac dress. Skirts twirl in rainbow circles, and the faerie lights reflect off sparkling jewels. It's a riot of color, and beauty, and music, and before long I get swept up in it, as though I am in a dream.

I don't actually know how to dance, but Harrisford clearly does, and his easy grace and confident movements mask my extreme lack of ability. Before long, I'm giggling, laughing so hard every time I take a wrong step that I have to cling to Harrisford's shoulders to avoid doubling over.

"Chan," he says, smiling in spite of himself. "What's so funny?" He raises our twined hands and twirls me. Below my knees, my skirt flies out in a perfect, plum-colored circle.

"I don't know," I choke out, trying to stifle my mirth. "This is all so serious. You look so serious. And I—" Despite my efforts to hold in it, I let out another giggle. "I think I'm just delirious because I hardly got any sleep." It's hard to imagine that less than twenty-four hours ago I'd had my entire arm up a qílín, with Harrisford standing next to me, coaching me on how to pull a foal. And now I'm in this glittering place, and actually dancing, like magic.

"You mean *we* hardly got any sleep. I, too, am severely sleep-deprived, yet you don't see me giggling like a drunken centaur." He's pretending to scold me, affecting a stern tone. But the smile on his lips and the shake in his shoulders suggest that he too is holding back laughter.

I stumble again, getting the dance step wrong, and to hide my error, he lowers me into a dip. Having not expected it, I let out a little squeal, reflexively winding my arms around his neck. As he rights me again, he sucks in a breath, and I let out mine—slow and shivery, heavy with longing.

The movement brings us closer than we've ever been before, our body heat enveloping us whole. Again, that electric tension builds between us, the thin sliver of air that separates us blistering with heat. Desire, molten hot, pulls deep in my lower belly, and we've stopped spinning, standing still amid the sea of couples.

The skin of his neck heats beneath my hands. His body, pressed up against mine, is scorching, his eyes burning behind his mask. My eyebrows knit as I analyze his features, my heart thundering as I search his face.

It's starting to feel awfully hot in here.

"Chan—" he starts, then pauses.

I feel feverish; I can barely breathe. "Yes?"

He doesn't respond. Instead, he raises his hand, the tips of his fingers skating across my cheek so softly that I shiver. Then—very gently, and very purposefully—he pushes up my mask so that it perches atop my head like a feathery sort of fascinator.

Sudden, incredulous laughter bursts from my lips. "What are you doing?"

"I wanted to see your face." The low pitch of his voice sends a thrill right through my body.

I tilt my face to his so that our mouths are almost touching. His hot breath fans my lips. His fingers—splayed against my lower back—twitch, just once, before he flattens his hand against the curve of my spine, crushing me harder against him.

Everyone around us is still dancing, but I barely notice. It's as though we're alone, just the two of us, standing at the center of a snowstorm.

My pulse pounds in my ears. All of a sudden I'm oddly nervous. And when I finally speak again, my words are a whisper, almost without sound. "What if I want to see yours?"

It's incredible he even hears me.

He gives me a smile that's all sharp angles and wicked promise. Then he goes completely still as I slowly raise his mask. I let my fingers linger at his temple, then slide them down to graze his jaw, relishing the faint feel of stubble that covers it.

Our eyes lock. We're jammed up against each other, our bodies rigid with tension. Silhouetted by the faerie lights above his head, his irises are pools of shadow—I can't even tell they're different colors. But what I *can* tell is that they're fixed right on me, watching me so intently.

"Briggs," I breathe.

Only millimeters separate his lips from mine . . . but in this moment, it could well be miles. A distance that spans seven years, full of endless taunting, fierce rivalry, animosity, contempt—

But Harrisford . . . Harrisford doesn't seem to feel the distance, because he's leaning in, he's pulling my face to his, he's pressing his lips, which are unexpectedly soft, against mine.

His tongue sweeps against my mouth and I sigh, opening up to him, so that the kiss—which starts out slow, and tentative, and full of unexplored yearning—suddenly becomes so much . . . *more.*

Something seems to shift within him. He inhales sharply, grasping my face with both hands, taking control, angling us so that he can deepen the kiss. My knees almost buckle but there's nowhere to go because Harrisford is holding on to me so tight, every curve of my body melded seamlessly against the hard muscular lines of his.

Our kiss turns frantic, desperate, like a battle of wills. A dance of our own making, where neither of us leads or follows. My hands are crushed against his chest and his are tangled in my hair and I'm oblivious to everything and all I can think about is Harrisford, Harrisford, Harrisford. How he feels, how he tastes, the scent of him filling my nostrils. It's so wild and heady that I can't think, I can't breathe, I'm being swept away—

But then all of a sudden, he shoves me away from him and stumbles a few steps back.

I reel, somehow managing to keep my balance. "Briggs? What's wrong?" My voice is unexpectedly steady; I sound less panicked than I feel.

He doesn't answer immediately. Between us, the air congeals, turning frigid, until goose bumps prick down my arms.

"I'm sorry," he says, his eyes glazing over. Then he turns and pushes through the crowd, fleeing far away from me.

25

Gwendolynne

For a long time, all I can do is stare at the empty space where Harrisford had once been. Dancing couples continue to sweep and sway around me, but I barely notice. My pulse is roaring in my ears and my body is shivering and pricking tears are needling my inner eyelids.

Fucking bastard. I cannot believe I just did that. I let him kiss me. I kissed him back. And then he . . .

I resist the urge to scream. My theory was right: He *had* been playing me. I'd heard of him and his womanizing ways, and I'm so foolish to have thought it might be anything but.

Nothing has changed in my surroundings; the only thing that has changed is me. But now, everything has lost its luster. The lights are garish; the colors clash; the music is a cacophony of painfully discordant twangs. A roving magician conjures a fire, and one of the lantern-toting faeries meets its bitter end.

My shock is giving way to fury, and I bunch my fists in my skirt, lifting the silky folds so I don't stumble as I run off the dance floor. I try my best not to cry, but my traitorous eyes do it anyway. On my head, the feathers of my mask give a few feeble flaps, and in a fit of fury I rip it off and crush it inside my fist.

A sob heaves out from someplace deep within my chest. Tears detach from my lower eyelashes, splattering all over my dress.

"Gwen!" The shout comes from behind me. The hall is loud—what with all the voices, music, and the occasional drunken shout—so I can't quite hear properly. For a second, I think it's Harrisford and unthinkingly turn around, before realizing that he never calls me Gwen—only my surname, Chan.

Someone squeezes between two dancing couples, and then the last of my resolve gives way and I break down into ugly tears.

It's Heloise.

"Oh my god, Gwen, what's wrong? What's happened?" She puts both of her arms around me and folds me into a hug.

I can't even choke the words out, can't bring myself to admit how ridiculously stupid I've been. So I just cry into her shoulder until my sobs gradually peter out and I allow her to lead me away.

When I take notice of my surroundings again, we're in a gallery filled with taxidermied birds. Heloise and I are sitting on the floor, leaning against a paneled wood door, next to a display of stuffed white swans. I sniff and dab at my eyes with my skirt. Harrisford's glamour spell is getting weaker, and some of my mascara is flaking off.

"Percy was right," I wail, fresh tears welling. "Harrisford is shit at glamours."

From a distance, Percy's voice echoes. *I am always right. You should know that by now.*

There's a pause. Then he adds, his voice gentler this time, *Do not fret over that man, Hairless One. He isn't good enough for you. And trust me when I say I am right about that, too.*

My tears are gushing out by now. Percy's kindness is unexpected, and too much for me to handle; I cry even harder, burying my face in my hands.

Heloise rubs my shoulder. "Gwen, what did that arsehole do to you?"

Now that I've put some distance between myself and the dance floor, I almost feel ashamed to admit what had upset me. There's no sense in pining over Harrisford-fucking-Briggs. Or reading too much into the way he held me, the way he kissed me, or even the way he laughed. Our business here tonight was purely transactional—I'd agreed to help him find the source of the surge, and he'd agreed not to tell Dean Kaur about Percy if I did so. It was my fault I gave in to the whims of my body and kissed him right there on the dance floor.

Not to mention, I don't even like him! He's an annoying, arrogant, blackmailing git, and for the sake of my fucking future, I should stop forgetting that. I need to stop being such a baby, gather my wits, and hold up my end of the bargain . . . if only so he will hold up his.

I force myself to stop crying and dry off the rest of my tears. "It's okay, Heli," I reassure her. "I was up all night on a call, and I barely got any sleep. I think—it's all just catching up to me." I wipe at my eyes again. My lips sting with the sharp taste of salt.

Heloise's mouth turns down. "Honestly, the on-call rota is barbaric. I don't know of any other industry where we'd be forced to stay up all night, and then turn up to work a full day the next morning."

"It's only a few weeks until exams," I say faintly. After graduation, most mag.fam students end up working day shifts—unless you specifically opt to work in a twenty-four-hour center. Myth.creat vets, though, wind up being on call a lot, mainly because their hospitals are more often located rurally. And of course, I'm still hoping to be top of class, because that comes with the job at the Ministry. Cushy hours, better pay, and better opportunities for advancement.

And also a chance to save my family.

Heli shakes her head in wonder. "Can you imagine? We'll be done with on-call. Forever."

And I'll be done with Harrisford Briggs, forever.

Thinking about the exams, and Harrisford, causes my head to throb. I'm reminded, with painful clarity, why I came here in the first place: to look for tethers, and to search for information about the surges. I still haven't found any objects that seem to be pulsing with magic—the only traces of magic around were the ones streaming off the people. But, then again, Harrisford and I never made it to the opposite side of Hintze Hall. Plus, it might not even *be* in the hall. This museum is so vast. Where would I even start?

I turn to Heloise, who's watching me, her brown eyes sympathetic.

"Heli," I say, "I think I might need to speak to your mother. I need to ask her about the surges."

"Ah," she says, nodding. "It's because one happened here recently, didn't it?"

I give her a weak, watery smile in return.

She climbs to her feet elegantly, like a gazelle, and then holds out her hand.

"Come on, G. Get up. Let's go and find my mother."

Dr. Nora Chapman is laughing with a group of glamorous women when Heloise pulls her away.

"Mum," she says. "Gwendolynne wants to talk to you."

Dr. Chapman's expression brightens. "Ah, Gwen! It's so lovely to see you. It's been far too long since you last visited."

"Can we . . . go somewhere a little more private, Dr. Chapman?"

Heli's mum excuses herself, murmuring her apologies to the other women, and follows us into a side corridor.

"What do you want to discuss, sweetheart?" Like Heloise, Dr. Chapman has a smooth, comforting voice, and I immediately want to confess everything.

"I'm looking into the surges. Thank you, by the way, for giving Heloise all that info—"

Heloise's mother's eyes narrow, and she slides her gaze to her daughter. "Oh? All that was for Gwendolynne? I had thought that *you* were interested in the topic, Heloise."

My friend rolls her eyes. "No, Mum. I've told you a thousand times, I'm not interested in humans."

Dr. Chapman gives her a tight-lipped smile, then returns her attention to me. "Well, Gwen? Have you figured anything out about what's causing them?"

I press the toe of my stiletto against the tiled floor. I'm grappling with whether to tell Heli's mother about the tethers. In the end, I decide not to say anything. It's hard to know who to trust when anyone could be the culprit. "No, not yet. We're still just looking at the location and severity of the flares. I was wondering: Have you noticed any patterns, perhaps? Like, is it possible that there are a few bigger explosions, and then a series of smaller surges, like aftershocks?"

Dr. Chapman purses her lips, thinking. "No," she says slowly, drawing out the vowel in the word. "I don't think so. From what we can gather, based on the locations and magnitude, the surges are all roughly the same."

I frown. "So there's nothing that affects how strong they are?"

Dr. Chapman shakes her head. "When we've performed magical assays on people who are affected, they're all elevated, of course, but to roughly the same order: three or four times the upper limit of the normal reference range. And there doesn't seem to be a pattern in location, either. Other than the fact that most of them have been clustered in London, the rest have been scattered randomly across the country."

"Are they happening overseas?"

"Not that we know of," Dr. Chapman responds. "Or at least, there are no reports so far."

"Oh." My hope drains away, as though I've pulled the plug in a once-full bathtub. I'd been optimistic that Heli's mum would be able to help narrow down the possible locations of the tethers. "I guess we're back at square one, then."

"Wait." Dr. Chapman's gaze is piercing, even though her expression is warm. "There is something . . ."

My head jerks up. "What?"

Her brow furrows. "The Bristol group who've been monitoring the phenomenon have identified strange spikes in atmospheric magic, always close to what they think are the origins of the surges. They're a bit mobile, moving around within the area, but the explosions always happen close to where they're located."

I scrunch my face up, thinking. "So, like a magical storm?"

"No." Dr. Chapman's tone is cautious, as though she too doesn't quite know what to make of these revelations. "When they measure the readings, they don't follow the patterns typical of atmospheric storms. Nor are they fixed levels, like something you'd expect from an object. The magical traces are closer to what you'd expect from a mammal."

My chest feels tight. "Like . . . a familiar?"

"No," Dr. Chapman says. "A human."

My mind churns. I almost stumble, unsteady on my pencil-thin heels. I grab Heli's arm to regain my balance, my eyes wide.

Is this what the saboteur is doing? Using *people* as tethers to hold open the portals? Is that why people have died—they can't deal with the level of magic required to hold open the tears?

I try to swallow around the blocked feeling in my throat.

I must look slightly unhinged, because Heli's mother gives me a look of concern. "Gwen, are you quite well? Do you feel ill? I can check you over if you like—"

"No, thank you," I say quickly. "It's . . . thanks very much, Dr. Chapman. I really appreciate your help."

I drag Heloise away from her mother, who goes to rejoin her group. Heli is confused. I'll need to explain everything to her. But first I need to tell someone. Not Harrisford, of course—since he seems to have completely disappeared (and is also a raging arsehole).

So I text Conall instead, on my strap. Conall, I tap out, while Heloise frowns beside me. I think I know what the tethers are . . . And it's even worse than we imagined.

26

Harrisford

I escape into the men's lavatory, tearing my mask off so roughly that the ribbon breaks with a snap. My pulse is galloping at the speed of a unicorn, and my skin—everywhere—is burning up.

It takes me two tries to successfully push on the tap, lean over it, and douse my face with water. Cupping my hands, I gulp some down, washing away the lingering tastes of champagne and Gwendolynne's lips.

Then, bracing both hands on the counter, I let the droplets stream down my face and plink dramatically into the sink.

"What the fuck is wrong with you, Briggs?" I stare at myself in the mirror. My face is all flushed and mottled. I don't know why I feel so goddamned . . . *ill.* Am I coming down with a virus or something?

Deep down, I'm quite certain I know the answer, and the answer is Gwendolynne Chan. I can't remember the last time a woman had this much of an effect on me. I can't remember *any* time a woman had this much of an effect on me. Anytime I look at her, draw near her, or touch her, I go completely to pieces—as though my body is just a disparate cluster of cells held together by lust and longing.

At least now, being away from her, I'm starting to regain my bearings. I clutch at my chest, waiting until my heartbeat slows to an almost normal level. Then, turning toward the row of urinals behind me, I take a piss, wash my hands, and carefully adjust my bow tie.

My mask is the last thing I tackle. The black velvet ribbon is broken, but there's enough slack that I can re-knot it—I guess those knot-tying workshops in third year were handy for more than just restraint of animals.

Fixing it back on my face, I take a deep, calming breath, trying to settle my nervous system. I need to find Gwendolynne. It's incumbent on me to apologize for running out on her like that. My mind flicks back to the way she looked, clinging to my shoulders, her face all flushed and lovely. The curves of her body against mine. The feeling of her mouth as it moved—so soft and sweet—when I finally mustered the courage to kiss her.

I wanted to bite those plum-stained lips. I want to bite her elsewhere, everywhere. Something about her is bringing out my primal, animalistic side. After tonight, I doubt I can maintain my resolve to keep away from her much longer.

I let out a sigh. Of course my timing was, as usual, terrible. Have I blown it? Hopefully not—hopefully all I need to do is explain that I'd suddenly needed the bathroom, and we can pick up where we left off.

From back in my dorm room, Pudding sends her sympathies down our bond. *Don't worry, Harrisford,* she says. *Gwendolynne has a kind heart. She'll forgive you.*

Sure, she's kind and forgiving—to everyone except me. And honestly? I probably deserve her derision. Regardless, I square my shoulders, bracing myself as though I'm a soldier heading into battle. This isn't war, of course, but it's possibly just as bad, or worse. I'm going to have to go out there, push through the crowds, and confront a pissed-off Gwendolynne Chan.

But just as I leave the bathroom, a familiar figure steps into my line of sight. He is tall and rakish, with a mop of thinning gray hair above a full-face mask. He has his arm snaked around the waist of a platinum-blond woman. She's laughing, and she, too, is masked. But even with her face obscured I can still tell she is definitely *not* Mrs. Mason-Price.

"Harrisford," Nathaniel Price says, letting go of his companion to shake my hand. "It's good to see you, son."

Since Mr. Price is my father's boss, I can't very well turn down his offer to join him for a smoke on the upper level. We trudge up the steps, past Darwin's statue, the raucousness becoming more muffled as we climb up and away from the party. The entire time, Nathaniel keeps his hand on my shoulder like a conqueror staking his claim.

"How's your father?" he says, when we finally reach the top. After groping around his chest pocket, he draws out a cigar.

We're on one of Hintze Hall's famous internal balconies, overlooking the dance floor. It's dark up here—a stark contrast to the lights and music that relentlessly pulsate below.

"Still in a coma," I say, staring at Nathaniel as he flicks a magic-fueled lighter and lights the end. Is it even permitted to smoke in here? I think the answer is no, but *no* is not a word that Nathaniel bothers to pay much mind to.

"Pity," Nathaniel says, though he doesn't sound sorry at all.

I suppose I can't blame him, since it would be highly hypocritical of me. When I think about my father being in a coma, all I feel is numb. Which is slightly concerning—surely I should be feeling *something*?

But there's nothing.

What do people normally feel when their father's life hangs in the balance? Most people would feel sad, I'd expect, but not me. Has he—being so cold and distant my whole life—trained me to be cold and distant, also?

Perhaps we Briggs men are just far too pragmatic. It's not like Father and I ever had any semblance of closeness. There's no love there to mourn the loss of, nothing tangible to grieve over. And I refuse to feel sad over the purely hypothetical.

I keep my eyes on Nathaniel as he blows out a puff of smoke, wondering if *he* ever shows signs of sadness. Has he even noticed that Percy, his old familiar, is missing? And if so, has he already purchased himself a replacement?

The cigar smoke immediately dissipates, leaving a nebulous scent of tobacco floating in the air. Nathaniel once told me that magical cigars are exactly like regular cigars except the smoke is enchanted to evaporate instantly. I never thought to ask where it actually disappears *to*.

"You know, son." With the cigar still clamped between his teeth, Nathaniel pulls another from his pocket, offering it to me. With a wave of my hand, I decline, and he stuffs it back in his pocket and leans his elbows on the balcony's balustrades. "For a while I thought it was your father who was trying to sabotage my company. I thought he wanted to depose me. But then he got caught up in that explosion, and I realized that it most likely isn't him."

The thud of my heartbeat speeds up, and the back of my neck is clammy. I mirror the other man's movements by leaning down and also propping my elbows on the rail.

Nathaniel is wily—as Magecorp CEO, he has to be—and I must choose my words wisely if I'm going to get him to talk. "So it's someone external to Magecorp, then, sir? Who's trying to sabotage the business?"

He blows out another stream of smoke. His jowls wobble as he shakes his head. "Your guess is as good as mine, my boy. I hope it's not someone from within the company. You know, I try to be a good employer . . . But it's not always easy. Balancing the needs of thousands of people. Tens of thousands, if you count foreign branches.

"But I've always tried to do right by them. I'm not perfect, but I will stand by that statement. And if it is an insider job, then it would be very disappointing, Harrisford. Very disappointing indeed." He stares down at the revelers for a moment, lost in a cloud of gloom.

So our theory is right. It *is* sabotage, and my father was telling the truth. That's something, at least. "I'm sure it's not one of yours, Mr. Price," I say, trying to sound reassuring. "I'm sure it's just some fringe group with an irrational vendetta against Magecorp." Maybe the media is right. Maybe it *is* the MLO.

He sighs. "You're probably onto something." Giving me a sidelong glance, he adds, "You're a smart kid, Harrisford. And well connected. If you hear anything out there"—he waves his hand in the general direction of the museum's entrance—"you come straight to me, agreed?"

I nod, though I'm silently seething at the way he still treats me like a child. All the *son*s, and *kid*s, and *boy*s—he's trying to sound paternal, but it just comes across as naff. I already loathe my own father; I don't need someone else trying to step into the role. It's just another opportunity for them to let me down. To manipulate me. To use me as a pawn in their games.

Finally, I spot Gwendolynne, my gaze narrowing in on her from above. My gut gives an uncomfortable lurch.

She's found a friend—a Black girl wearing a silver sequined dress—and they're crossing the dance floor, weaving hurriedly through the crowd. For a moment, I fancy that she looks up. Catches my eye. But then I blink, and she's gone . . . it was probably just my imagination.

I'm temporarily distracted as Nathaniel pushes up off the railing and then turns to lean back against it. He studies me for a long while, still puffing on his cigar, until my collar feels several sizes too tight.

Finally, he says, "How's school going?"

"University is going well, sir. We're about to sit our final exams—"

"And then you'll what, join the Office of Magical Animals at the Ministry?"

I turn around to lean my back against the balustrades, too. "If I come first, then yes." Spying the grimace that flits over Nathaniel's face, I continue. "It's a good role for someone like me. The salary is well above anything a new grad vet makes, the work is interesting, there's ample room for promotion . . . Historically, most of the past recruits have gone on to have high-up ministerial positions."

I don't add the most important reason: the fact that it isn't Magecorp.

"Well, Harrisford, you know that if you don't win the position, then we at Magecorp will absolutely welcome you with open arms. Your father's been angling for you to join the business since you were barely out of nappies—"

"I know he has." I try not to sound too glum about it. The prospect of a lifelong career at Magecorp has been hanging over my head like a scythe for as long as I can remember.

Naïvely, I had thought that enrolling in vet school might show Father that I wanted something different—a different path, a different life. I had even let myself imagine days driving around the countryside, music turned up, showing up to farms in mud-splattered coveralls. Earning a wage that was entirely my own.

But my actions just solidified my father's ambitions, made him even more determined. The first week of the semester wasn't even over when he'd already approached Nathaniel and convinced the big boss to set up a brand-new magical familiars facility. A whole, separate business arm devoted to breeding animals. With me, Darghan Briggs's son, as the inaugural head of the Veterinary Department.

The last time we'd argued about it, my father had given me an ultimatum. Come first, and win the Ministry position, or else I'll have to do as he wants and join him at the company. And the worst part? If I don't win the Ministry position, and don't join Magecorp, my father had threatened to use his considerable influence to make my life elsewhere *very* difficult. His sway at the Ministry is limited to a few hefty donations, but any other business, any other workplace . . . Magecorp supplies the vast majority of them. With just one phone call, he could easily prevent my promotion, rendering me incapable of any career progression at all.

My jaw muscles clench at the thought, and my head grows hot. I force myself to breathe. Perhaps I'm not so numb about my father's condition after all. Perhaps the feeling I've mistaken for detachment is actually one of . . . relief.

If Father recovers and I don't win the Ministry role, then I'll be stuck at Magecorp for good, under his control and entirely subject to his whims. I'd do anything to escape that preordained fate. And the only thing throwing a wrench in my plan is—you guessed it—Gwendolynne.

Nathaniel is still talking. "And he's very keen to see you progress up the ranks. It's not every day a graduate can walk out of university and straight into a leadership role. Trust me when I say it would set you up for life. You could even find yourself in *my* job one day!" He booms out a short, sharp laugh.

"Thank you, Mr. Price. I appreciate it." I really don't. The last thing I want is to end up anything remotely like Nathaniel. Or my father, for that matter.

Nathaniel straightens, shoving his hands in his pockets. Rocking a little on the balls of his feet, he says, "I'd really encourage you to think about it, Harrisford. Imagine how thrilled your father would be if he awoke to find that his son had chosen a more lucrative path." He spreads his hands wide. "I needn't remind you how much . . . *impact* . . . someone with his connections can have on your career."

My heart drops like a stone, settling somewhere in my gut. Nathaniel says it like it's my choice, but in truth, it isn't. I have to consider the very real possibility that Gwendolynne will beat me and steal the Ministry job out from under me. And the thought is terrifying, because in this moment, everything becomes distressingly clear: I'm going to have to betray Gwendolynne, the woman who I'm getting uncomfortably close to. Or else I'm going to have to sacrifice myself to the capitalist machine that is Magecorp—and a lifetime of servitude beneath my father.

One of us will end up deeply unhappy and . . . I don't want it to be her. The issue is, I don't want it to be me, either.

I've been reckless, letting my little crush get in the way of my singular ambition, my lifelong goal . . . my *why*.

Suddenly, I feel vaguely nauseated. So I don't respond. I just turn back around and stare down at the dance floor, hoping to glimpse a certain plum dress, as Nathaniel Price claps me on the shoulder and leisurely strolls away.

27

Gwendolynne

She did *what*?" Harrisford roars.

He hasn't seen us. He's standing with his back to us, unleashing his ire on some poor young coat-check clerk.

The freckled boy quails. "She—she already checked out her coat, sir."

"Come *on*, Gwen," Heloise whispers, tugging me away from the scene. She all but pushes me down the entrance steps to where the valet is waiting with her car.

"Do we need to wait for your mum?" I say, breathless. I know it's foolish, but I'm half hoping I'll get the chance to go back and confront that prick who kissed, then abandoned me on the dance floor.

"Nah. She usually grabs a hotel room in the city after attending functions like these." Heli grabs the keys from the valet and slides into the driver's seat. She leans over and speaks to me through the passenger window. "And don't you even *think* about going back for him, G." Her voice is stern.

I sigh, clutching my coat tight around me, and climb into the passenger seat. Heloise's ride is a sleek little sports car, all smooth lines and black leather and tasteful silver finishes. As we zip through the city streets, I lean my head on the cool window, feeling the car's judders right down to my bones.

Heli checks her reflection in the rearview mirror, then throws a glance at me. "Are you all right? What happened back there?"

I quickly explain to her what I'd learned about the surges since she'd given me the scrolls from her mother. About how Magecorp uses tethers to hold open the portals that allow them to harvest magic, and how someone is trying to sabotage Magecorp by making them lose control.

"So the surges are being caused by some external party?" Heli says, concentrating on the road.

"Yeah." I frown. "I think so. I don't know who yet, though. But after what your mum said tonight . . . I think they're using *people* as tethers, Heli. And that's why we're seeing surge-related deaths."

Heloise sucks a breath through her teeth. "Wow," she says after a pause. "That's messed up."

"It is." I sigh, frustrated. "It's just—I feel like I'm stuck now. I've hit a dead end. We have a list of people who've died, but no way of telling who killed them."

Heli's mouth twists as she considers. "Maybe we should report it, G—"

"No!" I cut her off so abruptly that Heloise throws me a quick, surprised glance.

There's a long, awkward pause during which Heli focuses back on the road and I slump into my seat.

"Are you gonna tell me what's going on, Gwen?" she says eventually, smoothly swerving into the next lane to overtake a slow driver.

I hesitate. "Well, I . . ." I really should tell Heloise about Percy. "I kind of maybe stole a cat."

"A cat." Heli lifts both eyebrows. "*You* stole a cat?"

"Yeah. From Saint Gertrude's."

She gives a low whistle. "Well, shit, G. I'm impressed." Heloise has been trying to get me to loosen up for almost seven years now.

"And Harrisford—he knows I did it." The familiar feeling of dread slithers up my spine. "He's threatened to tell Dean Kaur if I go to the police."

If Harrisford reports my misdemeanor, then Percy will almost certainly be confiscated. And, despite the fact that Percy is mean to me ninety-five percent of the time, I'm growing irrationally fond of him. I will not—cannot—put him at risk.

It's tough love, Hairless One, Percy murmurs sleepily. *Sometimes one must be cruel to be kind.*

I roll my eyes; he yawns, audibly, and then goes silent. It's probably my tiredness he's feeling, since from what I've read familiars channel their owners' emotions, and I'm quite sure *he*—unlike me—has been sleeping the entire day.

But there was something else buried, hidden behind his fatigue. Something that sounded almost like . . . affection?

Heli's voice cuts into my thoughts, jerking me from my reverie. "What a fucking bastard," she says, referring to Harrisford.

I am in *complete* agreement.

She drives in silence for several minutes, frowning at the car in front of us. "What if we do some background research, then? See if there's anything connecting the people who've died or gone missing." Her brow creases. "Didn't you say some of them worked for Magecorp?"

"They did. But I'm not sure those deaths are related. According to Harrisford's dad, the employees who went missing were trying to figure out who actually was behind the surges." It makes sense. It would be in Magecorp's interest to stop the sabotage, because regulating the supply of magic is the basic foundation of the business.

Heloise steers the car onto the motorway and smoothly shifts up a gear. "Do you wanna look into it tonight, Gwen? We could take my mum's list, crack open a bottle, and see if we can dig anything up?"

"I would, but . . ." Now *I'm* yawning. The smooth rumble of the car motor is lulling me into fatigue. Being up for so many hours last night is finally catching up to me. "First I need some sleep."

I wake late the next morning, having overslept, and have to throw on my scrubs and pedal furiously to Saint Gertrude's. Conall, Heloise, and I are rostered onto procedures today—doing things like dental cleans, stitch-ups, and other small operations that don't require a sterile surgery theater.

Jenna Rutherford is just finishing up morning rounds when I burst into the prep room, shrugging on my white robes.

"Is everything okay, Chan?" she says, raising one heavily penciled eyebrow.

It's out of character for me to be late to rounds. In every other part of my life, I'm a disaster—a clumsy, nonpunctual disaster—but when it comes to my work, I'm usually dead on time.

"Just catching up after a call-out the other night," I mumble, and Jenna gives a curt nod.

"As I was saying," she says, to the group. "We have a cat here with an abscess. Which normally is due to?"

"Cat bites," says Heloise promptly. "From fighting."

"Right," Jenna says as we crowd around the cat's cage. It's a miserable-looking British Blue with a snarl of bloodstained, matted fur on his flank. "But what if I told you this cat is indoors only? And he lives alone?"

"Could he have escaped?" volunteers Conall a little nervously. He darts his gaze to the heavily tattooed Jenna and then back to the cat.

"Good thought, Peters. But the owner swears black and blue that didn't happen."

"What about a spider bite?" Heloise shudders; she hates spiders. "Or some other insect?"

Jenna purses her lips. "Could be . . . But I've not seen them look like this before. What else? Think, folks."

I draw nearer to the bank of cages. The cat is crouching and obviously feeling poorly, but he lifts his chubby little lips and gives me a soft, plaintive meow. He has a magical aura about him, which is usual for a familiar, but his seems rather . . . extreme.

Plus, now that I'm closer, the dark staining on his fur doesn't only look like blood. Yes, there's dried blood there, but some of the markings look more like scorch marks.

"Magiphilia," I say, more to myself than to Jenna. I raise my head and address the group. "I think it's magiphilia. Except instead of expelling the excess magic, the cat's body has just . . . walled it off."

Jenna slaps her thigh. "Bingo! His magic levels are off the charts. There are burn marks on his fur. It's an unusual presentation, but it fits. This cat's just managed to sequester the magic into one part of his body. Good work, Chan." She taps her strap.

There's a ping, and Conall, Heloise, and I all check our own straps. Jenna's given me an extra mark for diagnosing the British Blue.

After delivering the qílín foal, I'd already drawn ahead of Harrisford by three points, but I note, with some satisfaction, that I'm now ahead of him by four.

Good. The bitter, petty side of me wants to beat him even more, now that he's shown his true colors and confirmed he's an actual prick.

"Well, chaps," Jenna says cheerily. "You get started on the procedures list. I'll be back to check on your progress after lunch."

An hour later, the three of us have anesthetized the cat and are preparing the abscess for lancing. Heloise is monitoring the anesthetic, and Conall is shaving the hair and cleaning the cat's skin, while I scrub my hands and snap on a pair of gloves.

"Do you think the problem's getting worse?" Conall says, dragging a disinfectant-soaked swab in outwardly spiraling circles. When he reaches the perimeter, he discards the swab and then picks up another. "Gary died from that surge, and though I can't prove it now, I—I think he had magiphilia, too."

Heloise and I shoot each other a look. "I think so," I say. So far, I've only discussed the actual magiphilia epidemic with Harrisford and Heloise. And Harrisford and I are the only two Seamere students who know about the qílín. Everyone else has seemed to swallow Professor Pickering's assurances that the common room surge was a one-off.

I haven't wanted to talk to anyone else about how widespread the problem seems, because in a world where there's so much misinformation, it's hard to know who to trust. But Conall lost Gary and I like Conall, so I decide now's a good time to let him in on what we know.

Lowering my voice so that it's drowned out by all the beeping equipment—I don't want any passing staff to overhear what we're saying—I explain. "The media's not reporting on it, but there's been a definite spike in magiphilia cases all over the UK. In animals *and* people. Related to random power surges."

Heloise taps the cat's eyelids and checks his jaw tone to make sure he's properly asleep. "Yeah, my mum's been looking into cases. The incidence is definitely on the rise." The cat's not quite deep enough, so Heli channels some magic from her familiar, Lightning, and uses it to top up the anesthesia machine.

I slide the scalpel blade onto its handle and wait for Conall to finish prepping the skin. "We think that maybe someone is trying to sabotage Magecorp—and maybe Linksphere. And those tethers that Magecorp use to hold open the portals . . ."

Conall gives the cat's skin a final swipe. "You said they're not what we thought, right?

I lower my voice further. "We think that whoever is causing the surges is opening extra portals . . . using *people* as tethers."

Conall, still holding the final swab, gapes at me. "Using *people*?" He claps his hand over his mouth and darts a glance at the closest door. Fortunately, we're still alone.

"There have been a few deaths," Heloise murmurs, marking the cat's heart rate, respiratory rate, and blood pressure down on the chart.

Conall takes a spray bottle and spritzes the cat liberally with metho. "Do . . . we think it's the MLO? It's what they want, right? The surges would mean more magic flows to us from the Void."

"I guess so, but . . ." I let out a long sigh. "We don't know if the MLO's involved just yet."

Of course, if you asked any random granny on the street, they'd swear up and down that it *absolutely, definitely* is the Magical Liberation Organization. From the outset, the media has already acted judge and jury, blaming the MLO for both the gala explosion and the one at Magecorp. I feel a slight twang of guilt at the latter, since that explosion was caused by me, but at the same time . . . I'm not about to turn myself in. Clearly, the MLO can look after itself.

But despite an extensive investigation by the police, no links between the MLO and the explosions have been found—yet.

I start incising the cat's skin. The capsule of the abscess is thickened, and it comes apart in layers, so it's as though I'm slicing slowly through an onion. Conall is wearing a distinct look of disgust on his face, and I don't think it's because I'm about to cut into a semisolid mass of pus.

"I started looking more into the tethers, and what they could possibly be," Conall says, after a short period of silence, his nose still wrinkled. "Just . . . scientific curiosity, you know?"

I do know what that's like, so I remain quiet, encouraging him to continue.

"And I discovered something interesting." Now no longer preoccupied with prepping the cat for the procedure, Conall starts tapping away on his strap. "There are mentions throughout history of a recurrent object—in our language, it's called the Source. But in other cultures it's known as various things: the Coming, the Salvation, the Hand of the Gods . . . It was said to have crashed into our world sometime back in the Dark Ages."

"Oh?" Heloise and I dart glances at each other again, and I return my focus to the abscess. The skin is extraordinarily thickened, more so than a run-of-the-mill cat fight wound, and even with all this cutting I'm *still* not through the capsule.

Conall does that fancy projecting thing, from his strap into midair, and I really should ask him how to do it now that I can channel enough extra magic to try. But now's not the time; he's already flipping through various websites that depict photos of all sorts: leaves taken from dusty, crumbling books; pictures of ancient rock paintings; sculptures displayed in museums around the world. And they're all of a roughly circular structure, with a honeycomb appearance to its surface, much like—

"The circular room!" I gasp out. The pictures are all depicting something that looks precisely like what I'd caught glimpses of in the center of the Magecorp vault. Before Darghan Briggs chased me and stunned me unconscious, of course. Then, because Heli and

Conall are both staring at me, confused, I elaborate: "Magecorp were keeping one of these . . . Source things, did you call it? In the locked vault at the top of the tower."

Conall takes a while to close his gaping mouth, and when he does, he slowly turns his attention back to the projected pictures in the air. "Well, according to some very old scriptures, a rock just like this came crashing down to Earth some thousand or so years ago. There are old myths and legends from all around the world, referencing an object that sounds like a meteor . . . and it's known in every culture as being something that once, long ago, brought magic to the people of Earth."

"Like a sign from the gods?" asks Heloise.

Conall frowns. "Yeah, something like that. But what if it wasn't from the gods? What if it was—"

"—from the Void!" I finish Conall's sentence for him, excitement unfurling in my chest. "Someone must have figured out that they could use it to tether open the portals and harvest magic that humans could use." I chew on my lip, thinking. It still doesn't explain how the saboteurs are using people instead of the Source. But at least we have a lead, now. "Magecorp must have somehow got hold of it—or part of it, if Linksphere also uses the same."

"Maybe whoever's opening the illegal portals somehow managed to steal some of this Source," Heli adds as she casually feeds more magic into the anesthesia machine. "Do we need to look into who has access? Find out if there have been any breaches of Magecorp security?"

I ponder this for a moment. Percy had said Nathaniel Price's mansion had been broken into, too. If some of the rock was stolen, it might not have even been from Magecorp HQ; besides, I really don't want the authorities to start poking around Magecorp's security records. That might implicate me, and I definitely don't want to get done for it. "Maybe we should start by profiling the victims. We could see if any of them have anything special about them . . . Like suspected ties to the MLO, or something."

Figuring that I'll dissect this information later, when I don't have an anesthetized cat in front of me and can therefore properly concentrate, I turn my attention back to my task. "Conall, you're brilliant, by the way. How did you find all this?"

Looking sheepish, he turns bright red. "I've spent the whole week trawling through the library archives. It's in none of the modern textbooks. I had to search right back to old editions, and look up some really obscure references."

"Wow. You're amazing." Heloise's praise is completely genuine, and wholly justified.

"Like I said, I was just really fascinated by the Magecorp blueprints and wanted to get to the bottom of how they do it." Conall shifts on his feet, clearly uncomfortable with the praise. "How they actually harvest magic, I mean. I should have been studying for exams, but . . ." He shrugs.

I think about the stack of IDs in Darghan Briggs's drawer. The deaths recorded on Nora Chapman's lists. The qílín foal that Harrisford and I saved with my hands (and his body).

And mostly . . . Mostly I think about Gary the guinea pig: his stiff little legs and Conall's palpable grief as he cried over his friend.

"No." Finally, I manage to stab through the outside of the abscess with the blade. A torrent of foul-smelling, partially inspissated pus pours out, and we all gag.

Ugh, says Percy, from a distance. *That is* disgusting. This is followed by the marked sound of him retching up his breakfast. I don't know what he's vomiting on, but I'm willing to bet it's my freshly washed laundry—or something roughly equivalent.

I frown. *You're not even here, Percy.*

True, he replies. *But remember: I feel everything that you feel, Hairless One.*

This is true; I can feel everything he feels too. It's unsettling, since I've always kept my emotions so walled off: behind my mask, inside my chest, in the cuts I make on my skin.

I shake my head to clear my thoughts, focusing on the trapped magic that is unfurling from the cat's incision. It hits me at once—the potent swell of too much magic, combined with a gangrenous stench. The magic has been trapped for so long that it's turned all black, so concentrated it is actually noxious.

"This," I say to Conall, voicing words that I never *ever* thought would come out of my own mouth, "is *way* more important than a bunch of bloody exams."

Later, Heloise and I lounge on her bed with glasses of red wine and an array of expensive cheeses arranged artfully on a cheese board. Percy is present too—now that I've finally told Heli about him, I thought he'd appreciate a change of scenery.

Heloise's dorm room is in the east wing, which is not quite as fancy as the truly posh south wing, but still much nicer than mine. (*Agreed*, says Percy, his tail flicking back and forth. *She has far better taste than you.*)

I scowl. Kind Percy is gone and Snarky Percy is back, apparently.

It's a bright, comfortable, cozy room, which Heloise has decorated in a multicolored riot of varying patterns and textures. Technically, it should clash—but somehow it just works. It's the exact type of room you'd expect Heloise to have, given her personality.

We're trawling through Heli's mother's lists, our laptops propped open—mine old and clunky, hers new and sleek. The aim is to research as many of the dead people as possible and see if we can turn up any clues. Any patterns. Absolutely anything whatsoever. I've been feeling crushed by the weight of frustration since leaving the gala; it's as though the information we need is dancing just beyond our reach, and only dribbling through in tiny increments that don't give us the full picture.

I draw in a deep breath. *It's no different to working up a case, Gwen. You just have to take each little bit of information and put it together to formulate a diagnosis.* Then, letting my sigh whoosh out of me, I type the next name into my browser's search bar.

"It was the surges, wasn't it?" Heloise says suddenly, fixing her gaze on me.

"What was the surges?" I mumble, preoccupied with clicking through the dozens of listings the search engine has on *Benjamin Purcell.*

"The reason you agreed to go to the gala with Harrisford Briggs."

My head snaps up. Hearing his name spill from Heloise's wine-stained lips makes me so irrationally angry. "Yes," I say, indignant. "We were trying to look for tethers. We figured there might be some remnant of one where the last big explosion happened—"

"*I knew it!*" she says, slapping my shoulder. "I *knew* you'd never agree to go anywhere with that prick voluntarily."

"Of course I wouldn't." My mood has abruptly soured, thinking about how Harrisford had abandoned me midkiss. "He's an arrogant arsehole and I want nothing more to do with him. Ever, *ever* again."

Heloise gives me a sly half smile. "Don't know if he would say the same thing, G."

I fix her with my most withering glare. "Yes, he would. I hate him. He hates me. We only agreed to work together because we're both trying to come first."

And I'm going to beat him, I add silently.

Even if it kills me, I'm going to wipe the floor with Harrisford-fucking-Briggs. I'm still four points ahead of him; I gained an additional two points for successfully treating the magiphilic cat's abscess, and he gained two points for something I don't know, and don't care at all, about.

"Mmm-hmmm." Heli takes a sip of her wine, that infernal smile still on her lips.

"Anyway," I say, distressed by the unpleasant turn our conversation has suddenly taken. "Have you found out anything interesting about the dead folk?"

After placing her glass carefully onto her bedside table, Heloise tugs her computer further up her lap. She screws her face up in disgust, then looks up. "There've been more deaths."

"Shit," I say. "More?"

Her eyes are glued on her screen. "Three in the past two days. This is getting *bad*, G." Her fingers fly across the touchpad as she scrolls, squinting at the social media profiles she's pulled up on the screen.

"Got 'em." She stops scrolling and swivels the computer to face me. She's enlarged pictures of three different people: two women and a man.

"Who are they?" I ask her, staring at their grim expressions. Clearly, they are mug shots.

"These three," Heli says, tapping the edge of the screen with one finger, "are all allegedly connected with the MLO in some way."

I lean forward to squint at the screen. In some ways, the Magical Liberation Organization would be the simplest explanation. Their stated purpose was always to help magic reach the masses. To distribute it equally and increase its accessibility. It's very plausible that they'd make a concerted effort to sabotage Magecorp. For the MLO to rip open multiple portals that increase the flow of magic into our world would be consistent with their cause.

Never mind that they staunchly deny any involvement. Never mind the fact that at least three of their own have been actually killed. History has shown us that they're A-OK with sacrificing themselves—and members of the public—in order to achieve their ends.

Yes. It could definitely be the MLO. Sometimes I need to remember that a stone is just a stone, a horse just a horse. One of the first things you ever learn at vet school is not to make things more complex than they outwardly seem. *When you hear the sound of hooves*, one of our first-year lecturers had said, *assume it is a horse, not a Pegasus*. It means: Always go for the simplest explanation first—the most common. Horses are common. Even unicorns are. But, being both shy and extremely rare, Pegasuses are almost never seen, even by the most experienced myth.creat vets in the world.

This looks like the MLO. It smells like the MLO. Logically, it probably *is* the MLO.

"I suppose that's our next step, then," I say, gripping the stem of my wineglass.

I have no idea how, and no idea when, but we're going to have to sneak into one of the MLO's super-top-secret meetings.

28

Gwendolynne

Unfortunately, I have no idea where to start looking, and neither does Heloise. Despite the fact that we spend half the night fruitlessly scouring the internet, we cannot find an ounce of information about how to contact the Magical Liberation Organization. I suppose being an underground extremist group requires utmost secrecy at all times.

At the dean's lecture on Friday morning, Professor Pickering is running things—once again, Professor Kaur is off sick. It's a little odd, to tell the truth. The dean seemed fine during clinics on Tuesday, and now suddenly she's ill again?

Usually, she doesn't get sick so often. In fact, apart from her paid time off, I have *never* known Professor Kaur to take a day off, ever. It makes me wonder if she's just avoiding official events like lectures, for some reason.

The vice dean's speech is so damn long that soon enough most of the student cohort have dozed off. Those who haven't are shifting in their seats, playing on their straps, or staring off into space, daydreaming. At the end, to a chorus of audible groans and indignant whispers that echo throughout the hall, Professor Pickering informs us that the on-call rota will still apply even during exam week—no exceptions.

He waits for the rabble to die down before he adds an addendum: We should not be viewing on-call weeks as being *disruptive*, he pontificates, but rather an *opportunity*. "It is, after all," he says, "your best chance to have full involvement on a wide variety of cases before being unleashed into the wider world."

Heli and I are only half listening, since we're using the time to scroll through hundreds of social media profiles of people with alleged links to the MLO.

It's when Professor Pickering is explaining, to one particularly disgruntled student, that we "shouldn't expect time off, not even for exams, because animals still need medical treatment" and besides, we "need to get used to working nights and weekends" that Heli suddenly sits bolt upright. She's wide-eyed, her mouth hanging open, and when she finally glances up, she shuts it.

"What's wrong?" I whisper.

Heli doesn't answer, just tilts her strap screen toward me. It's a profile picture from a social media account, framed by the glossy black casing of her latest-model strap.

The picture is angled weirdly, the focus is fuzzy, and most of it is out of shot—but it's still recognizable. Familiar. The account name, though, is strange.

I raise one eyebrow as Heli scrolls through the hundreds—or maybe even thousands—of cat memes on the person's profile. It's all very innocuous. But then, why the fake name?

"Burner account?" I murmur, under my breath.

Heli and I both slide glances toward the far side of the hall, where the person in question is sitting—face bored, their head propped on their fist, completely unsuspecting that there are two people sneaking them surreptitious looks.

Pen? I think, shaking my head in disbelief. *Pen Ferguson?*

Sweet, unassuming Pen . . . part of the MLO?

I try to ignore the aggravating blond who happens to be sat behind them, slouched in his chair with his arms crossed. But it's difficult, since the shaft of sunlight that's streaking across the hall is inconveniently spotlighting him. The light glints off his golden hair, making him look almost . . . angelic.

I snort. Harrisford, angelic? *Ha!* What a bloody joke.

Suddenly, though, he looks up, his gaze snapping onto mine. Inadvertently, I gasp. My fingers curl around the seat of my chair, gripping it with desperate strength. It feels a bit like the floor has fallen away—and if I don't hold on for dear life, I'll fall.

Harrisford clocks my movements, and the corners of his lips quirk slightly. Not quite a smirk, but close enough. I narrow my eyes to slits and, with a huff, pointedly face forward again.

"It could be a burner," Heli muses, thankfully distracting me from thoughts of Harrisford-fucking-Briggs. "Or someone just impersonating them." She lowers her voice to a whisper. "Whatever it is, we should investigate. This account is following almost everyone we've got listed as potentially linked to the MLO."

"Miss Chan, Miss Chapman," Professor Pickering barks, suddenly, from up on stage. His thin lips twist into a sneer. "Care to share with the group whatever it is that you find so interesting?"

"No, Professor," Heli mumbles as I go red and slide down farther into my chair.

A few minutes later, when Professor Pickering has lulled us all back into a stupor, I sneak another look at Harrisford. He's no longer looking at me. Instead, he's watching the stage . . . but there's an unmistakable tilt to his lips that suggests he's suppressing a smile.

By now, Pen seems to have dozed off. Their head has slipped off their hand, their chin resting on their chest.

Once again, I turn to face the front. It really is hard to imagine

Pen Ferguson being involved in the MLO. In fact, as recently as a week ago, I would never have believed it.

But this week? Everything's changed.

And I have to remember that anything—*anything*—is possible.

Later, when we knock on Pen's dorm door, they open it so it's only slightly ajar.

"Oh, hi, Gwen, Heloise." They exhale, seemingly in relief. The door swings open wider. "D'you need something?"

I smile at them. "We need to speak with you."

A pause. "About what?" they say slowly.

"About the MLO," Heli says.

Pen's face flushes red, and they go to slam the door shut.

Heli's too quick, though. And strong. She catches the door handle and keeps it cracked open. "Hey! We're not gonna get you in trouble, you know."

"We're just searching for information about the MLO," I add. "We thought maybe you could help."

Pen just stares at us, red-faced. Heli and I exchange a look, then turn back to them, both of us sporting our most winsome smiles.

"All right, all right!" Pen's flustered, their words coming out all tremulous. They shoot a nervous glance up and down the empty hall. "Just stop saying it out loud!"

"Saying what?" I frown. "'ML—'"

"Shush!" Frantically, Pen reaches out, grabs both our shirts, and drags us into their room. The door snicks shut behind us with an audible click.

Pen's dorm is absolutely crammed full of electronic equipment. Given their retro style of dress and their romance book obsession

(I'm pretty sure they're a book influencer in their spare time), I hadn't expected anything so . . . tech heavy.

But in complete contrast to the electronics, their decor is all vintage. Fussy, even. Large-print floral curtains, crocheted rugs, and lace doilies, all in tones of pink and green. Books cover every surface. In the center is the pièce de résistance: a shiny, chrome-legged 1950s-style laminate table with four matching hot pink chairs.

It's incredible, because two weeks ago I'd never ventured into anyone's room at Seamere except for mine and Heloise's. Since then, I've been inside Harrisford's, Conall's, and now Pen Ferguson's room. And I think, of all of them, this one might be my favorite.

Pen shifts a stack of books off their sofa to clear a space and gestures at us to sit. They're still looking rather harried.

I sink onto the green velvet surface and pull up the picture we'd been staring at during the lecture. "Is this you, Pen?"

Pen doesn't answer immediately; they just give a nervous laugh. But finally, they say, "Well, go on, then. How'd you find me out?"

"It's clearly you," Heli says, suppressing a smile. "The cardigan, the tattoos—"

"The cat memes," I add.

Pen pulls a tissue from a lace-covered tissue box and mops at their sweat-sheened forehead. "Jesus, I'm bad at this. I only used that pic because I've only just joined and I thought it would be helpful to other members to know who I am because otherwise they'd not accept my follow requests, you know? It's all so hush-hush and I just really want to be involved . . ."

My insides give a leap, as though I've swallowed a live fish. "So it's true? You *have* joined the MLO?"

Pen doesn't answer for the longest time. They just stand there, their face mottled red, twisting the tissue in their hands. "Y-you're not going to report me, are you?"

"No! Of course not. We're just—"

"I know you think I'm not the type." Pen cuts me off, and continues rambling, all in run-on sentences, as they try to explain. "I just . . . I've never agreed with the way the corporates restrict the supply of magic. It disproportionately affects marginalized folk, like you two, and Conall, and Alice, and Danny . . . and me, of course. And I don't want to go through life just *accepting* that, you know?" Pen's making short work of the tissue; it's almost disintegrated to pieces. "Since I've been book blogging I've discovered how powerful it is to have a platform and now we're so close to graduating I figure I should leverage that platform, it's almost my responsibility, I mean I want to be a good vet, of course, and all I wanna do is work with cats, but also I feel really strongly that—"

"It's okay, Pen." I hold up a hand to stop their panicked monologue. "We understand. Trust me, we're not looking for any trouble. We just want to go to the next meeting."

Their expression immediately brightens. "Oh! You want to join?"

Heli says "Yes" at exactly the same time as I say "No." I grunt as Heli elbows me painfully in the gut.

"We're thinking about it," Heli says, giving me a pointed look.

Pen's shoulders drop in relief, and they crush the tissue in their fist before tossing it into the bin. "Oh. Well. I can definitely help with that."

They cross to their desk and start scribbling something down on a piece of paper. As Heloise and I both wait, my mind turns over everything that Pen just said.

I'd always thought of the MLO as being radical extremists; apart from the occasional news story, I'd never had much reason to think about them. But lately, all I'm hearing about is the MLO. The MLO this, the MLO that, and—considering what I suspect they *might* be doing with human tethers, it's honestly surprising that someone so, well, *nice*—like Pen—would think to associate themself with them.

My thoughts are interrupted when Pen thrusts the piece of paper into my hand. "I won't be going to this," they mumble. "I'm too behind on study. But I've written down the address—it's a place called the Galloping Gytrash. It's tonight, at eight . . . You'll find them in the back room. The password to enter is 'codswallop.' Just . . . don't tell anyone it was me who said, okay? I'm giving this to you because I trust you, but the others don't know you, and . . ."

Heloise raises her eyebrows as she scans the address on the paper. "I know the Gytrash. I've been there before." She lifts her head and looks at Pen. "And don't worry, we won't say anything."

Heli and I both stand to leave.

"Thanks, you two." Pen turns their attention to their strap, unlocking it with shaking fingers. "I guess I should change my profile pic. And maybe delete the cat memes."

Good idea, Percy mutters. He's been listening in on the entire conversation. *Those memes are horrible, slanderous, blasphemous things, full of lies and untruths and . . .*

Percy doesn't stop ranting until I'm back in our room and he realizes I'm about to feed him. He tucks in immediately, eating and purring, all thoughts of cat memes instantly forgotten.

It's been a long week, and I really don't want to run into Harrisford Briggs. It's easy enough to avoid him during classes, since he's myth.creat and I'm staunchly mag.fam, but the common areas are a different story. Today, apart from the dean's lecture, I'd seen him exactly one other time, while Heli and I were crossing the courtyard. Panicking, I'd yanked her behind a pillar in an effort to hide from him, but he'd seen us both crouching there, much to my chagrin. Luckily, he'd made no effort to approach me, or even make eye contact, and had just kept on walking until he was well out of sight.

Now it's teatime, and I really don't want to risk running into him in the Heywood Hall dining rooms. And since I have a few hours to kill before the MLO meeting starts, I decide to take a plateful of food and wander down to the paddocks—to eat and check on the qílín foal. Earlier, I'd seen the gangly little creature capering about his mother, looking none the worse for his ordeal. But I want to take a closer look, make sure his vitals are okay.

The grounds staff have modified the main paddock to accommodate the qílíns—since they refuse to walk on grass, tarpaulins have been laid all around the perimeter with only a small patch of green exposed at the center. The air is muggy, hanging heavy on my skin like a wet blanket, and the evening sun sprinkles the grass with gold.

As I approach the qílín and her foal, though, I realize there's someone else there, someone who is also seemingly avoiding the dining rooms at Heywood Hall.

It's Harrisford, of course.

He's inside the paddock, sitting on one of the tarpaulins, his back propped against the reinforced wooden fence. His long legs are stretched out in front of him, and he has a plate balanced on his knees. In his hand is a half-eaten apple; as I watch, he takes a final bite and then holds it out to the qílín, who is nuzzling at him hopefully, letting out little whoofs of air that blow his golden hair about. The qílín snatches the apple core off him and crunches it noisily, and Harrisford laughs.

I scowl at the scene. Harrisford was right. The idea that qílíns are only drawn to *nice* people is grossly misrepresented.

Hastily, I try to retreat—but too late. He's spotted me. Raising his head, he stares as the qílín continues to nose into the crook of his neck, as though he might be hiding more sweet treats there.

I don't want to go over, I really don't. But equally I don't want him to get the wrong impression and think that I am afraid. After he'd left me, bereft, at the gala, I'd worked hard to convince myself that I truly *did not care*. That, in my quest to untangle the mystery of Magecorp's saboteur, it means nothing to me whether Harrisford comes along for the ride. If I run away again, after he's spotted me, then it'll negate the laissez-faire attitude I've been carefully cultivating for days. It had irked me all afternoon that he'd got the better of me in the courtyard.

Hiding hadn't felt like a victory. It had felt like defeat.

So I steel myself. Raising my chin, I grip my plate, straighten my shoulders, and approach.

"Chan," he says when I'm near enough to hear, and his voice has become all lofty again, like it always used to be when speaking to me. "What's a mag.fam student like you doing here?"

His condescension raises my hackles, and I glare at him and his half-buttoned shirt and his stupid fucking plate. But despite the fact this exchange has made me instantly defensive, it's also somehow a little . . . comforting? It's comforting to know that in spite of everything that's happened over the past one and a half weeks, we will always default to this dynamic: being each other's rivals. Enemies. Competitors. Nemeses. That nothing will stop things from going right back to the way they were.

It's comforting because, on the balance of it, hating Harrisford Briggs is much, much easier—and far less painful—than falling for his empty charms.

"I'm here to check on Chili." I'd nicknamed the foal Chili because it sounds a bit like *qílín*. "What are *you* doing here?"

Confusion flashes across his face, so fleeting it's barely noticeable, but he quickly smooths his expression back into its usual disdainful mask. "The foal? That's not even his name."

I ignore him. "It doesn't matter that I'm not myth.creat, Briggs.

I'm still allowed to come and check on the foal that *I* delivered." I narrow at my eyes at him, daring him to challenge my statement.

He gives a long, grievous sigh. "Look, there's plenty of room for us both. I'm quite sure the qílín will be happy for the extra company."

I glance at the golden creature, who is clearly simping over Harrisford, and frown. "I don't know. I'm pretty sure she likes you better."

Regardless, I hand Harrisford my plate and awkwardly climb over the stile. When I drop to the ground on the other side, I sit down beside him, my bum on the tarp and my back against the fence.

Harrisford hands me my food, and we sit in silence for a while, eating. I'm surprised to see that his plate is absolutely loaded up with desserts: trifle, bread-and-butter pudding studded with tiny currants, and a generous side helping of custard. How on earth does he *eat* like that, and still manage to stay so ripped?

It's probably all the large-animal work, I conclude. Wrestling with enormous beasts and such.

"Still like pudding, huh?" I pick up a piece of pasta and nibble on one end. I've lost my appetite, even though ten minutes ago I was absolutely ravenous.

He glances down at his plate, then gives me a lopsided grin. "I guess you've discovered my little secret."

"That you have a raging sweet tooth?" My voice cracks on the word *sweet* and I cringe internally, wanting to kick myself.

His grin widens, until it holds an almost-wicked edge. Leaning in, he murmurs, "Not very macho, is it?"

I hate myself for it, but that smile still makes my heart skip a little, so I tear my gaze away and force myself to watch the qílín. She's now trotting around the far corner of the paddock, stopping every now and then to let her foal suckle some milk.

“Where is Pudding, anyway?” I’ve become so accustomed to seeing Harrisford with the bearded dragon atop his shoulder, he doesn’t look quite right without her. Briefly, I wonder what it must be like to have a such a close and loving relationship with one’s familiar.

I barely see Percy, really. Every morning I let him out super early, before anyone else is awake to notice, leaving my window ajar so that he can make his way back. Every night he swaggers in, cool as a cat who isn’t scared by randomly placed cucumbers.

Percy’s indignant voice interjects my thoughts from wherever on campus he is: *I’m not scared of cucumbers, Hairless One.*

Of course you’re not, I think soothingly. He doesn’t reply, just huffs down our telepathic bond.

I don’t know where Percy is currently, but I don’t mind him roaming of a daytime. Being far too lazy, he’s not much of a hunter—plus, he’s always home by tea. I’m quite sure that by the time I go back to my dorm room tonight, he’ll be standing over his empty bowl, yowling.

Harrisford, on the other hand, seems to be particularly averse to being separated from his familiar. I suppose he *has* had her since he was four—perhaps she’s his emotional support animal as much as a conduit for magic.

Harrisford frowns. “Pudding? She’s in my room.” He pauses for a moment, the silence pressing, and then gives me a sidelong glance. “She’s lecturing me right now, actually. Telling me I should apologize.”

My mouth goes dry. “Apologize? To who?”

I sense him turning to face me but stay resolutely facing forward. “Why, to you, of course.”

My traitorous body flinches, and I involuntarily turn to face him.

We're uncomfortably close in this position, our knees slightly folded and pointing in toward each other, our shoulders resting against the fence's wooden posts.

And his face . . . His face is no longer cold, his look no longer supercilious. There's a warmth and energy in his eyes that I haven't seen since the night of the gala.

He rakes his fingers through his hair, pushing the loose locks out of his eyes as though trying to see me better. "Listen, Chan," he says. "I'm sorry I ran off on you like that. That kiss—"

"Don't worry about it." I cut him off, wanting to say it before he does. "I get it. It was nothing. We just . . . got caught up in the moment." I look down to hide my flushed face and stab a piece of pasta so violently it splits. Then, trying to affect nonchalance, I say, "Where'd you go, anyway?"

His jaw tightens, and he uses his own fork to shift the food on his plate. "Right. Well, I had to use the lavatory, and then I ran into Nathaniel Price—"

"You spoke to Nathaniel?" Hearing that name sets my pulse hammering; has Harrisford discovered new information that could help us figure out who is targeting Magecorp?

"Yes. I got him talking about the sabotage, and he told me . . ." Harrisford trails off. His eyes are locked on me, staring. And even as I hold his gaze, the fleeting tenderness in his face just . . . dissipates. His expression turns cold. Stern. He clamps his lips shut, setting them in grim determination.

What the hell just happened?

"*What* did he tell you?" I'm kind of reeling at how mercurial he's being, at how much his demeanor altered in less than half a second.

The muscle in Harrisford's jaw jumps and he looks away. "Nothing," he mutters. "It isn't important."

My own lips thin in annoyance, and I turn back to face front. "Are you sure? I hope you're not holding anything back that could help us figure out who's behind the surges."

Harrisford's shoulders tense further, frustration coming off him in waves. "Oh, give it up already," he mutters. "You're still banging on about those surges? Why are you so bloody bothered?"

"Bothered?" My voice is rising. Has Harrisford seriously just got sick of the investigation and moved on to the next shiny new thing? Does he really treat life-threatening, world-ending dangers the same way he treats his women?

I take a deep breath, my fingers tightening around the edges of my plate, willing myself not to fling its entire contents at him. "I'm *bothered* because the surges are hurting people. I'm *bothered* because someone is interfering with the *system*, and that's—"

"Well, maybe they're right to," he snaps, cutting off my tirade. There's a stubborn set to his mouth that wasn't there mere minutes ago. "Maybe the system is broken."

"The system is *Magecorp*, Briggs," I hiss. "It's your legacy."

He flicks at a stray blade of grass that is peeking around the edge of the tarpaulin. He's suddenly turned all sullen. "Fuck my legacy."

I stare at him for a moment, open-mouthed. "But . . . But . . . We *need* Magecorp. We need it for magic, we need it to do our jobs. We need it to *create* jobs, to stimulate the economy, to keep the price of magic down. Yes, your dad is an absolute arsehole, but that doesn't mean we should lie down and just . . . accept defeat! We're facing surges that could destroy our way of life, Briggs, and you're just going to . . . give up?"

Harrisford snorts. "Seriously? You actually believe that? That Magecorp helps the economy?" He lets out a bitter laugh and shakes his head. "And here I thought you were supposed to be the smart one."

I glower at him. For a brief, infinitesimal moment, it had felt like

Harrisford and I might come to some understanding. That we'd be able to get past whatever the hell had happened—or not happened—between us, and start working together again. I'd been so close to divulging what Heloise, Conall, and I had discovered, in the vague hope that we could maybe help each other figure out the mystery of the surges.

But I realize now that I'd been completely deluded; we will never get past the awkwardness, we will never be able to work together, and we will never not be archenemies who want to throttle one another. I want to throttle him now, to shove his head right into his plate so that his smarmy face gets caked in custard.

But I'm not an animal, so I don't. Instead, with as much dignity as I can muster, I climb to my feet, gripping my plate with both hands.

"I must say, Briggs." I don't even bother to hide my contempt. "Your excuse of needing to use the loo? It's particularly piss-poor." He stares up at me, open-mouthed, while I continue. "Perhaps, if you ate some *actual* food, you'd find it easier to control your bowels."

I spin on my heel and—plate and all—scramble over the fence, and leave.

I'm still so keyed up after my run-in with Harrisford that Heloise almost cancels our trip to the city to meet with the MLO. I wave away her concern, desperate to get away from Seamere and put Harrisford Briggs as far as possible from my mind.

We arrive on the street where the Galloping Gytrash is, apparently, though I see no evidence of its entrance. We're in a divey sort of neighborhood, where the buildings are crammed close together and the walls are covered in graffiti.

Heli stops in front of a manhole in the ground, then turns to me.

"Ready?" She fusses with my collar and pats down my hair.

Tonight, Heloise has put a glamour on me. Unlike Harrisford's glamour, which made me look a million times better than my usual self, Heli's glamour has effectively turned me into a completely different person. I don't know why, but she's made me look a little bit like the actor who plays Loki—and I'm not a hundred percent sure I'm comfortable with it.

Still, I'm not planning on being here long. I just want enough time to gather some intelligence. Then we'll get out as soon as possible.

"I'm ready," I say, bracing myself. I'm not really being honest—my heart is thumping so hard that it could almost escape my chest. Going undercover and infiltrating a secret meeting of what is apparently a terrorist organization was never on my final-year bingo card. Yet here we are.

"All right, then," says Heli. She's glamoured to look like one of the sixth-year students—a big, burly Black man whose name escapes me but who is really, really good at Flaugball. "Let's go in."

I cast a look around, frowning. There don't seem to be any open shop fronts, and no secret entrances to speak of. "How?"

She gives me an enigmatic smile, then points at the ground—at the manhole.

I knit my eyebrows. "There?" I say skeptically.

Heloise clamps her arms straight down against her body and takes a brisk step forward as though she's walking off the end of a diving board.

And then . . . she's gone. Just, disappeared.

My head swivels, my mind rebelling against what I've seen. Then, her voice floats up from somewhere below the manhole. "Come on, Gwen!"

I step forward myself, expecting to be sucked down into some sort of magical chute. But nothing happens. The sole of my shoe meets solid metal, and I stamp on it in frustration.

"I can't," I call down. "It . . . it won't let me through."

A disembodied laugh echoes right up through the grate. "Yes, you can, Gwen," Heli says. "You just have to believe."

Believe? Oh no. Not that mumbo-jumbo esoteric stuff. Yes, I'm studying magical veterinary sciences—*sciences* being the operative word in that sentence. I believe in magic, of course I do, but only when it's contextual and framed in a logical way.

But this? *Believing* in oneself? That sounds more like something you'd see being flogged by some fundamentalist church guy in a cheap polyester suit on early-morning Sunday television.

I suppose, though, if I'm going to make it to the MLO meeting, I'm going to have to put aside my judgment.

"Here goes nothing," I mutter to myself, crossing my arms over my chest. Then, letting my eyelids flutter closed, I take a deep, steadying breath—and jump.

Surprisingly, I go right through the solid metal, landing in a lumpy, wing-back armchair. The bar itself is cozier and less shabby than the streetscape above suggested. There are overstuffed couches upholstered in dated floral tapestry lined up against the walls. Before them, low tables are set with tiny magelights flickering in terracotta holders, and there are bare bulbs swinging from a slightly cracked ceiling. The wall is emblazoned with tastefully done graffiti art that displays the name of the venue. At one end of the room, an overstuffed set of bookshelves contains haphazardly stacked books, and at the other end a dimly lit bar is manned by a bartender who might actually be an orc.

After giving Pen's password to a security guard who's wearing a baseball cap pulled down low, Heli and I sidle into the crowded back room. There's someone sitting in the middle, murmuring in a low voice. I can't see their face, but they look like the leader—the rest of the MLO members are listening in rapt attention.

And then, finally, in the dim light of this divey bar, the speaker raises their head. They have thick black hair that cascades down to their waist, brown skin, and a golden nose stud. And I gasp, and grab Heloise's arm, because, because . . .

Because the MLO woman who's leading the meeting is none other than the Dean of Seamere: the esteemed, the venerated Professor Anika Kaur.

29

Harrisford

Danny has noticed that I've been in a foul mood since the gala and has basically forced me into coming out. So Friday evening after class, I go to meet him. My head is still spinning from the disastrous interaction I'd had with Gwendolynne when we'd run into each other at the qílín's paddock.

The conversation had been going—if not well, at least tolerably—until I'd mentioned Nathaniel, and remembered the Magecorp CEO's barely veiled threat. The memory had brought home the fact that I need to keep my distance from Gwendolynne Chan if I want to have any hope of staying motivated enough to get through final exams. I'd got too fucking close to her, close enough to want to throw myself at her feet and let her step all over me. I'd already willingly given her the qílín delivery. She'd earned far more marks than I had, once I'd sent in the report.

The truth is, if I spend any more time with this woman, I'll probably end up purposely failing the exams just to avoid seeing her disappointed.

My mood is enveloped in a cloud of gloom as I push my way into the crowded pub. Right away, I spot Danny sitting at the bar. He waves at me, his arm still bandaged—the bite he'd sustained from his snake, Artemis, is taking longer than usual to heal—and I weave between the clusters of tables until I drop down into the seat beside him.

"Drink up," he says, pushing a pint of beer toward me. It's a pale ale, the exact type I like, but tonight it tastes like cardboard in my mouth.

"So, mate," Danny says after we've both drunk silently for a while. I swipe beer froth off my lip with a napkin. "What's the deal between you and Gwen?"

I splutter, coughing up flecks of beer, and Danny has to thump me between the shoulder blades until I stop. "Nothing," I say, when I've finally ceased expectorating the entire contents of my lungs. "No deal. Absolutely nothing."

"You two've been spending a lot of time together, though." Danny half turns to face me, leaning one of his elbows on the counter, and calmly takes a swig of beer. "Bridie tells me you've been seen going in and out of her room."

"Tell Bridie to mind her own damn business." I glower at my drink, my shoulders hunched, fingers flexing around the glass. The condensation is cool and damp beneath my palm. "If you must know, Danny, she . . . Gwendolynne helped me patch up Pudding. On the night of the first gala. That's all."

His eyes spark with amusement. "You brought *Pudding*? To a gala? Man, oh man, you just can't help yourself—"

Cutting him off, I snap, "Yeah, well, Pudding's kind of hard to say no to."

Danny chuckles. "Don't I know it."

I heard that, Pudding says, from where she is curled up inside my pocket. Her voice is unamused.

"Go back to sleep," I grouse at her, only half jesting.

Danny polishes off his beer and signals to the bartender for another. "So Gwendolynne really isn't . . . up to anything? Even though there've been abnormal magic fluctuations coming from her dorm room for the past one and a half weeks?"

Why is he asking about Gwendolynne? "Not that I'm aware of." I give a grim smile. "Perhaps it's just the residue from my vastly superior magic levels."

My friend shoves me in the shoulder, and I chuckle. But inside, my gut is clenching. My chest feels tight. And I am pretty sure it's because what I'm telling Danny is true: that Gwendolynne and I aren't "up to" anything. We haven't been "up to" anything since the disastrous events of the gala.

In fact, after tonight's conversation, and the absolute contempt she'd shown me before she'd climbed the fence and stomped off . . . Not to mention the way she'd dismissed the kiss we'd shared as being "nothing" . . .

I don't think we'll be "up to" anything—possibly ever again.

Once Danny takes his leave, keen to get back to Bridie, I shove my hands in my pockets and begin the slow trudge to London General Magical Hospital, which is just up the street from the pub.

I haven't been to visit my father since Sunday, the day after the explosion. It feels remiss of me, but I'd been too caught up in investigating the surges with Gwendolynne. Besides, the daily updates from the nurses told me that Father still hadn't woken up, so I figured he wouldn't care whether I was there. Though, truth be told, he probably wouldn't even care were he *not* in a coma.

Today, though, I'm supposed to sign some paperwork to extend the duration of his stay.

The lift doors *ding*, and I stride out. As I draw closer to his room, my footsteps start to drag.

Stopping before the vending machine, I lean my forehead on it, the cool glass freezing against my flushed skin. Then I purchase a drink with my strap, almost jumping when the aluminum can crashes to the bottom.

Now that I know about the tethers, and have been soundly unsuccessful in my search for them, I rather wish I could just straight up ask my father. Surely he knows more than he was letting on when Gwendolynne interrogated him at the vault?

If he dies, we'll never know.

But then again, if he survives, it's likely he wouldn't answer anyway—conscious or unconscious. And I can't very well search his strap since the police confiscated it following the explosion.

I gulp down the drink in one go, tossing the empty can into the recycling bin before swiping at my mouth with my sleeve. The carbonated liquid churns in my stomach, and I have to stop myself from doubling over in front of my father's room and being sick all over the linoleum.

There's really no point. No point going in. My father is in a coma, with zero awareness of the outside world. And truth be told, I dread it: Seeing him is just like holding a mirror up to all my flaws and defects.

Whether he lives or dies has no bearing on *me*.

I'm just about to turn around and leave when a nurse sticks their head out of the room. "Ah, Mr. Briggs," they say. "Glad you're here. We need you to make a decision on signing the DNR."

My gut gives a lurch. A DNR—do not resuscitate—order would mean the staff wouldn't attempt to revive my father if he went into cardiorespiratory arrest. Not that the probability of recovery is very high, of course. But choosing whether or not they'll even try? That feels significant.

The nurse raises their eyebrows expectantly. To keep up appearances, I have no choice but to follow them inside the room.

The door closes behind me with a low-pitched squeal. And there he is, my father, his body making peaks and valleys of the sheets. His face looks more wan and sunken than it did just five days ago. The wheeze of the ventilator and the beep of the monitoring equipment are like screams that punctuate the still, dead air.

I have no idea how I'm going to make the decision. Do I want my father to live . . . or die?

Deciding on his fate feels like too much responsibility, and I don't quite know if I'm up to the task. If you'd asked me straight after he'd attacked Gwendolynne and held a gun to her head, or after my conversation with Nathaniel had reminded me of him and his blackmailing ways, I would've signed the DNR with absolutely no hesitation. In fact, if you'd caught me at the right moment, I might even have come into this room and unplugged his machine myself.

Is that the rational decision, though? According to my (many) therapists, I can be impulsive, irrational, and prone to making bad decisions. Is this one of those situations? I can't tell.

And can I judge him for blackmailing me, when I—in an act that truly cements me as his son—did the very same to Gwendolynne? My memory strays to the multiple times I'd threatened to tell Dean Kaur about Percy, and my heart seizes with guilt, as though it's been clamped in a vise. Thinking about our fight in the drug cupboard is like twisting the key. Tighter, tighter. I clutch my chest. Fuck, I was a right arsehole.

I have to admit, once and for all, that my father and I are the same—whether or not I wish to believe it.

Staring at him, I half fancy that if I watch him for long enough, perhaps I'll be able to read his mind. To know what he is thinking. To, once and for all, figure my father out.

But I can't. He's just as locked up as ever, even before the coma.

He'd been lying to me: lying about being in Wales, lying about his role at Magecorp, lying about the employees who had died on his watch.

Standing beside his bed, looking down at him, I'm suddenly transported back to my childhood. I'm four years old again, watching him from the corner as he stampedes through the house in a rage, discarding all of my mother's things. I'm twelve, and he's shunting me off to boarding school without so much as a backward glance. I'm eighteen, and he's rebuffing my offer to kick back with beers and watch a game of Flaugball. And the feeling that washes through my body isn't sadness because of his condition. It isn't even the pure rage I feel for what he did to Gwendolynne. It's a deep and wretched nostalgia for a life that has never been, for a future that never will be, for a father-son relationship that he's never deemed us worthy enough to have.

My fingers clench into fists, then uncurl, then clench again. The room tilts, and white spots cloud my vision.

There it is: the emotion—the *rage*—that I've been missing, cresting through my body: a deadly tidal wave.

I lean forward and brace my hands on the bed, breathing through my fury. The room is silent, save for the incessant beeping of the machines and the constant whir-pump of the ventilator. I stay like that for what feels like eons, though when I raise my head to glance at the clock, only a few minutes have passed.

Eventually, ignoring the way my body is shaking, I push myself up to standing, turn, and walk right out the door.

I don't pause. I don't look back. I've made my decision about the DNR. If my father stops breathing, if he goes into cardiorespiratory arrest . . .

Then so be it. I'm going to let him die.

I'm almost out the front entrance when someone shouts my name from behind me. Well, they shout "Mr. Briggs" several times, in escalating pitch, until I'm forced to turn around.

I finally pivot to see a young nurse in tight pink scrubs pushing her way through the crowds in the lobby. "Mr. Briggs," she says again, rather breathily, having evidently pursued me through the corridors.

It's late, and I'm exhausted, and I'm still so *fucking* angry, so I frown and say, "Please, call me Harrisford. Mr. Briggs is my father."

"All right . . . Harrisford," she says haltingly, testing the weight of my name on her tongue. Then she blushes prettily, her eyelashes fluttering as she blinks up at me.

I'm used to this reaction from women—whenever they talk to me, or I talk to them, or sometimes even as soon as they see my face—but for one of the first times ever I'm completely immune to it. She's objectively attractive, with smooth tanned skin and dark glossy hair, and about the same height as Gwendolynne Chan—

Stop it, Briggs. Good lord, why am I comparing everyone and everything to Gwendolynne lately? It's like I can't get that goddamned woman out of my mind, even for a fucking second.

I sigh again. "Do you need me to sign more forms?" As I'd passed the reception desk, I'd dutifully signed the hospital paperwork . . . including scribbling my signature, pressing the pen harder than truly necessary, at the bottom of the Do Not Resuscitate form. Perhaps—in my hurry to exit the hospital with its glaring lights and crowds of people and its sanitized smell of death—I'd missed one.

"No," she says, flushing harder, her gaze sliding down to my shoes. I'm making her so nervous that she cannot even look at me.

"It's just—my boss has asked me to check if you could possibly see a centaur."

The nurse continues to shoot covert glances my way as we walk side by side to the emergency wards, where the centaur is apparently waiting.

Centaurs are an ethical conundrum when it comes to medical treatment. Seeing as they are half-human, half-horse, debates have raged for centuries as to whether they're under the purview of human medicine or should be treated by us vets. Throughout history, both laws and public opinion have swayed from one extreme to the other: sometimes categorizing centaurs as human, and other times classifying them as beasts. More recently, in the twenty-first century, the laws have been updated to officially define them as both. Hence, the official policy is that they attend human hospitals for anything pertaining to their heads and torsos, and veterinary hospitals for problems related to anything else.

The issue is, the centaurs don't always listen. For one, they consider themselves entirely above the common laws and tribulations of humans. And second, they often get mixed up and show up to the wrong kind of hospital. Especially when they happen to be—

"Barnabus," I mutter as I round the corner to find the dark-haired centaur inside the pen.

"All right, Harrisford?" he says, grinning, then lets out a loud belch. His hair and tail are both tangled and snarled with leaves and sticks. "Old friend."

Barnabus isn't my friend, really. It's just that we have something of a tumultuous history. He's shown up to the veterinary hospital before, repeatedly, drunk to the point of collapse. Many times I've had to either bundle him into an ambulance to be taken to the hospital, or patch him up as best I can with the materials that I had on hand—while simultaneously trying *not* to alert Seamere management to the fact that I'd illegitimately treated the front half of a centaur.

I only do it because when he drinks, which is almost always, he can become aggressive without any warning. And a bucking, belligerent, seven-hundred-kilogram centaur is not something to be blasé about.

Therefore, it's usually just easier to do what needs to be done as quickly as humanly possible and then send him off on his merry way.

Most of his injuries are simple: cuts and bumps and scrapes from his constantly inebriated state. Most of them can be healed by magic, but occasionally he also needs stitches. Tonight, though, I immediately notice that he's not putting weight on one hoof. It's his front left limb, and he's toe-touching it, lifting it every now and then as though it is really sore.

Why'd you come here, *Barnabus?* I want to groan at him, but he's got that vicious glint in his eye that tells me that if I question it, he may well decide to kick my teeth out.

Raf Malik—the poor sod of a junior doctor who seems to always be on duty, and therefore has also dealt with drunken Barnabus many a time—crams his stethoscope in the pocket of his lab coat. "All yours, mate," he says, giving a quick wave as he takes his leave. It's clear he cannot get out of here fast enough. The door eases shut behind him with a whine.

After placing Pudding carefully on top of a stainless steel trolley, I sigh, roll my sleeves up to my elbows, and get to work. The nurse who accompanied me hangs around, giving obsequious smiles and offering to assist me "in any way she can," so I make her useful by asking her to fetch some coveralls and the tools they keep for this exact purpose. The hospital stocks things like hoof testers and hoof knives just in case—though the tools look at least fifty years old and are horrendously inferior to what I'm used to.

Once equipped, I lift Barnabus's foot, propping it on my knee, and lever off his shoe. Then I palpate his pulses and, with Pudding helping me to harness the atmospheric magic, check his aura for a localized area of pain. Once I find it, I start digging away at the sole with the hoof knife, while the nurse hovers around us, making awe-struck eyes at me. She's apparently never seen anyone do veterinary work on a centaur before.

"Ow," Barnabus bellows as I hit a particularly tender spot. "Easy, now, mate. You'll take me bloomin' foot off!" He hiccups, and for once I'm kind of glad that's he's so utterly drunk, as it'll make this entire process far less unpleasant for the both of us.

"I won't be much longer," I say, my breaths puffing. Centaurs are bigger than normal horses—and far bigger than fine-boned unicorns—and their legs are fucking heavy.

Barnabus lapses into silence for a few minutes, the only sound the soft scraping of my knife. Then his voice turns pensive, ponderous, brooding.

"Death stalks you, Harrisford Briggs."

The nurse gasps, but my movements barely falter; I've heard all this before. I can never treat Barnabus the centaur without him predicting some horrific fate for me. But everyone knows that centaur astrology is hazy science at best.

"The stars of your birth are—"

"—shrouded in misfortune. Yes, I know, Barnabus." Finally finished draining the abscess, I busy myself with applying a poultice. Once it's in place, I lower his hoof and start brushing the debris from the legs of my coveralls. "You've told me that before."

He squints at me blearily as I scribble down doses of pain relief for one of the doctors to dispense.

"But, mate, the stars've shifted since last I saw you." His golden eyes are slightly unfocused. "Things've changed for you, and trust me"—he leers—"it ain't for the better."

I raise my head to look at him as he sways on all four of his feet. This actually *is* new. I can usually recite all of Barnabus's and my conversations verbatim, since they're pretty much always the same. This, though, is the first time he's ever deviated from our usual, well-trodden script. "Oh?"

He lets out yet another alcoholic belch. I fan my face, trying not to inhale the stale, acerbic stench.

"Yes," he says finally, a hand pressed to his belly, trying to force out another burp. "It involves a person who you care for . . . very much."

Someone I care for? Not my father, surely? My gaze strays upward, to the ceiling, as though if I stare hard enough, perhaps I will penetrate the fifteen layers of concrete that separate us.

Do I care for him? That's a complicated question. I'm furious at him; I feel like I'll never forgive him. I've just signed a Do Not Resuscitate order, for Chrissakes.

The distance between us is a yawning chasm, the gap impossible to traverse. He's still my father, yes, but one can feel a pull toward one's blood relatives without actually *caring* for them one whit.

Yet . . . who else could it be? My mother? I did care about her, once—but she's been gone for so long that I doubt she even counts.

And while I'm friends with Danny, and we hang out a lot, it's more a friendship of convenience. I wouldn't say we particularly care much for one another.

Then, of course, there's Gwendolynne. Considering how little I know her, and how much she openly hates me, it seems ludicrous that the centaur could be talking about her. But then again, if you took all the people I associate with, bottled up my feelings for them, and then put said bottles in a line . . . Gwendolynne's would be the only one even remotely full.

In fact, as much as I'm loath to admit it, her bottle would be overflowing.

If it *is* Gwendolynne, by some stretch of the imagination, then what is Barnabus trying to say? Will he tell me that Gwendolynne will actually forgive me? Will he tell me not to worry, I can associate with her and still manage to pass my exams? Or will he tell me that she and I—my heart skips a beat—are actually destined to be together?

My gut is churning, my palms sweaty. I swallow, my Adam's apple feeling abnormally large, then wipe my hands on my robes. The nurse side-eyes me, clearly wondering at my reaction. "Well, what is it, Barnabus?" The words burst from my lips, brittle with impatience. "Spit it out. Tell me what is going to happen."

Suddenly lucid, Barnabus fixes me with both of his bloodshot eyes.

"According to the stars," he says, "the person you care about most will betray you."

30

Gwendolynne

Heloise and I follow Professor Kaur out of the bar once the meeting has finished. We hadn't learned much at the Galloping Gytrash, except the names of MLO members who had died—a detail we already knew. Plus that there is an MLO leader, someone even higher up than Anika Kaur, who is currently officially at large. It's all highly classified, apparently, but the missing leader is still on the run.

We trail the dean and her dog, Lenny, for three and a half blocks. They turn into a dingy alleyway before she finally turns around and sighs. "Miss Chapman, Miss Chan, you can come out now. I know you're there." Lenny sits on his haunches, his nose raised, sniffing the air.

We emerge from the shadows, chagrined. I thought we'd been pretty stealthy, but my career pivot into a life of petty crime would have to wait, I guess.

"How did you know it was us?" Heloise seems genuinely shocked.

"Come on, ladies." She gestures to her face. "Legally blind, remember? I've learned to recognize people by their auras, not by their appearances. Your glamours don't work on me."

We shuffle our feet. The fact that this didn't occur to us is actually a bit embarrassing.

"What are you doing here, anyway?" The dean puts her hands on her hips. "Are you thinking of joining the MLO?"

"No," I say quickly. "It's just . . . We were . . . We were . . ." I'm grasping for an excuse. Professor Kaur knows that I don't usually go to places like the Galloping Gytrash.

"We were wondering how you are," Heloise interjects smoothly, obviously the better liar of the two of us. "Professor Pickering said you were too ill to attend the lecture, and we were just . . . you know . . . worried."

Professor Kaur's face softens, and she gives a tinkling laugh. "Ill? Is that what they're telling you?" She shakes her head. "Heavens, Thomas is really a vile, sneaky little . . ." She trails off into a series of vulgar curse words.

"Thomas?" I blurt out. "Do you mean Professor Pickering, the vice dean?"

She grimaces. "The very same. I should have seen it coming. He's been trying to get my job since he first started."

"He lied?" Heloise's eyes are wide, the moonlight glinting off the sclera. To Heli and me, an actual *professor* lying is so ludicrous it's unbelievable.

The dean sighs. "Yes, Miss Chapman, he lied. I haven't been ill. I was formally suspended."

"Suspended?" I gape at her. "But why?"

Professor Kaur shrugs, then turns slightly to lean her back against the alley wall. "I'm quite sure it's got something to do with Magecorp. He's been in their pocket for *years*. They've been bidding to provide funding to Seamere for almost a decade, and I've blocked it every time. Thomas would *love* to get rid of me and let them make him their Seamere puppet."

"And they suspended you . . . why? Because of your involvement with the MLO?"

"They can't prove anything—not yet, anyway—but they suspect. If I were just a regular member, they probably wouldn't have a legal case. But if they find out how high up I am—"

"You're leader of the MLO?" asks Heli slowly.

"Acting leader," the dean says. "I stepped into this role twenty-one years ago, when the actual leader was forced to go under cover."

"Who's the actual leader?" I'm not expecting a straight answer but still feel it's worth a try.

The professor gives a small, tight smile. "Only a select few people are allowed to know that, Miss Chan. For safety reasons. We've kept the secret for decades—we're not about to give it up now."

I deflate a little, though truthfully it was a bit delusional to even bother asking. "So, why the MLO? Is it because you're anti-Magecorp?"

Pen Ferguson's involvement is one thing, but this? The fact that our honorable, upstanding dean is involved with the Magical Liberation Organization is seriously spinning me out. If the media is to be believed, the MLO are a bunch of radicalists. Degenerates. Terrorists. And to be fair, they *have* spent the past few decades sowing discord and blowing the living shit out of things.

And now, they're possibly killing people in their efforts to sabotage Magecorp. How could Professor Kaur align herself with . . . with that?

Crossing her arms, Professor Kaur purses her lips. "I'm a scientist, Miss Chan. I've devoted my whole career to investigating how magic works, how we can best use it to help as many animals as possible." She raises her head, and it strikes me how tired she looks. How pale and drawn her face is, how deep the lines are between her brows. "I'm anti anything that prevents magic from getting to those who need it."

"Like Magecorp." I clutch my head, which is starting to hurt.

"Yes," Professor Kaur says. "You'd be shocked if you knew what really goes on behind the scenes. Linksphere's slightly better, but not by much."

I brace myself, gathering courage, not wanting to let the opportunity to quiz Professor Kaur go to waste. "Is it Magecorp, then, that's behind the surges, Professor?"

"The surges aren't caused by Magecorp," she says, but she's looking cagey.

I raise my chin. My palms are sweating, but I have to ask. "Are they caused by the MLO?"

Professor Kaur stays silent for what feels like a very long time. "If you really want to know what's happening, Miss Chan," she says. "I'd suggest you go to the sixteenth floor of the London General Magical Hospital. I think you'll find it . . . illuminating."

Heli straightens her posture. "We will do, Professor. Thank you."

The dean grabs ahold of Lenny's harness and turns to leave. But at the last moment, she says one final thing to us over her shoulder.

"Listen—keep your ears to the ground. I'll send you both notice of the next MLO meeting. I know you're both smart young women with your heads screwed on straight." She presses her lips together for a moment before adding, "I'm quite sure that once you're better informed, you'll both want to attend."

Then she strides right past us, exiting the alley.

Security at the hospital is normally tight, but since everyone knows that Heloise is the daughter of the famous Dr. Nora Chapman, they let us walk right in.

In the bathrooms, we re-assume our glamours—not even Heloise would be allowed to enter the top-secret sixteenth floor—and change into the spare pairs of scrubs we'd luckily stashed in our bags after class.

It's a short ride up in the lift. The doors *ding*, opening to reveal a stark white corridor lit by garish fluorescent magelights. Ahead of us is a set of double doors. We try them, but they're locked. Fortunately, I still have Harrisford's *resignio* spell, since I'd never successfully used it at Magecorp HQ.

After using the spell to illegally unlock the door, we slip inside. The door shuts behind us with a soft click. Reflexively, I try the door handle—it doesn't budge—and my heart flips in my chest.

With the door locked behind us and no more *resignio*, we're stuck here. I guess we'll just have to make sure we don't get caught.

We creep forward. Directly ahead of us is an operating theater, visible through a large viewing window, with perhaps a dozen doctors and nurses, all in surgical gowns, operating on a patient. The room is abnormally bright, even for a theater; all of the surgeons' faces are lit up by an incandescent glow.

The patient is completely covered with sterile drapes, so I can't see what part they're operating on. But then I'm hit with that feeling again, the same one I had on the top floor of Magecorp: something sirenlike calling to me. It slithers beneath my skin, at once both invasive and strangely pleasurable.

The Source. The rock that Conall found in his research. I understand now why the room is so bright, why the lights are so dazzlingly intense. Whatever these doctors are doing in the theater, it has something to do with the Source. Is this what Professor Kaur wanted us to see?

The sound of voices sends Heloise and me scurrying behind an enormous bin on wheels that is piled high with discarded drapes. We crouch behind it, watching as two men in suits stroll to the viewing window.

My chest tightens. My heart thumps. I feel like I can't breathe.

I recognize the taller of the two men. I recognize his shock of gray hair, his pointy nose, his slightly undershot chin.

The man is my familiar's ex-owner, Mr. Nathaniel Price. But what is the Magecorp CEO doing *here*?

Inside the theater, the surgeons have finished closing the patient's wound, and nurses are moving around the surgical table, removing the sterile drapes. As the person beneath is exposed, I see that the incision is on the back of their neck, right at the base of their skull. I swallow, feeling sick.

If I'm interpreting the scene correctly, it seems the surgeons have just finished implanting a fragment of Source into a human. One look at Heloise's horrified expression tells me that she's come to the same conclusion.

Does it mean what I think it means? That we've been looking in the wrong place: It isn't the MLO that have started using humans instead of objects to tether portals. That it's actually *Magecorp* doing it?

I don't have time to mull this over, because already the patient is being transferred to a gurney and wheeled into the recovery room next door. The head doctor pulls down his mask, shucks off his surgical gown and mask, and tosses them into the basket.

"That's the last of them for today, then?" the doctor asks Nathaniel Price.

"Yes," Mr. Price says. "We have more tethers, but since the explosion—not enough Source."

The doctor gives a tired sigh. "You'd better figure out a way to keep this one alive, then. Or else there's going to be a worldwide magic shortage."

"You think I don't know that?" snaps Mr. Price.

Heloise and I shoot each other a glance. There's been nothing—*nothing*—in the news about a global shortage.

The shorter suited man—who I assume is Nathaniel's assistant—pulls out a tablet and starts tapping at it. "Have you thought about using one of the reserve tethers, sir?" He talks very fast, all the while pulling up file after file, which I can't see clearly at a distance. "Patient 39 might be a good candidate. Their Source was implanted so long ago, it will have built up a significant capacity. They might be the only individual capable of holding a long-term tether." He tilts the tablet toward Nathaniel, showing him something. "If we station 39 as the tether *inside* the Void, then our models suggest that they could hold the portal open for quite some time. We can just swap out the tethers on the outside as they burn out. This, at least, would reduce our need for new tethers and Source by something approaching fifty percent."

There's a pause. Mr. Price clasps his hands behind his back and rocks slightly on his feet. "Patient 39 is proving somewhat . . . difficult at this stage."

The short man frowns at his boss. "Will you reveal their identity to us, sir? I can have my team pay them . . . a *visit*. See if we can apply some pressure in a *different* sort of way."

"No." Mr. Price's voice is decisive. "Not yet, Jarvis. I know your thugs are champing at the bit to get their hands on this one, but I've got it covered."

"But, sir—"

"I have it covered." His tone brooks no argument.

I shiver. So the tethers are humans implanted with the Source, who help to keep the Void tears open. And not only that, they need *two* per portal: one inside, one out.

How long has Magecorp been doing this? It sounds like a while.

Perhaps it's always been the case: Magecorp exploiting human beings as tethers in order to plunder the Void. Sweat has sprung out across my forehead and along my upper lip. I swipe at it, keeping my eyes trained on the men, not wanting to miss anything.

"Perhaps you can look into magic-rationing spells," says the doctor. "They're a little unconventional, but they work. You'll need blood, though, and lots of it, if you want to amplify your stores of magic enough to meet current demand."

Mr. Price unclasps his hands from behind his back and scratches at his chin. "Good thought. This place has a well-stocked blood bank, doesn't it? Perhaps we can come to some sort of . . . arrangement." It's obvious he means a monetary arrangement. "Jarvis!"

Jarvis starts, almost dropping his tablet. "Yes, sir?"

"Schedule a meeting between myself and the hospital director."

"Yes, of course, very good, sir," Jarvis says, swiping his finger across his screen.

The doctor tugs off his surgical cap and goes to put it in the bin. But for the first time, he's looking right at us. At the angle he's now at, the bin's not quite large enough to obscure both Heli and me.

"You two," the doctor says, his voice commanding. "What are you doing just standing there? This bin is overflowing. Take it down to the garbage disposal, now."

We're sufficiently glamoured that neither of them recognizes Heloise—and I wouldn't be recognizable to them either. Thankful for Heli's spell skills, we hop to it, wheeling the bin through the hallway and into the open lift.

The three men continue to converse in low voices as the lift doors slide closed. As soon as we're shut in, we sag against the wall.

"Did you hear that, Gwen?" Heli says, wrinkling her nose. "It's *Magecorp* using the people as tethers."

"I know." My mouth pulls down. "That must have been what

Professor Kaur meant when she said we'd be shocked by what was happening."

Heloise turns her big brown eyes toward me. They're glinting with a sheen of tears. "How have they kept this covered up so long? All these people . . . *dying*?"

I shake my head, thinking of Hani Nguyen. Elouise Forrester. Benjamin Purcell. All the other Magecorp employees and MLO members who have died. Have Magecorp always killed people so that the rest of us can have a convenient source of magic? Was it just that they'd managed to cover it up—with their powerful connections and influence?

"Money buys silence, I guess," I say, suddenly bone-weary, and Heli and I stay quiet for the rest of the ride down.

I'm so preoccupied with our revelation that I don't even see him leaning against the hospital reception desk until it's entirely too late.

We've taken off our glamours—it would be suspicious for Heloise to have been seen going in, but not seen coming back out again. So I'm looking like myself once more when I crash into Harrisford Briggs's broad back.

At first, I'm irate—*what is he doing here?*—before I remember that his father is still in a coma following the Magecorp vault explosion. I suspect he had come for a visit, even though Darghan Briggs is a murderous maniac and doesn't deserve any sympathy at all. But that's Harrisford for you, I guess. He'd made it clear he'd prioritize his family over anything else when he'd stopped me from going to the police.

Harrisford half turns. At least he looks shocked at seeing me; his eyes widen, his mouth hangs open. I look between him and the nurse he'd been chatting to, who's still staring up at him with cloyingly lovesick eyes.

It only takes me a second to register what is happening. The two of them are standing next to the reception desk. Harrisford is leaning against it, one elbow propped atop its surface. The nurse, a pretty young woman dressed in hot pink scrubs, is nestled close to him, her hand resting on his shoulder. The name tag displayed prominently on her chest reads LUCY. As we'd approached, I'd noticed her—not realizing it was Harrisford she was speaking to—and she'd been chatting animatedly at him, before she'd reached up and adjusted his shirt collar.

It's an intimate sort of gesture, and something inside me twists painfully. But then I grit my teeth. I don't care who Harrisford speaks to, or how many cute nurses he flirts with. This is all *exactly* in line with what I've heard about his personality—that he's a player, a ladies' man, someone who toys with people's hearts as though they're nothing more than battered Flaugballs.

I'm half expecting Percy to say something snarky, but he's oddly silent. The emptiness resounding in my head is jarring. Perhaps he's preoccupied somewhere and not bothering to read my thoughts.

Harrisford opens his mouth, as though he's about to speak. But I grab Heli's arm and push right past the two of them—before he has the chance to say anything at all.

When I arrive home, it's to a darkened room and a conspicuously absent Percy. Normally, he'd be stalking back and forth in front of his empty bowl, meowing loudly, as if to announce to the world how cruel I am for only feeding him at regular, twelve-hour intervals.

But tonight he's not here. He's not in front of his bowl. He's not curled up on the bed. The desk chair is empty, as is the space on top of the bookshelf—one of his favorite surveillance spots.

My stomach clenches as it dawns on me: He's been oddly quiet all evening. After he got snippy about my cucumber comment, he'd lapsed into an extended silence. I guess I'd thought that maybe he was stewing over my insinuation that he was a scaredy-cat, but since I'd unofficially adopted him, he's never gone *this* long without intruding on my thoughts.

Heli comes up behind me as I take a shaky breath, trying to stem the rising tide of anxiety beating in my chest. "G, what's wrong?"

I don't answer immediately. "It's Percy. He's . . . he's not here."

"That's weird." Heli's lips pull down slightly. "Can you feel him down your bond?"

"What?" I stammer, flustered, staring unseeingly at my best friend. I'm so new to owning a familiar that psychically feeling for his presence never even occurred to me.

Heli's voice is soft, sympathetic. "Just . . . close your eyes and see if you can feel him."

Scrunching my eyes shut, I reach for him through the silence. There's nothing. Absolutely nothing. And I realize, too late, why I'd been so panicked.

The emptiness inside my head *isn't* just Percy sulking. It's a total absence of his life force. My mind feels like it did before I even adopted him.

How? How could our bond be severed? As I search my tiny room for a second—and then a third—time, my brain goes into overdrive, flipping through every possible scenario.

But when it fails to come up with another rational explanation, I turn to Heli slowly, my entire body beginning to tremble.

"He's gone," I say, unable to hide the wobble in my voice. "Percy is gone."

31

Harrisford

It takes me a few seconds to register what I've just seen.

Gwendolynne is here. *Gwendolynne is here.*

The nurse who's been rabbiting on for the past five minutes about goodness knows what—I was only pretending to listen to be polite, since she'd helped me so much with Barnabus—slides her hand further up my shoulder. "Harrisford?" she says, looking up at me. Just before Gwendolynne had rammed into me from behind, the nurse had giggled and said I still had some centaur hoof fragments dirtying my collar. And before I'd had a chance to stop her, she'd reached up and started vigorously brushing imaginary bits of debris off.

And then Gwendolynne had run into me. *Literally* run into me. And I'd been jolted out of my thoughts as I'd stared at her, shocked, looking like a total pillock.

"Excuse me, er—" I push the nurse's hand off my shoulder, realizing I don't even know her name. "I've got to go." The nurse looks stricken as I sprint off, having not asked for her name *or* her number.

By the time I make it to the top of the front steps, skidding to a stop, Gwendolynne is nowhere to be seen. I stand, panting for a few seconds, scanning the crowds for a glimpse of her. But she's gone. Well and truly gone.

A few minutes later, I've jammed on my helmet, climbed on my motorbike, and am speeding along the motorway toward Seamere.

As I ride, clouds of dust billowing around me, I think about what an idiot I've been. I'd thought the best course of action would be to maintain my distance, keep my head down, and focus on exams. Then, once we'd graduated and I've secured the Ministry position, I'd never have to see—or yearn for—Gwendolynne again.

But tonight—seeing her, feeling her body up against mine, catching the scent of her perfume . . . Even that fleeting touch, that briefest of looks, has ignited all of my past feelings back into sweltering intensity.

I'm being utterly foolish. I know I am. There are so many reasons why chasing after Gwendolynne is a fundamentally bad idea. It's not just because we're each other's number one rivals, and have been for the past seven years. But it's also the fact that the more I think about it, the more I'm starting to suspect that Barnabus *was* talking about Gwendolynne. I can't think of anyone else whom I care about, who is also in a position to betray me.

How will she betray me? Was it something to do with the hospital? Is she still thinking of going against my request and taking my father's confession to the police? I mean, it's not that I don't want my father to get his comeuppance—I do. But to have the police sniffing around my family's affairs?

It's too risky. There are too many secrets, too many skeletons in our closets . . . Plus, it would put Gwendolynne herself at risk. The police might figure out she caused the explosion at Magecorp HQ. Or whoever is sabotaging Magecorp might get wind that she's investigating and turn their focus onto her.

No. We can't involve the police. The stakes are far too high.

And yet, even with all these reasons, I'm still desperate to see her again. It's a bit of a shock, honestly, to realize that as concerned as I am for my safety, I'm even more worried about hers. This is . . . unprecedented. I've never had to concern myself with anyone outside my small, privileged bubble before.

You've lost it, Briggs, I tell myself. My stomach is churning, bitter bile coating the back of my throat. *You're a wretch. You will never, ever escape her now.*

She's walked away from me twice tonight, and it's excruciating how that made me feel.

It's not a trap, Harrisford, Pudding says gently, from where she's perched up on my handlebars. *Loving someone is not a trap.*

Do I love her? Maybe I do. I've never had to love a person before, not since I was four years old. And I don't quite know how it's supposed to feel.

For twenty-one years, I've been channeling what little compassion I have into caring for my bearded dragon, because when you're four, and your mother disappears suddenly, and then a few days later you get a pet, that's the only thing that keeps you from going completely off the edge.

Pudding is my familiar; most of the time, I can keep her with me. I can care for her, I can protect her, I can control every aspect of her environment. And part of me has always believed that if I don't care about anything else—well, then, I can't get hurt again. Can I?

But this? This is beyond my ability to control. Gwendolynne Chan makes me feel like every ounce of self-restraint is just slipping through my fingers.

And that thought . . . It fucking *terrifies* me.

Loving someone is not a trap, Pudding said.

"Then why," I say aloud, gritting my teeth as we weave and dodge through traffic, "does it feel like it is?"

I spend at least fifteen whole minutes pounding on Gwendolynne's door. The time passes both quickly and unbearably slowly. All I am thinking about is what I'm going to say to her when she finally opens up that door. I need to see her. I need to confront her. I need to know if she's the one who'll betray me. I'm burning up with frenetic energy that is trapped in my body with nowhere left to go.

My furious tangle of emotions has me thinking that I might actually throw myself to my knees before her and beg for her forgiveness. But equally, if she *is* the betrayer that Barnabus was alluding to, then perhaps it's best I keep my distance. Either way, she's not in her room, or else she's actively avoiding me.

I pound on her door again, then place my ear against it, listening for any signs inside.

"Back again?" It's Danny, hand in hand with Bridie, sauntering down the hall. They're clearly about to head into Bridie's room, probably to shag, since that's what they seem to do ninety-nine percent of the time they spend together.

"Is Gwendolynne in?" I ask, slightly breathless from my hasty ride here and the quarter of an hour I've spent knocking on her door.

Danny gives me a conniving grin. "Why? Is Pudding hurt again?"

"Shut up, Danny," I snap. "I just need to talk to her."

Danny is still snickering, but he stops when Bridie whacks him in the gut. She looks at me, her expression sympathetic, and says, "She's out. She left about twenty minutes ago. She said she was looking for something . . . something she'd lost."

32

Gwendolynne

Heloise and I crash through the undergrowth, shouting Percy's name.

We're in the forest surrounding Seamere that borders the outer paddocks. "Percy," I call out, angling my magetorch higher. "Percy!" In desperation, I even try "Lord Percival the Second, Purveyor of the Flesh of Small Defenseless Creatures, Destroyer of Carpet, Scratcher of Doors, and Usurper of Recently Vacated Chairs!"

But the only answer is a deep and resounding silence.

Heloise dangles a piece of premium smoked salmon from her fingers, brushing aside bits of bracken, while I shine my torch into every crack, crevice, and shadow that we come across.

There's no Percy.

"Perhaps he just fell asleep somewhere and forgot to drop his shields," suggests Heloise, though her expression tells me she doesn't really believe it. From what I've read, mental shields don't feel like communication is completely severed.

I swallow the lump in my throat. "I guess we should head back. Maybe someone will pick him up and hand him in to a vet clinic."

It's too difficult to voice my real fear: that Percy has been hurt. Or worse, killed.

But even if he hasn't—even if for some strange reason it's just that our bond was broken—it's still terrifying. If someone finds him and figures out who he is, they might return him to Nathaniel Price. They'll realize that I never euthanized him like I was supposed to. I'll get in trouble not only for going against a client's wishes but also for illegally adopting a familiar.

What will they do to me, if they find out?

What will they do to *him*?

I swallow, my mouth dry, and take Heloise's arm. My fingers dig into her biceps, but she doesn't say anything.

When we arrive back at my dorm room, the corridor is all dark. It's late enough that everyone is in bed, sleeping—except for Bridie and Danny, of course, who from the sounds of it are in bed, not sleeping.

I catch a whiff of men's cologne as I unlock my door. It reminds me of Harrisford's scent, though that can't be. He's probably gone home with that nurse from the hospital and is already busy peeling off her pink scrubs. Has he gone back to her place, or are they here at Seamere, cozying up in the south wing? My pulse rate spikes at the thought, my head growing so hot that my scalp actually prickles.

Grinding my teeth, I force my mind to think of something else. Why the hell would I care where Harrisford Briggs is? Or whose scrub pants he's currently getting into? Right now, the only thing I care about is Percy and his safety.

As I push open the door, however, the reason for the men's cologne smell suddenly becomes clear.

"Miss Chan," a man's voice says, from behind us in the corridor.

I spin round. Professor Thomas Pickering is standing before me, an unctuous smile upon his goatee-framed lips. He must wear the same brand of cologne as Harrisford. As I stare at the professor, he slides his hands into his trouser pockets. "Are you looking for something?" he says. "Or should I say, some*one*?"

Percy. Oh shit. "What do you mean?" My voice wavers as I try to feign ignorance.

His smile only widens. "I mean the illegal little kitty cat you were keeping inside your room."

My heart starts to pound, thrashing wildly in my chest like a bucking unicorn trying to escape its stall. "I don't know what you're talking about, Professor."

He takes two steps toward me. Beside me, Heloise stiffens, her fingers curling into fists. It's actually quite comforting knowing that my friend is willing to punch this loser in the face for me.

"I think you do," he says, his voice all oily, his eyes shadowed by the overhead fluorescent magelights. "I think you've stolen a patient from Saint Gertrude's and have been housing it in your room."

My entire body goes cold, as though it's been drenched in ice water. "Wh-what makes you say that?"

"We had an anonymous tip, of course," the professor says. "And when we came to your room and opened up the door, the report was proved to be right." He shifts slightly, so that he has a clear view into my sad, bare little dorm. "Your illegal cat was right there—curled up on that chair."

He's pointing at my desk chair, and my heart drops into my stomach.

It must be Harrisford. It must have been Harrisford who dobbed me in. No one else knew about Percy. I'd taken such pains to keep him hidden, only letting him out before dawn. And if he'd stayed out, he knew to check that the coast was clear before sneaking back in through the window. Only Harrisford knew that he was there—and Heloise too, of course. But Heli has been with me all night, and Harrisford . . .

Fucking bastard. Not only did he have the audacity to flirt with some tart from the hospital in front of me, he's also deemed it appropriate to casually destroy my life.

"Please," I say, my voice thick. "Is he alive? Please, just let me know he's safe."

The professor's lips thin. He doesn't answer straightaway. I wait, holding my breath, trying not to be sick.

Eventually, he says, "The cat's alive, Miss Chan. He's been sent to the pound, something that should have occurred in the first place."

The pound. My stomach unclenches, just slightly.

He's alive.

Tears needle my eyes, threatening to erupt. "I just . . . couldn't stand to see him euthanized, Professor. It was a mercy thing. I had . . . a moment of weakness. It won't happen again, I promise. I *promise*. Please, just find a good home for him, and I will *never* do anything like this again."

Professor Pickering regards me for several long and painful moments before finally, he sighs. "You've never been in trouble before, Miss Chan, and for this reason we'll extend you some clemency."

I let out a sigh, my shoulders sagging with relief.

"We've severed your human-familiar bond."

I swallow, then nod. "I understand, Prof—"

"And," he continues, cutting me off. "You're suspended until further notice."

For a moment, his words don't fully make sense, and all I do is stare at him, numb.

But then it hits, like an axe cleaving open my chest. At last, I lose the battle against my tears, and when I blink, two of them detach and flash down my face.

If I'm suspended, *now*, right before exams, I won't be able to continue accruing points. Which means that I'll stall at the level I'm at, while Harrisford—

Anger rips through my body. Harrisford's marks will continue climbing, until they've eclipsed mine. Until that privileged, cologne-wearing, floppy-haired, strumpet-bedding git gets top marks and breezes through all his exams and fucking steals the top position from me.

"Suspended?" My voice catches in my throat; I can barely choke it out. My tears flow faster, thicker, as the significance of his words becomes clear.

Suspended. There's seven years of wasted effort packed into that word. A lifetime of my parents' hopes and dreams, crushed.

"Yes, Miss Chan. Suspended." His cold, fishy eyes gleam behind his smudged wire glasses. "Unless, of course, you can obtain a permit to legally adopt the cat."

33

Gwendolynne

Three days later, I'm slumped on my parents' couch in our poky Manchester flat.

Professor Pickering had allowed me to stay one more night in my dorm room. But at first light on Saturday morning, I was forced to pack all my things and catch the train up north. According to Heloise, by Monday, *everyone* was talking about why *the* Gwendolynne Chan was no longer attending classes.

It's almost bedtime. My tea is cold—curry and chips from one of the takeaway joints a few doors down from my parent's restaurant.

I have no idea where Percy is. My only solace is the fact that no one seems to have discovered that he once belonged to Nathaniel Price. But I don't know how much longer it'll remain a secret.

Heli has been trawling through animal rescue sites, sending me pictures of all the black cats. None of them are flea-bitten, one-eyed, or scruffy enough to be him, and all it does is compound my grief. At night, I cry myself to sleep hugging a pillow, alternately imagining it's Percy . . . or Harrisford.

It's shameful, but now that I'm more than three hundred kilometers away from London—and Seamere—I've recklessly allowed my Harrisford-related fantasies to run rampant. On more than one occasion I've fallen asleep, still shuddering from my self-induced orgasms, with images of Harrisford's perfectly proportioned face crowding my muddled mind.

It feels okay to be imagining him, since I'll probably never see him again. We'll be enemies forever, after he betrayed me so badly, but soon enough the memories of him will fade to pale and shadowy echoes. And, surely, my hatred will eventually simmer down to a brooding sort of contempt.

In fact, I don't have to feel at all guilty about objectifying him, because he means nothing to me. *Nothing.* He's ceased to be an actual person. He's just a face, a body, a collection of physical attributes that trigger a purely physiological reaction. Dopamine, oxytocin, serotonin: chemicals that activate the pleasure centers in my brain.

Or perhaps I'm self-sabotaging, fancying the one person who I hate the most, the one individual who has so thoroughly ruined me. Like a stress fracture that won't heal because I stubbornly continue to run on it.

Stop thinking about him, Gwendolynne. Sighing, I sit up, pushing aside the plate of soggy chips.

Tonight is the night I usually video call my parents, a weekly ritual we started because their restaurant closes every Monday. It's fortunate that this week they're away, visiting family in Kent, unaware I'm back in Manchester. Ignorant of the shame I've brought to the family by being unceremoniously suspended a literal week before graduation.

When my parents answer, my mum is on the screen, though it only shows the upper half of her forehead, the majority of it being bare wall. My dad is somewhere offscreen, his voice coming through just fine. No matter how many times I've tried to teach my parents how to video call, somehow they manage to routinely mess it up.

Still, my heart fractures at the sound of their voices, talking excitedly at me.

"Guiying." Having obviously saved up all their news to tell me on our weekly call, my mum launches straight into it. "Your father saw nice man speaking on the TV today—Minister for Magical Agriculture. You should write letter to this man, he could get you good job."

The screen shifts, and my father comes into view. He's sat beside my mum, nodding solemnly, dark circles carved into the spaces beneath his eyes.

"Mā," I say, resisting the urge to roll my eyes. My parents tell me about completely unattainable job and networking opportunities on a semiregular basis. "I can't just write a letter to a minister and get a job, it doesn't work like that—"

"You get Ministry job anyway, Guiying," my father says, cutting me off. "Because you come first, yes?"

"Bà ba, I . . ." I stop short, my hands curling into fists. What am I supposed to say to *that*?

I've been kicked out of university.

I'm going to fail my degree.

I can't help you save the restaurant.

I am a . . . disappointment.

My insides shrivel at the thought of admitting the truth, so instead I just say, "I'll . . . try my best." There's still time to turn things around. Isn't there?

My dad's eyes soften. He raises a triumphant fist. "We are so proud of you. Our daughter, best at Seamere College!"

Surreptitiously, I sniff, swiping at my eyes with my sleeve. "Thanks, Dad."

"Have you eaten?" It's my mum now, once again making sure I'm not wasting away from severe and sudden malnutrition.

"Yes"—I glance at the half-eaten box of chips—"I've eaten."

After my mother has filled me in on all the family gossip, including how appalled she is that my younger brother is threatening to pursue a theater degree, the call finally clicks off. I bury my head in my hands. Tonight, my mother's incessant chattering was kind of a good thing—it meant I didn't have to say much, which kept me from bursting into tears. Plus, it's killed some time, helping me to delay the thing I've been dreading.

But it's time now; I can put it off no longer. Without Percy to channel magic for me, I've had to restart my nightly rationing spells, though with each passing day it's becoming harder and harder to care. There's no chance I can afford to get a familiar permit: The cost for one permit is more than half of what my parents make over an entire year. And it's only six days until exams start. I'll almost certainly miss sitting them and fail the entire course.

But still, like a fool, I'm unable to completely let go, so I go through the routine every night on the off chance that a faerie godmother will appear in my living room and tell me that it was all a dream. That I can go back to Seamere and finish my degree . . . *without* my family finding out.

Plus, I'd be lying if I said the pain didn't provide some semblance of distraction from the absolute shit show that is my life.

I've just dragged the blade across my skin for the first time, reciting the rationing spell as I go, when my doorbell rings.

I freeze. No one should be here. It's almost eleven p.m. I haven't ordered any takeaway deliveries, nor am I expecting visitors. The neighbors usually keep to themselves, and my parents are at the other end of the country and wouldn't use the doorbell anyway.

Tightening my hold around the scalpel handle, I creep to the door and look out the peephole. *Fuck.* I pull away, spinning to the side and flattening myself against the wall.

What the hell is Harrisford Briggs doing at my flat?

At least, I think it's Harrisford—it's hard to tell through the fish-eye lens of the peephole.

The doorbell rings again, and I try to quell my panting breaths. If I stay quiet for long enough, maybe he'll think no one's home. Maybe he'll give up and go back to wherever the hell he came from. What is he doing in Manchester, anyway? Is he here visiting someone? Perhaps he's like one of those sleazy celebrities, with a side piece in every city.

There's a prolonged silence. I let out a slow breath, still trying to stay quiet. Has he . . . gone?

But no. A moment later, Harrisford's voice rings out, loud and clear, from the other side of the door.

"Chan," he says sternly. "I know you're in there. I saw you look through the peephole."

Shit. It *is* him.

I freeze, hesitating, wondering what I should do. Then I remember I'm holding a scalpel, which gives me some advantage, at least.

Before he's had a chance to react, I've already flung open the door, shoved him up against the opposite wall, and pointed the scalpel blade at his neck.

"What the *hell* are you doing here, Briggs?" I hiss. My forearm is pinned horizontally against his chest. Trying not to notice the hard lines of muscle beneath it, I lean into him harder, pressing him further against the wall.

He actually has the gall to *grin* at me. "I'm paying you a visit, Chan. What does it look like?"

Some of my hair has fallen over my face, so I blow it out of my eyes, frustrated. "Visiting me?" My eyes rove over his attire—he's wearing an actual suit, with a tie *and* an overcoat. Yes, we're up north, but it's summer—it's not *that* fucking cold. "Dressed like *this*? In Manchester? Are you *trying* to get beaten up?"

"If you have a problem with my clothing," he says, infuriatingly calm as his smile grows wider and even more cocky, "you're more than welcome to take it off."

I bare my teeth and growl at him, pressing the blade of the scalpel against his skin. "You're awfully flippant for someone whose life is in danger."

The smile falls away, and he gazes at me intently, the deep blue of his left eye glinting in the dim magelights of the hallway. "Then it's lucky, isn't it? That I don't much value my life."

My hand shakes, and I jerk the blade away from his throat. He must have been a little tense, even though he hid it well, because he actually loosens a breath in relief.

But his relief is short-lived when he sees what I'm doing instead.

"Would you prefer an open or closed castration?" I say evenly, my eyes narrowed, now pointing the scalpel squarely at his crotch. "A scrotal or pre-scrotal incision? Take your pick, Briggs—I'm well trained in *all* the methods."

He swallows hard, and I give him a smile as falsely sweet as sugar-free syrup. "I guess I've discovered what you truly value, huh?" I say. *Typical.*

"What do you want me to say?" he rasps out. Under my arm, I can feel the pulse of his throat, beating hot and steady beneath his skin.

My voice drops an octave, deceptively soft. But inside, I am seething. "I want to know why you betrayed me." I spit. "Or more to the point, why you betrayed Percy. You can hate me all you want—I don't even care. But Percy? He's *innocent*. He has nothing to do with the fact that you and I hate each other. He didn't deserve to be seized. He didn't deserve to go to the pound." My voice has started to vacillate, and I'm livid to discover that I'm crying. I squeeze my eyes shut, trying to curb my tears.

Harrisford is quiet for so long that I wonder if he's passed out from hypoxia or something. So I crack open an eyelid. Unfortunately, he's still conscious, and worse—he's staring at me in that disarming way he has.

"I don't hate you," he says softly, after a pause. "And I swear on my life, Chan—I didn't betray Percy."

I've seen many faces of Harrisford over the past seven years. The arrogant side, obviously, his usual default state. I've seen him angry. I've seen him joyful. I've even seen him nervous, when I was about to anesthetize Pudding after the museum explosion. But I don't know that I've ever seen him quite like this. He's . . . vulnerable. His expression so raw, so open, that I immediately know, deep in my bones, that he really is telling the truth.

The fight immediately drains out of me, and I push away from him, stepping back, the scalpel dangling loose in my fingers. I'm suddenly aware of how ratty I look: My hair's a mess, my feet are bare, and—goddammit—I'm once again wearing that stupid *Twilight* T-shirt.

I should order him to go. Slam the door in his face. Stop him from entering the cluttered chaos of the flat. But tonight, Harrisford has shown me a new side to his persona. And not only that . . . He didn't betray me like I'd previously assumed.

So I whirl around in a huff and stalk back into my parents' flat—leaving the door wide open.

A moment later, I haven't heard him follow, so I turn to look at him over my shoulder. "Well?" I say, raising an eyebrow, tetchy that I have to spell it out. "Are you coming in or not?"

34

Harrisford

I'm wary as I follow Gwendolynne into her flat. Or her parents' flat, I should say. She's standing in the center of the room with her arms crossed, watching me, as I quickly take in my surroundings.

If I were being generous, I'd call the flat cozy, but in truth, it's positively *tiny.* It gives the impression of an overstuffed cushion bursting at the seams: There are items on every surface, from the TV cabinet to the messy coffee table to the massive sofa that dominates the room. A Chinese calendar, red and gold and covered in advertisements, is the only adornment on the wall. Clothes are draped over furniture, books and papers stuffed into every shelf, and from a spot by the television a lucky cat swings its paw back and forth, doleful.

It's small and messy—the complete opposite of the sterile formality of the Briggs mansion. But in truth . . . I kind of love it. It's utter chaos contained in a small package, much like Gwendolynne herself.

"Do you want some tea?" Gwendolynne poses the question with a look of utmost distaste, as though offering me hospitality causes her physical pain.

"Please," I say, because I like to provoke her, and also because I am thirsty.

She disappears into an adjacent room as I move farther into the flat, loosening my tie and divesting myself of my overcoat and my jacket. These I drape over the back of a chair—to join another pile of clothing—before I hitch up my suit pants and sink onto the sofa. The sounds of banging and slamming cupboard doors float out from the kitchen, consistent, I suppose, with Gwendolynne's current emotional state.

My gaze sweeps the coffee table, which is stacked high with textbooks; she has clearly been studying during her period of suspension. Beside the books lies a sad-looking cardboard box containing the remnants of her supper.

She emerges some minutes later and slams a small porcelain teacup on the coffee table in front of me. "It's Chinese tea," she says, her tone curt. "It's all we have." There are no other sitting surfaces in the living room, so she perches on the sofa, as far away from me as possible. The action causes the T-shirt she is wearing to twitch up, exposing a considerable expanse of pale, smooth leg, and I hastily look away.

"Chinese tea is fine." I take a sip. It's good. Then, with my cup, I gesture at the TV, which is playing *Pride and Prejudice*.

The volume is turned down low. It's the scene where Mr. Darcy confronts Elizabeth in the pouring rain, and he's arrogant and she's belligerent and we're meant to hate Fitzwilliam Darcy, but I always felt kind of sorry for the poor, smitten, awkward bastard.

"This, though," I say, fixing her with a baleful look. "*This* is unforgivable."

She bristles. "What is?"

"The 2005 version? Honestly?" I place the cup on the table and fold my arms, feigning outrage. "When the BBC version is clearly *far* superior?"

She scowls at me, not wanting to rise to the bait, but I don't miss the scanty flint of a spark that catches in her dark brown eyes. "And is there anything else you wish to comment on in *my* house, Mr. Briggs?"

"The curry and chips. It's an abomination. It should be salt and vinegar only, you know . . . unless you are a miscreant who savors chaos and destruction."

She presses her lips together, and I know I've got her. "You uncultured *swine*," she says through her teeth, though her tone is playful. "You can get out, and leave *this* miscreant to enjoy her delicious meal in peace."

I chuckle and lean toward her. But she stiffens, a faint flush staining her normally pale cheeks. There's a sort of charged atmosphere between us, something that I've noticed seems to happen whenever one of us draws too near.

She opens her mouth, closes it again, then finally sighs. "What are you *really* doing here, Briggs?" It's the same question she asked me to begin with, except now her voice is soft, the expression on her face glum. Plus, she isn't pointing a size 10 scalpel blade at my jugular.

Seeing her sudden meekness makes my heart contract for a beat. I cannot forget that she has had her life completely turned upside down. This is a woman whose whole identity is built on academic achievement, and all it took was a tatty old cat and some unknown conniving bastard to bring it all crashing down.

"I came to see how you were doing," I answer truthfully. "And to bring you some practice papers." Reaching into my trouser pocket, I draw out an admittedly rumpled stack of practice exams that the lecturers handed out on Monday. It's Tuesday, so I'm a day late giving them to her, but then again I did have to buy a car to make the trip all the way to Manchester. I know from experience that my bike isn't set up well for long trips, and I didn't want to be conspicuous by using my father's Magecorp limo.

For a moment, she stills, seemingly frozen. But then she reaches out and plucks the papers from my hand. "Thanks." She's flushing even harder, staring down at the papers now sitting on her lap.

"Listen—" I pause. What do I even say to her? I've never had trouble talking to women, but whenever I'm with Gwendolynne, I feel completely lost for words.

"Yes?" She's still clutching the exam papers, her entire body tense. Her fingers are trembling. Mine would be too, if my arms weren't so tightly crossed. My body hums with nervous energy.

"I'm really sorry you were suspended." Even I'm surprised at how honest I'm being. "It's really not fair on you—or on Percy."

And then—oh shit—she's crying again. Great, big, splashy tears that stream down her face, skimming along her jawline and splattering right onto the exam papers. Without thinking, I scoot closer, and then our arms are touching, our legs are touching, my arm is around her, I'm drawing her to me, I'm tucking her head beneath my chin as she sobs into my chest, her tears dampening the crisp white cotton of my shirt.

Fucking hell. I'm hugging Gwendolynne Chan. And she's not recoiling. In fact . . . she's leaning into me.

"I really need this, Briggs." She says this against my chest, the sound vibrating right down to my core. Inside me, the dueling sensations of lust and pity are waging a war of epic proportions, my brain so utterly confused that all I can do is hold on to her tighter. I curl around her, cinching her closer into my body: a body that is now reacting, uncontrollably, to the smell of her skin, and her proximity. "I *need* to come first."

"I know," I murmur, using one hand to rub soothing circles on her back.

But then she scoffs and pushes me away, suddenly angry. "*No*," she seethes. "You *don't* know. *You*—with your money, and your privilege, and your—" She stops, covers her face with both hands, and starts properly sobbing, her shoulders shaking.

I don't know what to do or say, so I remain silent. My chest feels hollow, bloodless, as though she'd actually stabbed me with that scalpel in the hallway and exsanguinated me entirely. I keep one hand on her back because I'm not quite sure where else to put it.

Eventually, she speaks, her voice muffled by her hands. "My parents are going to lose their restaurant."

My brow furrows; I sit up straighter. "What?"

She drops her hands and raises her head. She doesn't look mad anymore; now she just looks . . . weary. "The Chinese restaurant downstairs. You would've gone past it to get to the stairwell. They own it. They've been running it for twenty-five years, since they first immigrated. They built it from scratch—from *nothing*, Briggs. *Nothing.* I used to spend every weekend there. Studying at one of the tables."

Slowly, the puzzle of Gwendolynne's life is becoming clearer, as though I'm finally piecing it together. "And you need the Ministry job," I say slowly, mulling over this new information. "Because of the money." My gaze meets hers, and though her big brown eyes are still sheened with tears, there's a steely determination in them that is making my heartbeat falter. "Because you want to help them save their business."

She nods, scrubbing away a stray tear with the heel of her hand. "It's just . . . rent has risen so much these past few years. And with more people ordering home deliveries, and fewer people eating out . . ." She trails off, then continues, her voice even stronger than usual. "They sacrificed so much for me, Briggs. For my education. For *years*, they broke their backs in that place to put me through school. Even with the scholarship, there are still significant costs involved. Costs they can't really afford. And if I get the Ministry position, then—then I can pay them back." Her eyes lock with mine, now completely bone-dry. "It'll still only be a *fraction* of what I owe them."

She lapses into a meditative silence, as do I, and when I reach out to take her hand, she doesn't pull away.

"Your parents really love you, don't they?" I murmur. Her hand feels so delicate in mine, which are calloused and covered with scars and burns from years of working with mythical beasts. Her frank and honest confession is forcing me to be candid, too.

"I guess so." She shrugs. "I mean—they never say it, but they do show it. I know they care."

I let out a long, slow breath and shake my head. "I don't really know what that's like."

She gives me a curious sort of look, her teeth digging into her lower lip, and goddammit, if I don't get to bite that lip sometime in the very near future . . . my fingers flex around hers, just slightly, and her gaze drops—sharp as a blade—to where our hands are intertwined.

"Your father . . ." She doesn't make eye contact again. "He's a bit of an arsehole, isn't he?"

I let out a snort. "That's quite the understatement, Chan." I let my gaze drift away for a second before landing it back on her. "He's trying to force me into Magecorp."

"For a job?"

I turn her hand over, faceup, letting it rest on top of mine. "Yes." With my thumb, I trace the curves and lines of her palm. "They're starting up a brand-new familiar breeding facility—"

"But that sounds perfect, doesn't it?"

I give a grim smile. "Not really. You've met my father, Chan. You know what a tyrant he is. He's pretty much blackmailed me into joining Magecorp . . . *unless* I win the job at the Ministry."

She frowns, the delicate arches of her eyebrows drawing down. Neither of us expands on the fact that we both really need that job. "Was he always like that?"

My collar feels too tight, even though I've already loosened my tie and undone my top button. "It got . . . worse after my mother was gone."

"Your mother," Gwendolynne murmurs. "She died when you were a kid, right?"

My insides shrivel to ice. Talking about my mother is . . . painful. But again, I find myself speaking, as though I'm not quite in control of my mouth. "It happened when I was four."

I should stop here. Should change the topic, segue the conversation into something safer. But there's something about Gwendolynne Chan that makes me want to lay myself bare; flay my soul open for her frank perusal. I don't quite understand it—why I'm suddenly ready to divulge my most closely guarded secret—but something is broken between my brain and my lips, and I'm unable to stop myself saying it.

"But she didn't die," I say, and take a deep breath. "She . . . she left."

35

Gwendolynne

It takes me several seconds to realize I'm staring. "Oh. I'm sorry."

My mind is reeling. Harrisford's mother left? I'd never heard that before—the official line is that she died. As far as I know, he's currently twenty-five. How the hell has he managed to keep this a secret for an entire twenty-one years?

"It's all right," he says, though he looks completely miserable. "I did get Pudding in her place."

Pudding. I knew it. That lizard *is* his emotional support animal. But then it dawns on me: She isn't here. Which is unusual. "Where *is* Pudding?"

"I left her in London." He shrugs and then adds dryly, "It's a rather long drive here, Chan."

I frown at him. "Aren't you worried about another surge?"

"To be honest, yes. But I couldn't not come and see you."

My heart stutters inside my chest, then resumes thumping at a higher pace, and all of a sudden I'm *very* aware of the plain fact that Harrisford and I are holding hands. I'm gripped by a sudden urge to tell him everything that Heloise and I found out—about the people Magecorp are using as tethers, about the Source, about the London General Magical Hospital doctors implanting fragments of

Void-origin rock into the back of people's necks . . . I want to tell him that somehow the MLO are involved but it's possible they're not the culprits and there's something—*something* I can't put my finger on—that I'm missing. And it frustrates me beyond measure that I don't know what it is.

But overriding all of this is another urge. A more bodily urge, stemming from where the smooth skin of my hand is touching the rough skin of his; from where the bends of our knees—his right one, my left—are just brushing one another as we face each other on the couch; from where his gaze drops down to my lips, lingering there, hungry. And these latter urges—the pining, compounded by all the nights I've spent falling asleep to hyper-realistic daydreams of moments such as these—are crowding literally every other thought from my lust-addled mind.

I lean forward so we're even closer, our knees ramming up against each other even more. And he leans forward too, so near to me that I can feel the touch of his ragged breath upon my lips. We stay there, our eyes locked on one another, not talking, not moving, our breaths coming fast and shallow.

My stomach seems to be doing a nonstop series of backflips. I shouldn't do this. I shouldn't. But my brain seems determined to ignore the alarm bells sounding inside my head.

Are he and I going to kiss . . . Again?

Harrisford clears his throat. When he speaks, his voice is hoarse. "Gwendolynne, I—" He stops, and swallows.

Everything below my navel clenches in response to the sound of my name on his lips. I don't think I've heard him say my first name, ever, and there's roaring in my ears and fogginess in my vision as I tug my fingers from his grasp, grab him by his tie, and roughly close the distance.

He gasps, once, against my lips. But then he groans, his hands coming up to my face, gripping it with a force that makes me almost cry out. As soon as my lips part, his tongue is there, sweeping against mine, and I let go of his tie and grab hold of his collar, pinning him in place as we kiss. And it's completely ridiculous but the thought suddenly occurs to me that I'm *really* glad I've already brushed my teeth.

I let out a giggle against Harrisford's mouth, and he pulls back suddenly, the corners of his lips tilting up in a grin. "What's so funny?" he says.

When I don't answer, he shifts me, so easily, like a doll. And then I'm sitting on his lap, straddling him, his calloused hands sliding up my bare back, caressing my skin in a way that makes every muscle in my body tighten. I gasp, twisting my fingers through his silky hair as our lips crash together again, my hips rocking in time to our kiss, and in my position I can tell he's either stowed a cattle prod in his trousers or he's very, very turned on.

My fingers find his tie, loosening it farther even though I don't really know how, and we break apart just long enough for me to pull it off over his head. Hurriedly, I undo his buttons, pinging one right off in my impatience, and push his shirt off him, almost going to pieces at the feel of his muscular shoulders beneath my hands. The very same shoulders that I've ogled many a time, whether clad in coveralls or straining against linen shirts or naked and bare, inside his room. I can't help but claw at him, my fingernails digging into his skin, my fingertips running over the scars marring his neck and back.

His hands slide down, tightening on my buttocks, and he groans again, into my mouth. "Fuck, Gwendolynne," he growls, skimming his lips along my jaw, then to my neck, nipping me on the sensitive part, right below my ear. I cry out, my hips flexing against him, harder this time, and I reach down, fingers scrabbling to loosen his belt, to undo his button, to tug down the zipper of his fly . . .

His hands abruptly leave my backside and gently encircle both of my wrists. "Stop."

The word is like a bucket of ice, immediately dousing my libido. I sit up, ramrod straight, and stare at him. "What?"

His jaw is clenched, his neck muscles straining, the vein on his forehead distended. "Not tonight," he grits out, sounding almost like he's in pain.

Oh my god. I'm an idiot. I'm an idiot who has thrown myself at Harrisford Briggs, the number one male floozy of final year, the rich, pretentious prat who keeps a girl in every city. I try to climb off his lap, but he clamps his hands on my hips, holding me in place.

I'm spiraling now, panic expanding in my chest like a gastric volvulus about to rupture. He . . . doesn't want me. I can feel that between my legs he's definitely hard, and yet . . . he's pushing me away?

I must be absolutely *repulsive*.

"I'm sorry. I get it." I'm floundering, blabbering, so far beyond embarrassed that I may as well be in another county. "I— You— Uh . . . It's fine, it's fine, it's totally fine—" The worst thought suddenly occurs to me. "It's the shirt, isn't it? I swear it's not dirty. I have more than one shirt, you know. It's just—it happened to be clean in the wash cycle—"

He cuts me off, his eyebrows knitting. "Chan, trust me—I am not even remotely thinking of your wash cycle."

"Is it because it's *Twilight*, then? Maybe you hate *Twilight*. You think it's campy and cringe and . . ." I draw a deep breath. "Yes, that's it, I get it now, it's that you hate *Twilight* . . ."

His lips twitch, amused. "I have absolutely no idea what you're talking about."

I stop ranting for a bit and gape at him, horrified. He's familiar with the BBC version of *Pride and Prejudice*, but he doesn't know about *Twilight*? Rich people really do exist in an entirely different stratosphere. "It was only the biggest vampire phenomenon to sweep the western world—" I start, then stop short, aware I'm actually rambling. "Oh, never mind."

He closes his eyes and gives a long, drawn-out sigh. When he opens his eyes again, he looks resigned. "Remind me—why are we talking about vampires, again?"

I blurt out unthinkingly, "Because we're talking about why you don't want to have sex with me." Then I add, somewhat sheepishly, "and I thought that maybe . . . maybe it's my shirt."

Both of his eyebrows shoot up, and his fingers tighten on my hips, his touch searingly hot against my bare skin. "If it were just the shirt," he says, and his voice is oddly rough, "I wouldn't hesitate to rip it off you."

Desire curls, hot and sharp, in my belly. "Then why?" I'm aware that I'm sounding plaintive, but at this point I'm beyond caring. Harrisford Briggs has a reputation for sleeping around, and I must be the most revolting person ever to be one of the few women he's rejected. My chest feels caved in; it's like I can barely breathe. And when I speak again, my voice is small. "It's me, isn't it? It's not the shirt. It's me. It's just that you don't want to fuck *me*." I'm almost in tears, and again I try to scramble off him. But he's too strong, and he keeps me pinned in place on his lap.

"You think I don't want to fuck you?" He stares at me. "Are you completely insensible to what is happening between my legs?"

I wilt under the force of his gaze. "Then . . . *why*?"

"Because it's late, and I drove for hours to get here, and I have to be up at four if I'm going to make it back in time for class. I desperately need some sleep—"

"Fuck me quickly, then, and then get some sleep."

Slowly, he slides his hand up my back, under my T-shirt, pressing me even closer until my chest is crushed up against his. "Oh, Gwendolynne," he says, his voice like liquid velvet, his lips brushing my ear. "When I finally fuck you, I don't intend on getting *any* sleep."

I try—and fail—to stifle a whimper. "What if *I* need you to fuck me to get some sleep, then?"

Harrisford's eyes darken, and this time it's *his* hips that flex against mine. For a moment, he does nothing. Says nothing. But then in one swift movement he stands—lifting me as though I'm a feather and not a full-grown adult woman—and throws me over one shoulder.

"Briggs," I gasp out. "What the fuck!"

"Where is your bedroom, Gwendolynne?"

I shudder, because I'm still not used to hearing him actually say my name. When I don't answer, he continues, louder this time. "*Gwendolynne.* There are only four doors leading out of here. Which one is it?"

"Why?" I snap. I'm humiliated—and also massively turned on—that he's carrying me like a sack of meat. "Why should I tell you when nothing's going to happen?"

He says, very deliberately, enunciating each word, "I said I wasn't going to fuck you, Chan. *Not* that nothing would happen. Now tell me, my little miscreant . . ." I hear the wicked grin behind his words. "Which one is your fucking room?"

36

Gwendolynne

He throws me on the bed—actually *throws* me onto the bed—and stands over me, looking like some sort of shirtless Greek god. His hair is all mussed up from where my fingers have tangled through it, his pupils are dilated, the defined ridges of his abs bracketed by the sharp edges of his narrow hips. Molten heat pools deep in my core; at the same time, my heart is hammering, beating against my ribs.

I lick my lips, suddenly nervous. Yes, I wanted this—I mean, I'd practically *begged* him for it. But now we're in my room, with the Hello Kitty bedspread that I've had since I was eight, and this all feels too risky. I can't afford to lose my head, to forget that only days ago Harrisford had been chatting up some nurse from the London General Magical Hospital. And while *he* might find it easy to change his lovers as often as he changes his sheets, I know from past experience that it's not at all how *I* function. I'm strictly a one-boyfriend-at-a-time type girl, and I tend to fall too hard, too fast.

And I'm pretty sure that if I let Harrisford Briggs get too far inside my head, then I'm in very real danger of losing my heart.

"Are you sure you want this?" I'm embarrassed by how breathy I sound. "Don't you want to go back to Lucy?"

He frowns, confused. "Who's Lucy?" Before I can answer, he's already crawling up the bed, caging me in with his warmth and his weight, the full length of his body pressing me down into the bed. Grabbing my face again, he pulls me to him, and we're kissing again—frantically, frenetically—all muffled moans and jagged breaths.

He breaks contact for a second, then starts to kiss down my neck and chest, stopping briefly to close his mouth around my nipple, right through my thin cotton T-shirt. I cry out, my body bowing off the bed, as he continues to make his way farther down.

I'm already panting, writhing under the overwhelming intensity of his touch. "Do you want me to . . . take off my shirt?"

He raises himself up on an elbow for a moment, staring at the cheesy *Twilight* cast photo emblazoned across my rapidly rising and falling chest. Then he shoots me a small half grin. "No. Keep it on. I think judgy Carlisle will help keep me in check."

I scramble up onto my elbows and glare at him indignantly. "You said you didn't know *Twilight*!"

His grin only spreads wider, and *good god* his smile is perfect. "I never said that, Gwendolynne."

I shiver. Whenever he says my name, it almost rolls across his tongue, as though he's savoring an exceptionally fine whiskey. Dropping back onto the pillow, I try to get out of my head. To let the whirlwind of sensations—Harrisford's hands on my hips, his lips on my skin, the tongue he's now running up one of my bare legs—take over. He kisses up my calf, my knee, pushing up my T-shirt until it bunches at my waist, and then I remember, too late, what he's going to find when he reaches my thigh—

"Gwendolynne." This time, my name doesn't sound sensual. It sounds . . . choked. He skims his thumb across the labyrinth of old scars marring my inner thighs. "What is this?"

I scrunch my eyes shut, wishing I'd never come in here. Wishing I'd never allowed him in my bedroom, in my bed . . . Wishing I'd never allowed him to come into my parents' flat at all. I'm sure he's slept with dozens of women who aren't permanently disfigured between their legs.

Everything inside me seizes up, and I snap at him. "You're so fucking ignorant, Briggs." But the words lack bite. I sound almost . . . fatalistic.

My eyes are still closed, so I don't see him move, but I feel him shift a little so that he's looking at my face. "What do you mean?" His tone is unexpectedly gentle.

"How do you think I've survived all these years?" Tears are starting to prick at my inner eyelids, and I clench my jaw, willing them to go away. "How do you think I've managed to . . . *afford* . . . all the fucking magic I needed to get through vet school?"

"I—I don't understand."

My eyelids spring open, and *fuck*, now there really *are* tears, and I really don't want to cry while Harrisford Briggs is lying between my ugly, spread-eagled legs. I try to wriggle out from under him and clamp my thighs shut, but he's got one of my knees secured against the bed, his thumb still caressing circles across my skin.

"It's a rationing spell." I don't even know why I'm bothering to explain. "It's the only way I can make the little bits of magic I can afford to buy last the entire year. It takes *blood*, Briggs. Without a familiar, I can't channel magic from the Void, so unless I ration it with the spell, it runs out too quickly. And performing the spell means I have to sacrifice some of my qì—my life force—just to have enough." I release a deep, tremulous sob, and shake my head. "It's okay. I understand. You can leave if you want." *You don't need to stay with a mess like me*, I want to add. *You can go back to pretty, perfect, scarless Lucy.*

But he makes no move to leave. Instead, he runs the tip of his index finger—gently, so gently—along the fresh cut I'd made right before he'd arrived. And when I finally realize what he's doing, why there's a sensation of warmth spreading languidly along the wound, more tears spill from my eyes and run down my face onto the pillow.

He's . . . He's *healing* me. He's fucking healing me. In a way I never bother to do myself because I can never spare the magic.

And where his finger goes, his lips soon follow, kissing me softly along the just-healed cut until he's dangerously close to the edge of my knickers.

"Gwendolynne." Resting his cheek on my inner thigh for a moment, he closes his eyes, just briefly. "Gwendolynne."

It's like he can't get enough of my name. His voice is so soft, it makes me weep harder. He looks up at me, blue-and-brown gaze penetrating. "Why are you crying?"

I don't know how to explain it. I don't really know how to explain that the cutting started out as a necessity, but now it's also something like . . . security. So instead I just sob out, "Because I'm hideous."

"Gwendolynne," he says, murmuring my name for the third time in just as many minutes. He shakes his head. "You're not hideous." He plants another kiss, gently, on my scars. "You're perfect."

I squeeze my eyes shut, willing my tears to stop. This scene is a fantasy that's played on loop in my head for *ages*—and here I am ruining it by sniveling like a baby.

"No, I'm not."

"Yes. You are. See?" He bends his head and drops another kiss on my other, equally scarred thigh. "*This* is perfect."

He shifts a little, kissing me softly on my lower belly. "And *this* . . . is perfect."

I squirm, my eyes squeezed shut, the stillness only fractured by my broken breaths.

"And this?" Harrisford whispers, running his lips gently across my underwear until his mouth is positioned right at the apex of my thighs. I feel the scorching heat of his breath as he leans down and kisses me—right *there*. "Perfect." It sounds like a prayer. A confession.

A . . . question.

All I can manage in response is "Please . . ." I breathe the word out on an exhale.

And with that, Harrisford reaches up, and I lift my hips reflexively as he eases my already sodden underwear down and down, until they're completely off.

Throwing them to one side, he settles himself back between my legs, his large hands wrapped around each of my thighs.

"I think, Gwendolynne," he says, his voice dropping low. "That perhaps you need a distraction."

"What . . . sort of distraction?"

He looks at me very seriously. "I'm going to make you come, now."

A small whimper escapes from my lips. I've never had a man tell me that, so simply and directly . . . and it's hot.

I'm a failure. A disappointment. My whole life is falling apart. But this?

Yes—this is exactly the sort of distraction I need.

"You seem . . . very confident about that." I'm speaking with bravado, but with the way he's looking at me, I'm already teetering right on the edge. Every inch of my skin is thrumming with unspent need, and I'm weak and shivery, mere putty beneath his hands.

He gives a low chuckle and says, his voice rough, "It's a challenge I'm willing to accept." And then he lowers his head again, and gives me a long and languorous lick.

I react instantly, my legs clamping around his ears. Any residual rational thoughts I might've had are immediately chased from my brain. I'm writhing, moaning, twisting my hands through his hair to keep him pinned in place; he keeps going, relentless, even as my body does its best to buck him off. At some point, he lets go of my thigh and pushes a finger inside me, quickly followed by a second. And the sensation—of his mouth on me, his fingers in me—is so overwhelming, the pleasure so heated, that I immediately go over the edge, screaming out his name.

He continues working on me as I come, riding me through my release, and it's only when I'm sated, legs shivering with the aftershocks, that he crawls back up my body and kisses me deeply. I can taste myself on his tongue, and it nearly makes me come apart once more.

"Say it again," he says huskily, his lips grazing the curve of my ear. His breath fans my skin, and I shiver.

I'm still panting. "Say what?"

"My name, Gwendolynne." He nips me on the earlobe. "Say my name."

I wind my arms around his shoulders, letting out a little moan as he sucks on my neck. "Harrisford," I breathe out, wrapping my legs around his waist. "Harrisford. Harrisford. Harrisford."

He shudders and kisses his way back up my throat until our lips find each other again. This time, when we kiss, it's no longer feverish—it's tender, like the sweetest-tasting honey; like the warmth of a setting sun; like the first scent of spring dissolving a frozen winter.

He called me perfect. He called me *perfect*. My heart is full to bursting, and as I kiss him back, I realize, in half a heartbeat: I am truly, deeply in trouble.

Because how many other women has he said those exact same words to?

"Harrisford," I whisper. My tone has changed sufficiently that it's enough for him to pull back slightly and give me a quizzical look. "This is just a . . . onetime thing, isn't it? Just for tonight."

He stills for a moment, gazing at me, one hand still twined in my hair. Then he gives the most minuscule of nods. "Sure," he says, lowering his mouth to my neck. "Just tonight."

I let out a sigh, relieved. This is just a transient moment; just something to purge him from my system. The kiss at the gala . . . was just an appetizer. This, what we just did, was a full and satisfying meal. And I should be satisfied—how many times have I imagined him joining me in this very bed? How many times have I come on my own, clenching around my own fingers that I desperately wished were his? Perhaps now, since the real-life Harrisford has given me what is arguably the best orgasm of my life, I can finally put to rest the ridiculous thoughts I've been having about him and our nonexistent future.

We have no future, Harrisford and me. In just over a week, he'll be graduating first at Seamere, and I'll be nothing but a vet school dropout. And we'll go our separate ways, and never see each other again, and he can bed as many nurses named Lucy as he wants without having to bear witness to my jealousy.

Perhaps, if I can't graduate, I can devote my life to figuring out the cause of the surges—and stop them. Harrisford can have his illustrious Ministry career, while I'll just carry on quietly in the background, trying to save the world.

I'd been so lost in my thoughts that I hadn't noticed Harrisford had moved, easing himself behind me. Both of his arms are wrapped around my waist, his nose and lips buried in my hair, my backside nestled snugly against the still-present evidence of his arousal. I give my butt an experimental wiggle, and his grip tightens.

"Chan," he growls warningly, his voice low at my ear. "Go to sleep."

I stop moving, deep, bone-rending fatigue making my limbs all heavy. I'm sated, I'm spent, and Harrisford's warmth is surrounding me, enveloping me like a cocoon . . . Yet somewhere deep in my chest, the tiniest crack appears, all empty and hollow inside.

The tears are back. I close my eyes, my heart fracturing, all too aware that now—post-orgasm—Harrisford and I are no longer on a first-name basis.

When I wake, sunlight is already streaming through the window, and Harrisford is gone . . . because of course he is. I curl up into a ball, my body going cold, the absence of his touch conspicuous.

Yes, I've been trying to convince myself that Harrisford Briggs means nothing to me. That after one night of mind-blowing oral sex, I'd be satisfied enough not to miss him. But I know now: I've been fooling myself.

I'm such a fucking loser.

It takes me a long time to roll over and face the empty space in the bed beside me, the rumpled bedsheets that still smell faintly like his cologne. But when I finally do, there's a slip of parchment neatly folded upon his pillow. Could it be . . . a note? From Harrisford?

My heart is racing as I unfold it with stiff, shaky fingers. The paper is heavy, almost as thick as cardboard.

It's not a note. The words on it are printed, not handwritten, except for a messily scrawled *XX* in the lower right-hand corner. And there's an address listed for somewhere in London.

I squint at it harder, my bleary, swollen eyes struggling to focus on the words, until finally, finally, my brain registers what I'm seeing.

LICENSE FOR A FAMILIAR, the card reads.

Then, on the next line: FOR LORD PERCIVAL THE SECOND.

37

Harrisford

I didn't want to leave . . . I almost couldn't bring myself to leave. But now I'm here, back at Seamere, and I cannot get her out of my head.

When I'd left, it was well before dawn. I'd stood over Gwendolynne's sleeping form for a moment, watching the way the slanting moonlight cast shadows across her face. She looked so peaceful, so beautiful, that it was all I could do not to climb back into bed with her, put my face between her legs, and coax out more of those delicious sounds she'd made the night before.

Harrisford, she'd whispered to me in the darkness, and I swear to god this woman is going to be the death of me.

And yet, she'd said it plainly: For her, it was a onetime thing. To her, the kiss we shared at the gala meant nothing. She doesn't want me in the way that I want her; for Gwendolynne, I was just a means to an end, a satiation of her desires so that she could get some sleep.

"Briggs, are you all right?" Marcus raises an eyebrow at me. "You seem a little . . . distracted this morning."

We're standing in the phoenix shed, assessing a bonded pair who—due to what I can only assume is related to the surges—are catching fire and then regenerating far too frequently. According to

Neck's seminal textbook, *Internal Medicine and Surgery of Mythological Beasts*, phoenixes usually regenerate once every five hundred years, at most. But this pair are doing it weekly. It's burning up all their energy reserves and making them unable to channel magic. I've donned a pair of fireproof gloves, the type we usually use for dragons, and I'm supposed to be grabbing one of them by the legs so that we can examine the bird more closely.

"I'm fine," I say, though it's a lie, for my head is still full of Gwendolynne's face; my nostrils still seared with her scent; my ears still ringing with how my name had sounded falling from her lips. "Just . . . had a late night, that's all."

Pushing open the gate to the pen, I prowl closer to the phoenix pair. They shuffle back into the far corner, letting out melodious wails, trying to escape me. When I'm close enough, I pounce—but not fast enough, for the phoenixes launch themselves into the air in a flurry of flying feathers before alighting at the opposite end of the pen, looking indignant. I land painfully on one shoulder, the shock so jarring I feel it in my teeth.

Marcus lets out a howl of laughter, and I scowl at him as I scramble back onto my feet. I still haven't forgiven him for the stunt he pulled with Gwendolynne and the qílín, but I have to keep the peace—from now until graduation, at least.

Even Pudding gives a small chuckle from where she sits atop a post, but she stops when I turn my most scathing glare on her. When they've both finished laughing at my expense, Marcus jerks his chin toward the pen. "Go on. Try again."

I really am off my game, because I have to spend a good ten minutes chasing the fucking birds. At one stage, the male phoenix decides to face me, puffing up his chest and flapping his wings in a threatening display of dominance, and I'm forced to back up a few paces. Phoenixes have a reputation for being protective, male phoenixes especially so, and I get the sense this one won't hesitate to peck out my eyes.

When I finally manage to catch the male bird, Marcus helps to restrain him while I collect samples of blood from his tiny wing vein. Then I siphon off the excess magic, storing it in a Magecorp-branded battery, and let him go, unharmed.

The female phoenix must realize that I actually am trying to help, because after this she voluntarily struts up to me and offers herself up to be caught. Marcus taps his strap, then gives me a sly wink.

Mine pings. He's given me five marks for this, more than he should, really. It's blatant favoritism, and it's nudged me well ahead of Gwendolynne—a fact that no longer fills me with triumphant exultation. But when I question it, he just waves off my concerns.

When we're done, Marcus leaves me to clean up and get the blood samples to the laboratory. I go to leave, but just as I'm about to shut the door to the shed, I notice that the phoenixes are embracing—or whatever you'd call the birdlike equivalent. They're standing close together, their long necks curved around one another, and it tugs at my chest to witness it. Like most birds, phoenixes bond for life, keeping one monogamous mate forever. And since they're effectively immortal . . . this is an even more impressive feat.

As I stride toward the pathology lab, I wonder when Gwendolynne will finally return. It's been five long days here without the chance of running into her or hearing one of her sarcastic comments. I could have easily express-posted Percy's permit to her, and sent digital copies of the practice exams via her strap . . . But last night, the agony of not having seen her for days had proven to be far too much. So I'd made the trip up north, sacrificing sleep, my sanity, and possibly also my dignity, just so I could see her face.

Not that I had wanted to give her the permit right away. First, I'd been harboring a secret, reckless hope that my visit would be an opportunity to kiss her again, and I didn't want to come across as though I was bribing her for physical contact. That too was the reason I stopped myself from having sex with her—as difficult as it was, it was safer to avoid it, to give her the permit the morning after, so that she wouldn't get the wrong idea about my intentions.

Plus, I also had to see if there was any trace, any evidence, that she was intending to betray me, as Barnabus had suggested. But after we'd had that open, honest conversation about our respective families, I'd concluded that Barnabus had probably got it wrong.

According to the stars, the person you care about most will betray you, he'd said. Thinking about it, he'd probably meant my father. It would make sense, since my father *had* betrayed me when he'd used the alibi of being in Wales to attack Gwendolynne on the top floor of Magecorp HQ. Perhaps the centaur just presumed that I care about my father . . . I suppose it's a fair assumption, since it seems that most people do care about theirs.

Or perhaps Barnabus was wrong altogether. Maybe there isn't anyone who's currently out to get me. I read once that centaur astrology is based on an outdated map of the stars made by an ancient civilization thousands of years ago. And since then, the stars have shifted. Centaurs, however, still cling to their archaic knowledge of the constellations, which explains why their predictions are so consistently imprecise.

Either way, I've come to the conclusion that Gwendolynne is definitely not planning to betray me. And that I should probably ignore drunken centaurs who are salty because I've just dug into their hoof with a knife.

I've arrived at the lab, so I approach the reception desk and hand over the specimen bag containing the blood. "Thank you, Harrisford," the pathologist says, taking the samples from me. "Do you have any other blood for me today?"

The mention of blood has my gut churning, and an image of Gwendolynne's scarred legs floats up in my mind. When I'd changed her into her nightclothes after the Magecorp HQ explosion, I'd noticed the few on her arms, of course . . . But I'd just assumed they were old cat scratches. And I hadn't seen the ones on her inner thighs because, while I may be many things—few of them good—one thing I am *not* is a fucking pervert.

"No," I tell the pathologist, before pushing out the door, my heart thudding dully in my chest.

I cannot believe I've been so ignorant about how less fortunate students procure their magic. It's so easy for me, with my privilege, to forget that magic is not freely available to all. And I'm seized with such compassion for Gwendolynne, my chest squeezing so hard I suddenly have difficulty drawing breath, that I come to the obvious conclusion . . .

I love her.

I love Gwendolynne Chan.

I realized after last night: I'm head over heels for her. I mean, why else would I bother to actually buy a fucking car and drive an eight-hour round trip just to see her face for one night? I've been so dense, denying my attraction for her, then denying my deeper feelings.

I'm so in love with her that it no longer matters which of us comes first. Not to me, anyway. Somehow, it feels less important. Working together to figure out the cause of the surges, losing myself in the taste and scent of a woman that I'm in love with . . . These things have taken precedence. And where my head is at right now, I'd willingly endure a Magecorp job forever if it would give me one more night with her.

This is what Gwendolynne has done to me—made me prioritize someone else more than I prioritize myself. Made me care. Made me *feel.*

And I have to say, it's fucking *glorious.*

I'm proud of you, Harrisford, Pudding says, her claws digging into my shoulder. *You're finally seeing some sense.*

"She'll probably hate me for it," I reply, somewhat sullen.

It's all right if she does. Pudding's voice in my head is kind, as always. *Nothing ventured, nothing gained. You'll feel worse if you never say anything at all. Especially since you don't truly know when you will see her again.*

My stomach clenches. "It might be never." We are, after all, about to graduate and leave Seamere for good.

She gives a sympathetic hum. *It might be.*

My strap buzzes, and I check it. It's my contact—the one who got me the *resignio* spells, the one who managed to get me a rush familiar permit, even though I only had half the payment up front and they usually take weeks to approve.

Briggs. I need the rest of the money, the message reads. Meet me in the postmortem room in half an hour.

The postmortem room has a permanent, lingering stench of decay, even though it's thoroughly scrubbed and hosed on a daily basis. Danny Wong is at one of the tables, performing a necropsy on a griffin. They're big creatures, so he's using a chainsaw, but when he sees me, he switches it off and uses his forearm to push up his goggles.

"Hey, man," I say, wrinkling my nose at the sour smell of blood and gore and putrefaction. "I have your money."

Percy's rush permit was eye-wateringly expensive, and Danny's not the type to let that sort of money slide. I'd had to move some funds between my accounts before drawing out the magecredits in cash, which is safer, since cash is more difficult to trace. I don't want my father's accountants to get suspicious and start sniffing around my accounts; after spending a heinous amount on the two *resignio* spells, I cannot risk any further scrutiny.

Danny tugs off his gloves, pulls his ear protectors down so they hang around his neck, then shoves the cash into the chest pocket of his coveralls. "Thanks, mate. How'd she take it?"

"I don't know. I left it behind when I cleared out this morning. I didn't get a chance to see her reaction."

He stares at me open-mouthed for a second, then laughs. "Mate, you didn't even *try* to claim credit?" He shakes his head. "You are *so* whipped."

"I am not," I snap, but my retort lacks a certain fervor. The excuses come, so well-rehearsed they roll smoothly off my tongue. "I just want her help to figure out the source of the surges. It is my father's company, after all, that's at risk. And she is the most brilliant mind in our year—"

"Whipped," Danny says, grinning, lowering his goggles, and replacing his gloves.

Shoving my hands in my pockets, I lean back against one of the other steel-topped tables, hoping Danny doesn't notice the way my face has heated. "Honestly, it's a travesty she was even kicked out in the first place." I'm trying to channel my mortification into something more productive, like anger. "Who the fuck would do that to her? To Percy?"

Danny doesn't answer; he just fits his ear protectors back on and starts up the chainsaw. But the look on his face—I know that look. I've known Danny for too long to miss it.

He knows something.

I push away from the table and stalk closer. "Danny. You *know*, don't you?"

Up close, the roar of the chainsaw is overpowering. As Danny resumes hacking up the griffin, I see that it's covered in burn marks; another casualty of the surges, I suppose. I'm suddenly gripped by the urge to get back to the investigation. Hopefully, now that she's acquired a permit for Percy, Gwendolynne will come back to Seamere, and I can convince her to start looking into it with me again.

"Sorry," Danny shouts, the teeth of the chainsaw splintering through bone. "Can't hear you."

Annoyed, I reach out and physically grab one side of his ear protectors away from his ear.

"Do you know who told Pickering about Percy?" I shout over the sound of the motor. Danny bats my hand away and switches his equipment off.

He stares at me, his eyes narrowed, for several long moments. "Maybe," he says, his demeanor guarded.

Yes. There it is. The tight chest. The rising heat. The controlled but rapidly expanding rage crowding out my thoughts. My next word is hissed. "*Who*?"

Danny drops the chainsaw onto the table with a deep, thudding clang and crosses his own arms across his chest. "Promise you won't get mad," he says, chin raised.

I rake my hand through my hair and give an irritated huff. "All right," I reply after a pause.

He levels a look at me. "It was Isla."

"Isla." My ex. I spit the name out like it's a curse.

"Now, Briggs, remember what you said about not doing anything stupid—"

"Fucking Isla! That devious little . . ." Now both my hands are buried in my hair. "*Fuck*."

Danny looks on sympathetically as I literally fall to pieces. I sink down into a squat, staring at the floor—even though it's spattered with literal gore—and take several deep, heaving breaths.

"She just . . . saw you getting close to Gwendolynne, that's all, and wanted to get her out of the way." Ah, Danny. Always the voice of reason. "You know Isla never got over you. And it's worse that it's Chan, after what happened in fifth year—"

"You don't need to remind me," I snap. What happened in fifth year was the final crack in Isla's and my relationship. The reason we ultimately broke up. It's also the reason why I no longer perform glamours (except, of course, in very specific circumstances).

But our relationship problems had already been there, prior. On the surface, Isla and I had been pristine, shiny. The perfect couple. But underneath, we were all wrong. The glamour I'd messed up had only served to expose the underlying rot.

Isla was never the right person for me. Nor I her. So who is she to come swanning in, getting between me and Gwendolynne, trying to fuck things up?

I don't care that I promised Danny, with my whole chest, that I absolutely would not get mad. I am mad. I'm fucking furious.

Going after Isla, though, isn't going to help matters. I know that.

I also know what I've got to do. And I know I should not put it off any longer.

Straightening my shoulders, I stand, forcing my breaths to slow. My fists uncurl. My jaw unclenches. Slowly, my resolve hardens.

Yes. I will *do it.* Whenever I next get a chance to talk to Gwendolynne, I'll tell her.

After so many years of running from the truth . . .

I will finally confess how I feel.

38

Gwendolynne

I take the train back down to London that very day to reclaim my now-legitimate familiar.

The pound stinks of cat pee, ten times stronger than anything I've ever smelled at Saint Gertrude's—and I've smelled some pretty rank stuff at Saint Gertrude's. I guess the high stocking densities and crowded facilities mean the stench just can't be helped.

At reception, I show them the permit, then sign all of the relevant paperwork. The staff—a bunch of exhausted, overwhelmed, animal-loving volunteers—are overjoyed that I have found him.

Percy's actual legal name is listed on the forms as *Lord Percival the Second, Purveyor of the Flesh of Small Defenseless Creatures, Destroyer of Carpet, Scratcher of Doors, and Usurper of Recently Vacated Chairs.*

Huh, I think. *He was actually telling the truth.*

As soon as the paperwork is completed, the staff perform the bonding ritual, and I feel the telepathic connection between us re-open.

As soon as he sees me, Percy leaps, shivering, into my arms. I squeeze him, just so *relieved* to have him back with me. I've missed him. I've really missed him. It's not even about the fact he can channel magic. It's that, even though it's only been two weeks, I've somehow managed to become attached to the obnoxious little fucker.

I heard that, he says, with a huff. *But I shall forgive you, Hairless One, since you are indeed my valiant rescuer come to save me from despotic jailers.*

I laugh as I start walking, carrying him out of the facility. "Was it *that* bad? Really?"

Percy sniffs. *It is most unfortunate, but I've discovered something even worse than tinned tuna-for-one. A substance so ghastly, so dreadful, so diarrhea-inducing that I do believe I shall never turn my nose up at your food again.*

It takes me a moment to understand he's referring to the cheap tinned cat food that the shelters seem to favor.

"We'll see how long that lasts," I say, while Percy bristles.

Conall, Heloise, and Pen are absolutely ecstatic to see me back. It gives me a warm, fuzzy feeling, because I've always felt a little like I don't quite fit in. That no one would really miss me if I was gone. But there's Conall, giving me a drawing he'd made just for me. There's Pen, hanging back, nervously chafing their hands until I finally crack and pull them into a side hug. And then, of course, there's Heloise.

Heloise is actually crying. She waits until Conall and Pen have left before she rushes at me, wrapping her arms around my neck. "I missed you so much," she whispers into my ear.

Percy gives an indignant yowl at being squashed between our two bodies.

"Oh, quit it," I tell him, pretending to be stern. But in reality I'm half laughing. "You should be thankful you're legitimate now. You won't have to hide out in my room so often."

Indeed. I must remember to thank the Bum Scratcher when next I see him. Percy's obviously referring to Harrisford's purchase of the permit. *He is my true savior, since frankly . . . your room is hideous.*

I roll my eyes, grinning. "You're such a drama queen, Percy."

Percy thinks for a moment, then says, in an extremely condescending tone, *You may add that to my list of names, Hairless One.*

Heloise is still hugging me, refusing to let go. "I've been so worried about you, G. How did you even manage to get a permit?"

Finally, we break apart, and I scrunch up my face, still not quite sure how—or why—it came about. "It was Harrisford. Harrisford bought one for me."

"Harrisford?" Heli's eyes widen. "He managed to get one that fast?" She shakes her head, astounded. "It must have cost him a *fortune.*"

I'm not quite sure how much a permit costs at short notice, but I can imagine a lot, since a standard permit is already so expensive. "He'll be fine," I say mulishly. "He can afford it."

Heloise is still staring at me with a funny expression on her face. "Sure," she says. "But it's pretty obvious—"

"What's obvious?" Straightaway, I regret asking, but it's too late. I didn't stop myself in time.

She gives my shoulder a playful shove. "That he wants to get into your pants, Gwen."

"He does *not*!" My face and chest prickle; I'm sure they've turned bright red.

I haven't had a chance to tell Heloise yet about what Harrisford and I did last night. In fact, I'm not actually sure if I *ever* want to tell her.

In the cold light of day, it honestly is extremely embarrassing. At the time, it had felt so normal, casually discussing sex with Harrisford as though we were discussing the weather. But now, when I think about the way I'd pleaded with him to fuck me, all I want to do is crawl into a hole and die.

"Oh, he does," she teases. "That boy is *pining* for you, G. He wants you *bad*."

I grimace. No. He doesn't. It was just a onetime thing—he'd readily agreed to that. We'd both agreed to it. Give it another few days, and he'll be joyfully bedding someone else . . . someone who is probably less work—and infinitely more attractive—than boring old me.

But the memories rise involuntarily inside my mind. The way he looked. The way he felt. The way his strong arms held me against him, cradling me as we slept. The calluses on his palms as he kneaded my bare skin; the way his faint stubble felt under my fingers and against my inner thighs; the scars covering his shoulders, his back, his neck.

Something lurches in my belly at the memories, though I can't quite put my finger on what. Shaking my head, I ignore it. There's no time to obsess over Harrisford's physical perfection—and imperfections—right now. Not when there's a corporate conspiracy threatening to destroy the world. One that we somehow have to solve before exams start in less than a week. I brace myself, actively pushing all thoughts of Harrisford right out of my mind.

We're in the hallway outside my room, so I glance around to make sure no one is watching, then drag Heloise through my door, shutting it behind us.

Percy immediately leaps out of my arms and begins pacing around the room, sniffing the walls and furniture intently. "Smell anything interesting?" I ask him, arching an eyebrow.

He's now moved on to the hem of my trousers, his little nostrils flaring as they suck in all the scent. *I can smell the Bum Scratcher on your clothing*, he says, then rubs himself contentedly against my leg, purring.

"All right, all right, that's quite enough," I grumble at him, before lifting him off the floor and depositing him on my bed.

After giving Percy a vigorous scratch behind his ears, I straighten to speak to Heli. "What are we going to do now, about Magecorp? About what we saw at the hospital?"

Heli turns to me, twisting one of her braids. "I've been thinking," she says. "The list my mother gave us wasn't just dead people, was it?"

"No, it also listed those who went missing, but—" Stopping short, I twist my mouth in confusion, trying to follow her train of thought. "What are you getting at?"

She gives a low chuckle. "Considering you're the smartest witch at Seamere, G, I'm surprised you haven't thought of this already. That man at the hospital—Jarvis—talked about using the tethers to hold open the portals, right?"

"Right," I say, casting my mind back to the conversation we witnessed.

Nathaniel Price, Jarvis, and the doctor had been discussing how to continue harvesting magic despite having inadequate Source. They'd spoken of a "patient 39" who'd been implanted with a Source fragment a long time prior. And Jarvis had said: *They might be the only individual capable of holding a long-term tether. If we station 39 as the tether* inside *the Void, then our models suggest that they could hold the portal open for quite some time. We can just swap out the tethers on the outside as they burn out.*

Reflexively, I reach out and grab Heli's arm. "Shit, Heli. You think that the missing people might be inside the *Void*?"

Heli nods. "Yeah. I think there's a chance that whoever's opening all the portals to steal magic is kidnapping people to use as tethers. Maybe they're using the tethers that Magecorp already implanted, or maybe they're new ones implanted with stolen Source. But either way, if we go in and rescue them—"

"—then we can close the portals and stop the surges!"

But then we both fall silent. I pace to the window, gripping the sill; Heli sinks onto the bed and starts stroking Percy's back. There's one major thing we're missing . . . and that is: How do we get into the Void?

I lean my forehead against the glass, my burst of exhilaration dissipating until it's thoroughly replaced by gloom. No one speaks for several long minutes.

That is, until Percy pipes up from where he's lounging at the foot of my bed. He's been listening to my thoughts, evidently.

If you want to enter the Void, Hairless One, he says, *you'll need to break into Nathaniel's house and steal a big black box.*

I swivel to face Percy. "A big black box?" Apart from the time he'd told me someone broke into the Price mansion, Percy has never spoken about his life there. And I'd never thought to ask, which in retrospect was a massive oversight.

He gives me a slow blink with his one eye. *Yes. I saw my ex-human open portals many times.*

"And once we get a black box, how do we open the portal?" I say, breathless.

You will need a Source, Hairless One.

I frown. "The black box uses the Source to rip open the portal?"

No, Percy says, with the long-suffering tone of someone trying to explain an extremely simple concept to a child. *The black box tears open the hole. The Source helps to keep it open.*

The Source. I chew my lip, thinking. The Source is the key. The tethers are only able to keep the portals open because they're implanted with bits of Source.

It takes a moment for Percy's explanation to sink in fully, but then I'm rummaging through my wardrobe. *Source. Source. I need a*

Source. My mind chants the phrase over and over as I search, like it's an affirmation.

After Harrisford had rescued me from the Magecorp tower, healed me, and put me in my *Twilight* shirt, he'd presumably stuffed his mother's suit somewhere.

When I finally come across it, I realize that *stuffed* isn't exactly the right word. He had, in fact, folded it up neatly and placed it inside a drawer. I shake out the tweed fabric. It's still covered with dust and debris from the explosion.

"What are you doing?" Heli asks, unfolding herself from the bed and coming to stand by me.

I don't answer her. I just continue my careful search of all the crevices in the tweed, running my fingers along all the neatly sewn seams. And then—

"Got it," I say, my heart giving a triumphant flip. Resting in my palm is a piece of Source: shrapnel from the explosion.

Percy tells us that Nathaniel Price has plenty of black boxes. He's not quite sure what they're called, how to work them, or even what they do, but he assures us that every time he witnessed Nathaniel tearing open a portal, he'd done so holding one of the boxes.

It takes the rest of the afternoon for Heli and me to sketch out a plan. Percy, having never had his bond formally rescinded from Nathaniel's control, still has the ability to enter the Price family mansion. Unfortunately, the protection charms and security wards won't allow either of us to accompany him, but he agrees to go in on his own.

That night, under cover of darkness, Heloise, Percy, and I sneak up to the tall steel fence of Mr. Price and Mrs. Mason-Price's enormous estate property. In the distance, the peaked roofs of the Price mansion are shadowed against the inky sky. Fortunately, it's cloudy and dark, so Percy blends seamlessly into the surrounding shadows.

I crouch beside him, nerves tying my stomach in knots. This is dangerous—so dangerous. "Be careful," I say, my mouth running dry. I only just got Percy back and I don't want to lose him again. "Don't make a sound. Don't be seen."

He narrows his eye to a slit. *You are severely underestimating a cat's ability to be stealthy.* His tail twitches, irritated. *It seems a conspicuous gap in your veterinary knowledge.*

I don't even have it in me to be annoyed by the snootiness of his tone. "Just . . . hurry back, okay?"

He spends some moments regarding me with a haughty look. *Do not fear. I shall hurry.* And as he turns away, he adds, *I do not want to lose you, either.*

I stare at him, open-mouthed. Did Percy just admit that he actually . . . cares about me? I don't have time to ask, because already he's squeezing into the minuscule space beneath the fence. Having demonstrated that cats actually *are* made of liquid, he trots off into the darkness. When he is a few meters away he all but disappears, swallowed whole by the night.

"And now we wait," I murmur. My chest feels constricted, as though I've zipped myself into a too-tight dress.

Heloise sits down, her back against the fence, and before long I sink down beside her.

"Do you think it's actually Magecorp behind the surges?" I ask, after we've sat silently for a few minutes. "And the explosions?"

"I dunno, Gwen." Heli's eyes are wide and dark, liquid pools in the moonless night. "It doesn't sound like using people as tethers is a new thing. I think"—she gives a small frown—"that maybe the surges and explosions are from something else, like Mr. Briggs claimed."

"Maybe whoever's sabotaging Magecorp is kidnapping the implanted people and using them up too fast." I scrunch my nose up in disgust. "I would say it sounds like something the MLO would do, but then Professor Kaur . . ." I trail off. It's beyond imagining to believe that the dean, my hero, would be involved in anything that shady. Not to mention someone as gentle, and as *noble*, as Pen.

"I *know*, right?" Heli says, tipping her head back against the fence.

I almost lean back too, but instead I leap to my feet, because Percy is back. "Percy!" I whisper as he slips back underneath the fence. "You brilliant, brilliant animal."

He trots toward us, a sleek black box around the size of a cigarette packet clamped between his jaws.

I stare at him, puzzled. "I thought you said it was a big box?"

It is big to me, Percy retorts, dropping the box at my feet. And it's true. The strange black object might be small to me, but Percy had to almost unhinge his jaw to fit it inside his mouth.

I pick up the black box off the ground and shove it in my pocket. It's heavier than I expected, and oddly cold. "You're right. And thanks. You can definitely have some baked beans for that."

Heli raises one eyebrow at me, and I chuckle. Then, after I signal to them both to start moving away, we begin picking a path through the overgrown grass, heading back to Heli's car.

We haven't made it far, though, before it happens: A gunshot rings through the air, cleaving the stillness in two.

Heli and I scream, and even Percy jumps. Mrs. Mason-Price, the same woman who'd ordered me to euthanize Percy on the first day I met him, is running across the vast expanse of her lawn, brandishing a magical gun exactly like the one Darghan Briggs had pointed at me.

"Run!" I scream. Dropping all attempts to remain quiet, we start crashing through the tangled undergrowth. My heart is pounding in my throat, my breaths coming in ragged rasps. We're so close, we're so close, it's only a few paces away—

Another shot rings out, and behind me, Heloise screams. I whirl around, yelling her name, and she stares at me, wide-eyed as she crumples. Her hand is clamped on her upper arm, and even in the darkness I can see that around it, there's a dark stain creeping slowly outward, seeping into the sleeves of her cream-colored shirt.

"Heli," I pant, sprinting back to her. "Oh my god, Heli." I fall to my knees, pressing my hands over the wound. Then, not even thinking about the fact I'm not technically allowed to do it, I perform a quick healing spell to cauterize the blood vessels, then seal the wound shut.

Percy lets out a plaintive meow, and I drag Heloise's arm around my shoulder. Together, the three of us stumble toward Heli's car, while behind us Mrs. Mason-Price screams obscenities at us. She must have thought we were trying to trespass—perhaps she's more paranoid after the last break-in—but at least she seems to have given up hunting us, now that we are at a distance.

Somehow, I manage to yank open Heli's car door. Percy leaps in and onto the back seat. He sits bolt upright with his tail curled around his body, shivering following the close encounter with his ex-owner.

I start to bundle Heli into the back seat, but she waves me away. "Gwen, I'm all right. You healed me already, remember?"

"But—but you were *shot*!"

"The bullet must've just grazed me. Get out of the way, G, I'm driving."

"Heli—"

Heli gives me a stern look, hands on hips, her eyebrows at a severe slant. "Be serious, Gwendolynne. *You.* Are not driving *my* car."

Percy pipes up from the back seat. *You should listen to the Beautiful One.*

"The who?" My mind is sluggish, not quite keeping up, but the next second, it clicks. "*Oh.* You mean Heloise." Of course Heloise is the Beautiful One, while I am deemed alopecic.

Yes, her. Percy's intonation is a mixture of conceited and concerned. *We have both witnessed your fast-twitch reflexes, and . . . well.*

Rolling my eyes, I concede defeat. Heli's right. My nerves are shot. I probably wouldn't even be able to work out how to start such a fancy vehicle anyway.

Heli and I tumble in, and I've barely managed to tug the passenger-side door shut when the mage-powered engine kicks in and Heli floors it.

Halfway down the motorway toward Seamere, as she's hunched over the steering wheel, gripping it with both hands, Heli lets out a giggle. She presses her lips together, giving me a sidelong look, trying to stifle her mirth.

She fails.

Catching my eye, she lets out a snort, then another giggle. A bubble of elation expands in my chest, and I start snickering too, then outright laughing. And then we're both laughing, tears leaking out of the corners of our eyes, me clutching the stolen black box in both of my hot little hands.

Maybe it's ridiculous to be proud of it, but I must say: I've got *pretty* good at rule breaking recently. The adrenaline and endorphins are pumping through my blood vessels like the headiest of designer drugs.

The electric windows slide down, Heli pumps up the stereo, and then we're zooming along, singing at the top of our lungs, completely off tune. Percy sniffs disdainfully, but even he can't hide the fact his tail is twitching in time to the music.

I've been reinstated at Seamere. Heli and I are almost graduated. We have a Source, *and* we've managed to steal one of Magecorp's black boxes. All we need to do now is get Conall to help us figure out how the fuck to use it.

And as the shadowed scenery zips past us, the glowing orange streetlights blurring in our vision, we belt out bad '90s pop into the night air, exhilarated.

I, Gwendolynne Chan, am going to ace my exams. I'm going to beat Harrisford. I'm going to win . . .

And I'm going to fucking figure out what's causing all these surges.

I, Gwendolynne Chan, am back in the game.

39

Harrisford

Unfortunately, I don't get a chance to confront Gwendolynne before exams, because straightaway we're launched mercilessly into our final revision period. Four days of study pass by like a whirlwind: a montage of cramming and late nights and far too many coffees.

I see Gwendolynne often, but at a distance, and usually insensible to the world because she's studying.

Her being so ubiquitous is a little unusual, I must admit. During every other examination period over the past seven years, she's spent most of her time shut up in her room. This time, though, she seems to be everywhere: the library, the courtyard, bolting down food in the canteen with her eyes glued to a book. Other times, I've caught her holding some sort of small black rectangular object, frowning at it. It's not something I've seen before—I can only assume it's some newfangled method of revision.

She's omnipresent, both in physicality and within my mind. The woman I simultaneously want, and want to beat. It's as though she's been put on this earth purely to torment me.

I manage—just—to keep my distance. With the specter of exams hanging over us, I tell myself that Gwendolynne is extremely stressed and needs to be left alone. Plus, I can't trust that I'll hold myself back from yanking her into my arms and kissing her, and never letting her go again.

On Monday morning, final examinations start in earnest, and all (well, most) of my thoughts about Gwendolynne are chased out of my mind. I've no time to brood, what with the examiners putting us through our paces.

A third of the exams are practical, involving wrangling dragons, or demonstrating suture patterns, or giving tablets to aggressive, fire-breathing chimeras (which are almost as difficult to give pills to as the common household cat). A third are oral, which means being stuck in a stuffy room with various associate professors who have affected perfect poker faces while flinging random, unrelated questions at us. And the last third are written, with the entire year sitting at rows of desks in the converted dining hall. It has had wards added to it so we can't cheat by asking our familiars to look up the answers. Officials from the Magical Education Regulatory Authority prowl up and down the aisles, scanning for evidence of other enchantments.

Since my surname comes before hers in the alphabet, Gwendolynne is always seated behind me, one row back and three to the right.

It's exceptionally distracting; I can't even count how many times the back of my neck heats, as I wonder if she might be looking in my direction. Usually, my mind flits there momentarily before I'm able to focus once again on my work, but during one of the last exams—an internal medicine exam—I find myself unable to concentrate.

The words swim in front of my eyes, the small black text blurring together. With one finger, I push my glasses up—the hall is stifling, the bridge of my nose sweaty—and utter a curse beneath my breath.

> Outline the etiology and pathophysiology of hypertrophic cardiomyopathy in the common garden gremlin (CGG) and its effect on cardiac function.

I wonder if Gwendolynne is looking at me.

> Explain how disease prevalence impacts the positive predictive value (PPV) *and* the negative predictive value (NPV) of a diagnostic test.

I wonder if she's thought about me much these past few days.

> Describe, in detail, the physiological basis for fire breathing in the dragon. The use of a diagram is permitted in your answer.

I wonder if she's thought much about the night we spent in Manchester, in her bed.

I wonder if she has, because I certainly have. Constantly.

After making a halfhearted attempt to scribble out an answer, I chance a glance over my shoulder at Gwendolynne. And I can't quite believe it, because . . .

She's looking right at me.

For a second she looks bewildered. Two red spots bloom on her cheeks, and she quickly ducks her head, staring hard at her page. A fraction too late, I turn away too, only to sneak another look a second later. She's still staring—or glowering, rather—at her exam paper, now furiously chewing the end of her pen.

Gods above, she is adorable.

When we're finally let out of the hall, I get swept along with the tide of students, feeling like an absurdly tall piece of driftwood being buffeted about by the sea. There is laughing and chatting and cheering all around me—we have just finished our last-ever exam, after all—but my eyes are trained on the crowd, looking for Gwendolynne's head of black hair. It must be my lucky day, because a moment later I spot her, weaving through the crowd toward me.

She's frowning, her brow creased, murmuring something beneath her breath, so lost in her thoughts that she doesn't see me until she's almost collided with my chest.

"Oh," she says, blinking up. Then her eyelids slide shut, as though she's trying to wish me away. "Briggs."

"Chan," I say, trying to keep command over my voice. I'm in too much danger of sounding overenthusiastic. I have a plan, something I've been carefully constructing over the past few days, but I have to tread carefully or I'll risk scaring her off.

She opens her eyes again, scowling when she sees I'm still standing there. Her eyes are lighter, almost hazel, in the brightness of the afternoon light. A shard of sun streams through a stained glass window, throwing a geometric pattern of colors across her hair.

"Would you mind moving, Briggs? I left a book behind." We're still crushed in a press of students, being jostled by the crowd. It occurs to me that with my height and broad stature, there's not much room to squeeze past.

I don't respond for a second; I just stand there, smiling stupidly. Then, before I can lose my nerve, I blurt out, "Do you want to grab a bite to eat?" *Goddammit.* So much for being cool.

Startled, she says, "What? Together?"

"Yes, together."

She doesn't answer immediately, just eyes me suspiciously. "What for?"

"To celebrate."

Her suspicion only grows. She narrows her eyes. "Celebrate what?"

I sigh. "The end of exams." Then I add, "*Obviously.*"

"But . . ." She rubs at her temple, seemingly flustered. "Why don't you just go to the party?" For weeks, a group of students have been planning a huge knees-up in Heywood Hall for end of term.

I shrug, aiming for nonchalance. "I just feel like doing something a bit more . . . private."

She gives a dubious sort of frown. "With me? Are you sure I'm who you want to celebrate with?"

I cock my head and squint at her. "Depends. Your name is Alice Chu, right?" I grin when she whacks me in the shoulder.

But then I step closer, into our shared space. She stares up at me with those wide, guileless brown eyes, and immediately, I am lost in them. "Yes, Chan, it's you I want to celebrate with." A thrill rolls right through me when I see her visibly shiver.

She seems to gather herself, her chin jutting up, her expression defiant. "Why?"

"Because, next week, one of us is going to be awarded the top spot. And since we don't know which of us it is yet, I figured we may as well celebrate us both."

"Fair." She pauses, as though contemplating my words. Then she flashes me a dazzling smile. "It'll be me, though. You know that, don't you?"

Fuck. I never realized how much of a turn-on a cocky Gwendolynne could be.

"That's it," I growl, grabbing her wrist. She lets out a little gasp but doesn't wrench away as I begin to tug her down the hall. "Gwendolynne Chan, you're coming with me."

40

Gwendolynne

Harrisford leads me to the Seamere car park. At one stage, Danny tries to corner him, pressing him to go to the party, but Harrisford just waves him off.

We arrive in front of a small black car. The lights flash and there are two little beeps before Harrisford swings the passenger door open.

"Get in," he says. A command, not a request.

I fold my arms. "How do I know you're not planning on murdering me and dumping my body so that you'll come top of class?" I'm trying to focus on Harrisford's face, though it's hard since today he's wearing a white V-neck T-shirt that hugs his chest and biceps as though he's something carved from marble. I didn't even realize Harrisford owned any T-shirts, but I suppose even Greek gods like to be comfortable for exams.

"Well . . ." One corner of his lip twitches. "I do prefer my women more . . . alive."

His response makes my skin tighten. *His* women? His *women*? I don't know whether to be attracted or repulsed.

Propping my hands on my hips, I arch an eyebrow at him. "Alive? Is that all? You don't have very high standards, Briggs."

He leans closer, caging me against the car. Heat radiates from his skin. His scent shoots up my nostrils, something beneath his cologne that is one hundred percent pure *him*. I bite my lip involuntarily.

Harrisford's gaze locks on my mouth. "My standards are higher than yours, it seems," he breathes, his voice so menacing it almost undoes me on the spot. He tilts his face closer to mine. "Since *you're* the one about to go on a date with a potential murderer." Then he straightens and raps the top of the car door, his expression turning predatory. "Now get in the car, Chan."

Is that what this is? A date? My limbs have lost all feeling as I surrender and fold myself into the seat. It's clean, it's comfortable, it's got that new-car smell. Harrisford slams my door shut.

"I thought you didn't own a car," I murmur as he slides into the seat next to me. I run a finger along the pristine dashboard.

He starts the almost-silent magic-powered engine, flings his arm around the back of my seat, and begins reversing out. "I bought it last week."

I raise my eyebrows at him. "You . . . bought a car?" I'm stunned by the idea that anyone would just go out and . . . *buy* a brand-new car. With cash, presumably. Without having to save up for literal years.

His eyes flash to mine for a second, and then away. "With graduation so soon, it was about time I got one."

I stare at him because his voice sounds strained—he's gripping the steering wheel, his knuckles blanched, and his ears have gone the tiniest touch pink.

I turn to face forward again, shaking my head. Harrisford Briggs is seriously weird.

We spend most of the drive in silence, me chewing my lip and watching the scenery slide by the window. It's summer proper now, and the air has grown even thicker and muggier than it's ever been before.

All I can think about is how irresponsible this is; now that we've finished exams, I really should be trying to figure out, once and for all, how to access the Void. Conall, Heloise, and I had spent every night during the exam period puzzling over blueprints and twisting the unmarked dials and knobs on the black box Percy stole. But nothing seemed to work, and Percy—though he'd witnessed the procedure many a time—didn't know anything beyond his vague, cat-biased recollections. Nathaniel, it seems, had been careful to shield his thoughts whenever he'd deemed it necessary.

It's only two days until the graduation ceremony. After that, we'll all go our separate ways. I'll lose access to Conall's brilliant mind, and Heloise's smarts and steadfast support.

The others are planning to go to the party anyway, I tell myself, trying to assuage my guilt. *You can work on it again first thing tomorrow.*

We drive past paddocks with grazing unicorns, their silver foals frolicking through the grass. The meadows are bathed in sunshine, butterflies (or are they cabbage moths?) flitting around the wildflowers. But I can barely appreciate it. First, because the surges—and the inaccessible Void—are still hanging over my head. Second, I'm ruminating over all the things I might have messed up in my exams. And third . . .

I still don't understand what Harrisford is doing.

The last time I saw him, he'd called me perfect, then made me come, spectacularly. The time before that, he'd been flirting with the nurse at the London General Magical Hospital—a woman whose name he'd forgotten mere days later.

And the time before *that*, he'd insulted me at the qílín paddocks and basically laughed in my face when I brought up the surges.

Which is the real Harrisford? And which version is the act?

Eventually, the countryside gives way to the city, and before long we're pulling into the car park beneath a restaurant. Inside, it's dim. The place is decked out all in black, multitextured layers of velvet seats, black-stained hardwood, glossy lacquered feature walls. The only sources of light are innumerable flickering candles, which are simply wicks inserted into little jars of liquid magic, and there are at least twenty pieces of cutlery laid out at every setting.

"We have a booking under Briggs," Harrisford says at the front desk, and my stomach does a little somersault at the careless way he'd said *we*. The maître d', also clad all in black, leads us to a table tucked way up in the back. I'm feeling out of place because I'm not wearing black, and also because I'm tragically underdressed. The only redeeming factor is that Harrisford is dressed casually, too.

Harrisford calls for the wine list as soon as we are seated, donning his reading glasses to peruse the menu. I watch him, studying the little indentation that appears between his eyebrows when he concentrates; at the way he absent-mindedly runs a finger back and forth across his full lower lip while he's reading. When he looks up, he raises his eyebrows at me, having caught me gawking. I bite my lip and look away.

Stay on your guard, Gwen. I cannot let myself feel. I cannot let myself get caught up in Harrisford's twisted games.

"Do you want white or red?" he says.

"Red, please."

He orders, and when the bottle arrives, he pours me a glass. I frown. "Aren't you having any?"

"No. I prefer white." He nudges my glass toward me.

I narrow my eyes at him. "You should order some, then. It seems unfair to have me drinking, and you completely sober. I feel as if it's putting me at a disadvantage."

He rolls his eyes but gestures to the waiter, who at Harrisford's request brings a second bottle.

We clink our glasses and drink, eyeing each other across the table. I still haven't asked why Harrisford has brought me here. It might be petty, but I don't want to give him the satisfaction of knowing that I'm curious. So instead, I just say to him, "We really can't agree on anything, can we?"

He had seemed lost in thought, but my question jerks him out of his reverie. "Whatever do you mean, Chan?"

I take a sip of wine. "Red or white. Mag.fam, myth.creat. Curry or vinegar. BBC or the 2005 version—"

He scoffs, cutting me off. "I'm sure we can find something we agree on."

"Oh yeah?" I say, challenging. "Let's try, then. Dark chocolate."

He shoots me a scandalized look. "White. It's so much sweeter."

"Coffee or tea?"

"Coffee," he says, then flushes. "I know that you prefer tea."

"Beach or snow?" I say, and at precisely the same time I say "beach," he says "snow." Of course he'd like snow, since he's posh, snobby, and stupidly rich.

I cross my arms and lean back in my chair. "All right then, here's the big one: Team Edward or Team Jacob?"

He takes a sip of his own wine, then purses his lips. "Neither," he says, after a beat. "Team Jessica."

My mouth drops open in an expression of mock outrage. "You *animal*! She's meant to be the bitchy one!"

He shrugs. "The actress who played her was hot."

I shake my head in dismay. "That's it. I think we'll have to stay enemies forever."

His eyes gleam with something like amusement. "Right, enemies. Of course."

Something has shifted in the atmosphere, as though a magical surge is happening here, right now, right at this very table, in the small expanse of space that separates us. It's like the delicate dance we're doing is bringing us closer and closer, in increasingly tight circles, and I'm finally facing Harrisford as myself, completely vulnerable, laid bare.

I sigh, defeated. I have to know, once and for all, what game Harrisford is playing. "What are we doing here?"

"We're drinking wine. And soon, we will be eating."

"No, I mean, what are *we* doing *here*." I gesture frantically to the space between us. "Why did you bring me here? What are you playing at, Briggs?"

He takes another sip of wine, eyeing me over the rim of his glass. Then he sets his wineglass down, very carefully, on the table. "Why, I'm wooing you, Chan."

I let out an incredulous laugh. "*Wooing* me?" Immediately, my heart starts to race, and my breath feels far too big for my chest.

"Yes, wooing you. Isn't that how people do it? Take them to fancy restaurants and ply them with food and drink?"

I stare at him, open-mouthed, still hung up on his archaic speech patterns. "That sounds like something straight out of last century!"

He leans forward, smirking, until our faces are only inches from one another. I realize, too late, that I'd been leaning forward too. "Would you rather I put it differently?" he says, and his voice has dropped so low that it makes me shiver, melting a pool of desire in my lower belly. "Would you rather I say that I'm courting you?"

"That's even worse. That's like something . . . they'd say in a Jane Austen novel." My words come out so breathless, it's embarrassing.

He leans even closer, until his breath caresses my lips. "Who would I be, do you think? Darcy, or Mr. Bingley?"

I'm admittedly impressed by his knowledge of Regency-era literature, although he's perhaps just familiar with the BBC TV miniseries. I give him a speculative look, then curve my lips into a wicked smile. "I think you're most like . . . Mr. Collins."

He gives a roar of outrage. "You evil witch! I don't think that *enemies* is strong enough a word." But he's grinning.

The sliver of air between us shivers; there's that electric charge again. He's talking as though he wants us to be an item, but everything I've heard about Harrisford is that he just sleeps around. How many women has he brought here? How many have come before me and been lured by the magic that he weaves with his words? My stomach has twisted around and around on itself; I take another gulp of wine just to calm my nerves.

The first dish arrives, startling us. We spring apart. Harrisford snatches up his glass and takes a hearty swig of wine.

As each course comes out—I learn somewhere during the third dish that it's a degustation menu—we skirt around several topics, not quite knowing how to earnestly land on a conversation. I try to discuss the examinations, but he shuts me down. "Not everyone enjoys dissecting everything as much as you do," he says.

I try to broach the topic of his mother, since the last time we'd spoken he'd revealed that, despite the rumors, she is still alive. But he shuts that down too, only confirming that his middle initial stands for Finlay because it was his mother's maiden name.

"Shame," I murmur. "I thought Harrisford-fucking-Briggs had a nice ring to it."

When he dares to bring up the night we spent in Manchester, it's me who vetoes the conversation, refusing to discuss it while blushing hot all over.

At one point, Percy cuts in, inside my head. *Ask him to scratch you on the bum.* I give an indignant shriek, which has Harrisford giving me a funny look.

"Shut up, Percy," I hiss back at him. "This conversation is *private*!"

Harrisford shakes his head, half amused, half appalled. "You really ought to learn how to shield, Chan."

It's all very awkward, full of stilted conversation. But finally, after we've polished off course seven, and the wine has loosened me up enough that I'm no longer as tightly strung as a cello, Harrisford finds the topic that we can both freely indulge in: what I know about the Void.

He asks me what I was doing, that time we ran into each other at the hospital. And, with my tongue freed by alcohol and an urgent need to fix things, I tell him. I explain how Heli and I had snuck into the MLO meeting, and how we'd discovered that Professor Kaur was the acting leader. I tell him about the conversation we'd overheard between Nathaniel, the doctor, and Jarvis. I tell him about the horrifying surgery that Heli and I had witnessed: doctors under Magecorp's thumb implanting bits of Source into the necks of humans so that they can be used as tethers.

And finally, I tell him about how Heloise, Percy, and I had broken into Nathaniel Price's mansion and stolen a device to enter the Void. But that, despite our best efforts, we still hadn't worked out how to use it.

Harrisford listens to all of this patiently, and by the time I've finished speaking, my words spilling over themselves in my hurry, I suddenly realize that he and I have reached across the table and are holding each other's hands.

The tenth course has finished. Degustation is over. And my "date" with Harrisford (the potential murderer) has come crashing to an end.

41

Harrisford

We walk out of the restaurant slowly. My pulse is racing and my palms are clammy because tonight has been perfect and I really do not want it to be over.

I hadn't realized how far Gwendolynne and her friends had got in the investigation. While I was moping around, worrying about Nathaniel's threats, she was busy sneaking into clandestine meetings, breaking into high-security mansions, and uncovering unethical, underhanded agreements between Magecorp and the medical establishment. In all honesty, Gwendolynne deserves to come first—she puts me to shame, quite frankly.

I turn to face her. "That was . . ." I start, but then stop. The degustation was delightful, but in truth it was an appalling lack of food. Every course was artfully arranged, the flavors delicate and nuanced, the ingredients fresh and seasonal. But put all together, it just wasn't very . . . well, filling.

She stares at me, and then her lips curve into a smile. "Puny? Minuscule?"

I break into an embarrassed laugh. "Infinitesimal."

She laughs too, and relief washes through me. And then she's grabbing my arm and tugging me along the street, saying, "Come on, Briggs. Let me show you my version of going out to dinner."

Twenty minutes later, we're standing on a street corner, devouring greasy burgers. Honestly, I'm impressed at how quickly she can cram that thing into her delectable mouth.

"This is amazing," she says, her voice muffled by the food.

"Agreed," I say, though I'm not talking about the burgers.

When we've finished, we scrunch up our wrappers and toss them into the rubbish bin that's right outside the burger joint. She's still in the baggy shirt and jeans she wore to the exam, her lips all slick with burger grease, and I think that she is perfect.

"I'm sorry you had to do all that on your own," I say. "Investigate the surges, I mean. Truly, I am."

She sighs. "It's okay. You were right." She scrunches up her nose. "Magecorp *is* evil. Whether or not they're causing the explosions, they're still exploiting people."

"Yeah." My tone is morose. "You can see why I don't want to work for them."

Gwendolynne is still silent, regarding me. She reaches up and touches a finger to one corner of my mouth.

At first, I flinch—my instinct is to duck away. But I hold my ground. The pad of her finger is scalding hot against my skin. My lips part, and I actually hear the breath hitching in her throat.

"You have something," she whispers. "On your lip."

I stand still as a statue as she swipes it away. I too am holding my breath. "Is it all gone?"

"No." She keeps dabbing at my lip, and eventually her movements slow, as though she's contemplating something.

"Is something the matter?" I say, alarmed, because her expression has suddenly shuttered.

"Is it strange for you? Standing out here, on the street, eating a burger from a greasy spoon? It's hardly what you're used to."

"I can honestly say that it was the best burger I've ever tasted. Why do you ask?"

"Because . . ." She takes a step back, folding her arms tightly, then flashes me a look. "I sometimes feel like you judge me. You know, for being poor and all."

I frown. Her words sting, deep within my chest. And it's because I know that she's not entirely wrong. I was a snotty little snob for most of my time at Seamere—but over the past two years, ever since I'd started noticing Gwendolynne in a way that was not strictly as an academic rival, I've been trying to slowly dismantle those prejudices. And while I might not always get it right . . . I *am* trying.

"Listen." I run my hand through my hair, trying to figure out how best to articulate my thoughts. "I might have done . . . Once. But I don't think that anymore. The truth is, Gwendolynne, I find everything about you utterly perfect. I wouldn't have you any other way."

Her gaze slides off to the side, and then she shrugs. "I guess it's mainly Percy, then, who judges me."

I reach out, gently tugging her arms away from her body, until we're standing face-to-face, her hands clasped in mine. "Percy," I say, drawing her closer to me, "doesn't know how lucky he is to have found such an exceptional human."

The deep mahogany of her eyes fixes on me. I can almost see myself reflected; I can see the mirror images of the mage-powered streetlights dancing across her irises. For a moment, I'm transfixed, almost as though I'm outside my body. An observer, watching us from the outside in, as we teeter on the cusp of our pasts and our future.

It feels like a moment that could go in a number of different directions, lead to an almost infinite number of possibilities. So heavy and so significant . . . that I freeze.

It's Gwendolynne, not me, who breaks through. She rises up on tiptoe, her hand lifting to my face. Her voice drops, until it is but a whisper. "I think, Briggs, that you might still have something . . . right here."

And then she's drawing my face down to hers, and I'm not fighting it, because my god this is what I want, it's what I've wanted for years, it's what I now realize I've wanted since that time in fifth year when Isla insisted I put a glamour on her as part of a role-playing game and I'd accidentally turned her into Gwendolynne Chan . . .

Gwendolynne's tongue touching the corner of my lip sends all my blood rushing to my lower body and it only takes a minor shift of my head position to be finally, finally kissing her again.

At first, it's slow, sensual, exploratory—but then she lets out a little sigh against my lips and I groan, curling around her, clasping her harder against my body so her chest is crushed against mine. Our kiss turns desperate, passionate, my hands roaming anywhere and everywhere and all over her body. I can barely think because all I want to do is touch her, see her, be inside her. Worship her.

I've booked a hotel room for the foreseeable future because exams are over, and I don't wish to go back to Heywood Hall—or my father's mansion—unless absolutely necessary. Both of them hold too many painful memories.

And more than anything, I want Gwendolynne to join me. At the hotel. Tonight. But it's her choice. It must always be, absolutely, enthusiastically, one hundred percent her choice.

So I break the kiss, crushing my lips against her temple.

"Gwendolynne," I murmur, my words vibrating against her skin. "There's no pressure either way. But . . . will you stay with me tonight?"

42

Gwendolynne

It occurs to me as we're riding up in the lift that maybe this has been Harrisford's plan all along.

Perhaps this whole thing has been a challenge for him. A conquest. A ploy to get me, his greatest rival, into bed. Perhaps he feels the need to bring me down a peg, to win this final game.

And you know what? In this moment . . . I don't care. In a way, even if it's just another one-night thing, at least I'll have won, too.

It's because I need this. I need the distraction. I've been so stressed out by exams. So defeated by my inability to figure out the black box or how to enter the Void. If one night of sex with Harrisford is what it takes to numb those feelings temporarily, I'll take it.

We're standing shoulder to shoulder, not talking, as we ascend to the twenty-second floor.

"Don't you need to go back and get Pudding?" I say, to break the oppressive silence. "Isn't she like, your emotional support lizard?"

"She's not my emotional support—" Harrisford starts to snap, but then he catches sight of my grin reflected in the mirrored walls.

"You cheeky witch," he laughs, bumping his shoulder against mine.

Then his smile sharpens. He half turns, his arm snaking around my waist, and leans in close to speak into my ear. "Trust me, though . . ." His voice has deepened to molten liquid. "With what I plan to do to you, I'd prefer not to have an audience."

At that precise moment, the lift doors slide open and he strides out, leaving me to scramble after him, my face flushed beetroot red. How is it that I started out teasing *him*, yet *I'm* the one who's wound up flustered?

When we enter, he shuts the soft-close door behind us. I only have a second to take in the room. Or, not a room rather, but a *suite*, bigger than anything I've ever seen before, bigger even than my entire flat. I don't get a chance to register any details because Harrisford is already on me.

He's kissing me furiously, and I'm kissing him back, our movements clumsy, harried, unbridled. He walks me backward farther into the room, his lips chasing me through space as my body arches, his hand splayed against my lower back.

It takes mere seconds before we've tugged off my T-shirt, and only another second before he's pulled his own off, too. He runs his lips along the angle of my jaw, to my neck, kissing me down it, then biting me, hard, at the angle of my shoulder.

I cry out, half in lust, half in pain, and his mouth captures mine again, swallowing my scream. Another strangled moan follows, also into Harrisford's mouth, as he slips his hand beneath the cup of my bra and kneads my breast, skimming his calloused fingers across my nipple. My whole body jerks, my legs almost giving out beneath me, but one of his muscular legs is shoved between both of mine, and then I'm grinding against him, finding both too much and too little friction between the fabric of our jeans. He groans out my name and grabs hold of my butt, kneading it, clasping me tighter to him.

When he slips the straps of my bra off my shoulders and starts kissing across my décolletage, I quip, "No judgy Carlisle this time."

He raises his head just a fraction, just enough to say, with a sinful gleam in his eyes, "I don't think I need him to rein me in tonight."

My desire surges from a current into raging river rapids, and I adjust my stance to let Harrisford take off my bra. He leans back for a moment, his gaze sweeping down my body, and then drops to his knees, undoing my jeans, easing them down my legs, and good god I'm glad that I wore some decent knickers. It's my own personal end-of-exam celebratory ritual.

He gives a low hum of appreciation at the already dampening silk, skimming his nose along my waistband before impatiently tugging that down, too. Palming my hips and digging his fingers into my backside, he shoots me a lascivious look before clamping his mouth between my legs.

I cry out, my knees buckling, but Harrisford is there to hold me up. I twine my fingers through his hair, rocking my hips against his mouth. His touch, his lips, his tongue are urgent, uncompromising; he approaches giving me pleasure with the same enthusiasm as he did that night in Manchester. He teases sounds out of me that I never even knew I could make. And when my pleasure breaks, I cry out his name, and he keeps going, which makes me explode again, and again.

I'm still shaking with the echoes of my many orgasms when he pulls me up and lifts me into his arms, kissing me again. Automatically, my legs wrap around his waist, feeling the considerable length of his hardness slide against the slick evidence of my pleasure. "I'm wrecking your jeans," I whisper against his lips.

"Fuck it," he manages to grind out. "I like it."

He walks me to the bed, dropping us both down, the hard planes of his torso jutting up against the soft curves of mine. With frantic hands, I help him remove his own jeans, pushing them down his long legs until they're off completely, and then I do the same to his underwear until he, like me, is completely naked. He sits back to grab a condom out of the pocket of his discarded jeans, and grins when I raise an eyebrow and say, "You were a bit overconfident about fucking me tonight, weren't you?"

He smirks and rips the packet open. "I believe you've got me exactly where you wanted."

He rolls the condom on. And I stare at him. My gaze rakes the full length of his body, tracing the dips and bulges of his muscles—he's built, but not too built; lean, but not too lean. My eyes linger on his cock, which is looking imposingly big. And then I reach out, my fingers grazing his six-pack, trailing down his abdomen, then skirting sideways until they skim the sharp V of his hips . . .

"Gwendolynne," he groans, and everything inside me tightens. I am so, so ready for him.

He leans over me, easing me back onto the pillows. I'm nestled in down and linen and the lighting is soft and Harrisford's body is warm and hard, and he's braced himself on his arms above me, supporting his weight so he doesn't crush me, and I put a hand on his chest and realize that he's shaking. Realize that his heart is beating about as fast as mine.

"Are you . . . nervous?" My tone is disbelieving.

"I'm not nervous," he says, too quickly. Then he concedes. "Okay, maybe I'm a little nervous."

I scrunch my brows in confusion, even as my legs curl around his thighs, tugging him even closer, until the evidence of his arousal slides—both hard and soft and oh so warm—against my abdomen. "But . . . why? I mean, you've done this before . . ."

"Yes, of course." A look of alarm flashes across his face. "Why, haven't you?"

"Of course I have!" But then I add, "Not very much, though. I was always too focused on study." I don't add that while I *have* had sex, it's never been good. It's never approached even a fraction of the intensity that I feel when Harrisford and I merely kiss.

Harrisford leans down and kisses me, tenderly this time. "I've done this before, Gwendolynne . . ." His eyes lock on mine; his hold on me tightens. "But never with someone I care so much about. So yes, I'm nervous."

I almost snort, but I don't. "You care about me. Right." It's still impossible for me to reconcile the Harrisford Briggs I've known for seven years with the words coming from his mouth.

"I do." He lowers his head, brushing his lips along my jawbone, making me inhale sharply. "Do you want me to prove it to you?"

"How?" My voice comes out unusually high; I squirm.

"How many ways can I prove it, Gwen?" He cradles my face, presses a soft kiss at one corner of my lips. "Shall I tell you about how I only bought that car to drive to Manchester, because I couldn't stand another twenty-four hours of not seeing you?" His fingers tighten as his nose skims along my cheek; he plants another light kiss at my temple. "Or how about the fact that I lied about the qílín foal? I always knew you could do it. I wanted you to. I wanted you to have the win."

My breath catches; I can barely comprehend what he's saying because everything—his words, his touch—is all so overwhelming.

He feathers kisses down my face. One of his hands runs along my collarbone before twisting possessively into my hair. "Or perhaps I should tell you how I don't even care about the Ministry job anymore." At this, he takes control, angling my head and kissing me on the neck, until I let out a little whimper. "If selling my soul to Magecorp is what it takes for me to be with you, so be it."

He stills, his last words whispered against my skin. So raw. So vulnerable. "The truth is, Gwendolynne, I've wanted you for so long. Years, in fact. I was just too much of a coward to admit it."

There's a prickling at my inner eyelids that means tears are coming, so I blink hard, then say, "But . . . that makes no sense. Why me? I mean, there's absolutely nothing special about me . . ."

"Chan." He raises his head, completely exasperated by now. "You're the smartest witch at Seamere—"

"You know what I mean. I mean . . . physically. Personality-wise. I'm dead average in every way." And there it is: me laid bare. The insecurities I've had since forever, on full display for him to see.

"Average!" Harrisford repeats. He shakes his head at me. He's silhouetted by the light, and his eyes are dark, smoldering with an intensity that curls my toes. "You know, Chan, for an intelligent woman, you really do have a poor grasp of the word 'average.'"

My lips part, and I'm going to say something snarky in return, but the words never leave my lips because he's positioning himself, his eyes fixed on mine.

He pauses for a moment, staring down at me, his breaths coming ragged. He brushes away a strand of hair from my face. And for the second time ever, his expression is one of complete vulnerability. It's as though I've died and exited my body because I never, never envisioned him looking at me . . . like *this*.

Our lips find each other again, raw and tender and sweet and unhurried. And then he's pushing himself into me, so slowly, so gently, and I'm stretching and stretching and he's murmuring my name against my lips and I'm full, so full of Harrisford, both in my body and in my heart.

We both stay still for a moment, our shuddering breaths mingling together, fracturing the hotel room's somber silence; he rests his forehead on mine for a second, his eyes closed. "Gwendolynne," he says, teasing my name out on his tongue, and involuntarily I clench around him, making us both gasp.

And then he's moving. He's moving in me, and he's kissing me all over my cheeks, my jaw, my chin, the tip of my nose. I wrap my legs around his waist and tilt my pelvis, meeting him stroke for stroke . . . inviting him to go even harder, even faster. He responds in kind, and with each thrust I cry out, because he's nudging me higher and higher and closer to the precipice until suddenly . . .

He pulls out.

I gasp, bereft at the sudden emptiness. Is he . . . done? I can't believe it would be over so quickly, and yet . . .

But he's not done. He's standing, his face flushed, his expression oddly furious, and he pulls me almost *roughly* to him and then rasps in my ear. "Hands on the desk, Chan."

"What?"

He spins me around. "Hands on the fucking desk."

I hadn't noticed the desk before; it's much like Harrisford's own desk, all sleek shiny wood and tasteful stationery and—oh god—he's behind me again, lining himself up, positioning us in such a way that I'm forced to brace myself on the desk's surface.

With a single movement, he buries himself inside me again, all the way, and as he begins to move he leans over, his chest nestled against my back. I let out a shivery moan from the sensation, and he grabs my chin and turns it to give me a frantic kiss, before letting my face go.

"All those times you said you were chained to the desk," he says into my ear, his voice rough, "and all I could think about was holding you down and fucking you just like this."

Still buried in me, he drops his hand and starts working at me between my legs. I cry out again; the pleasure is so intense, building so rapidly. Every nerve ending is on fire, my body singing with unleashed desire. He clamps a strong arm across my torso and tugs me against him so that our bodies are flush, my upper thighs sliding against the shiny wood of the table, his fingers rubbing as he starts thrusting faster. "Tell me when you're close, Gwendolynne."

"I—I'm close. I'm close."

He flips me around and maneuvers me back to the bed, climbing over me and pinning both of my wrists down with one of his large, rough hands. He slides himself back into me, his thumb once again rubbing at my clit. "Come for me, Gwen. I want to see your face when you come."

It only takes two more thrusts and then I'm falling apart, shuddering and boneless. "Harrisford!" His name explodes from my lips like a prayer. "Oh my god. Fuck. Fuck. Fuck!" My final curse morphs into a scream.

He speeds up, unrelenting, until he's groaning my name into my ear and his movements have turned erratic and his hand tightens around my wrist almost hard enough to crush me.

But he doesn't crush me. He goes motionless, so still, settling carefully against me so he doesn't hurt me, his cock still buried deep inside. He presses a kiss against my lips, softly, like a salve for their bruising, and then another kiss right by my ear.

"Congratulations, darling Gwendolynne," he says. "On finishing final year."

43

Harrisford

In the half-light of the encroaching dawn, Gwendolynne's skin glows.

She's lying on her back, her face half-turned away from me. Our limbs are intertwined, my gaze tracing the gentle planes of her features. I can see the tiny baby hairs lining her cheeks—normally invisible but now silhouetted by the growing light.

My body stirs, reminiscing on last night. Remembering how I'd poured myself into her, both literally and figuratively, as she arched her back and cried out my name. How we'd taken a long shower together, and afterward—with the streetlights slanting through a gap in the curtain—she'd straddled me as I marveled at her, entirely under her thrall.

I'd worried, beforehand, that our physical chemistry would fall short of my (admittedly high) expectations. That things might just feel awkward and anticlimactic.

I'd been wrong.

Sex, it's clear to me now, is just sex. It's like candy floss, tasting sweet at the time but dissolving quickly, leaving only a faint trace of its presence on the tongue. But *sex with someone I truly care about*—now that is something else altogether.

It wasn't just the way Gwendolynne had clawed at my back, her legs wrapped around my torso, or how her body felt beneath mine as we both edged toward our climax. It's the way that being with her gives me the sort of deep fulfillment that I have *never* previously experienced.

It hits me with sudden clarity: I only slept around because I was searching for something. And that something was her. It was always her.

I was just too much of an idiot to realize.

My strap buzzes, wrenching me from my musings. Holding my breath, I ease my arm from underneath her. She looks so peaceful, her breathing deep and even, and I know she's probably exhausted. After all, we've just finished a grueling week of final exams, and last night we barely slept.

She murmurs and rolls over, away from me, and I take a moment to admire the view before checking who's messaged me at such an ungodly hour.

It's Danny. *Strange*, I think. He's usually not up this early, especially not after a party. Perhaps he went hard all night and never went to bed at all.

Unlocking my screen, I open the message. Briggs. Wanna go for a run?

I flop onto my back and groan. Not really. All I want to do is stay here, in bed, naked, next to Gwendolynne. But the longer I lie beside her, the more I want to touch her, kiss her, roll her over and take her again, from behind. And despite my wants, I don't wish to wake her prematurely.

I tap out a reply: Can't mate, sorry. I'm in London.

A few seconds pass before my strap buzzes again. I'm in London too.

Sitting up, I swipe my disheveled hair off my forehead. Danny's in town? That's odd. He never said anything about that yesterday.

I scrub at my face with both hands and blow out a slow breath, thinking. At some point I'll need to return to Seamere and pick up Pudding, but not just yet. Perhaps a run *is* a good idea. I'm jittery, I'm anxious, and I'm still so fucking turned on. If I head out, I can work off some of my unspent energy, then pick up some breakfast from my favorite pastry shop—I want to introduce Gwendolynne to everything, all at once—and bring something back for her.

Then, after I've settled my nerves, and I've satiated her in other ways—with fancy boxed sugary carbs—then . . . Then I've decided: I will grow some balls, harden the fuck up, and *finally* tell Gwendolynne how I feel.

I refuse to be coy or circumspect any longer. There is only one day until our graduation ceremony; one day before university ends for good. After that she'll head back to Manchester for the summer, until she commences her first postgraduate job. With each passing day, my opportunities to admit that I am so desperately in love with her are rapidly diminishing.

Even if she rejects me, even if she laughs in my face . . . Even if last night was another "onetime thing" and she never wants to see me again. If I don't work up the fucking courage to tell her before we graduate, I know I'll regret it forever.

Having made my decision, I roll carefully out of bed and tug on a pair of shorts.

Taking a deep breath, I cast one last look at her sleeping form before going to the desk and scribbling a note. *Gone for a run. Be back soon. H xx.* Then, I shrug on my discarded T-shirt, lace up my trainers, and quietly slip out the door.

As I run, I re-open the bond between Pudding and me. For obvious reasons, I'd put up shields last night, but now that I'm at a distance from Gwendolynne it seems safe to check in again.

You're up early, Pudding says as soon as the bond snaps open.

"Just going to meet Danny," I puff.

Danny? Pudding gives a murmur of approval. *That's good.*

I've just turned in to my favorite running track, which loops around Green Park and St. James's Park, when Danny joins me. We've run this route many a time, so he just merges onto the pathway and starts keeping pace beside me.

A good quarter of an hour passes before my chest begins to burn. I slow to a jog, then stop, bracing my hands on my knees. I'm more tired than I realized, since I—like Gwendolynne—didn't get much rest last night.

"You good, mate?" Danny says. Usually I have more stamina.

"Yeah. Just tired." I straighten and rub my temples, trying purposefully to slow my breathing. A faint headache is starting to brew somewhere behind my left eyeball.

He grins. "Not enough sleep?"

I shove his shoulder but say, "Something like that." Glancing sidelong at him, I add, "What are you doing in London, anyway?"

Annoyingly, Danny doesn't seem in the least bit out of breath. "Actually, to be honest, I was trying to find you."

He's giving me a funny look—full of pity and resignation—and I'm just about to ask him what's going on when he digs into his pocket and pulls out a half-full syringe.

"Wait. What is that?" I eye the syringe. Why is he holding it? Is it some sort of drug he filched last night in order to get high for the party?

But if it's just that, then why is he moving closer? Why is he holding it like *that*?

"What are you doing?" I back away. My head starts to throb in time with the alarms going off in my brain.

Danny doesn't answer. Undeterred, he just continues advancing on me, even as I retreat. "What *is* that?" I say. "Danny? Danny!"

Still not speaking, he closes the distance, his expression one of dogged determination.

My heart is thumping, my back so clammy that my T-shirt is clinging, slicked against my sweat-soaked skin. Raising both hands, I shove him, hard, in the chest. "Get the fuck away from me!"

"Briggs." He shakes his head. "I'm really sorry, mate."

Then he lunges at me, slamming the syringe into my shoulder.

When I wake I'm in . . . my own dorm room? I'm groggy; it's like I'm hungover. Pudding is here, on her custom-made perch, basking beneath the UV light I'd mounted over the top.

"Wong," I spit, unamused. "You *sedated* me? Is this some sort of joke?" I've heard the stories, of course—final-years pulling last-minute pranks on each other before the year is out.

"Not a joke, Briggs." He takes out some sort of device—a black box, identical to the type that I'd seen Gwendolynne with—and switches it on.

I gape at him, lost for words. At first, nothing happens. But then the still air inside my bedroom starts to waver like a mirage. It's like the shimmering mirages you see rising from the roads during a heat wave.

"What the *fuck* is going on?" I say, stumbling backward. I jiggle the door handle, but it's futile. It won't move. I grind my teeth; Danny has locked us in. Inside my own goddamned room.

Twiddling a dial on his device, Danny gives a most nonchalant-looking shrug. "I'm opening a Void portal."

"Opening a portal?" I splutter. How the hell does *Danny* know how to open a portal? When actual geniuses like Gwendolynne and Conall Peters couldn't?

Since I can't leave the room, I instead march over to Danny, trying to grab the box. "Seriously, Wong, stop this fucking farce this instant, or I'll—"

With lightning-fast reflexes, Danny jerks it away. "You don't understand, Briggs," he snaps. "Surely you know what that scar is? The one on the back of your head?"

"The *what* on the back of my head?"

"Your scar." Moving behind me, he shoves my head forward, pushing up the hair at the nape of my neck. "You were implanted. With the Source. Don't you see?"

He lets me go, and I recoil, my mouth sagging open in horror. "I—what?" Shaking my head, I continue. "No. No. You've got it all wrong, you . . ." I trail off. My gut starts to churn, and I heave a breath, willing myself not to vomit.

"Nope. It's true. You're a tether." He goes back to twiddling the dials on the box. "Your father, and Magecorp, have been cultivating you as one for decades." His eyes flick to me, then back to the box.

My mind immediately jumps back to the fancy dinner in London, when Gwendolynne told me what tethers were. I sink onto my bed, everything inside me crumbling. "I'm . . . I'm a tether?" I can't believe this, I don't want to believe this.

And yet . . .

"Yeah, mate." Danny pulls a sympathetic face. "Sorry."

I finger the scar at the base of my skull. My limbs are numb, my hands shaking. I don't—I can't remember any of this, at all. The scar has been there for as long as I can remember. I'd never taken much notice . . .

"Fuck." I clutch at my head, staring blankly at Danny. "Wait. Are *you* a tether?"

"No. I'm a caster." He holds up the black box and shakes it a little.

"I'm meant to tear open a hole to the Void with this thing. Tethers like you are designed to keep the Void open while Magecorp and Linksphere harvest magic."

Trying to breathe, I scrunch my eyes shut, panic tearing through my veins. "But . . . that still doesn't explain why you're opening a portal. In my fucking *bedroom*."

"I can explain," Danny says, his voice rough around the edges. "It's actually—"

He gets cut off, because at that moment, the very fabric of the world ruptures, a split appearing in midair. The center of it is so black, it seems to be absorbing all the light. A deluge of raw, unrefined magic floods from it, and I cough. It smells like ash.

It feels . . . wrong. I'm used to the magic that companies like Magecorp and Linksphere sell in neat packages—not this wild, unbridled energy that comes pouring from the Void.

"*Danny*," I scream, doubling over, my hair blowing about in the Void's maleficent wind. As I crumple to my knees, the back of my skull prickles, expanding into a pounding pain, and all of a sudden a deluge of memories drenches me, like a tsunami. Just before it pulls me under, the logical part of my brain clicks: Apparently crude, unprocessed Void magic can trigger deeply buried memories.

I'm three years old. I'm on a table, thrashing. But I can't move because there are adults around me. They're holding me down.

I'm three years old. A man in a white coat carries a syringe. The needle is pointy, and I am scared. He slams it into my arm. I scream. Everything goes black.

I'm three years old. I wake, groggy, a mask fitted over my face. The air I breathe is cold. I cry for my mama, but she doesn't come. She isn't allowed to come.

I'm three years old. My hair is shaved. My head feels spiky. The back of my neck hurts, and when I try to turn my head, stitches tug at my skin.

I'm four years old. It's bedtime. My mother is hugging me. "I wish I didn't have to do this, Harry," she says. I squeeze her back. I don't really understand. But by the time I wake in the morning, she's no longer there to hug me.

The memories slam out of me again, and I'm weakened by their effects. Danny is hauling me through the cleft that's splitting reality in two. And as I'm dragged through the rippling opening, all I can think about is Gwendolynne, back at that hotel room, reading the note that I scribbled . . .

Promising that I would come back.

Pudding stares at me from where she's sitting, stone-still upon her perch.

"Pudding." My voice is choked. "Help me." I don't know how she could even save me, but I'm rapidly running out of options.

She just tilts her head slightly, a look of despair clouding her beetle-black eyes.

I'm sorry, son, she says, as I'm pulled right into the Void.

44

Harrisford

When I next come to, I'm tied to a chair, my hands bound behind its back.

My eyesight is blurry, as are my memories. At some point, when Danny was dragging me through the portal, I'd woken. He'd looked at me for half a second before whacking me on the side of the head. Lights had exploded in the outer corners of my vision before my consciousness slid back into blackness.

I shake my head, trying to clear it. And as my eyes begin to focus, I realize: My vision isn't hazy because my eyesight is poor. Everything is hazy because I'm in the Void.

I'm ensconced in what appears to be a cavern, entirely clad in stone. There's a small steel table set up beside me; an unopened autoclave bag, presumably filled with surgical instruments, sits atop its surface. The air is opaque with curling spirals of mist that choke my throat and nostrils.

I raise my head when I hear footsteps. Danny Wong, my oldest friend, bends over me, frowning.

"Sorry about the hit, Briggs." He touches his hand to the side of my head. "And the little whiff of ketamine. But you were struggling pretty bad."

I bare my teeth at him, chafing against my bindings. "Can you blame me? You sedate me, kidnap me, drag me into the Void, then fucking *knock me out*, and you want me to accept your apology?" I shake my head, incensed. "Unbelievable!"

"Listen, Briggs." Danny sighs, then straightens, crossing his muscular arms over his chest. "This isn't what you think it is. We haven't kidnapped you—"

A second voice sounds in my head. Pudding's voice, slightly echoey, as though she's speaking to me from a distance. *We've saved you.*

I gulp, my mouth all dry. "Puds." The word sounds choked in my head. *Pudding* is involved, somehow? What the fuck is actually happening?

She's still in my dorm room, I assume. I clearly remember my last view of her on her perch. It's hard to believe that she and I can still communicate so clearly across the Void.

I struggle against my restraints again, to no avail. "What do you mean 'we'? Who is 'we'?"

Danny looks away from me before sliding his gaze back. "The Magical Liberation Organization."

I gape at him. "You're in the MLO?" Something dawns in my drug-hazed mind. "Wait. You're opening portals. Are *you* behind the surges? *You're* trying to bring down Magecorp?"

Both of us are, Pudding cuts in.

"*Both* of you?" My mind is buckling, not comprehending that my childhood friend and my familiar are behind the Magecorp sabotage. Can familiars even be part of the MLO? I had no idea.

Calm down, Pudding says. *Let me explain . . .*

I let out a roar and thrash, the ropes rubbing raw lines in my skin. "Explain what? That you're trying to destroy my father's company? The one he's devoted his whole life to? That you've been lying to me this whole time?"

How the hell did I not know? I thought Pudding and I knew everything about each other. But now it just feels like, all this time, I've had a stranger living inside my head. The betrayal is a punch to the gut.

Harry, please. Pudding's voice is pleading.

I stop. My mouth drops open.

I am . . . gobsmacked.

Harry. She called me Harry.

All my anger bleeds out of me as I slump into the chair, completely shell-shocked. There's only one person who has called me Harry. Ever.

When I next speak, my voice tremors. I hardly dare ask. "Who *are* you?"

Pudding is quiet for so long that I can almost hear static buzzing inside my head. But then she speaks, and when she does, all she says are three words. Her name.

Theodora Finlay-Briggs.

Everything inside me freezes.

At first, I'm unable to talk. Unable to wrap my head around it. A shudder runs through me, so violent I almost convulse. And then I choke out, in an almost inaudible whisper, "Mother?"

Oh, darling. Pudding—my mother—is talking to me, but I barely register. Her voice is just a droning noise whirring inside my mind. *I wanted to tell you so many times, I really did, but if you'd known, it would've put you at risk . . .*

Fury expands, tearing through my chest, and I explode. "You. Pudding. Are my *mother*?"

"She's not just your mum, Briggs." Danny rubs at the back of his neck, his face all red. "She's the leader of the MLO."

"She . . . she what?" I sag, folding into myself. Feeling small. Feeling four years old again. I shake my head. "No. *No!*"

I'd learned about it all, of course, during history lessons at school. About how, around twenty-five years ago, a series of high-profile murders targeting civilian witches had rocked the magical community. At the time, the media and the general public had pinned the blame on the MLO. A media frenzy had ensued, and some underhanded political maneuverings led to the MLO being classified as a terrorist organization—even though none of the murders could be directly traced to the MLO itself.

Under duress, and in response to public pressure, the Ministry had formed an Anti-Terrorist Task Force, headed up by a group of particularly vocal anti-MLO individuals—one of whom was my own father. The task force, in conjunction with the British Magical Police Force, had been dispatched to round up all of the MLO leaders and get them arrested, tried, and summarily executed, or else thrown into jail.

Over the ensuing years, the task force had rooted out most of the main suspects—all except one. The big boss, the anonymous head honcho, who had gone into hiding and never been found . . .

And Danny expects me to believe that's my *mother*?

My heart beats out an erratic rhythm, the pain like a brand in my chest.

I was four when my mother disappeared.

I was four when I got Pudding.

And I'd never put the two together.

"Mum." My voice cracks on the word. I slump forward, weak against my bindings. "Come in here. Let me see you. I need to see you."

I can't, Harrisford, Pudding says gently. *I'm acting as the tether, on the other side.*

The space behind my eyes has grown hot, so I squeeze my eyelids shut. "Father made you a tether too?"

No, Harry. Your father never got to me. I've been in hiding for twenty-one years. Am I imagining it, or is my mother's voice sounding choked? *But . . . you're my son. I volunteered to do this. I swallowed some Source so I could be here for you.*

My familiar—my own mother—became a tether to what . . . kidnap me? And even worse: She *lied* to me. For twenty-one fucking years.

"So you could be here for me?" I spit the words out. "That is . . . dragonshit." I try, and fail, to clutch my head, my arms still bound to the chair. "I *protected* you!"

I'd stopped Gwendolynne from going to the police to prevent her from becoming a target, yes. But it was also because my mother's disappearance had given me a healthy hatred for the police. I still remember being a kid, clutching Pudding in my lap, glaring at the officers who returned day after day to question me about my mum. At the time, I'd regarded them suspiciously. I had *despised* them. I was four years old, barely out of nappies, saddled with responsibilities no child of that age should have to deal with.

"Your mum has been working behind the scenes this whole time, Briggs, trying to take down Magecorp," Danny says defensively. "It was them, not us, who were behind those deaths."

Harry, my mother says. *I'm sorry it had to come to this. But your father—*

"Father is in a coma," I grit out. In a coma, and, like me, completely oblivious to the fact that his wife—and my mother—leads the very organization he'd been ordered to hunt down. "This is . . . *highly* unnecessary." The revelation hits me: Barnabus the centaur had been telling the truth. The person I most care about—my mother—has betrayed me.

Looking back, did I ever have the slightest inkling? That Pudding was my mother? Even just a tiny bit? Perhaps . . . perhaps the thought had flitted through my mind once or twice: the times when Pudding seemed to know more about me and my past than I even knew myself.

But I'd always quickly quashed those feelings, putting it down to the human-familiar bond. It was easier not to think too hard, easier not to know. All I'd done was cling to Pudding tighter, because she was all I had left in the world, and I couldn't stand to lose someone else I loved, the way I'd lost my mum.

"Listen, you dolt." Danny gives an exasperated huff. "We're not trying to hurt you. We're trying to help you. Our intelligence told us that Nathaniel Price was making plans with your father to recruit you into Magecorp as a tether. Even before the explosion."

Danny's words bring me back to why I'm here, in the Void, in the first place, and my entire body flushes cold as my unburied memories rush back. It's like an incoming tide, engulfing me, pulling at me, threatening to drag me back to their deep and fathomless depths . . .

My mother continues. *And now that they're running out of Source, we're assuming Nathaniel will speed those plans up. Especially since you're about to graduate. We're trying to hide you in here, where he can't find you.*

"So, what?" I squeeze my eyes shut and shake my head. "You're just expecting me to accept this? And stay here, stuck in the Void forever?" Immediately, my mind jumps to Gwendolynne. Was it only yesterday we'd finished exams? Only last night that I slept with her? Just one day ago that I foolishly believed I had everything I'd ever wanted?

It's just temporary, my mother says. *We'll conceal you in here until everyone assumes you're dead. Then, once they're off your trail, we'll release you back into the real world under a new identity.*

A new identity. No. *No!*

With my reputation, Gwendolynne will probably assume I tricked her into sleeping with me. That I deceived and then abandoned her. When she wakes in the hotel room to find me gone . . . What will she think?

You don't have to worry about Gwendolynne, since you won't be seeing her again, my mother says. My mother has heard my musings, traced the trajectory of my thoughts. Her tone is remorseful, deeply apologetic. *I'm sorry, Harrisford.*

Anger rises like a rush of hot air beating against my skin. "You were the one who encouraged me to go to her!" I'm yelling. "*You* told me that love isn't a fucking trap!" Again, I struggle at my restraints, the ropes cutting into my biceps and across my chest. Damn it. Why does Danny have to be so bloody good at knots?

I did say that. I can picture Pudding—my mother—now. Almost visualize the regal rise of her chin. *But you'll see, with time. It's better to have loved and lost than to have never loved at all.*

"That's a fucking lie, and you know it." My head is pounding. Shards of grief are slicing through me, right into my core. "You cannot honestly expect me to believe that was true of you and Father."

She's silent for a long moment. *Your father and I were a different story.*

Oh yes, I want to sneer. I know their story. I know how the two of them, both from wealthy families, married each other for status, power, and money, not for love.

I may not know much about relationships, but I know this: I do *not* want what my parents had. I want something different. That's why I broke things off with Isla Ennis, even though everyone thought we were the ideal couple. I didn't love her, not truly, and for me? That is a total dealbreaker.

But I don't say it. Instead I say, aloud, "Why should I trust you? When you've lied to me? Betrayed me? When you and the MLO have been causing the surges? When you've been *killing* people?"

"Mate, you've got it all wrong." It's Danny again, and he's gesticulating with jerky movements. "We haven't been killing people. We've been doing to them what we're doing to you. Hiding them out in the Void until the authorities presume they're dead, and then letting them assume a new identity so Magecorp can no longer find them."

I stare, nonplussed. "So." I swallow. "Hani Nguyen *isn't* dead?"

Hani Nguyen is the only name I can remember from Nora Chapman's long list of the "deceased." And I can only remember it because I'd spent so long staring at her photo ID. I'd gone to such great lengths attempting to make Gwendolynne look like her (not that she ever did, of course; Gwendolynne can't really look like anyone else when she's easily the most beautiful woman ever).

"Hani is now Samantha Lai," Danny says. "A twice-divorced executive who lives a life of leisure in Australia on her considerable alimony payments."

I'm shocked into silence, contemplating, while I try to fit all these fractured epiphanies together in my mind.

"So the portals stay open because the Source is magnetized to the Void." A statement, not a question. I know this because I can currently feel the way my own Source is being called to by the Void.

The Source wants to get back to its own dimension, my mother says quietly. *And yours is particularly strong, Harrisford. It's been there, accumulating power, for decades.* Her voice sounds thick; I think she's crying. *I tried to stop them putting it in you, my darling. I really did. But your father was just too powerful.*

I let my head bow, chin to chest. My eyelids flutter shut. "I understand, Mother." I understand, but I can't forgive her.

I was four. You left. I can't forgive you.

Then again, she didn't leave, did she? Not really. This whole time she's been with me, as my familiar, protecting me in whatever limited capacity she can.

When I speak again, my voice sounds weak. I'm empty inside; just a hollow shell. "So the power surges are because . . . you open portals for the people you're hiding to get in and out? Do you open more portals than Magecorp do?" More portals mean more power, I'm guessing.

We have to open more of them to rescue people, yes. There's a trace of regret edging my mother's words. *But unlike Magecorp,* we *don't make the tethers hold portals open for extended periods.*

Bile churns in my stomach, and I force myself to take a few breaths. "Is that how Magecorp kills people?" I ask. "The tethers, I mean. Because they have to hold the portals open?"

Tethers—like me. Implanted by Magecorp; saved by the MLO. What I really want to ask is: Is there a chance that *I* might die?

A pause. *Yes,* my mother says. *Many of the tethers burn out. And Magecorp doesn't care if they do, as long as they get their magic.* Her voice is bitter.

"That is—" I cut myself off and shake my head, unable to find adequate words.

It's greed, Harrisford, pure greed. My mother's voice is rising. *They worked out years ago that humans are the most effective tethers, as opposed to objects, or familiars. Objects are inert, and animals absorb the magic, making it harder for Magecorp to harvest. But people? The Source fragments interact with a human's magical abilities, augmenting the Source's power. Magecorp discovered that when human tethers implanted with the Source are placed on either side of a tear, they can keep the magic flowing from the Void for longer than the Source alone.*

"So they need a tether for each portal," I say, trying to comprehend it all.

"*Two* tethers per portal," Danny explains. "One stays on our side—that's your mum, in this case. The other goes into the Void—that's you."

My mind is getting tangled. "So I'm holding the portal open now?"

Danny shakes his head. "We've closed it for now. We didn't want to risk the portal becoming too unstable and collapsing."

But when we re-open, Pudding continues, *it needs to be in the exact same spot. If any of us moves, or the portal collapses while it's open, the two of you could get trapped.*

I stare at Danny, aghast. "People get trapped inside the Void?"

Rarely. My mother pauses, hesitating. *We usually stay in one place for as long as is feasible, in order to throw the authorities off our trail. Then we remove the victim's Source and help them escape. Mostly it works as planned; sometimes, though, there's insufficient time to get everybody out safely.*

My heartbeat stutters. "MLO is risking its own members to save civilians? Why?"

"We're not making them risk themselves, Briggs." Danny sounds impatient. "MLO members volunteer, to further a cause they believe in."

"*A cause they believe in*," I repeat, scrunching up my face. "That Magecorp shouldn't exploit people?"

Danny squares a look at me. "That magic should be available to everyone, *without* needing to exploit people."

I clench my jaw, ruminating on this for a moment. All of a sudden I feel very tired. The ropes around my wrists and torso continue to cut in. "So the surges, the excess magic, the magiphilia, and the explosions . . . You're causing all this because you're trying to save people from Magecorp?"

The explosions aren't caused by us, Harrisford, Pudding says.

"Who, then?"

There's a long pause. Eventually, my mother speaks. *They're caused by you.*

45

Gwendolynne

The next morning, Harrisford is gone.

The painful pang that jolts through my body transforms into a warm, fuzzy feeling when I spot the note he'd left: *Gone for a run. Be back soon. H xx.* His writing is so messy it's almost illegible; I guess it's appropriate since soon he'll graduate as a doctor of sorts.

While I'm waiting for him, I take another shower—uninterrupted this time—making use of all the upmarket toiletries. I dry my hair to smooth silk with the fancy hotel hair dryer. I wrap myself in a fluffy robe, brush my teeth, then settle down in front of the enormous TV to wait for Harrisford.

By ten a.m., my stomach is growling, so I order room service. I order twice as much as I would usually, because I assume Harrisford will be back soon. He doesn't show up, so I eat too much, feeling faintly sick by the time housekeeping shows up at noon.

"He must be training for a fucking marathon or something," I grumble, and Percy sends an *Ugh!* down our bond. Ugh, indeed, since why would anyone want to run *that* far? Though at least I finally understand how he keeps himself so fit.

By two p.m., Harrisford still hasn't returned, and I'm picking at the cold remains of my breakfast. It barely fills the hollow ache gnawing at my stomach—an ache that's there not because of hunger, but because I'm now coming to the cold, stark conclusion: Harrisford isn't coming back.

He's fucking left me. *Again.*

Even after we'd had mind-blowing sex. Even after he'd whispered the sweetest things, deep in the dark of night. Even after he'd caressed my face, kissed me oh-so-tenderly, looked at me as though I was the center of his entire universe.

He's lied to me. Again. And again. And I fell for it. Again. I should have gone with my gut instinct: that this was all part of his strategy, his scheme . . . to triumph. To achieve one final victory.

My chest feels like it's all caved in. My heart is thumping pitifully fast. The hotel is surrounded by high-rises that block out the afternoon sun. I shiver, my teeth chattering in the darkening room, once again feeling like the world's biggest fool.

At three p.m., I finally get dressed, gather my things, and exit the hotel, too angry to even cry.

The next day, after seven grueling years of training, the senior cohort of the Seamere College of Magical Veterinary Sciences finally graduates.

It's a short timeline; since we're all assessed by magical means, they can calculate the results almost immediately. It means they can also kick us out faster, I guess.

It's a bittersweet feeling; I'm happy to be moving on, of course, but I'm also frightened, apprehensive, sad. Plus there's the fact that, only two nights ago, I'd pictured myself celebrating graduation alongside Harrisford, and now—after he abandoned me in the hotel room—I won't be.

The afternoon is warm, not hot. The other students buzz with excitement. Everything is swathed in the unmistakable aura of magic. I've no idea why, but there have been no more surges for the past twenty-four hours—the elevated atmospheric magic seems to have eased to its normal low-level hum. At least the brief respite gives me, Heli, and Conall a bit more time to figure out how to enter the Void.

The ceremony is outside, so that both familiars and mythical creatures can attend: The qílín and her foal stick their muzzles through a fence; Arkany flies lazy circles overhead; I even spy a dark-haired centaur swigging from a suspicious-looking flask. Percy snoozes, curled on my lap.

My neck is sweaty beneath my gown, and my hat makes my head all itchy. Although I'm terrified of seeing Harrisford, when I take my seat in front of the stage, my gaze involuntarily drifts to his chair.

It's empty.

My stomach twists itself into knots. He's probably rolling out of some other woman's bed in a sort of postcoital daze, and will arrive at the last minute looking impeccable, as usual. I clench my hands into fists and force myself to swallow the scream that's lodged inside my throat.

Don't think about him, Gwendolynne. I grit my teeth. He means nothing. *Nothing.*

Professor Kaur is still suspended, so that awful man, Thomas Pickering, is presenting the degrees today. He gets up to speak, droning on about the honor of Seamere and the next generation of bright young veterinarians.

But I'm not listening, because I'm wondering: Where the fuck is Harrisford? The ceremony has started, and he *still* hasn't shown up. I try to keep myself from repeatedly checking his empty chair but fail miserably.

His absence is just so . . . odd. Today, we'll find out our final scores. We'll find out who is being proclaimed top of Seamere. And I know Harrisford. I know he wouldn't usually miss an opportunity to gloat if—by some cruel trick of fate—he manages to beat me.

The vice dean is nearing the end of his speech. I sit up straighter, trying to focus, pushing Harrisford to the back of my mind, as Professor Pickering clears his throat and unfolds the parchment that holds the thread of my entire future.

"And this year the top student of Seamere College, who won by one single point, is . . ."

The audience waits with bated breath. "Dr. Gwendolynne Chang!"

"*Chan*," Heloise, who is next to me, mutters indignantly. But I barely register her. I hardly notice the way the crowd ruptures into applause as I stand and edge my way along the row of seats, wondering the whole time where on earth my biggest rival is.

Afterward, when Heloise spots me, she rushes at me and gives me an enormous hug.

"Congratulations, Dr. Chan," she says, beaming all over her face. She takes a step back and gives me an illustrious bow, with a flourish. "The greatest, the most fantastic, the hottest-ever top graduate of Seamere."

"Thanks, Heli," I mumble quickly, and then I grab her forearm and pull her close. "Listen, you haven't seen Harrisford around anywhere, have you?"

"Harrisford? No, why?"

My eyes scan the crowd, checking one last time for his distinctive golden head. "He didn't show up to the ceremony."

Heli's eyes widen. "Really?"

My cheeks flush. The fact that she didn't notice is a little embarrassing. No one else seems as observant about Harrisford's movements as I am.

I ignore that thought. "Yeah. He missed the entire thing. Heli, you don't think—"

I stop short. I haven't yet told Heli about what Harrisford and I did two nights ago. Or how I've fallen hard for him, even though he doesn't feel the same way back. I haven't had the chance to tell her how he'd fucked right off the morning after we'd had the most incredible sex—*twice*—and I'd seen him in all his perfect, naked glory.

I freeze. My brain has snagged on something, and my mind is churning, sifting through my recollections as though I'm perusing books inside the library. At the hotel, I'd been so delirious with desire that I hadn't noticed, hadn't registered what I was feeling.

I press my fingers to my lips, recalling some deeply buried body memory of the way his skin had felt beneath my hands. After our second time, he'd fallen asleep before me, snoozing on his stomach, and I'd taken the opportunity to spend a considerable amount of time ogling him. I'd run my fingers through his soft blond hair. Caressed the scars that covered his shoulders and his back.

He had many scars, yes, but also a specific one. One that was more raised and less irregular than the ones that marked his back. And if I recall correctly, it had been high on the nape of his neck, just at the base of his skull. It's one I'd subconsciously noticed when he'd undressed in his room at the Briggs mansion, because it looked different from the others. A very straight scar, in a very particular place . . .

"Gwen?" Heli says, uncertain.

I pace away from her, one hand clamped on my forehead.

Now that exams are over and my brain is no longer in panic mode, my memories are unlocking, answers to all my questions slotting into place. And the sound of Nathaniel Price's subordinate, the man who Mr. Price called Jarvis, echoes through my mind: *Their Source was implanted so long ago, it will have built up a significant capacity. They might be the only individual capable of holding a long-term tether.* They'd been talking about a particular patient, someone who they referred to as patient 39.

A patient 39 they intended to use to ration their remaining Source.

"Heli—" I choke out, my throat closing over. "Harrisford . . . His scar . . . Oh my god."

Heli's brow creases. "What's wrong? What about Harrisford's scar?"

"I think it's an implant scar." I raise my eyes to meet hers. "I think . . . I think that Harrisford is patient 39."

Heli and I corner Pen and Conall at the postgraduation cocktail function. They're slightly tipsy on champagne but agree to come immediately. We need them both: Conall because he's brilliant in all things to do with the Void. And Pen because they're the only one out of the four of us who knows how to pick a lock.

With me cradling Percy, we rush through the hallways, heading to Harrisford's room. Thankfully, the south wing's main corridor is empty, since most of the students are still at the function. The last time I was here, most of the mahogany doors were open, hanging off their hinges with holes blown through them from the surge. But now they're pristine: Magical Maintenance have clearly been through and repaired every single one. It's different to our wing, which still bears loose locks and ill-fitting doors and scorch marks all the way up the walls.

Figures. I'm slightly bitter—but not surprised—that they've prioritized the rich folk over us.

As we hurry along, I ask Pen, panting, whether they or the MLO know about Magecorp's plans to kidnap Harrisford. They shake their head. "Sorry, Gwen, but the MLO are secretive about all their intel, even if we're members. They say it's best to keep information siloed so we're not a risk if one of us gets caught."

When we arrive at Harrisford's door, I bang on it, but he doesn't answer. So I give the signal to Pen, who slides a bobby pin out of their elaborately curled hair and inserts it into the keyhole. It takes a few minutes, a lot of jiggling, and several choice words from Pen's mouth before the lock clicks and the door swings ajar.

My heart starts to pound. I haven't been in Harrisford's dorm room since that fateful morning, around two weeks ago, when we'd been prepping to break into Magecorp HQ.

It's exactly the same as it was then, with the exception that Harrisford's bedclothes are smooth, having been neatly made up.

And there's something else there; something *extremely* worrisome.

There's no Harrisford.

But there *is* Pudding, sitting on a platform, watching us with unblinking eyes.

A few minutes later, I'm actually pacing, both hands buried in my hair.

"He never goes *anywhere* without his familiar," I tell the others. It's not strictly true, of course—he'd come to Manchester without her. And to dinner, and the hotel room. But for him to miss graduation *and* leave Pudding behind . . . This is very much out of character.

"Could he be at the hospital?" Heli asks.

I stop moving for a second, chewing my lip. "I doubt it," I say, after a pause. "From what Jarvis said, it really sounded like he'd been implanted ages ago."

Was this something that Darghan did—to his own son? Is that why he was pressuring Harrisford to join Magecorp, so he could use him as a tether?

I feel sick. In the cavernous depths of my mind, I picture Harrisford as a small boy, a white-blond mop of hair on his head, being held down on a surgery table and forcibly sedated while his father stands at the viewing window, looking on . . .

"I'll call them anyway," Heli says, and while she makes the phone call, I draw nearer to the bearded dragon, feeling all fidgety with worry.

"Where did he go, Pudding?" I say to her, aloud. But she can't communicate with me. The only people familiars can speak to are their bonded humans.

Heli hangs up, the corners of her mouth tugging down. "He's not at the hospital."

Percy has been silent the whole time, curled up tightly on an armchair. But now he pipes up, his aloof voice echoing through my brain. *Can you not smell the Void magic?*

My gaze falls on him, sharp and pointed. "No?" I've never been able to smell Void magic. I didn't know that magic even *had* a smell. Is this another thing, like detecting ketones and being able to easily diagnose DKA, that I'm not genetically equipped to do?

I remember suddenly that the others can't hear Percy and me communicate, so I turn to them, to ask if anyone else can smell it.

They all respond in the negative. Like me, none of them could smell Matilda the DKA cat's ketones. The only one who could smell them was Harrisford. Perhaps the two abilities are related, somehow.

Percy gives a disdainful sniff. *Well, it absolutely reeks of Void magic in here. I could also smell his life force. The trail was strong, leading to this room, but in here it just . . . disappears. Which means that—*

I don't wait for Percy to finish before I spin to face my friends. "He's been kidnapped." My memories are raking through the other things Jarvis had said to Nathaniel at the hospital, about patient 39. *If we station 39 inside the Void . . . we can just swap out the tethers on the outside as they burn out.*

My voice wavers as I add, "I think that . . . Harrisford has been taken into the Void."

46

Gwendolynne

The Void?" Conall gasps out. "But . . . how?"

"He's got a piece of Source implanted in his neck." I touch my own neck involuntarily; the pitch of my voice rises until I'm sounding borderline unhinged. "I guess they used him to hold open the portal and then, what . . . just dragged him right through?"

Conall's eyes widen. "He's got a *Source*? How'd he get a Source?"

Heloise tugs on a loose braid before winding it back into her bun. "Magecorp put it in, we think. The fuckers."

I push back my own hair with shaking hands. "We need to find him. Quickly. The surges are *killing* the human tethers, and—" Tears spring to my eyes. I can't believe that after everything that's happened, I'm crying over the possibility that Harrisford Briggs might die. If you'd asked me three weeks ago what I wished for Harrisford's future, I'd have probably said that I wanted him dead. Hell, if you'd asked me this morning, I would've offered to strangle him myself.

But that was before I figured out he hadn't left me—he'd disappeared. And now he's in danger. Fear is clawing up my insides, gouging out a gaping hole. I chew the inside of my cheek so hard that it bleeds, and the metallic taste of blood floods my mouth, centering me.

"Perhaps we need to open the portal again," Conall suggests. "In the same place where he was taken." He frowns, then murmurs, "There must be a weak point in here, somewhere."

"Okay." I draw in a shuddering breath. "But how do we open one? We haven't been able to figure out how the black box works."

"Well . . ." Conall rubs his temples, thinking. "We're assuming the portal is here, in this room, where his life force disappears, aren't we? So long as we find the right spot, we can use our bit of Source to tether open this side. Hopefully, he'll be on the other side." He frowns. "We'll need the exact coordinates, though."

"Right. Okay." I nod my head, which feels barely attached to my neck, like I'm one of those spring-loaded bobblehead dolls. We have a plan. If we have a plan, I can distract myself from falling into an anxious heap. "Percy, can you find the weak spot? Can you smell where Harrisford's life force disappears?"

Percy twitches his whiskers, ducking his head slightly as if to nod. *Yes, Hairless One*, he says to me. *I am fairly certain that I can.*

Ten minutes later, we've gathered our supplies—including the black box—and Conall is fiddling with its dials, the tip of his tongue sticking out. Pen is at the door, keeping watch. Percy is pacing around the room, sniffing everything intently, trying to find the exact location of the previous tear: the one that Harrisford would have been snatched through when he was kidnapped into the Void.

I'm standing on Harrisford's plush cream carpet, Heli's arms around me. I'm quaking. My body is nothing but adrenaline; my organs feel too big for my skin.

"Do you think I'll find him?" I say, after a prolonged period of silence. I can't hide the slight tremor in my voice.

Heloise gives my shoulders a squeeze. "What do you mean, 'I'? *We* will find him, Gwen. Of course we will. Have faith."

I sniff and blink back tears. "You don't have to come. Into the Void, I mean."

She huffs out a soft laugh. "Don't be daft, Gwen."

"But . . . it might be dangerous."

She reaches up to give me an affectionate pat on the cheek. "G, you're my best friend. Of course I'll come."

"I'll come too," Conall says, still focused on the black box. It makes sense—he would never pass up the opportunity to study the infamous Void up close.

Percy interrupts his search for half a second to interject, *I too shall accompany you.*

A tiny ember of warmth sparks within my chest. As much as I don't want any of my friends to risk themselves, I'm kind of glad I won't be alone.

Everyone falls quiet again, the only sound the clicks and whirs from Conall fiddling with the box.

"But," Heloise continues, breaking the silence. Her voice has turned unusually stern. "If we go in there and find him, G, then you have to promise one thing."

Suddenly wary, I say, "What's that?"

She crosses her arms and gives me a knowing look. "That you'll finally shag him."

I groan and bury my face in my hands. "*Heli* . . ." Will she see the way my face has flushed red? Will she figure out I already did?

"Don't 'Heli' me, Gwen. You just need to do it already. I mean, I've seen you. You've been making sex eyes at him for *weeks*."

I open my mouth to explain, but she holds up one finger to stop me. "Yes, you have. Don't deny it. Now, I don't care whether you two fall in love and get married and have perfect biracial babies, or whether you fuck like rabbits exactly once to get it all out of your systems, but, girl—if you don't promise to do at least *one* of those things, then I am *not* going to help you get him. Do you know how much of a cranky-arse bitch you've been since that man started chasing you?"

I know what she's doing. She's trying to lighten the mood by distracting me. Still, I rise to the bait, scowling at her. It must be so obvious by now that I'm blushing. "He *has not* been chasing me—"

"Oh yes he has." She gives me a gentle smack on the side of my head. "What planet have you been living on? Because whatever sex eyes you've been making"—her lips curl into a wicked smile—"he's been making them *ten* times worse. At *you*."

She gives me the smuggest, most satisfied smile, and I'm so annoyed that I feel the need to finally confess . . . everything.

I fold my arms and raise both eyebrows. Irritation has chased away my despondency, at least. "Well, you've got it all wrong. I'll have you know, we kind of . . . already did . . ." I taper off in embarrassment.

Her mouth falls open, and she gives a shocked sort of laugh. "You *didn't*."

"We did." It's my turn to look a little smug now. "Where do you think I was, the night of the end-of-exams party?"

She tips her head to one side, scrutinizing me through narrowed eyes. "Being grumpy and antisocial in your room? Like usual?"

I bristle, about to retort, but I'm interrupted by Percy, who lets out a sharp, high-pitched meow. He's found something. It's next to the desk I'd marveled over the first time I'd been in here. Climbing to my feet, I slowly creep over to the empty space that Percy is scratching at.

He continues to cry, sounding strangely catlike, and scrabbles at a specific point in midair.

Almost like it's a door.

"It's here, is it?" I say.

He meows again, and then in my head, says, *Indeed it is, Hairless One.*

Sitting back on his haunches, he keeps pawing at the air with his front foot. He seems *desperate* to get through. I remember the strange luring sensation I'd felt when faced with the Source back at Magecorp HQ. Do familiars feel the same pull? Does the Void magic call to them, even harder and stronger than it does to us humans?

"How are you doing, Conall?" I ask, my insides seizing up with ice. Conall presses a couple of buttons, and then finally the box whirs to life.

"Good," he says, triumphant. "I think I've got it." Now that we have the right conditions, a designated weak point, and tethers both inside and outside the Void, he's finally been able to figure out how it works.

"You're amazing," I say genuinely, and he blushes a dark shade of pink.

Pen lurks by the entrance, peering through a crack in the door. They're too nervous to enter the Void itself but have volunteered to keep watch. This leaves Heloise, Conall, Percy, and me to go in and rescue Harrisford.

This is it.

"Are we all ready?" I say, and everyone gives me brisk nods. Conall and Heloise clasp hands, and Pen tenses by the door.

Sinking onto one knee, I crouch down to address Percy. "It's time. You take the Source and stand in position, and Conall will open the portal." We only have a tiny scrap of Source, and Conall has hypothesized that at such short notice, only Percy, with his ability to channel and amplify magic, will generate enough energy to hold open the Void. I present the small glowing Source fragment sitting on my flattened palm to him, and Percy tilts his head so he can reach it. His rough little tongue tickles as he licks up the Source and swallows it.

"Thanks, Percy," I say.

Percy's eye slits to half-mast. He gives me a low, throaty purr and, like the first time we'd met, tilts his head and bumps it against my hand. I let out a sob, choked with tears . . . This cat, who I've known for just a shade over three weeks, is risking his life to help me rescue a man he knows only as the Bum Scratcher.

I scratch him on the head and chin while his purr rises in volume, until it sounds like the engine of Harrisford's mage-powered bike. Then I give him a final stroke—from the top of his head to his tail. He arches up into my touch, then turns and slinks toward the unopened portal to take up his position.

Conall presses another button. A whirring sound fills the room, and the air begins to ripple and shimmer. A deep feeling of dread—and euphoria—grips me, which I attribute to the effect of the Void. Percy stands waiting, his crooked tail sticking straight up, the very tip of it flicking back and forth.

"We stick together," I tell everyone, including Percy. I grasp the scalpel I brought along for self-defense so hard that my knuckles hurt. "None of us leaves without the others, understood?"

Everyone steels themself as the universe splits wide open. We adjust our footing, bracing ourselves as violent pulses of magic stream out from the tear. It explodes out: raw, untamed power, making our hair stand on end.

A stream of light spikes out from the rupture in reality. Sparks fly, splattering Harrisford's wallpaper with tiny scorch marks. Conall and I shoot a glance at one another. Is it supposed to look like this?

I don't get to ask, because just at that moment, Pudding leaps off her perch and latches onto my face. "Fuck!" Reflexively, I scrabble to get her off me. Has the influx of Void magic affected her, too? Or is she just scared?

To avoid my flailing scalpel blade, Pudding scrambles to the top of my head, her claws gouging scratches in my scalp. I've never seen her move so fast. "Pudding, stop!"

It's Pen who manages to save me, darting forward, plucking Pudding off my head, and flinging her into the walk-in-wardrobe. They shut the door firmly. "That'll help," they say, then give a wobbly laugh.

"Thanks, Pen." I rub at my tender head, then call out to Pudding. "I'm sorry, Pudding! I promise I'm trying to help Harrisford, not hurt him!"

The rip grows wider, and we all fall silent again. Percy turns his head, and when he speaks, his voice has taken on an unusual gravity.

Hairless One, he says, staring at me, his single eye wide and unblinking. He almost sounds . . . mournful? *I want you to know that if anyone here dies, then I . . . I shall be sure to eat you last.*

This is . . . oddly touching. Warmth flushes through my chest. Darting forward, I scoop him up, kiss him on top of his head—hard—then let him back down to the floor. He lands, looking undignified and bedraggled and very much the worse for wear.

The portal is several feet wide now, the power from it streaming out in gusts of wind that buffet us around. Percy struts forward, his head and tail held high, and right at the entrance to the other world . . .

He stops.

He looks left, then right, then left again, then stands staring straight into the Void. We all watch with bated breath, waiting for him to go through. But he just . . . doesn't.

Ugh. I think. *Cats.* So typical. They scrabble and scratch to go through a door, and then when it finally opens, they just bloody well stand there.

"Oh, for fuck's sake," I say, scooping Percy up in my arms and striding resolutely through the gateway. "Come on, everybody. We're going in."

47

Gwendolynne

We charge into the Void: me brandishing my scalpel, Conall and Heli close behind. Percy, who is tucked under my arm, squirms as we pass through the portal until I'm forced to let him go.

At first, everything is so gloomy, it takes my eyes a few seconds to adjust. We're in a sort of cave, the walls, floor, and ceiling all made of rough-hewn gray rock. Mist swirls all around, obscuring our vision, and I creep forward cautiously, swiping at it with my free hand.

When a gap finally opens up in the thick, tenacious fog . . . I see him.

My stomach drops.

Harrisford is bound to a chair, ropes crisscrossing over his torso. His head is bowed. I cannot tell if he's conscious.

Behind him, wielding a blade in one hand and a pair of forceps in the other, plunging the latter into a bloodied incision at the base of Harrisford's skull—

Is . . . Danny?

He's wearing a surgical mask that obscures the lower half of his face, but I can still tell it's him.

Danny raises his head, but too late. When he sees me, I've already lunged at him, my teeth bared, and pressed my scalpel to his neck.

"Get. Away. From him," I snarl through gritted teeth.

He raises both of his gloved hands, bloodstained instruments and all. "Chan," he says evenly. "Put the scalpel down and I'll explain."

"Explain what? That you kidnapped Harrisford and are—" I grapple for the words, my eyes darting to Harrisford and back. "Exactly what the fuck are you doing, Wong?"

I'd already worked out that Harrisford had been implanted with a fragment of the Source. And if Danny is operating on him, then that must mean . . .

"I'm removing his implant," Danny says. His next words come out as a hiss. "Now *put the scalpel down*."

I jerk my chin at him. "You first."

Danny lets the scalpel and forceps clatter to the ground. I too drop my scalpel and take a couple of steps back.

Tearing my gaze away from Danny, I draw closer to Harrisford's chair. I can see he's breathing—deeply, evenly, despite the restraints around his torso—and his head is flopping down, his chin resting on his chest.

I'm close enough now that I can reach out to him. Cupping his chin, I raise his head. His eyes are closed, his face slack-jawed, and when I raise his left eyelid, the blue eye is blank. "You anesthetized him?" Involuntarily, my thumb sweeps across his jaw, stroking it.

"Of course I did," Danny says irritably. "We surgeons aren't as evil as you think, Chan."

Danny's always been a cutter more than a medic. Apparently, he's hoping to specialize in dragon surgery.

"You're as thick as a typical surgeon, though," I snap. "Why have you not secured his airway? Don't you know how obstructive his head position is?"

The cocky expression on Danny's face falters, and he looks away and mumbles, "He's fine. I've been monitoring his breathing, all right?"

I glare at Danny, incensed at his stupidity. But then again—I have to remember that Danny is Harrisford's friend. I still don't fully understand what's happening, but it seems that he's actually trying to help. "Well, go on, then. I'll protect his airway while you finish off."

Danny scrutinizes me for a moment, as though he's wondering if it's a trap. He must finally decide that it isn't, because he moves closer, still wary.

"Are you still sterile?" I say, gesturing to Danny's gloves with my eyes. "You haven't touched anything?"

"No, ma'am." I stiffen at the condescending nature of his tone but don't say anything.

Heli, looking very solemn, peels open a fresh pair of forceps for Danny. With both of my hands, I cradle Harrisford's chin while Danny resumes digging around in the incision. Harrisford's face is pale, his long eyelashes fanned out on his upper cheeks, and I've never noticed this before . . . but there's a faint dusting of freckles across the bridge of his nose.

He looks young, so young, and my heart clenches at the thought of him as a boy, on the operating table, being surgically implanted with something he was too little to understand.

I'm so focused on Harrisford's face that I don't notice at first. Nor does Danny, who has an intense look of concentration as he fishes around in Harrisford's flesh for the Source. It's Conall who speaks, from the corner where he's still clutching Nathaniel's black box.

"What's that noise?"

I look up and around at our surroundings. It's quiet at first, but getting louder—a deep rumbling that's vibrating the mist. Danny raises his eyes, leveling a look at me. Beads of sweat are springing out on his forehead and running down under his mask. "It's the portal. It's starting to collapse. It happens when things get too unstable."

The portal is about to collapse? My heart gives a lurch. "And what—that'll trap us?"

Danny nods, using an elbow to wipe his forehead. "Yeah, until someone on the other side opens up another one. And even then, we'd need to be in the right place at the right time. The Void is a funny place . . ."

Panic tears through my chest. "Well, hurry up, then!"

He starts working faster, his fingers moving beneath Harrisford's skin. I swallow, trying to tamp down the nausea that's washing right through me. I've seen plenty of surgeries, of course, but it's different when it's someone you care about.

Because I do care about Harrisford. It may be stupid, and reckless, and for sure I'll get my heart broken . . . But I can't help it. The past few weeks have changed my opinion of him forever.

"I can't find it." Danny's still looking for that goddamned Source. "I'll have to extend the incision. It was implanted so long ago—I think it's migrated."

Shit. I guess it happens with microchips too. Generally, we implant them between an animal's shoulder blades, but movement and time can shift them elsewhere. Sometimes we find them slipped down one leg; Conall once scanned one that had lodged itself just below a dog's left ear. "Do it, then," I hiss. "Quickly!"

The rumbling gets louder. Danny sweats harder. He's muttering obscenities beneath his breath. "Fuck, fuck, fuck," he says. "I don't understand why the portal's collapsing so quickly. We normally have more time than this."

I look at Conall in desperation. Conall's the smart one here, the one who understands the most about Void engineering. "Why would it be collapsing?"

Conall's mouth twists. "Not sure, Gwen. Could it be . . . because we brought a tether in here? When there was one in here already?"

My stomach drops. *Percy.* I brought Percy in, when Harrisford was already in here.

Danny splutters. "You brought a *tether*? A tether with a second *Source*? There's only meant to be one on either side of the portal, Chan. Bringing a second one in will—"

Conall has gone deathly pale. "Short-circuit things. And it's too late to reverse it. We have to hurry!"

I hold my breath, my heart thrashing in my chest. I'm shaking; a wave of dread expands in my body, permeating every inch of my flesh. "Hold on, Briggs," I whisper to him. My hands are clasping both sides of his face. "I've got you. I've got you."

Finally, Danny pulls out and gives a frustrated growl. "Fuck! I can't find it! We'll have to get him out and continue looking for it later." With quick movements, Danny performs a healing spell.

Shit shit shit. My anxiety is spiking through the roof. "Should we suture the incision?"

"No point." Danny is panting. "We don't have time for stitches. And even the healing spell will need to be done again. It'll all be reversed by the time we go back through the portal."

"Going through the portal undoes magic?"

"It strips any spells, healing, enchantments . . . The theory is that the Void wants to reclaim the magic."

I have to assume it makes sense, because I don't have time to think about it. Already the rumbling has become deafening, the mist swirling around us in rapid circles. Our hair is all staticky, like it gets immediately before a lightning strike.

"Help me cut his ties," I say to Danny, swiping my dropped scalpel off the floor and starting to saw through the ropes.

We release Harrisford, and together, we haul him up to standing, one of his arms around each of our necks. Percy winds around our legs, purring. Bits of debris from I don't know where are starting to rain down on our heads.

Harrisford stirs as we prop him up, his head lolling to one side, his eyelids fluttering open. He blinks blearily at me, the pupils of his brown and blue eyes dilated.

"Gwendolynne," he slurs, giving me a stupefied smile. "You . . . came."

My heart stutters and I swallow. I can't dwell on his words. There's no time to think, no time to feel. "Hang in there, Briggs," I say, curt. "We're getting you out."

Conall and Heloise fling themselves out of the portal as the ground judders and more fragments of rock plummet down upon our heads. Holding himself low to the ground, his tail streaming behind him, Percy too sprints toward the opening and dives through it.

Supporting Harrisford, Danny and I stumble closer, aiming for the tear.

"Wait." Danny stops just before we go through. "We need a Source on both sides to keep it open."

I whip my head around to look at him, over the top of Harrisford's head. "We *what*? Why didn't you say that earlier?"

He reddens. "I forgot. I was so focused on rescuing Briggs."

My throat is so thick, my chest so tight, that I feel like I can barely form words. "But . . . the Source. It's still in Harrisford . . ." I trail off, my mouth going dry. The only other bit of Source I know of is inside Percy.

Danny gives me a rueful look. "Yeah. If we'd got it out, we could've left it here, as the tether."

Harrisford scrunches his eyebrows in confusion, and says to Danny, his voice thick, "You never got my Source out?"

"Sorry, mate, couldn't find it. Must've migrated."

"Well, shit." He sags against me. "Fucking dragon's balls."

There's a loud bang, and something crashes to the ground, startling us. Panicking, I ask, "What'll happen if he doesn't stay behind?"

"If he goes through before us, the portal will collapse and trap us here," Danny says, distraught. "And if *we* go first, and he tries to follow"—he grimaces—"the portal will collapse on him as he's passing through."

All the blood drains from my face. "It'll kill him?"

"Possibly." Danny swallows. "Probably."

God-fucking-dammit. My heart races and my limbs turn to jelly and it's a miracle I even manage to keep Harrisford propped up. "This can't be the only option." It can't be, it can't be. My brain scrambles to find something—anything—that will solve this problem. But nothing comes to mind. This isn't like studying, where every question has a logical solution. I cannot think of a single answer.

I heave a shuddering breath, in and out. My chest is so tight, it feels like it could explode. For once in my life I am . . . stumped.

And then Harrisford is there, holding me up. He has let go of Danny and has taken my face in both hands, gripping it.

"Gwendolynne," he says, and he seems more lucid than he has this whole time. "You need to leave—"

"What?" I blink at him, distracted; I'm still trying to figure out how to fix this.

His fingers dig into the swell of my cheeks. "You have to go, love, you—"

He pauses, because another deep rumble rolls through us, shaking the ground. When it finishes, he speaks to Danny but keeps his eyes locked on me. "Danny, take Gwendolynne out. Please."

It finally clicks in my brain—what he's saying. My fingers bunch in Harrisford's shirt. "*No.*" I tighten my grip on him.

Danny, who's lingering near the portal, uncertain, speaks up. "Come on, Gwen, we need to go—"

"*You* go!" I'm screaming at Danny, but all I can see, all I can focus on, is Harrisford.

Something detaches from the ceiling and crashes to the ground, narrowly missing our heads. Harrisford lets go of my face and throws his arms around me, shielding me—just as he once shielded me from the flaming qílín.

When I blink my eyes open again, we're covered in dust. My head is still tucked beneath Harrisford's chin, his hand pressing the back of my head.

When he speaks, it's in a voice of deadly calm that rumbles right through his chest. "Wong. Go on. Get out of here."

Danny edges toward the opening. He already has one leg out. Yet still, he hesitates. "You sure?"

"Yes. But, if you can . . . hold the portal, will you?" Harrisford's arms tighten around me. "I've just got to say goodbye to my girl."

48

Harrisford

Danny stares at me for a second as we conduct a silent communion. Then he gives us a quick salute and scrambles out of the shrinking hole.

A cracking sound explodes around us, like thunder, and the ground tremors even harder. My head spins; the sedation is wearing off, and lucidity is taking over, but the movement still brings on a disorienting sort of dizziness.

"This *isn't* goodbye." Gwendolynne looks up at me, her eyes hard, her jaw set. "I'm not leaving you."

I tighten my hold on her. "Don't sacrifice yourself for me. I—"

"It's not a sacrifice. It's a choice." She balls her fists in my shirt even tighter, her expression so full of grim determination that I almost fold, right then and there.

But I can't. I cannot renege on my swiftly sketched plan.

"Listen to me." My words grind out, painful as a serrated knife. "You have to, because—" Another rumble reverberates through the cavern, sending showers of debris tumbling around us.

When the air clears, I try again. "Because you're better off out there, figuring out how to stop me from causing the explosions—"

She twists out of my arms, takes a brisk step back, and stares at me, her entire expression one of disbelief. "What? Stop *you*? Explosions?" There's another crash, and a bit of the roof detaches, shattering when it hits the ground. Our heads whip around, our attention caught by the sound.

Only for a sliver of a second, though. I don't want to waste these precious seconds looking at some fucking rocks. I snap my gaze back on her and take a deep breath.

There's no time for me to explain properly, but I need her to believe me. To understand. "Yes, me. I'm the cause of the explosions."

"*You?*" She shakes her head, so vigorously. "That's . . . not true."

"It is." My voice almost falters, but I hold steady. "There's no time to explain. The MLO opening too many portals was causing the surges, but it was my Source that was blowing things up. It was implanted too long ago, Gwendolynne. It's just . . . too strong."

"It's not." She's forcing the words out, her body so tightly wound it's a wonder she hasn't imploded. "You said the explosions were happening places your *dad* went—"

"I was wrong. They were places *I* went. My father's been dragging me around to all his events lately. For 'networking.'"

She stares at me, aghast. When she raises her hands to her temples, I can see that they are trembling. "No. *No.*"

There's another bang, and we reach for each other, clinging together as the world tilts sideways. The air is silty, full of vaporized rock.

"This is for the best." The grumbling has escalated to a roar, and I now have to shout to cut through the noise. I pull her to me, crushing her in the tightest embrace, so that my next words are muffled against her hair. "I can't continue hurting people. I can't continue hurting *you*."

And it's this that seems to hit her, makes her start trembling. I clutch her head to my chest, my hand on her upper back, trying to quell her shivering. Trying to channel enough calm for the both of us.

Inside me, though, everything is writhing, crumbling, disintegrating into dust.

I steel my resolve. There is nothing left for me on the outside. Nothing. No more university. No job. No family. My father is in a coma, and even my familiar—my own mother—has betrayed me. The only thing left that's worth anything is Gwendolynne. And whatever it takes to convince her to save herself—I need to do it.

It's what we tell clients sometimes, when it comes time to euthanize their pets: Sometimes, the kindest gift we can give a loved one is to let them go.

"If you're out there," I continue, my voice fueled by urgency, "you'll have a better chance of figuring out how to fix this. Then, when you have, you can come back in and rescue me."

I'm lying, of course, about her coming back to save me. There's no way I would want her risking herself again. But I'm hoping that once she escapes, she'll realize how much she still has to live for. Out there, outside the Void.

And even if she never figures out how to stop Magecorp, or the MLO, or save everyone from my Source, I am hoping that eventually she will move on. Come first. Get the Ministry job. Just . . . live.

I cannot let Gwendolynne sacrifice herself for me. Can't let her throw away her dreams. Perhaps it's never been a priority for me in the past, but falling for Gwendolynne has taught me that there's more to life than winning, than always being the best.

I mean, she put herself at risk to save Percy. She relentlessly pursued the top spot—not because she wanted the money or the glory, but so she could save her family. And even though I don't deserve it, even though I'm a shitty person, she still finds it in her heart to want to save *me*.

I would be an absolute fucking fool if getting closer to her didn't force me to become a better man.

She's silent for so long, while the cave quakes around us, that for a moment I think I've got her. That she's seen the merit in my plan and has agreed to leave. But then her shoulders straighten. She pulls away from me, and I'm surprised to see that, even though her whole body is still shaking, she's not crying.

"I *will* figure it out," she says through clenched teeth. "In here. With you."

The entire cave judders, so violently, and another chunk of rock crashes to ground. It sends plumes of dust into the air, coating our hair, clothes, and faces.

But I barely notice. Instead, a bleak sort of resignation clicks into place inside me. It's determination. Purpose. Resolve. My gut feels hollow to the point of aching.

Already in my mind, a new plan is forming. I'm switching approaches. Analyzing my options. Doing a risk assessment.

Strategizing.

For in the end, I cannot escape it: I *am* my father's son.

Ignoring the noise and the chaos around us, I pull her closer and kiss her forehead—hard. I want to clasp her to me and tell her it will be all right, that everything will work out. I want to hold her and never, ever let her go. But I can't. I cannot fail her.

And to be honest, I hate myself; I hate that I have to do this. I would never, in a million years, willingly betray her. Yet here we are. And even though every last cell in my body is screaming at me not to do it—the thing that will fucking *destroy* me—I must keep reminding myself that this is what's best for her.

This . . . is the *right* thing to do.

With both hands, I cradle her face. "Okay," I whisper, into the infinitesimal space that divides us. "We'll figure it out . . . together."

Her brown eyes are wide, her eyelashes all caked with dust. As I watch, two single tears slip down each of her cheeks. Staring at her intently, I commit her face to memory. Even covered in grime . . . she is beautiful.

I can barely form more words. But somehow, I manage to choke some out. "Gwendolynne." Finally, tears well in my own eyes, making my vision as opaque as a blurry, rain-washed window. I lean my forehead against hers. "The portal is going to close soon."

"I know." She reaches up, her hands around my neck, and pulls my face down.

We kiss. Her lips taste like salt and sadness. I don't know if it's from her tears or mine. Perhaps it's both.

We stay like this, locked in an embrace, her arms thrown around my shoulders, my hands gripping her waist. And the whole time, cracks are feathering along the walls, rocks are raining down upon us, and the entire ground is shuddering. The Void, now, is on the cusp of collapse . . .

I can't let her go. *Fuck.* I love her so much and I'm a complete imbecile for not having realized sooner. I should tell her. Tell her everything. Before it's too late.

But . . . it would only make matters worse. And the portal is shrinking farther. I'm running out of time.

I've messed up so many things in my life. Put my trust in the wrong person: my mother. I'd always thought of her as guiltless, a pure, shining light illuminating my early years. Until I learned that everything I thought I knew was a lie. That she'd betrayed me.

I've been emotionally alienated from my father, burning up with hatred and vengeance, not caring that he was on the cusp of dying, even wishing I could kill him myself.

I've been ignorant, so ignorant, about how my actions impact others. I've used my privilege to manipulate people, to hold them hostage to my whims. I've used my wealth and my power to exploit those who I felt were beneath me.

And, of course, I—and the Source that Magecorp implanted against my will—have put both animals and people in danger, causing surges that disrupt the world's flow of magic.

I've made so many mistakes in my life. Too many.

But this, saving her, is the one thing I can get right.

The portal has shrunk so much; it's now alarmingly small. The cavern ceiling shatters, breaking into fragments, mirroring the cracks that are cleaving my heart. An enormous explosion sounds above our heads, reverberating painfully through my ears. It's my last chance. It seems as though everything—this reality, this universe, this Void cavern, my life—is collapsing.

So I break away, ending our kiss abruptly.

She gasps at the suddenness. Overbalances. And before she has a chance to realize what I'm doing, I put both my hands on her shoulders . . . and give her a firm shove.

"Harrisford!" she screams as she tumbles through the tear.

Not a second too soon, for at that precise moment, the hole shrinks to a tiny circle.

Her eyes lock on mine. Now her expression is full of something else entirely:

Betrayal.

It's all I catch before the portal blinks entirely out of existence.

One last view of Gwendolynne's stricken face.

And then she's gone.

49

Gwendolynne

The air gives a few more feeble ripples. And then the portal just . . . disappears.

As though it had never existed.

Heloise rushes to me. I'm shaking so hard that my teeth click together. "Gwen," she murmurs. "Oh, Gwen."

"Open it!" My voice is hysterical. Animalistic. My fingers claw at the carpet. "*Get him out!*"

"Can we, Conall?" Heli asks, her voice edged with worry. She squats next to me, rubbing circles on my back as I double over on the floor. "Can we re-open it?"

Conall frowns. "I'm sorry, Gwen," he says gently. "Since it imploded on its own, this particular weak spot is now just too unstable."

I collapse then, and finally burying my face in my hands, I burst into sobs. Hot, stinging tears run through the gaps in my fingers, splattering dark stains onto the floor.

Bastard. That fucking *bastard*! He tricked me—again. Tricked me into believing we would stay together. And then, at the last moment, he betrayed me.

When will you ever learn, Gwen? I was ready to give my entire existence up for Harrisford Briggs, and . . . he didn't even want me to stay.

The pathetic thing is, even despite all this . . . it still doesn't make me think less of him. It makes me think less of *me*.

All I can think is that this is all my fault. I should never have taken Percy into the Void, because then the portal wouldn't have collapsed, and we'd have had more time to find and remove Harrisford's Source.

I shouldn't have assumed Harrisford had left me when he'd disappeared from the hotel room. Perhaps I would've started looking for him sooner—before the graduation ceremony, even. What if I'd gone looking earlier? What if I had found him in time?

I shouldn't have let him push me through the tear. I should've realized, should've reacted faster, should've fought harder to stay.

And I really shouldn't have denied my feelings for so long.

I should have told him how much I cared.

The room falls into silence for several loaded minutes. I don't speak; I just continue kneeling on the carpet, weeping into my hands, while Heloise tries unsuccessfully to comfort me. It's Pen—sweet, nervous Pen—who ends up dragging me back from my almost-inconsolable state.

"Um, Gwen?" Pen says. "What do you want me to do with this one?"

I raise my swollen, tearstained face. Pen is holding Danny Wong hostage against the wall, a loaded syringe in their shaky hand, pointed at his neck.

"I wasn't sure what was happening," Pen says, their voice tremulous. "He came out all bloody, and I didn't know what'd happened, so I kept him here until one of you could tell me what to do."

This is so unexpected that I almost gasp a laugh. But grief quickly snuffs it out. Instead it emerges as a strangled sort of wheeze.

Of course Pen wouldn't know what had happened in the Void. All they had seen is the three of us—and Percy—go through the portal to rescue Harrisford. Then we'd all come out again with Danny, but no Harrisford.

"It's okay, Pen," I finally manage to rasp. My throat is scratchy, my limbs all weak; the crying has exhausted me. "Wong was in there trying to take Harrisford's Source out. You can let him go."

Pen shoots Danny a loathsome look before grudgingly stepping away. Danny lets out an audible sigh, rubbing at his neck.

"You're not off the hook yet, though, Wong." Fury is beginning to displace my sadness, beating a tattoo inside my chest like a drum. Angrily, I dash my tears away and scramble to my feet, advancing on him.

Even though Danny's much taller than me—almost as tall as Harrisford—he must feel the scale of my wrath, because he backs up against the wall, pressing himself flat.

"*Why* were you in there with Harrisford?" Eyes narrowed, I ram my finger against his sternum, hard. Rage is bursting from my pores. I'm almost *spitting*.

"I was—" he starts, but I cut him off and continue to hurl questions at him.

"Did you kidnap him?"

"I didn't—"

I lean in close, my face only inches from his. "How did you *know*?"

He swallows. "Know what?"

I bare my teeth. "*About his Source*, dammit!"

"It's because . . ." Danny is stammering; he can barely look at me. When he finally speaks, his words come out all in a rush. "It's because I'm from the MLO, okay?"

"The MLO?" I repeat, reeling. Could it be true? Was it the MLO all along? *When you hear the sound of hooves, assume it is a horse, not a Pegasus.*

My finger is still jammed against Danny's chest. I can barely process what it is I'm hearing.

"Wait." Pen whirls around, their fists clenched by their sides. "*You're* MLO?"

"Yeah." Danny frowns. "Why, are you?"

Pen's red-painted mouth sags open before finally, they say, "I—uh . . . Yeah. I just joined last month." On shaky legs, they stagger backward and sink onto a chair. It's like the entire foundation of their world has collapsed, and Conall clasps Pen's rounded shoulders as they take several heaving breaths.

Ignoring Pen, Danny continues. "I was meant to rescue Harrisford, Chan. The plan was"—he lets out a shuddering exhale—"to remove his Source and send him into hiding. To give him a new identity." He slumps against the wall and shakes his head. "Man, I really *fucked up* in there."

Heli snorts from behind me. My head whips around at the noise. She has both eyebrows raised in an expression that clearly says: *Hell yeah you did.*

I turn back to face forward and scrunch my eyes shut, trying to process everything. "I don't understand." My voice tremors. "Harrisford said he was causing the explosions. But the common room . . . for that first surge . . . he wasn't there . . ."

"He was," Danny says. "Just briefly. He stopped by after the explosion at the museum gala." He raises his eyes to mine. "He was looking for you, actually."

My pulse starts to hammer. My hand trembles. Releasing Danny, I bring my palm to my forehead, trying to retrieve my murky, panic-fueled memories of that night. "For me? Why?"

Danny stares at me for the longest time. Finally, he says, "Bloody hell, you're as bad as he is."

My fingers twitch, and I almost slap him but manage to stop myself just in time. "What do you *mean*?" I've had enough of people talking in riddles.

Heloise pipes up from across the room. "Jesus, Gwen, haven't you noticed?" She's preoccupied with trying to heal the wound she'd sustained from Mrs. Mason-Price's gun. It's bleeding again, which makes sense, since Danny said exiting the Void strips all magical enchantments. But because it's on the back of her shoulder, she's having trouble reaching it.

I stalk over, jerk down her shirt collar, and with a perfunctory flick of my wrist, I heal her again. "What haven't I noticed?" I snap, more terse than I intended to be.

Everyone falls silent. Pen shuffles their feet. Conall suddenly appears very absorbed in inspecting the Magecorp box. Heli rolls her shoulder, her eyes flicking between me and Danny Wong.

The room is completely quiet except for the rhythmic ticking of Harrisford's grandfather clock.

"Well?" I fold my arms and scowl at everybody. "Is anyone going to answer me?"

Finally, Danny does. "Isn't it obvious, Chan?" he says, and gives a hollow laugh. "Harrisford Briggs has been in love with you . . . for literal fucking years."

50

Gwendolynne

I've almost finished packing up my dorm room when I finally get the call.

"Good afternoon, Dr. Chang." A tinny, female voice emerges from the speakerphone of my strap.

"It's Chan," I correct, slightly irritable. "Dr. Chan."

"Oh. I'm sorry, Dr. Chan. This is Marilyn Hindley from Ferguson's Recruitment. I'm calling to discuss the job application you sent through a few days ago."

I drop another stack of papers into an already overflowing box. "Yes, of course. Thanks for calling me back."

"I'm pleased to say that we've reviewed your application and we were impressed with the strength of it. Normally, we would ask you to go through an official interview process, but your references all speak so highly of you. Plus, of course, being the Dux of this year's graduating class . . ."

My heart flips in my chest, then starts thumping so quickly that I almost feel it in my toes. "Does that mean I've got it?" I'm kneeling on the floor among the bare, empty remains of my room. "I got the job?"

"Yes, Dr. Chan," Marilyn confirms. "We'd like to formally offer you the graduate position that will start on the thirteenth of August. Congratulations."

My stomach fizzes with something that feels like both excitement... and guilt. Here I am, accepting my first job offer, while Harrisford—poor Harrisford—is still stuck inside the Void.

I tuck my hair behind my ears with trembling fingers and squeeze my eyelids shut. My guilt is gathering behind my eyeballs, threatening to spill out as tears.

No. I blink hard, several times, and swallow down the feeling. This is what I *want*. What I've been aiming for. There's a reason I sent that job application off, and I cannot afford—at the last minute—to lose my focus.

"Thank you," I whisper, ignoring the way the words catch on my tongue. "I'm . . . very happy to accept."

"Excellent. I'll send over the contracts and all the salary information shortly. And, Dr. Chan?"

I'd been on the brink of ending the call, but something had changed in the woman's tone that stopped me. "Yes?"

Marilyn's voice drops lower, as though she's actually whispering into the microphone of her strap. "Are you *absolutely* sure this is what you want?" she asks. "This position? You know, as the top student from Seamere College, you'd have the pick of any role you wanted . . ."

I pause for a moment. Lick my dry lips in an effort to distract my mind. My thoughts are churning, and just for a moment—a single, crystalline moment—I wonder what my life would be like if I chose a different path.

A whole lifetime flashes through my head. Achievements. Promotions. Rising through the Ministry's ranks. Even becoming Britain's first-ever female Chief Magical Veterinary Officer. The thought is so ludicrous it almost makes me laugh.

But then again . . . *What if?*

I shake my head, dispersing the visions. Those are just flights of fancy. Dreams of a life belonging to a different woman—one who'd never met Harrisford Briggs. Who'd never fallen for him. A woman with so much potential, so much ahead of her, and a burning ambition to join the Ministry.

But that's not my life now. I am no longer that woman.

The day after I graduated as the top student of Seamere, I received the formalized offer to join the Ministry. The same offer that is extended to the top student every single year. The job I'd been working toward for seven fucking years.

And, very politely, I'd thanked them for their consideration . . . and respectfully declined.

I declined it because I have a new focus now: to infiltrate the Void again and rescue Harrisford Briggs. The man who, according to his oldest friend, loves me—even though he'd never worked up the courage to say it. The man who chose to sacrifice himself so the rest of us could escape. So that *I* could escape.

Now, with hindsight, I can appreciate it with burning clarity. The way he'd tried, using several approaches, to convince me to save myself. And when I didn't agree, well. He made the decision for me.

The man who, once I figure out how to find and remove his Source, I still hope to go in and rescue, and bring him home.

And I *will*. Bring him home, that is.

I am Gwendolynne Chan, the smartest witch at Seamere, and now I have a new goal. To stop Magecorp, and everything Nathaniel Price stands for . . .

From the inside.

"Yes," I say, more firmly, more resolutely. "It's the job I want."

This will be a good job. It may not have the prestige of the coveted Ministry role, but at least, being private sector, the salary is almost as high. With some extra weekend shifts, it'll be sufficient for me to live on, with just enough left over to send to my parents so that they can save their restaurant.

And I can use my position to achieve my objectives. To rescue Harrisford, and then the world.

Marilyn clicks off the call, and I take a moment to blow out a long, slow exhale. Then I go to dump the final few objects into the last empty box. An indignant yowl alerts me to the fact that the box is already occupied.

Percy's furious little face pops up. His ears are flattened, his whiskers pulled right back.

My box, he hisses.

I roll my eyes. "Unless you're going to help me fit more into *that* box"—I gesture at the one next to it, which is already full to bursting—"then I'm gonna need you to hop out of this one, quicksmart."

Very deliberately, Percy crouches back down. I poke his chest. He grumbles.

Finally, though, he grudgingly starts to channel me a little bit of extra magic.

"*Thank* you," I say, with only a touch of condescension. Then, using Percy's magic, I perform a charm to expand the already full box.

After sealing it with packing tape, I straighten, hands on hips, and survey the bare bones of my room. Although I've lived here for four of my seven years at Seamere . . . it's never truly felt like home.

Now that he's finally secured ownership of the box, Percy props his paws up on its edge. He looks around, surveying the state of his looted kingdom from his stately cardboard castle.

I hope that wherever we're going, he mutters, the tip of his tail flicking, *the accommodations are better than* this.

I think of my flat in Manchester, where I'm planning to go until my new job starts. I think of the clutter, of the daggy carpet and the old TV and the giant pile of shoes stacked beside the door.

"I wouldn't get your hopes up," I say, deadpan, and Percy growls, his tail swooshing even harder.

I grin at him before turning to pick up the full box. Balancing it on my hip, I tug open my front door, keeping it ajar with my foot. Then I pause.

This feels . . .

Momentous.

After seven brutal, punishing years, I'm no longer a Seamere student. I'm walking out this door as a graduate, with nothing but a trove of memories, a single box, and a lovable arsehole of a cat.

Oh, and Pudding. Since Harrisford never returned from the Void, I figured I'd better adopt her, temporarily. Keep her safe for as long as needed.

We can't communicate, of course, but I know all about reptile health and husbandry—so I think I'll do a pretty good job of looking after her until Harrisford comes back.

And he *will* come back.

I'll get him back.

"Percy, Pudding, let's go," I say. Then—more to myself than to anyone else—I add, "Wait for me, Briggs. I'm coming for you."

I take a deep, steadying breath, steel myself, and step through the open door . . .

As the newest employee of Magecorp, Limited.

ACKNOWLEDGMENTS

When I set out to write *Strange Familiars*, pulling experiences from my own time at veterinary school (but making them far more *magical*), I was planning to write it just for me. At the time, I didn't have an adult literary agent, I didn't have a publisher . . . all I had were memories, a rough concept, and a gaggle of characters who simply would not shut up. It's been incredible to witness the pathway this book has taken: from the fragments of an idea to a real, full book, and I have so many people to thank for that journey.

First, I'd like to pay my respects to the Traditional Owners of the unceded land on which I live and work, the Wurundjeri people of the Kulin nation, and pay tribute to Elders past, present, and emerging.

Thank you to my literary agent, Lauren Spieller, assistant Hannah Teachout, and everyone at Folio Literary Management. From the moment we first spoke, I trusted you both implicitly, and I'm SO thrilled we got to work together on this book (hopefully the first of many)!

A HUGE thanks to my editor, Kristine Swartz at Ace/Berkley, for falling in love with Gwendolynne, Harrisford, and Percy as much as I did! It's such a dream to have an editor who just "gets it"; I'm truly grateful to have found such an incredible partner. Thank you also to Mary Baker, production editors Megan Elmore and Alaina Christensen, and the rest of the copyediting team, as well as Stephanie Felty, Elisha Katz, and Jessica Plummer.

And to everyone at Hodderscape: my original editor, Calah; my new editor, Charlie; editorial assistant Marina Dominguez Salgado; publishing director Molly; Kate from publicity; as well as everyone else behind the scenes, it's been a privilege to work with you in the past, and I'm so thrilled to work with you again. Thank you!

Massive props to artist Addie (@klimtsonian) and art director Katie Anderson for creating the cover of my dreams! It's magical and romantic and whimsical with just the right touch of darkness—i.e., it fits the book *perfectly*. I feel like the luckiest author ever to have had such beautiful covers throughout my career, and it seems that this trend is set to continue!

This wouldn't be a veterinary book without acknowledging the animals: thank you to Achtung, my dapper black cat (sadly passed), who was the inspiration for Percy and has thus been immortalized. And to Wasabi, my Ragdoll, who provides the most effective distraction in the form of cuteness and stealing-my-chairness, thank you for making the writing process that much more difficult.

As a veterinarian myself, I must also acknowledge all of the animals I've treated, both at vet school and throughout my career, who were often the only reason I got up and went to work each morning. Thank you also to all of my clients over the years for trusting me with your pets. (Except the ones—and there were many, sadly—who inspired the portrayal of Mrs. Mason-Price in the opening scene. Those people are expressly *excluded* from these acknowledgments, for the record.)

To every single veterinarian, vet tech, and vet nurse out there: Thank you for the work that you do. You are HEROES.

An extra-special thanks to veterinarians Dr. Kate Thompson (equine extraordinaire) and Dr. Tegan Stephens (exotics expert) for lending me your knowledge in all things horse (centaur) and reptile (bearded dragon) related. For context, I'm a registered specialist in feline medicine, which means my expertise is basically "cats" and not much else; these two were instrumental in plugging the gaps in my veterinary knowledge. Thank you also to Dr. David Neck, who authored the book mentioned in the text, *Internal Medicine and Surgery of Mythological Beasts*, which I found to be an extremely informative and interesting reference.

To my beta readers, Marina and Shaylin: I'm so grateful for the feedback you gave me, which made the book so much stronger! To Frances, for fact-checking my British terminology. And to the rest of my writing friends, both online and in person: THANK YOU. I simply could not survive the wild ride that is publishing without you all.

These acknowledgments will probably have been written, finalized, and gone to print by the time I put together any sort of street team, so instead I will acknowledge the street teams I've had for my last two books: the No Reflection Street Team and the Mortal Creatures. Thank you for being the best hype squads an author could ever ask for! I appreciate you all so much!

Thank you to my mum, dad, brother, sister, and mother-in-law, for all the times you helped me through my various veterinary exams. Thanks also to my kids, Ada and Callan, who are growing up to be book lovers like me and animal lovers like both of their parents. And of course, the hugest thanks of all to my husband, Lachie, who I met in my third year of vet school, and who thankfully has never been my rival but only ever my biggest support.

Last but not least, thank YOU, dear reader, for picking up this book. I appreciate it more than you can possibly know.